Treason, Treason!

by Josh Langston

DEDICATION

This is dedicated to three of the people, in addition to my bride and our two wonderful children, who were absolutely indispensible in the writing of this book. To my brothers, Lloyd and John Langston, and my sister, Karen Langston Boyce, I can only begin to thank you for the many hours you invested in this project, to say nothing of the continuing love, support and encouragement you have always lavished on me.

For all those years when I tried to convince you that being the youngest made my road the toughest, I apologize. I'm glad you never believed it.

Just know that I consider myself thoroughly blessed to have you in my life. Thank you for always being there when I needed you.

--Josh

ACKNOWLEDGMENTS

Special thanks go to Kathi L. Schwengel who not only created a remarkable cover, but who read an early draft of the manuscript and helped keep me sane while I worked on it. You're a special person, Kathi, and a damned fine writer. I'm proud to be counted among your friends. (And yes, the Guinness is on me!)

Visit her at:
http://myrandommuse.wordpress.com

A portion of the Hudson River Valley, 1780.

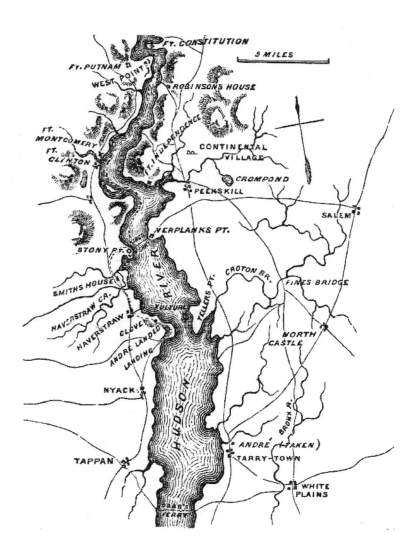

~ Part I ~

"She looked and there was the king,
standing by the pillar, as the custom was.
The officers and the trumpeters were beside the king,
and all the people of the land were rejoicing and blowing
trumpets.
Then Athaliah tore her robes and called out, 'Treason,
Treason.'"

The Holy Bible
King James Version
2 Kings 11:14

Chapter One

*"Remember that all through history, there have been
tyrants and murderers, and for a time, they seem
invincible. But in the end, they always fall. Always."*
                                          --Mahatma Gandhi

At age 52, Raines Kerr had almost everything
he wanted: a well-paying position, a secure future,
and a loving daughter. But the loss of his wife had
put a hole in his heart that would never heal. After
ten years the ache remained.

He'd hoped to feel a moment of peace
knowing that at long last he would either make her
greatest dream come true, or die trying. Instead,
turmoil churned his insides like a blender. Unlike
Raines, Beth Kerr hadn't feared death. She hadn't
feared anything. For her, death would be the start of
"just another adventure."

A physicist and rational thinker, Raines
admired his wife's attitude despite harboring doubts
about her vision of the hereafter. Nevertheless, he

was committed to the project, to his wife's dream, and to the possibility that the course on which he was about to embark would change the world.

Dramatically.

And forever.

And with a little luck, something far outside his normal area of control, he might even survive.

He had already set the machinery in motion, quite literally. In a few moments, the cloth-bound package on the ground in front of him would--if all went according to plan--disappear. Precisely ten minutes later, he would, too.

His daughter, Leah, stood a few meters away, wide-eyed and apprehensive. He tried to exude confidence, but his involuntary bodily functions betrayed the truth. Sweat glands and sphincters made damned good lie detectors.

He had great faith in his lab, his equipment, and the accuracy of his calculations. Still, he would have preferred to do more testing. Unfortunately, the power required to generate an Event made it impossible to run as many tests as he would have liked without bringing undue attention to his experiments. Even though he chaired the physics department, and enjoyed the considerable benefits of the accomplishments of his early career, he had no desire for scrutiny. He required secrecy. The project demanded it. If the Crown had any inkling of his intentions, he'd be thrown into a cell from which he'd never escape.

In that event, death would be a much preferable outcome.

Thus he stood on the threshold of the

greatest scientific discovery of all time, and he could share it with no one except his twenty-five year old daughter, Leah. And not only was she sworn to secrecy, she would soon be joining him, and the equipment which made it all possible would be reduced to a smoldering puddle of slag.

A faint whirring sound got his attention as well disguised receptors gathered the high-voltage charge that would power the Event. Raines looked at the pitiful sack containing what would soon become all his worldly goods.

Bon voyage, he thought in the moment before his lumpy baggage winked out of existence.

The pop which heralded the disappearance sounded ominously loud. So loud, in fact, that Leah jumped backwards in surprise even though she'd been expecting it.

Ten minutes remained. Either he would join the recently departed bag of stuff, or he'd be dead. He *had* to show confidence. He owed it to Leah. He owed it to Beth. Hell, he owed it to himself.

He squinted at the watch he'd placed on the ground just outside the targeting circle he'd scribed for himself in the rock. The circle he'd cut for his supplies stood empty.

It would soon be time to crouch down and grab his ankles.

And close his eyes.

And pray.

Nine minutes to go.

~*~

Joel's leg hurt. Again. He grunted as he massaged the deep scar in his thigh through thick wool trousers. The damned thing rarely *stopped* hurting. Whiskey helped, and he had an array of sympathetic pub-mates willing to self-medicate alongside him. Some of them also bore scars from the never-ending war.

"Bloody damned colonials," observed a red-cheeked Oliver Leahy as he lowered his bulk onto a barstool at the Small Arms, Joel's favorite watering hole. Rather than prove his ability to read Joel's mind, Oliver's comment merely restarted a long-standing conversation. He gave Joel's shoulder a comradely nudge. "Leg still acting up?"

"A bit." Joel raised his glass and looked at Oliver through the liquid lens, then tossed the amber fluid to the back of his throat and swallowed. The sudden surge of alcoholic heat made his eyes water and caused him to shift his thoughts away from his damaged leg, and the lie. He wondered if he should indulge in another.

"At least ya got the bugger what shot ya," Oliver said. "They grow snipers out there like we grow weeds. German guns, Spanish ammunition, and French--"

"Diseases," Joel said, though they'd shared the joke so many times neither man laughed at it any longer.

Oliver continued with hardly a breath. "They call themselves Americans. As if they're the only ones living on this continent! Death mongering bastards."

"To be fair now, we shoot at them, too." *If*

only you knew.

"Aye, but they *deserve* it! We're merely protectin' what's ours." Oliver took a sip of beer. "Most o' the time, anyway. Besides, they started it."

"That was a long, long time ago."

"Well it won't go on much longer from what I hear."

"And what's that?" Joel asked. "Suddenly you've got an ear at the Ministry of Defense? I thought you ran a bookshop."

"There's no end of uniforms popping in and out of that shop. I hear them talking. Come to think of it, maybe you should drop in and buy a book from time to time. You might learn something, too."

"Fiction bores me."

"Ruddy Philistine! It's not *all* fiction. Buy something about philosophy, or cooking, or--I dunno--art!"

"I've always fancied history."

"Then, come by! I've got a huge selection."

"Maybe I should. God knows there's nothing worth listening to on the radio. It's all about the fighting; what the colonials are up to, or what we're going to do in reprisal. Nobody talks about how it all got started. Nobody cares anymore."

"Ha! Don't get me goin' about the colonials declaring their bloody independence. They started the damned war; that's all I need to know. And let's not forget they cost us the homeland."

"They've got no sense of history," Joel said. "All they want to do is fight."

Oliver bumped his beer glass on the bar. "Ain't that the truth! Even those what call 'emselves

Torries don't share an ounce of loyalty to the crown. They just stopped shootin' is all. The rest have been at it for two centuries."

"Almost two and a half."

"They're worse than the bloody French. Why won't they give it up? They'll never win."

"They think they can wear us down," Joel said. "They want it all--the midlands *and* the coast. I swear--"

"Phone for ya, Joel," said a slender young woman behind the bar. She held out a handset for him, its cord draped across the bar and out of sight.

"Dawkins here," he said, covering his open ear with his palm. He listened to a brief message then responded with, "Right. Be there in ten," and handed the phone back to the barmaid.

"So much for lunch," he sighed, then waved his empty glass at the Union Jack behind the bar and shoved himself to an upright position. "Love to stay and chat, but I've gotta get back to work." *Besides which, we've already had this conversation a thousand times.*

Joel dropped a two-pound note on the dark wood bar and winked at Mollie Evans, the Small Arm's proprietor. Everyone loved Mollie, and those who didn't lacked the stones to try and take advantage of her. She'd fought her way to New England in the last wave and, according to rumor, left a pile of dead Germans behind to prove her mettle. She put the cash in her apron and wiped the bar clean in a single, well-practiced motion. "Thank you, Inspector," she said.

The thickset bookseller raised his beer in a

parting salute. "Yer a noble public servant, Joel Dawkins. Slow as a slug, and ugly to boot, but noble just the same."

"I love you, too," Joel said and limped to the door. He took a cautionary look around before pushing it open. One could never be sure if a Yank was lurking nearby. Being a cop in Boston was hard enough. He had no intention of posing as a target for some knuckle-dragging colonial terrorist.

~*~

Leah Kerr stood in the shade of a monstrously large oak tree and watched her father try to look nonchalant, as if he weren't in the least bit concerned that he was attempting something never done before. No big deal. Another day at the office. Another walk in the park.

Bullshit.

Even though she knew it was coming, the ear-splitting *Pop!* that signaled the departure of his supplies came as a shock. He never said it would be so damned loud. She rubbed her ears and watched as he tried to maintain a confident and good-humored expression. He had to be scared shitless. She felt that way for him, and when it was her turn, she had no doubt she'd feel that way for herself. It wouldn't matter that her turn would only come if the system worked--and worked flawlessly, an assurance he certainly didn't have.

"Five minutes," he said. "Everything's going to be fine. I'm sure of it."

Five minutes. Not nearly enough time to tell

him all the things she needed to say. How much she loved him. How much she needed him in her life. How much she admired his intellect and his devotion to her mother's dream. How much she feared she would never see him again. How the hell could she pack all that into five minutes?

"I love you, Daddy."

He gave her that slow, wide smile that had always been a source of strength, confidence, and love--a smile that erased pain, restored faith, and promised hope.

"I love you, too," he said.

He kept looking at the watch lying on the ground just outside the target circle. Her mother had given it to him, and Leah couldn't remember a time when he hadn't worn it. Now, of course, that was out of the question. She wondered if he really needed to see the seconds ticking away, or if he was trying to draw comfort from the memory of her mother's gift.

"Don't forget what I told you about adjusting the settings," he said. "Don't take any chances."

"I won't."

"Promise?"

"Promise."

"And be sure to flip the Doomsday switch to On."

She smiled at the reference. It would only be Doomsday for the equipment he'd built. Once she was gone, the power surge signaled by the pop would be directed back to the lab rather than into the power grid which serviced most of Massachusetts. As intended, the massive voltage spike would melt down the Event generator and pretty much everything connected to it. With any luck, the building would escape serious damage. After all, neither of them wanted to see anyone hurt.

"Will do," she said. "That's the big orange one on the wall next to the picture window, right?"

He looked up in sudden alarm, then saw her mischievous grin. There were no windows in the lab, nor any large orange switches for that matter.

Sitting on his haunches inside the scribed circle, he twisted his lips to one side and raised an admonishing finger. She was waiting for him to shake it when the whirring sound she'd heard previously started up once again.

Raines Kerr wrapped his arms around his shins and lowered his head.

"Daddy," Leah cried, "I love--"

Pop!

"--you."

Standing alone in the now deserted clearing, Leah took a deep, shuddering breath. Phase One, as her father had called it, was complete. It would soon be time to determine whether or not it had been completed *successfully*.

~*~

Buried deep within the walls of the Ministry of Defense headquarters in Annapolis, Maryland, two aging senior officers sat at a table on which rested a high-definition map of the so-called midlands, an area defined by the Appalachian mountains in the east, the Mississippi river in the west, Canada on the north, and the Gulf of Mexico in the south. Most of the residents therein called it "America." The generals, like most citizens of New England, had other names for it, few of them pleasant, but all of them descriptive.

"I'd like to see this mess resolved once and for all," said General Sir David Fitzwilliam, Chief of the Defense Staff. He leaned back in his chair and squinted at his highest ranking subordinate, General Sir Malcolm Nash, Chief of the General Staff.

"I certainly share that goal," Nash said.

"What I'm saying, Malcolm, is that I want to see it done. Finished! Completed during my lifetime. And, to be utterly candid, I don't have a great deal of time left."

Nash appeared instantly, and deeply, concerned for the welfare of his superior. "My condolences, General. I had no idea you were ill."

"I'm *not* ill. I'm old. Should have retired ages ago."

"Ah. Well. That's a very personal decision we must all--"

Fitzwilliam held up his hand. "Spare me your insight, please. Now, while I still have some time left, let me tell you what I want."

"Of course, sir."

"Simply stated, I want a plan. And I want it spread out on this table within a week. It must spell out, in detail, what we need to do to put an end to this war."

Nash pursed his lips and exhaled through his nose. "With all due respect General, if it were that easy, don't you think we would have done it before now?"

"I'm quite sure you could have," said Fitzwilliam. "Many times! I imagine there have been countless plans, mapped out in exquisite detail."

"But--"

"Yes, that's the problem, isn't it? There's always a 'but.'"

"I'm afraid I don't understand."

Fitzwilliam shook his head. "I'm talking about the politicians. They don't have the balls to see a real war through to the end. And that's what it's going to take to put an end to this absurd rebellion."

Nash cast about for something to say but came up empty. Fitzwilliam knew he would. Just as he knew the wobbly bastard would run to the prime minister the moment their meeting ended.

"Here's what you're going to do." Fitzwilliam tossed a thin file on the table. The cover bore the General's seal along with the usual hash marks denoting information of the most highly classified nature.

"Look that over, Malcolm. It spells out what I want done and who I want put in charge of every major element in the plan."

Nash left the document on the table. "It sounds to me like you've already got your plan, General. What is there for me to do?"

"I've merely outlined it in the broadest terms. You'll have to flesh out the details." Fitzwilliam carefully cut the end off a Cuban cigar, licked the seam, and struck a match. He puffed until nearly obscured by clouds of tobacco smoke. Nash waited in silence. "Pick up the damned file, Malcolm."

"Of course, sir!" Nash stood, put the folder

under his arm, and turned toward the door.

"Where the hell do you think you're going?"

"To start work on the plan, sir."

"You'll read that file in here," Fitzwilliam said. "Nothing leaves this room."

"But--"

"Or would you prefer to retire?"

"Retire?"

"Yes. Right now. This bloody moment. I've no doubt I can find a dozen people to take your place."

And do a better job than you've ever done.

"I'd prefer to examine your plan first, sir. I need adequate time to--"

"You haven't been listening, Malcolm. I can't spare any more time. Either you get to work, now, on my terms, or you get out. Either way, that plan stays in this room. Furthermore, only the men and women I've listed in the file are to have any knowledge of this operation. Should anyone in parliament, or God forbid, any of the Royals get wind of it, I'll have you shot. Protocols be damned. Is that understood?"

"I-- Uh, yes sir."

"So, what's it going to be--'into the breach' or off to the beach?"

"You make it sound so easy."

"It is."

Nash returned the folder to the table, unopened. "I believe it's time for me to step down."

Fitzwilliam smiled. "Excellent decision." He pressed a button on the underside of the table. In response, an armed guard entered the room. "Sergeant, kindly escort General Nash to his office

too soft for a classroom.

He coaxed the usual personal information from her and entered it all on the form. With the preliminaries done, he sat back in his chair and gave her what he thought was a reassuring smile. "Now, who's gone missing?"

"My fiancé," she said. "William Smithers." She handed him a wrinkled and slightly faded snapshot then put herself back to work twisting a damp handkerchief into cordage. "I call him Billy, but to everyone else, he's William."

Joel glanced at the photo of a paunchy, slightly balding man in his early thirties sporting a wispy Van Dyke. The expression on his face could have been either a smile or a smirk. Joel doubted he'd like the bloke if he ever met him. "How long has he been missing?"

She glanced at her watch. "Almost two hours."

Joel fought the urge to close his eyes and shake his head. *What had Billings been thinking?* The 48-hour rule had been in effect since before Joel made it to Special Branch, and that meant a person wasn't technically "missing" until they'd been gone for at least two full days.

"Miss Doyle," he said, "I don't understand why you weren't informed when you first came in, but we have a policy--"

"My Billy disappeared into thin air," she wailed.

Of course. Didn't they all? "I don't mean to seem rude, Miss Doyle, but we--"

"He was right in front of me," she said,

suddenly blushing. "Well, above me, actually. And then he was just... gone!"

"Above you? Like on another floor in your building?"

"No. I mean directly above me."

"Where you could see him?"

"Well, yes. Of course. Although I didn't have my eyes open the whole time." The distraught woman's complexion shifted from rose to radish. She lowered her voice to a barely audible whisper. "I believe it's called the missionary position."

Joel had spent nearly ten years investigating missing persons and assumed he'd heard just about everything, but this claim left him speechless.

"Please," she said, "swear to me that detail won't be included in the official report. If my mother ever saw it, I'd die."

Joel cleared his throat. "We often find it prudent to hide certain facts we uncover during an investigation. This one certainly fits that category. We needn't mention anything about it to anyone not directly connected to the case."

"Thank you." Miss Doyle's face gradually shed much of its color.

He shrugged. "Now then, let's go through this again, shall we? In, uhm, detail."

The blush returned with a vengeance, and Joel instantly regretted his word choice. "Forgive me! That's not-- I didn't mean--"

"I understand you have to do your job, Inspector." She gamely cleared her throat. "I'm-- I'm prepared to provide any details you think will help. But please, you must find Billy. I can't possibly go on without him."

"A little clarification, then, if you don't mind," Joel said, striving to be tactful. "Is it possible Mr. uh--" he checked the form "--Smithers merely left the room afterwards, say while you were--uhm--recovering from... you know."

"No. It's like I told you, he disappeared *during* our... activities."

"During?"

"Yes."

"In the uh--I'm trying to be delicate here--middle?"

"I think the proper term is *in flagrante delicto*."

Joel coughed. "You were actually, sort of, that is to say, intertwined?"

"Inter-*connected*," she whispered.

He sat back and looked at her with a mixture of shock and admiration. It took a moment to collect his wits before he could continue. "I don't suppose Mr. Smithers is a magician by trade, is he?"

"Certainly not! He's a chemist, not some tawdry stage charlatan. And, I might add, a third cousin by marriage to Lord Middlebury."

"Middlebury, yes, I see. But he actually *works*, you say. In a laboratory?"

"A pharmacy."

"Of course. Has he ever done this before? Disappear, I mean."

She shook her head. "He's a very cautious, conservative, methodical man. He never does anything unusual. He doesn't like surprises. He positively thrives on routine."

"And yet, you're saying he disappeared." Joel snapped his fingers. "Just like that?"

"Well, no," she said. "It wasn't that sudden. He sort of just... faded away. He had a funny look on his face, but I suppose that could've been from--" Another furious blush. "--uh... Well, I think you can imagine."

"Right," Joel said. "He just faded away."

"That's about the size of it."

"Into nothing."

"Yes."

He squinted at her. "How on Earth could that be possible?"

She blinked at him. "Isn't it your job to figure that out?"

~*~

Chapter Two

"Time is an illusion."

--Albert Einstein

Leah Kerr strolled into the rare books section of the Millburn College library which she had visited often in the weeks leading up to her father's Event. Her presence having become common, she no longer rated a glance from the cramped room's guardian, a bespectacled crone with an uncanny knack for annoying anyone wishing to do research among the crowded shelves. The room's odor bespoke more than rotting paper and fading ink. Leah suspected mold, most likely the sort that attacked brain cells which God intended to stimulate original thought, that being the rarest commodity on the ivy-covered campus.

Leah feigned interest in several malodorous tomes before making her way to the shelf upon which rested the Lancaster family Bible. Though printed some 300 years past, the leather-bound book remained in stellar condition. And for good reason. It had been hidden away for most of the 19th and 20th centuries in a privately owned vault. When the Lancaster family estate was liquidated, the executor's charge required him to distribute anything of historical value to "worthwhile educational institutions" near the original homestead. As the only such entity within an hour's drive of the now crumbling Lancaster manse, Millburn College got the Bible along with an astonishing number of oil portraits featuring profoundly unremarkable people.

The Bible, however, was amazing. Leah's father had taken an interest in it the moment the holy book arrived on campus. The elder Kerr had long been on the lookout for just such a find. Once the novelty of owning it had worn thin, and the school dedicated itself to being busy with something new, Dr. Kerr altered the library's catalog and related indices. Now known simply as "The Lancaster Book," the magnificent Bible took up residence among volumes of poetry, most of which had been self-published and donated to the school. The Lancaster Bible was no more likely to be examined at Millburn than it had while hidden in the safe.

Just as she had practiced during earlier visits to the library, Leah carefully opened the Lancaster's ancient King James edition and turned to a passage in Ecclesiastes. She had no need to read it; the scripture had been engraved in her heart:

Treason, Treason!

*That which hath been is now;
and that which is to be hath already been;
and God requireth that which is past.*

What changed Leah's life forever was the number scrawled in the margin beside the passage.

~*~

Joel opted not to work late as he usually did. He had no reason to rush home, no wife or children or pets required his attention, but the mystery of William Smithers' disappearance had thoroughly taxed his imagination.

People didn't just dematerialize. Especially not during sex. Afterwards, maybe. In fact, quite often. But considering Miss Doyle's charms--though unlikely to inspire chaps to queue up for a go--and "Billy" Smithers' goat-like appearance, the two seemed reasonably well suited.

Joel frowned; his own romantic record consisted of no wins and several losses. Perhaps he could learn something from Miss Doyle, but he doubted it. Still on the hopeful side of 35, he could count his successful dating attempts on one hand. Though he hardly considered himself unattractive, he knew he wouldn't be sought out to appear in any adverts for men's fashions.

And then, of course, there was the limp. He might've enjoyed dancing if not for that. Or perhaps not. All he knew was that he'd never get the chance to find out. A bullet from someone he should have been able to trust made sure of that.

He found himself standing outside the Small Arms. Though not an alcoholic, at least not yet, he found the public house to be more of a home than his flat. He could find the former in a blizzard. If the same storm blew the latter away, he wouldn't feel much of a loss.

It was a Friday after all, and Mollie Evans was bound to be around. Just looking at her would improve his mood, and besides, he needed a bit of her insight. She might not have a degree in psychology, but like most bartenders he'd known, she could smell bullshit a mile away. Unlike most others, she always knew how to deal with it.

Mollie smiled at him as he made his way through the maze of tables and chairs crowding the room. Dark wood and heavy furniture gave the place a feeling of solemnity.

"Yer early," she said.

"I missed you."

That got him a chuckle. "Hungry?"

"Starved."

"For love, right?"

"I have everything else."

"Poor dear. All I've got are bangers n' mash. Will that hold you 'til you find yerself a lass?"

Joel smiled. "It'll have to do."

Mollie patted him on the head like a puppy then sent his order into the kitchen. With neither a word nor a wasted motion she poured him a tall lager and sent it sliding down the bar. It came to rest with only minimal disturbance to the head, a wide dollop of which floated down the side of the chilled glass.

"That jar's on the house, luv," Mollie said. "You look like you could use it."

He smiled his thanks and took a sip.

"So, what's it about this time?" she asked. "Somethin' juicy?"

"I'm not supposed to talk about active investigations."

Mollie pulled away in a stunningly overdone rendition of shock. "Blimey! I've stumbled onto an *active investigation*." She put a hand on his forearm as if acting out the last two words. "Beer doesn't buy as much as it used to, does it? I seem to remember a time when we discussed a number of your more interestin' cases. I'd pour out me ales, and you'd pour out your tales."

"Very poetic."

"Stick around. I'm just gettin' started." She paused to make change for another customer, then gave Joel her full attention. "If you're going to faff around about it, I'll find a blonde to dissect the tricky bits for you."

"All right," Joel said. "It's like this: a woman pops in and reports her boyfriend's gone missing. Happens all the time, right? That's what I thought. Only this time, she claims he disappeared while they were making love."

"Before or after?"

"During," he said. "She was quite specific."

Mollie stared at him as if he'd grown an extra head. "Get on with ya."

"I'm serious."

"Was she sober?"

"I think so."

"On drugs?"

"Not likely."

"She's a headcase then," Mollie proclaimed. "Completely bonkers. You'd be better off checkin' the wards to see who's short a nutter."

"If only it were that easy. It's official business now. I've gotta follow it up."

Mollie's cook strolled out of the kitchen with Joel's sausages steaming on a plate beside a mound of mashed potatoes. He threaded his arm past Mollie and deposited the repast next to Joel's beer.

"Eat up," Mollie said. "With cases like this one, you're going to need your strength."

~*~

Leah Kerr stared at the number and the initials scrawled in the margin of the ancient Lancaster family Bible. It had nothing to do with Ecclesiastes, nor would anyone else understand the meaning behind it. The number was meant for her, and only her, and its very existence proved her father's brilliance. Much more importantly, it proved he had *survived!*

Leah recognized his handwriting, as short and shaky as it was. There could be no mistake. She read the number aloud, softly, to herself. Then, two more words tumbled out in a short, excited whisper: "It works!"

With that, she carefully closed the holy book and returned it to the shelf. She nodded to the crone behind the wire spectacles. They would not be seeing each other--ever again.

Leah's spirits soared even as trepidation nibbled holes at the edges of her resolve. All the decisions had been made, all the plans set in motion. She had but to carry them out, and toward that end she left the library and walked across the modest campus to a bike rack just outside the Jefferson Building, an edifice bearing the right name if the wrong lineage. None of that mattered any more. The time had come. *The time had come!* She laughed at the very thought.

That which hath been is now;
and that which is to be hath already been...

Oh, yes, Leah thought. Oh yes, indeed!

She wanted so much to climb on her bike and make a mad dash to the drop site her father had indicated. They had located three possible sites, none of which were likely to be disturbed during the long wait between the time Dr. Kerr left his message and the time Leah received it.

They had left the selection up to him, based on conditions at the other end, and he had indicated his choice via the number in the margin of the Lancaster Bible. As it turned out, he'd chosen site number 1, the very same spot from which he'd departed.

With night rapidly approaching, Leah realized nothing would be gained by a frantic search in the dark. Waiting until morning wouldn't change anything for him, and would give her a chance for one last night of sleep before she began the final preparations for her own departure into the unknown--or nearly unknown--to be with him.

Leaving her bicycle chained to the rack, she turned her steps to the Jefferson Building, home of the Millburn College physics department.

The lights in the building had been turned off long before she arrived. The building stood empty, as usual. Her father's office occupied the northeast corner of the structure, and she walked briskly through dark corridors and shadowed stairwells to reach it.

Key in hand, Leah opened the departmental door and entered his lair. Still full to bursting with excited energy, she danced past the secretary's desk. The well-meaning but nosey old Mrs. Flaherty had been given a sudden and quite unexpected vacation. Seconds later Leah reached the door to Dr. Kerr's private office.

Another lock.

Another key.

No problems.

She entered a smaller room, closed the door, and flipped on the lights to reveal a dignified, well-organized space. Absolutely nothing looked out of place. The orderliness extended to an array of pencils arranged on the desk blotter. Small to large, they huddled together like the boards in a privacy fence.

"Precision," her father had so often said, "begins with the little things." He proved it relentlessly, and while she loved him for it, his students often cited it as a sign of something dark and psychologically wrong, if not simply psychotic.

Screw 'em! We'll never have to deal with students--or faculty--ever again.

Friday evenings rarely saw many people on campus. This night proved no exception. Though still relatively early, Leah knew she'd need a good night's sleep to be ready for the next day and what likely would be the start of her adventure.

Helping herself to a glass of water from the sink in her father's private washroom, she swallowed a pair of sleeping tablets and stretched out on the leather sofa which filled one end of the small office.

She briefly considered running around the school's track a few times to tire herself, but she had just taken the pills and had no desire to lessen their impact. She would just have to be patient and concentrate on being relaxed. She ignored the simple fact that the tactic had never worked in the past. However, the sleeping pills had come from her father, and therefore they would work.

They had to.

Sprawled on the couch with her eyes closed, Leah mentally reviewed their preparations. Though likely a fool's errand, it occupied her mind until she eventually dozed off and entered a deep and dream-free sleep.

~*~

Perhaps if Joel had someone or something else in his life, he might not have dragged himself to the precinct offices seven days a week. But at most times of the year, Saturday was just another day.

The superintendent certainly never complained that Joel put in extra time for which he never earned a shilling. But by the same token, on those rare occasions when he did take some time off, no one said a word.

Linwood Billings seemed to operate on a similar system. For as long as Joel could remember, the towering, well-postured sergeant seemed to be perpetually on duty.

When Joel lumbered into the precinct, Billings handed him a file folder with a note attached from the squadron's "research" staff--two over-worked clerks hoping to make detective someday without the benefit of blood relatives in high office. They were charged with gathering and verifying basic information--addresses, credit reports, phone records, etc. Joel glanced at the note they'd left him, then back up at the towering sergeant.

"Is this a joke?"

"I've no idea what you're talking about."

"Surely you remember the woman you opened a case file on yesterday afternoon. Sharon Doyle?"

"Vaguely."

"For God's sake man, you waived the 48-hour rule for her. You must've had a reason."

"Ah yes," Billings said after a moment of reflection. "Right! Odd little bint. She'd been doing some chap from the south side and claimed he'd gone missing. 'Faded away like a fairy mist.' Or something like that, wasn't it?"

"Something like that, yes." Joel waved the slip of paper in his hand. "The man's name is William

Smithers. But, according to the boffins down the hall, he doesn't exist."

"Oh."

"*'Oh?'* That's it?"

"Indeed. Seems to me you can close the file, mate. The lady's got 'er hat on backwards is all. Happens all the time."

"But you *saw* her. You talked to her. She had you convinced."

Billings wavered. "I admit I felt sorry for her, but I'm no shrink. I sure as hell don't get paid like one. Chalk it up to sympathy, I say. Waste of time for a copper."

Joel turned away and opened the Smithers file. He'd left it with the researchers the day before. It contained the form he'd filled out with data provided by Sharon Doyle. The photo she'd supplied had been stapled to the inside cover.

Joel squinted at it. Far from a work of art, the picture was at least reasonable. Or had been. It had faded significantly overnight. Though it lacked detail, Sharon Doyle's mysterious lover remained front and center.

It was all far too odd. Joel was on his way out the door to pay Ms. Doyle a visit when Billings called him back.

"Phone call for you, Dawkins."

"I'll take it at my desk."

Dropping the Smithers file, Joel turned to a fresh page in his notepad and picked up the phone. "Missing persons," he said. "Inspector Dawkins."

An annoying female voice responded, "That's Dawkins? With a D?"

Joel stared at the receiver in his hand. *No, you twit. That's Dawkins with a bloody Q.* He exhaled, slowly. "Correct. How may I assist you?"

"My name is Francis Flaherty. I'm the secretary of the physics department at Millburn College. I understand you're in charge of Missing Persons?"

Me and my legion of minions. He sighed. "I am indeed."

"I would prefer to turn this over to someone local, but apparently the district isn't interested in missing persons."

"Sadly, that seems to be the way it is in all of the rural areas. It's a manpower issue." He didn't bother to add that the situation was only slightly better in Boston proper. "All such cases come here, to me. Did you wish to report someone missing?"

"I do," she said. "Our departmental chair, Doctor Raines Kerr."

"And your name again, please?"

"Flaherty. Francis Flaherty."

He couldn't resist. "That's Flaherty? With an F?"

"Yes," she said with a prolonged sibilance.

Joel scribbled down both names before asking the critical question. "And how long has doctor Kerr been missing?"

"I don't really know," she said. "I've been on vacation myself. I got back yesterday and have been trying to reach him ever since. He should've been in his office or the laboratory, but he doesn't answer his phone, and no one's seen him since I left."

"I should think his students would have

reported it if he failed to show up for his classes."

"He spends most of his time doing research," she said. "He doesn't have any classes this term."

"And what is he working on?"

"Well, physics, of course."

"Of course. But could you be just a tiny bit more specific?"

"Not without a great deal more education than I have," she said with an implied harrumph. "I've worked for Doctor Kerr for most of a decade. Ever since his wife died, as a matter of fact. Oh, I should tell you, when he didn't return my calls, I tried to get in touch with his daughter, Leah. No luck there, either. I've left messages for both of them."

Joel dutifully jotted down the third name. "So, it's been several days since the... since you last saw him?"

"It's been three weeks, exactly."

"I see. Could he be staying with friends?"

"Doctor Kerr keeps to himself. He and his daughter are very close, but I've never heard him speak of any other family or friends. Well, except for someone at a thing he called the dojo. Utter nonsense, I say. One thing I can tell you, he isn't on the best of terms with the rest of the faculty at Millburn."

"And why is that?"

"Politics. He and Leah don't hold the same opinions as most other staff members."

"Ah. So, Miss Kerr works for the college, too?"

"She's a graduate student, not an employee. History department. She's waiting for her thesis to be approved, but from what I've heard, that's not likely to happen anytime soon, if at all."

"Shoddy work is it?"

"Certainly not! She's nearly as smart as her father, and he's brilliant!" She lowered her voice. "It's all about politics."

"For a *history* major?"

"*Especially* for a history major. She has some crazy ideas about what might have happened if the colonials had won the rebellion way back in the beginning." She let out a long breath. "I don't know all the details. If they're important, you can get them from someone else. I just called to report that Doctor Kerr is missing, and for all I know, so is his daughter. I would hate to think something has happened to either of them. At heart they're good people. Misguided, perhaps, but good."

"I will most certainly look into it," he said.

"Excellent," said Ms. Flaherty. "I'm available this afternoon if you need me. I have keys to Dr. Kerr's office and lab."

"I'll be there first thing Monday morning."

"*Monday?* Why the delay? What if he's in trouble?"

Joel shifted in his chair and rubbed his leg. "Do you think anyone in the history department will be in their office over the weekend?"

"No, I suppose not."

"And you can't think of anyone other than Miss Kerr with whom I should speak?"

"Other than me? No."

"Monday it is, then. Unless you have some reason to suspect foul play."

"Heavens no! The Millburn community may

be a bit narrow-minded, but no one here would take drastic measures just to silence opposing thought."

"You're quite sure of that?"

After a pause, Flaherty said, "If I were to suspect anyone of foul play, it'd be Leah. She's the most radical person on campus."

~*~

Leah stretched as the sun broke through the window in her father's office and bathed her eyelids. Time to get moving.

After a quick pass through the lavatory, she left the building and jumped on her bike. Having skipped dinner the night before, she pedaled toward the campus dining hall where she grabbed coffee and biscuits to go. She could have used a much bigger breakfast, but she was too eager to dig up the message her father had left for her.

Though tempted to try eating en route, she had learned from experience that dining while biking was a losing proposition. Instead, she crammed the food into her mouth and chased it with the hot beverage. She disdained tea just like her parents, but she thoroughly enjoyed coffee, the drink of choice for colonials. Even after all this time, they refused to consume the Crown's preferred beverage as if the taxes were still in force. The very thought made her giggle.

Some things never changed.

After finishing her coffee, she climbed back on her bike and rode directly to the Event site. Not surprisingly, there were no distractions. The location was remote enough to discourage anyone who had no specific business there--a description that fit virtually all of New England, from the frigid bays of Nova Scotia to the fetid swamps of coastal Georgia.

She and her father had discussed any number of ways to pass messages. Sadly, the communication could only be one-way--from him to her. Confounding the issue was the subjective delay in the delivery, at least for him. That required the better part of 232 years.

For Leah, of course, the wait was immaterial so long as the message survived. Toward that end, they'd decided the best method would be to store the missive in a ceramic jar, sealed with wax and buried in a pre-determined location. They'd selected three such sites not knowing which might be the most easily accessible for Raines.

Leah finished the short ride to the rocky plateau from which her father had so recently departed. The area appeared undisturbed since her visit the day before.

Leaning her bike against the same old oak which had sheltered her from the sun the day before, Leah stepped gingerly to the edge of the rocky cliff overlooking the slow-moving stream some wag had dubbed the Pinckney river.

She'd seen more--and faster-moving--water in drainage ditches. But that was largely the point. They needed an area that was both remote and undesirable; it had to remain undisturbed for a long, long time. A low cliff overlooking the Pinckney was just the thing.

Treason, Treason!

Leah scrambled over the ledge and down toward the turgid green water, home to countless millions of mosquitos, frogs, and even less hospitable creatures.

She worked her way down to a spot just below the granite slab on which her father had marked the target circles. The mass stood easily four feet thick. She had no idea how long it had been since any Pinckney floodwaters may have reached the spot, but she seriously doubted it had occurred during her lifetime, or that of anyone she knew.

Using a trowel, she began digging at the tightly packed soil beneath the rock. Somewhere in there her father had buried a jar containing instructions. Hopefully, he'd added a bit more-- about what he'd been doing, where he was living, and what she might hope to expect when she arrived later on.

The digging seemed to go on forever. She loosened small shards of rock and sent them tumbling downhill to the wet soup below. Gravel, dirt, insects--some of them dead--followed suit. Since she and her father hadn't preselected the *exact* spot, she started on the left and worked methodically toward her right.

Somewhere near the middle she found the digging easier. Soon, she was reaching well into the bank beneath the granite. The ground was cool there, and though she scraped her knuckles during the excavation, she had a sense that all was well. This was the spot.

It had to be!

But it wasn't.

After digging to a depth of some three feet--the length of her arm plus the trowel--she concluded he would never have buried anything deeper than that. Annoyed, and more than a little weary, she climbed back to the top of the ledge for a rest.

The sun had drifted to the center of the sky, and while she had been in the shade most of the morning, any efforts she made in the afternoon would be done without that benefit. Fortunately, she'd brought a bottle of water with her and used it to slake her thirst.

Then she crawled back over the side and kept digging.

Though she perspired significantly more than she had in the morning, the digging actually proceeded more quickly. Still moving to her right, the soil seemed as loosely packed as it had been in the center. Rocks and other debris cascaded past her and down the hill in miniature avalanches which she totally ignored.

And then she hit something that didn't sound like rock. In fact, it sounded hollow.

She forced herself to pause and take another long drink of water, then attacked the site. Within minutes she extracted a cylinder made of light brown pottery. The top had been closed with a wooden stopper, and the upper quarter of the vessel had been sealed in wax.

Leah's hands trembled as she held the odd little jar and the message she was sure it contained--a message from 232 years in the past.

~*~

Chapter Three

"It is not known precisely where angels dwell--
whether in the air, the void, or the planets. It has not
been God's pleasure that we should be informed of
their abode."

--Voltaire

Raines Kerr lay face up in the afternoon sun. Something hard and sharp dug into his shoulders as he struggled to clear his head. He soon realized more of the same afflicted his back and legs. The pain drove him to an upright, cross-legged sitting position, but the discomfort found a new focus in his buttocks. Too dizzy to stand, he shifted left and right and manually swept the offending objects--stones and pebbles, he realized at last--from beneath him.

"You're not exactly as I expected," said a nearby voice.

Raines looked up and squinted in the general direction of the speaker. Though the Event left his senses clouded, he made out a slender black male in his mid-teens holding the reins of a horse. At his feet lay the bag of supplies Raines and Leah had so carefully assembled.

"That's my stuff," Raines said, wondering why he felt the need to state the obvious.

"I assumed as much," said the youth, "but I cannot fathom why you'd stand in need of anything."

Puzzled, though not ready to admit it, Raines tried to stand and quickly abandoned the idea. Immediately, the boy stepped forward to assist him. "Allow me," he said and took a firm grip on the physicist's arm. With surprising strength, the lad easily brought Raines to his feet. Not trusting his balance, Raines thanked him and leaned against the horse.

The boy smiled an acknowledgement, then appraised him as if he were a statue. Raines offered his hand, but the boy frowned and stepped back.

"My name is Raines Kerr. I'm uh, new around here."

"Of course you are," the boy said with a conspiratorial smile. "I'm Gabriel. The Colonel's wife says I was named after an angel." His smile grew still wider.

Raines felt certain he was missing something, as if the boy's introduction hid a deeper message. He assumed his mental fog accounted for the inability to solve the riddle. Had the boy seen him materialize? And if so, why wouldn't it have frightened him? Fortunately, the physicist's wits *and* his equilibrium returned in short order. "How long was I out?"

That earned him a blank look. "Out?"

"Unconscious--asleep."

"Ah. You slept not a whit," Gabriel said. "You began moving moments after you... arrived." He seemed suddenly nervous. "If you'll pardon my saying so, uhm, sir, your entrance seemed to lack... What I mean to say is that I would have expected something more... Well--"

"Out with it!" Raines barked, and then immediately regretted his outburst. None of his students had ever reacted to him with such alarm. He felt like a tyrant.

"I apologize," he added hastily. "I didn't mean to bite your head off."

Gabriel gave him a puzzled look, his fear quickly replaced by curiosity. He put his hands to his ears as if to reassure himself that everything remained where it should be. "My head, sir?"

Figures of speech, idioms. Leah had warned him about them. *Two hundred years of slang and verbal shorthand, gone up in smoke.* "I didn't mean to shout. I just wanted you to get to the point--to say what you meant."

"About what?"

"About my arrival. Evidently it didn't meet your expectations." *How could he have had expectations?*

"Ah. That. Yes, well, it seemed somewhat--"

"Go ahead. You can say it."

"--undignified."

"I see," Raines said, though he clearly didn't.

He made a determined effort to push the issue from his mind and concentrate instead on his surroundings. The first thing he noticed was a man lying spread-eagled on the ground a short distance beyond Gabriel and the horse. "What's wrong with him?"

"I'm no physician," Gabriel said, "but I'm fairly certain he's dead."

"My God! How?"

Gabriel eyed him with some suspicion. "I'd have thought you'd already know that."

"What?" Raines shook his head. "I have no idea what you're talking about!"

"Forgive me," Gabriel said, "my education has not prepared me properly for this moment. T'would help if you advised by what title you should be addressed."

"Title?" Raines was still looking at the man on the ground. "Uh, doctor, I suppose."

"Mysterious ways indeed," the youngster whispered. "Even so, I'd never have guessed *that*."

"Guessed what?"

"That an angel would wish to be called something so... ordinary. But then, I suppose you require a certain anonymity to blend in."

Of all the scenarios Raines had contemplated for his arrival in 1780, none of them included a greeting committee comprised of a corpse and a lunatic.

"I'm not an angel," he said at length.

"Of course not," said Gabriel, his agreement dramatically overdone.

"I'm serious," Raines said. He pointed at the

unmoving man. "And I have no idea what happened to that poor soul."

Gabriel smiled knowingly, and Raines vowed to chose his words more carefully from then on. Rather than compound the problem with still more words, he approached the body and knelt to examine it.

"His horse reared when you arrived, and off he flew. Landed just like that, with his head turned nearly backwards. He hasn't moved." Gabriel peered down at Raines with undisguised wonder. "I didn't know what to expect when you showed up, but it certainly wasn't that. And... I--" He shuffled his feet, nervous once again. "I mean no disrespect, but uhm, I have to know. Where are your wings?"

"Wings? Right." *At least he's a sincere lunatic.* "They're uhm... ceremonial. In fact, we almost never use them anymore. When we have an assignment, we simply *appear* wherever we're sent."

The boy frowned. "The sound surprised me most. Like a very great cork pulled from a monstrous bottle. So strange. And--forgive me--not at all *heavenly.*"

Raines briefly pondered the observation. "I suppose you were looking for trumpets."

"Why, yes!"

"And perhaps a huge flash of light?"

"Exactly! I've studied the Bible, sir. Ask me anything!"

"There's no need. I believe you. As for the sound and fury, such theatrics are just too expensive." He dismissed the topic and turned to check the prostrate man for a pulse.

"Even for *God?*"

"He has more pressing concerns than accounting."

Gabriel chewed on that while Raines lifted the deceased's eyelids to see if the pupils reacted to the light. Seeing no change, he blew gently across them to spark an involuntary blink. Nothing. "I'm afraid he is dead."

"As I thought."

"You don't seem overly concerned."

"Pardon me for not grieving," Gabriel said. "But the man planned to sell me as soon as he married my mistress."

"Sell you?" *Mistress?*

"Aye. The moment Miss Chastity Cotswold became Mrs. Elihu Smithers, he planned to use her dowry to establish a shipping business."

"And you're part of her dowry?"

Gabriel nodded. "The thought of exchanging my books and letters for chains and tools drove me to my deepest prayers. But of course you already know all this."

Raines got to his feet, a plan coalescing in his mind. He hadn't anticipated dealing with slavery in Massachusetts, nor would he have imagined bumping into one who thought him an angel. "Not even angels know everything. It doesn't work that way. Sometimes we don't see the whole picture."

"Why else would God have sent you?"

"Most of the time those we're sent to help don't see the whole picture either."

"I'm confused," Gabriel said. "I thought you were the answer to my prayers."

"Well, yes and no."

"Sir?"

"You can't find answers until you understand the questions," Raines said. "And we've both got a good bit of understanding to master. Now, how far is it to town?"

"Town?"

"Or wherever Mr. uh, Mr.--" He gestured at the deceased.

"Smithers."

"Right. Wherever Mr. Smithers lived."

"It's a long walk," Gabriel said.

"Then help me load Mr. Smithers across his saddle. Your mistress will need to be informed."

"Would you accompany me?" Gabriel asked, clearly concerned. "I fear she will be sorely vexed. And having a doctor to hand, even one who's not quite what he seems, would be a comfort."

"Of course," Raines said. "After we get Mr. Smithers tied to the horse, I'll gather my things, and we can be off."

"You are truly a godsend," Gabriel said.

"Let's keep that between us, all right?"

"Of course, sir. You may trust me with anything."

Raines prayed that was true.

~*~

General Sir David Fitzwilliam ran his finger down the list of names he'd chosen to carry out the tasks which would end the insanely prolonged rebellion. Though it had been decades since they had fought any battles in the traditional sense, the colonials had managed a guerilla campaign which kept too many crown resources tied down. That situation had gone on far too long. It had to end.

Swiftly.

And permanently.

His plan would do that. The royals and the politicians wouldn't like it, of course. Despite the never-ending nature of the conflict, there were many who sympathized with the rebels even if they didn't support them directly. Almost everyone paid lip service to the idea that the rebellion had gone on long enough. More than long enough! But few leaders in memory were willing to anger the public to achieve the victory they all *said* they wanted.

Bloody hypocrites.

Fitzwilliam would fix that. During the Great War the Germans had taught the world a serious lesson about winning battles: fight to win, and use everything at your disposal to do it. Don't hold back, and for God's sake, don't split your forces on two continents! Fitzwilliam was not alone in blaming the colonies--and the Irish, of course--for the success of the German invasion of the British Isles. The mere thought of Kaiser Wilhelm redecorating Buckingham Palace infuriated him.

Alas, all that had been before his time; he'd had nothing to do with it nor any hope of changing it. That would be the task for his heirs. There was something he could do now, however: end the goddamned rebellion so the army could focus on reclaiming the homeland.

Recruiting the people whose names appeared

on his list would be the next step. And a relatively easy one. Every last one of the candidates was connected to a bona fide member of the peerage. Some, like Fitzwilliam, had historical ties to the never-ending war. Others were simply ready to make names for themselves.

He hesitated briefly. After all, it was Saturday, and nearly everyone on his list would be at home, resting up for a return to the monotony of a protracted conflict which had lost all but token support.

No, by God, it's war! And it's time we ended it.

He reached for the phone to summon the first person whose name appeared on the list: Murchesson, Gerald B., Major, MI5. The man had spent half his career in Military Intelligence. Section 5, as everyone knew, handled domestic espionage.

A man with that sort of training was precisely the type of person he needed. And, because of a surprising discovery, Fitzwilliam had to put his plan into action immediately. He couldn't allow a single day's delay. Murchesson would have to do. There was no time to recruit anyone else. Fortunately, the General had reason to be confident.

Based on his record, the Major had earned his reputation as a rising star. Fitzwilliam had never met him, but he knew his father. The elder Murchesson, while sorely lacking as a strategist, had been a bulldog when it came to a fight. He had strange eyes: one blue, one brown. As a boy Fitzwilliam had a Great Dane with similar eyes, *and* temperament, come to think of it.

He sighed. Like so many other fine men, his

friend had been cut down by a colonial sniper. His son would want revenge. And if the younger Murchesson was anything like his father, he'd understand how his role in the plan would provide all the vengeance he could ever want.

~*~

Joel took a west-bound trolley to the address Sharon Doyle had given him. Because it was a Saturday, he could have used an official police vehicle, but aside from the bother of dealing with machinery that was balky at best and certain to be ill-maintained, he needed the time to think. And he certainly didn't need to deal with Boston's legendary traffic snarls. Literally hundreds of privately owned automobiles crowded the narrow roads every day. He had no desire to put himself at greater risk.

The trolley sped along at a reasonable pace, across the Charles River via the Benedict Arnold bridge. The route extended all the way to Watertown, far beyond his destination.

Doyle lived in a modest home just off the main street in Brighton. She answered his knock almost immediately.

"Good day, Ms. Doyle. I'm just following up on your visit," Joel said. "I don't suppose you've heard anything new."

"About what?"

"Mr. Smithers, of course."

She seemed puzzled.

"You reported him missing yesterday," Joel prompted.

"I did?"

"Yes. I took the report myself." He reached into his pocket and produced the photo he'd removed from the official file and handed it to her. "Here's the picture you provided."

She accepted the snapshot and carefully examined both sides, then looked up and examined *him*. "Is this some kind of joke? There's no one in this picture." She shifted position to get more light on the image. "There's no doubt it was taken in my parlor, but--"

Joel plucked the photo from her hands and studied it himself. Though the likeness of Smithers had completely disappeared, the fading had no effect on the background.

"If there's a joke involved here," Joel observed with no effort to hide his irritation, "it's on me, not you. And it's not very funny. I have important work to do."

"Are you implying that I'm somehow involved in this nonsense?" she asked.

"That's rather obvious, isn't it? You were the one who came into my office with your lascivious fable and photographic trickery. We've checked, Ms. Doyle, and there *is* no William Smithers." He gave her his darkest stare. "There's no Billy Smithers, either."

"I have no idea who, or what, you're talking about. I came into the police station to inquire about employment. I spoke to a charming sergeant there. Billings I believe his name is. Extremely tall fellow. Ask him. I recall seeing you, but if we had some sort of conversation, I've no recollection of it. Nor, I might add, do I have any desire to speak with you further. Good day, sir!"

With that she slammed the door in Joel's face.

~*~

Though sorely tempted to tear open the wax seal on the old jar and extract the message from her father, Leah could no longer stand the swarming mosquitos which had plagued her since she began excavating beneath the rock ledge above the Pinckney slough. Despite arms and legs peppered with red welts, she recognized her most immediate needs included a shower, food, and clean clothes.

The message could wait. It had done so for over 230 years. What difference would a couple hours make?

She gathered her gear and piled it into the basket on her bike, then pedaled hastily back toward the campus. It wouldn't be a long trip to her new address. The apartment she shared with her father was nothing like their old home. That building occupied an expansive, heavily wooded lot close to the college without being part of it. She missed the place, and all its memories, but they had a greater need, and selling the house helped them meet it. Though the apartment lacked almost all the amenities of their old home, it was superior in one respect: proximity to the Event site.

Near the corner of Burgoyne and Cornwallis streets, near the main entrance to the campus, Leah slowed to a halt.

A twin column of uniformed children,

directed by a pair of boys in their early teens, were queued up to march through the Millburn grounds. The uniforms, though wrought in kiddie sizes, captured in detail the outfits worn by British soldiers during the early years of the war. Accompanied by young drummers and a flag-bearer, the little parade had drawn a sizeable crowd of sympathetic adults.

Their parents, most likely, Leah theorized. *Yet another generation of redcoat invaders.* She felt a familiar scowl settle her features as she waited for the procession to pass.

Rather than merely provide spectators for whom the children could march, the crowd had apparently walked alongside the columns. Considering the tender age of some of the uniformed "soldiers," Leah thought that quite reasonable.

A woman from the ranks of admirers stood with a boy in his late teens or early twenties. He gestured at Leah, rolled his eyes, and whispered in the woman's ear.

"I've heard about you!" the woman said in a loud voice. "You're the one who thinks the rebels should've won the war." Her brows were drawn down accusingly, and her lips scribed a tight line.

"What?" The comment took Leah by surprise. "I... It's... This is silly. No one cares what I think."

"It's that sort of attitude that keeps us at war," accused the woman. "Traitors like you can't give it up."

Leah eyed the children in 18th century military attire. "If I had kids, I surely wouldn't want them doing anything like this."

The remark caught the attention of other adults.

"You don't approve of patriotism?" Heads all around shook up and down, background noise slowly faded as the volume of muttering went up.

"I don't approve of treating invaders as if they were heroes," Leah said with all the calm she could muster knowing how poorly her comment would be received.

"*My* child is no invader!" shrieked the woman. "He was born here."

"Mine, too!" said another.

Others jostled closer, eager to demonstrate their loyalty to king and country.

"Who *is* this bitch?"

"Get her off the street!"

"She's attacking the parade!"

"Slut!" Cried someone else.

Another added, "Make that *filthy* slut. Look at the dirt on her."

"Colonial whore!" groused a man on crutches.

"Don't use that language near *my* children," the first woman said. "Even if it's true."

Due to the surly knot of people surrounding her, Leah couldn't get away. All paths were blocked. Soon, angry people began poking and grabbing at her. Two men vented their anger by kicking her bike. She desperately wanted to strike back, just as she'd been trained, but a lone woman against a small mob stood little chance, and she knew it.

"Stop!" She screamed, but the entreaty only made them attack harder.

Fully engaged in fending off the worst blows,

she could only watch helplessly as someone wearing a shirt modeled after the British flag reached into her basket and grabbed the ceramic jar she had spent so much effort recovering. She had little time to register details, but the thief was male and could have been a Millburn student. Shoving the bike away to create some space, she fought to break free and follow him.

The effort proved futile. Too many people stood in her way, and none of them showed any inclination to disengage.

A few moments later the crowd's attention shifted back to the parade where the liveried children shuffled into step accompanied by a merry pipe and drum tune.

It wasn't "Yankee Doodle."

With the ruined bike at her feet, her hair tussled and clothing torn, Leah scanned the area for any sign of the thug who'd stolen the message from her father.

A cheer went up as the children's brigade passed under the Millburn College arch where the school's motto--*Home of scholarship, bastion of tolerance*--had been inscribed in multiple languages.

~*~

Joel remained angry all the way back to Boston. He considered returning to the precinct but had no compelling reason to waste the rest of his day there. Besides, the weather promised a pleasant weekend for anyone wishing to stay outdoors. That normally didn't appeal to him, but he knew there was a football match scheduled for later in the day, and the thought of catching the game with Mollie definitely appealed to him.

He wasn't as crazy about the sport as Oliver Leahy or the other lads at the pub. Someone had said the boffins in New York were working on a device to send pictures through the air, much as they sent radio waves. He wasn't about to hold his breath waiting for something like that, though it would be nice if it were true. Imagine watching a match from the comfort of a pub chair!

Rubbish, of course.

Technology had advanced quite fast enough to suit him. Most of it, anyway. Perhaps a little more work in the realm of reconstructive surgery would be nice. He'd dearly love to get rid of his limp.

Even more than the limp itself, he'd like to get rid of the need to explain it. He was tired of the lie and tired of relying on it just to keep his job.

The trolley dropped him off near Oliver's bookshop. Joel went in for a look around and noticed a pair of uniformed army officers in deep conversation near the back of the store. Oliver wasn't in sight. Ordinarily he had no interest in military men, most especially officers. But Oliver had said something about changes afoot. Changes that might affect the never-ending conflict.

Joel wandered closer pretending to be interested in a book on photography, which turned out to be less of a ruse than he'd first intended. After all, hadn't he just been made the butt of a photographic joke? Perhaps he could figure out how someone managed to create a photo print with disappearing ink, and limit the disappearance to only a part of the picture. How could the foreground image--supposedly of the fictitious Billy Smithers--have been supplanted by the background, completely filling in for the missing male lover? How bizarre! Who even *thought* like that?

A glance over his shoulder confirmed the two army types were examining a book that also focused on photography, the type that featured unclothed females in lewd poses. He recognized the style from some French postcards Oliver had once shared with the lads at the Small Arms.

Mollie had not been amused.

He wondered if she liked football.

There seemed to be but one way to find out.

~*~

The walk seemed interminable, and not merely because the flies had discovered the remains of the late Elihu Smithers.

"If Mr. Smithers intended to *start* a shipping business," Raines asked, "what other occupation did he have?"

"He called himself an entrepreneur, and he specialized in horses."

"He was a rancher?"

Gabriel looked about as if someone in the surrounding woods might overhear him. "He didn't raise them. He stole them."

Raines cut his eyes at the youth. "You're joking."

"That's one of the reasons we were out this

far from Miss Cotswold's home. Or, rather, Colonel Cotswold's home. Master Smithers wouldn't conduct *business* where someone might catch him in the act."

"You're saying he was wanted?"

Gabriel's brows dipped in confusion.

"If he was a thief, wouldn't someone be out to arrest him?"

"Forgive me if your manner of speech confounds me from time to time. We here on Earth are given--"

"Stop." Raines held up an admonishing palm. "Please. Don't think of me as an angel. Think of me as just... just someone who showed up from, say, a long way away. An unimaginably long way away."

"I shall try."

"I need you to promise."

"Done."

"Good. Now what about Smithers? Surely there's a sheriff or a constable looking for him."

"Quite possibly," Gabriel said. "But not anywhere near the home of Colonel Cotswold. Master Smithers would help himself to a horse from a paddock in one county and sell it to someone in another county. Then, knowing where the stolen animal was stabled, he would steal it a second time and return it to the original pasture before the first owner ever knew it was gone."

"How devious."

"He once bragged that he'd sold the same horse five times."

"Then someone must have been on the lookout for him. Such a swindle couldn't be kept a secret for long."

Gabriel gave his shoulder a slight nudge. "I suspect that's the case. Few would risk the punishment for theft in this colony."

"Imprisonment?"

The teen chuckled. "The stocks and a lashing at the very least. Then a brand if not a hanging."

"A *brand?*"

"Of course! On the cheek where it can be seen by everyone--a great 'T' for thief. I can't imagine how painful it would be. And then there's the nailing, too."

Raines squinted at him. *Nailing?*

"Of course," Gabriel said, smiling with understanding. "There's no need for this sort of thing where you come from." He casually adjusted the strap holding the dead man to his saddle. "For those judged of multiple crimes, their ears are often nailed to the stocks. Sometimes it's easier to remove the ears than the nails."

Raines felt himself blanche. "I image that cuts down on repeat offenders."

Gabriel didn't get the joke.

"Right. Well then," Raines said, "can you tell me a bit more about Miss Cotswold and how she got involved with such a sinister fellow?" *Dear Lord, I'm beginning to talk like him!*

"That's a sad tale, indeed. Colonel Cotswold and his wife had seven children, all girls. Miss Chastity is the youngest and the only one not married. The Cotswolds have long been associated with the finer folk in Boston, but his business suffered as the war went on."

"He's serving the colonies?"

"The Colonel is a proud member of the Sons of Liberty. But his participation is limited due to his age and the wounds he sustained fighting the French and the savages." He paused in sudden thought. "Do you suppose you could examine him? As a doctor, especially one with such powerful connections, perhaps--"

"Sorry, I'm not that kind of doctor."

"Oh."

"I'm not allowed to perform miracles simply because it might be convenient."

"I see."

"Besides, I have another important mission. I have to get to New York."

Gabriel looked at him in amusement. "Wouldn't it have been easier to simply *start* there?"

"And what would that have done for you?"

The boy responded with a broad smile.

"I'm wondering if Colonel Cotswold might be able to help me in my journey."

"I'm sure he would." Gabriel patted the dead thief's leg. "Once we've seen to Master Smithers' needs."

"I doubt he's expecting much," Raines said.

"On the contrary," said Gabriel, "I suspect he has a great deal to look forward to where he's going. But none of it will be pleasant."

~*~

Leah finally reached her tiny, furnished apartment on foot. With no personal belongings in it, the place felt foreign. Just getting there seemed strange. Her bicycle had been damaged too much to ride, and she lacked the strength to drag it back. Let the rubbish men collect it, she thought. She didn't really need it anymore.

After a long, hot shower, she changed into clean shorts and a blouse, then fixed herself a hot meal. The entire exercise, from the moment the crowd lost interest in her until she sat down at the kitchen table and ate, was managed with the dispassionate competence of a robot. And like an automaton, nothing registered. Her senses were all engaged in getting her hands on the message from her father.

They had discussed many plans, and many options, but it always came down to one basic problem: no matter how much they prepared, they couldn't know in advance what really awaited them in the summer of 1780.

According to her research, there had been no battles in the area at that time, and likely very little activity of any other kind--all of which was to the good. Unfortunately, most of what she "knew" came as a result of deduction and not from verifiable intelligence.

Simply put: they could not know with what they would be faced when the Event left them in the past. She would have one chance to collect anything they might need. Whatever else her father deemed necessary for the success of their mission had been written down and passed along via the crockery she'd dug up that morning.

And lost that afternoon.

She considered going to the local police to

report the robbery, but she knew they had more pressing matters than the recovery of an old jar, especially one belonging to a crazed radical and known sympathizer of the self-proclaimed Americans. And, even if they did find it, the relic would likely have to remain in police custody as evidence of the crime. Knowing how slowly the courts operated, it could be years before she got the damned thing back.

Of course, none of that would matter to her father. Owing to the power of an Event, she would simply show up at the date and time they'd anticipated, assuming her father's machine was calibrated correctly.

Until then, Leah was on her own and would remain so until she embarked on the next stage of the mission. Getting there meant finding the jar.

Finding the jar meant searching the campus--a largely hostile campus.

Surely there was someone she could call on for help. She couldn't possibly have pissed off everyone at Millburn.

But try as she might, she couldn't think of a single person.

~*~

Chapter Four

"Mumps, measles, and puppy love are terrible after twenty."

--Mignon McLaughlin

Having wasted the morning on the Doyle/Smithers affair, Joel decided to take the rest of the weekend off. It wouldn't surprise him if Ms. Doyle took out her resentment with him by contacting his superiors. Not that he cared too deeply. He'd held his position long enough, and with sufficient commendations, that he should be able to keep it for as long as he liked, even without the aid of his "patron." Just how long he *wanted* to keep it, he really didn't know.

Perhaps he had put too much of himself into his work, and the time had come for other pursuits. Mollie Evans might be a good bet. Though they'd never seen each other outside the pub, they'd always gotten along well enough inside it. She had a charming sense of humor and flirted with all the lads, but never, as far as he knew, took any of them to her bed.

Standing on the walk outside the Small Arms, he shot the cuffs on his shirt, mostly to hide his Black Watch tattoo. No point in displaying something that might dredge up ancient history. He brushed invisible debris from his chest and walked in.

He immediately spotted the enchanting Miss Evans in her usual spot behind the bar, her Siberian blue eyes constantly on the move to spot potential trouble. Though he'd never personally seen her in action, he'd heard from Oliver Leahy, among others, that she wasted neither time nor sympathy on anyone making mischief.

God, what a woman!

Threading his way through the tables and chairs crowding the floor, he eventually found a vacant stool at the bar and parked himself there. Mollie cocked an eye at him and swiveled her index finger from the beer taps to the booze in bottles behind the bar. He nodded, twice, when she pointed at the whiskey.

Grabbing a pair of shot glasses, she filled them both to the brim from a bottle beneath the bar, and delivered them with a smile warm enough to melt an iceberg.

"You're a luv, know that?"

"I do," she said as if she hadn't already heard it ten thousand times, that day.

"Do you ever take any time off?"

"Of course! You think I live here?"

"Sometimes I wonder."

She batted her lashes at him, but he couldn't help notice she'd also kept a wary eye on a table near the front window.

"What's goin' on there?" he asked.

"Prob'ly nothing. One o' the lads there has met his quota, and he's spoutin' off 'bout the bliddy war. You'd think they'd find somethin' else to talk about, wouldn't ya?"

It soon became clear the foursome at the table had taken sides, and all indications put the ratio at 3:1 in favor of the loyalists. "Want me to calm them down?" he asked, feeling for the darbies on his belt. "I've got cuffs."

"No need."

"I don't mind."

She smiled at him. "Neither do I."

He watched as she gave the bar a quick wipe, then floated through the room as if riding on a magic carpet. Nothing stood in her way or even slowed her passage.

Joel strained to hear what was said at the table, but noise from the intervening crowd made that impossible.

Suddenly, and without any dramatics, Mollie had a grip on the ears of two patrons. Both twisted at the waist, their faces reflecting an agony he couldn't imagine as she led them to the door and launched them into the summer air. The third member of the pro-crown trio followed his mates outside leaving behind a tiny cloud of one-pound notes.

Mollie leaned over the dazed pro-colonial still seated at the table, spoke to him for a few moments, then helped him up. He smiled his thanks, and she walked him to the door.

Joel had finished the first of his two shots by the time she returned and was well on his way to finishing the second. "What was that all about?"

"The usual: who started what."

"And you took the rebel's side?"

"I know what it's like to face invaders," she said, her face blank.

"Huns?"

"Aye."

"Listen," he said, offering a far less emotional topic, "what d'ya say we take in a Cobber's match tomorrow? I've got a mate who can get me tickets. Good seats, too."

"Aren't you a love!" She kissed him on the cheek. "But I've already got a date." She bobbed her head in the direction of the dark-haired barmaid who'd delivered the phone to him the day before.

"For football?"

She eyed him with amusement. "We've got a very different game scheduled for tomorrow."

Sometimes, Joel decided, life just wasn't fair.

~*~

Sunday morning found Leah eager to begin her search for the stolen ceramic jar. Unfortunately, she had no idea where to begin. Why anyone would be interested in something like that puzzled her. She supposed there might be a market for stolen antiques, but who'd be interested in an old jar? And where might one go to find a buyer for such a thing?

The only logical conclusion she could think of was The Barn.

After a hurried breakfast, she dressed casually and wandered over to the two buildings which comprised the history department. One contained offices and classrooms; the other, a house formerly occupied by Millburn headmasters, had been thoroughly gutted and remodeled. A combination of antique furnishings and clever lighting gave the interior the appearance of an old English manor house. Officially dubbed Chumley Hall, it not only served as the focal point for social events, it housed a sizeable collection of 18th century artifacts donated to the school by Millburn faculty and alumnae. Shortly after its renovation, some wag had dubbed it The Barn, which name never failed to draw scowls from administrators. No doubt the admin types had hopes of milking still more funds from Lord and Lady Chumley. Leah thought the unofficial name fit perfectly.

She reached the office and classroom building first. Newer and larger than The Barn, it was also securely locked. This didn't prove terribly disappointing, as the building would have been locked during and after the parade as well. She doubted it harbored any clues to the thief's identity.

Next, she moved on to The Barn, which normally would not open until the afternoon. Instead, it buzzed like a hive under assault. She wandered about the periphery hoping to discover what drove all the excitement. Her patience earned its reward much sooner than she expected.

Dr. Lillian Plouth, head of the Millburn history department, stood in the center of the melee directing traffic. Leah watched from behind a curtain as Dr. Plouth sent her disciples to various locations in the main hall. Tables and chairs were arranged, covered in white cloth, and prepped as if in anticipation of a royal visit.

Just what I need--the bloody Queen and her Prince of (occupied) Wales.

The titles had not been officially changed, of course, but everyone, regardless of their views on the rebellion, knew the Royals had little going for them beyond the Crown Jewels and claims to real estate long occupied by Germans. And yet all of New England--from Nova Scotia to Florida--seemed intent on worshipping members of the bloodline. Leah couldn't imagine a greater waste of time and energy.

Avoiding the hubbub, Leah stayed on the outskirts of the activity and kept an eye on the people involved. Big events drew big crowds and might provide a glimpse of the man who stole her ceramic jar.

Though she scrutinized everyone who came in sight, she concentrated on the males. Late in the morning, as the workers and volunteers neared the end of their frenzied preparations, she spotted someone wearing a shirt just like the one worn by her thief.

He stayed in the room only long enough to confer briefly with Dr. Plouth, then left by a side door.

Leah hurried to catch up with him.

~*~

Raines Kerr had never fully appreciated his 21st century bed until he spent the night in one from the 18th. Though he never considered himself particularly tall, his six-foot frame dwarfed that of everyone else in the Cotswold home, where he'd spent the night--mostly awake and wishing he could extend the bed a foot or two.

His physical discomfort might have been worse if he'd been forced to sleep outdoors, something he assumed would be required so early in his mission. Forced wakefulness gave him time to fully consider his situation. That events in general, and *the* Event in particular, had gone so well left him nervous. Careful planning and attention to detail had always been his hallmark, but experience had taught him the truth of the adage about the best laid plans. His may not have been subject to quite as many unforeseen circumstances, but they were hardly immune.

The Cotswolds were a pure joy, and falling into their domain had been such a positive turn that he began to think in terms of actually completing the task he and Leah had set for themselves. He felt so confident, in fact, that he'd begun to wonder if he should warn her not to make the trip. Despite his good fortune, it could have gone wrong in countless ways, many of them fatal. Here, in the past, there was no way he could guarantee her safety. Millburn had its drawbacks, certainly, but she'd be far less vulnerable there and then than here and now.

But that's insane!

His mind raced. If she never took the one-way journey into the past to join him, she might not survive the changes to the world resulting from his tinkering. Would she even be born? She certainly *had been*, in what was now for him, the far future. Verb tenses became surly and uncooperative when used in conjunction with time travelers.

What if something he did in order to carry out the plan later caused one of his own ancestors to marry a different person, or not have any offspring at all? Would *he* suddenly disappear? It seemed likely, since he wouldn't have been born under the altered circumstances. But then, if that were true, how would he have existed to alter them in the first place? It made his head hurt.

Though rife with theories, observations, and experimentation, physics as he knew it didn't have answers for everything. His own fallback position, though he couldn't prove its validity--yet--was that the universe would adjust to an altered past. If something changed, there would be a ripple effect moving forward through time to realign everything from memories to memorabilia.

Maybe it wasn't the bed that kept me awake after all. He frowned so hard *that* hurt, too.

Thinking about the Cotswolds, however, made him smile. The colonel and his wife reminded him of the Fezziwigs, pleasant characters from his favorite Dickens novel, *A Christmas Carol*. Mrs. Cotswold, short, plump, and giggly, had an irrepressibly bright outlook. For her, everything would "work out all right." She had no idea why that might be, but failure, doom, and dire consequences had no place in her lexicon.

Colonel Cotswold, though marginally less gregarious than his wife, fully shared her physical characteristics *and* inability to see a dark horizon. It just couldn't happen. It never had before, ever. At dinner the previous evening the Colonel had even called upon Gabriel for confirmation.

As if on cue, Gabriel dredged up and recited a passage from Matthew, Chapter 6: "'Behold the fowls of the air: for they sow not, neither do they reap, nor gather into barns; yet your heavenly Father feedeth them. Are ye not better than they?'"

And yet, based on what Raines had gathered from conversations with the boy, the rebellion had cost the Colonel dearly and left him dangling over the abyss of bankruptcy. They assumed the marriage of their daughter, Chastity, to Mr. Smithers, would assure her well-being, and that eventually "all would be well."

"They're on their way to debtor's prison," Gabriel said, "and they don't even realize it."

"Surely you told them Smithers was a horse thief?"

"Of course," Gabriel lamented. "But what proof did I have? Master Smithers told them I harbored ill will for him, and that I was not to be trusted. He claimed I was innocent in the ways of enterprise and couldn't recognize the difference between a trade and a tort."

"Amazing. And they sided with *him*?"

"They did indeed, sir. I had thought of myself

as a member of the family. After all, I grew up alongside Miss Chastity. From the time we were five, we had the same tutors, ate the same food, and slept under the same roof. I thought they loved me. But I was being foolish. I see that now."

"Maybe not," Raines said. "Smithers may have clouded their judgment. It wouldn't be the first time such a thing has happened. Where I grew up we called them 'con men.'"

"An odd phrase."

You have no idea.

Later, when they reached the Cotswold home, Raines stood by Gabriel and confirmed the youngster's story about Smithers' demise. Just as the physicist had urged, the Cotswold's servant abbreviated the tale saying the poor man had simply been thrown from his horse.

Chastity Cotswold appeared a short while later, passing through the front entryway and walking stiffly toward the remains of her fiancé. Raines had been utterly unprepared for the sight of such a lovely young woman. Smithers must have been at least thirty years older.

What a lecher! Any feelings of remorse Raines might have harbored for causing the death of the horse thief evaporated on the spot.

Chastity took the news of his death in stride, however, and he thought, with more than a touch of relief. The Colonel and Mrs. Cotswold remained solemn.

"This is a great tragedy," Colonel Cotswold said after Gabriel had introduced everyone to Raines. "Thank you for your assistance, Dr. Kerr."

"Does he have any family nearby?" Raines asked.

"No," Chastity said. "He was somewhat secretive about that. I asked him about bringing his relations to our nuptials, but he claimed they all lived far away."

"Most likely in prison," Gabriel suggested in a cautious whisper meant for Raines. In a louder voice he added, "It's too late to take him to Master Lennox."

"The mortician?" Raines asked.

Colonel Cotswold gave him a puzzled look. "Hiram Lennox makes caskets, among other things, and tends the graveyard."

"He made our armoire," Mrs. Cotswold said. "He's quite clever with tools."

"Gabriel," Colonel Cotswold said, covering his nose with the cuff of his shirt, "make Mr. Smithers comfortable in the stable. We'll decide what to do with him on the morrow."

"Shouldn't we bring him inside?" Mrs. Cotswold asked.

Chastity made no pretense of holding her nose. "No!" she said with a nasal wheeze. "He's starting to st--"

"He may have stepped in something," said her mother.

"I agree with you, Colonel," Raines said. "The stable will do nicely. Gabriel, may I be of assistance?"

The boy's look of relief spoke volumes.

"That's hardly necessary," said the Colonel.

"I insist." Raines put his hand on Gabriel's elbow. "To the stable, then."

"You'll join us for supper?" Mrs. Cotswold asked.

Gabriel paused. "He has nowhere else to go."

Please Gabe, no talk of angels now!

"He put his own needs aside to help me," the young servant said. "And does so even now."

"Then you'll not only stay for supper, you'll stay the night," the Colonel said.

Raines would have been completely content at that point but for the actions of the intoxicating Chastity Cotswold. Far from playing the role of grieving fiancé, she had maneuvered close enough to him that he could feel her body heat through his thin shirt. Pressing her chest into his arm, she looked up into his eyes and gave him the sort of come-hither smile for which heroes leapt off cliffs.

"I look forward to learning more about you, *Doctor* Kerr," she said, eyelashes aflutter, "much, much more."

~*~

Joel left the Small Arms less steady on his feet than he'd been when he went in. He managed to get home in one piece and fell asleep on the sofa. On Sunday morning he dragged himself through the shower and otherwise made himself presentable. Having given up cooking for himself long ago, he went back out to select a cafe.

The search ended quickly and left him at a cramped table in the rear of a delicatessen which catered to a largely agnostic clientele. The spot he occupied provided a good view of the street, plenty of hot coffee--he'd never cared for tea--and the constant aroma of fresh-baked bread.

All of which gave him time to reflect. His last foray into the Small Arms hadn't been a total loss. If nothing else, he'd managed to distract himself from the healed wound in his leg and the open one in his ego. Ladies had turned him down before, and probably would again. He had to keep reminding himself not to stop trying, although the temptation was strong.

Perhaps he was setting his sights too high. He thought about Sharon Doyle for the first time since he entered the pub the day before. Where had she set her sights? Or had she given up, too? The elaborate fiction about Billy Smithers still rankled him, mostly because he couldn't fathom any motivation for it. What was the ruddy point?

He glanced at a newspaper left behind by a neighboring agnostic: *The Boston Globe & Mail*. A slight shift in his chair allowed him to read the headlines. Apparently, and to no one's surprise, the Royals were once again on the move.

He had never bothered to join the game of guessing where they might appear next. They certainly had a great variety of official functions, representing the people of New England *and* a government in exile, but for many they were famous simply for being famous. He wondered what that might be like, and then decided he didn't want to know. He could bloody well bait his own hook, assuming he ever went fishing.

Fishing?

Why the hell not? It would get him out of the

city, into the sunshine, and away from the Small Arms--three things he never did often enough.

And he had a whole day to waste doing it.

~*~

Very few things would have motivated Leah less than participating in a gathering to honor Her Royal Highness or any of the horde of entitled lordlings birthed over the last few decades. She felt certain that's why God had created people like Dr. Plouth--people who could be counted on to pander to the Queen.

Good for her.

Better still for Leah. It meant that while security for the affair would be increased, no one would be looking specifically for her. It didn't matter that her name would probably be included on a list of suspected colonial sympathizers, she wasn't about to present herself as a threat to anyone.

At least, not until she located the miscreant who stole her ceramic jar.

Did Dr. Plouth have something to do with that?

The question intrigued her, but she didn't give it much credence. Besides, she was busy racing around the outside of The Barn to catch sight of the man in the flag shirt she'd seen talking to the Royal-loving department head a few moments earlier.

Amidst the general confusion and flurry of last-minute emergencies, her jog around the building turned no heads among the security types she could see. The others, and she assumed there were many, didn't concern her. If she'd been carrying anything that might be considered a weapon things would undoubtedly be different, but the Crown had been quite successful in limiting the right of commoners to own firearms other than fowling pieces.

The privileged class, of course, had access to a wider variety of weapons. Most were dubbed "sporting arms" although their lethality wasn't particularly sporting for their targets. More than one such weapon had found its way into the on-going rebellion--on both sides.

Leah and her father had discussed at length the pros and cons of sending weapons into the past, for personal protection if not as a means of tipping the scales of war in favor of the colonies. Several issues caused them to abandon the idea. For one thing, the amount of power required to transport such things was enormous, and they needed every erg they could drain from the power grid to transmit hard currency. Secondly, they lacked the underworld contacts from whom they might obtain guns and the irreplaceable ammunition they'd also need.

And, as if they required still more reason not to avoid armed time travel, Raines had no idea what effects such travel would have on explosives. Nor did either of them care to find out first-hand.

So, assuming Leah could track down her thief, she would have to deal with him barehanded. Fortunately, she was prepared. Knowing they'd be forced to rely on little more than wits and talent, both she and her father had spent considerable time learning and practicing hand-to-hand combat techniques.

Over the years, Millburn had built quite a reputation for its wrestling and martial arts teams, and Raines played a major role in helping to recruit the best coaches. He'd even lobbied for improved practice and competition facilities. The school had never objected to the coaches taking on students for private lessons.

Leah did well in those studies and could have been a valuable member of the school's varsity martial arts squad, but she had little enthusiasm for representing Millburn in *any* sort of competition, physical or intellectual. Though she couldn't punch or kick as hard as her father, her reflexes were much faster. Fast enough to strike her instructors even when they expected it. She knew she could take care of herself. Just as she intended to take care of the bastard who ran off with the message from her father.

Sadly, he was nowhere in sight.

After wandering the campus for another hour, she gave up the search. Leaning back against one of Millburn's countless hardwoods, Leah put her elbows on her knees and prepared for a massive attack of self-pity.

"You're Leah Kerr, aren't you?"

Leah sprang to her feet as the speaker stepped out from behind the tree, a lanky man in his late twenties wearing slightly worn and definitely out of date clothing. He needed a shave and a haircut, but given those, and proper apparel, he could have passed for a graduate student.

"Do I know you?" she asked.

He shook his head and gestured for her to join him on the ground beneath the tree. When she paused, he sat first.

Though tempted to leave, Leah's curiosity caused her to stay. "How do you know my name?"

"From your reputation," he said. "You're not very well liked around here."

She squinted at him without responding.

"We've been watching you for a while now," he said.

"Who has?" she asked. "And why?"

"A few good people--people interested in freedom."

Oh, good Lord! First the Royals and now a bomb-thrower? What next, an elephant ballet? "What do you want? I'm very busy."

"I can see that."

"I'm just taking a little break, that's all."

"From looking for your lost pottery?"

She dropped instantly to her knee and grabbed him by the throat. "*You* took it? I want it back. Now!"

Despite her sudden attack, he remained calm and tapped the point of something frighteningly sharp against her left breast. She released him.

"Thank you," he said and folded the knife blade back into its handle. "There's no need for that. We're on the same side."

"I don't have a side."

He laughed.

"I want my jar back. It's... it's an antique."

He nodded. "Appears so."

"It's quite valuable. Especially since it's

unopened."

"*Was* unopened."

"Bastard! You had no right to--"

"Mind telling me how your father signed a note to you and sealed it in a jar that's got to be-- hell, I dunno--a hundred years old?"

Two hundred and thirty-two to be exact, you moron. "That's absurd!" she said.

"Oh. Then, perhaps we've made a mistake." He got to his feet and brushed off his pants. "Sorry to trouble you."

She put a restraining hand on his arm which he casually inspected. "I want it back," she said.

"The jar?"

"The note."

"Why?"

"Because it's mine, damn it!"

He appeared to contemplate her demand. "We might consider a trade."

She glared at him, muscles tense. His throat looked pale, and ever so vulnerable. She could incapacitate him with ease, leave him gasping for air through a windpipe no longer capable of supplying his needs. But he obviously wasn't acting alone. There would be others to avenge him, and if not kill her, slow her down. None of those options were acceptable.

"What kind of trade?"

With no one else around, there was no need for him to even lower his voice. "We need your help to blow up the Queen."

~*~

Chapter Five

*"It is the mark of an educated mind to be able to
entertain a thought without accepting it."*
                                                    --Aristotle

   His wallet twenty quid lighter than it had
been before he went fishing, Joel did have a little
something to show for it: a serviceable rod, a valid
angling permit, and an empty creel. Other than
providing a buffet of O-negative for the mosquitos
which had multiplied a thousand-fold since his last
such trip, Joel accomplished nothing. And after
prolonged deliberation, mostly while distributing
bait to unreceptive aquatic creatures, he concluded
that his proficiency with the fair sex was only
slightly better than his skill with hooks and worms.
   On the way to his Monday morning
appointment with Frances Flaherty, he deposited his
newly purchased tackle in a collection bin for the

Children's Society near the Anglican church he passed on his way to the train station.

For once, he had timed things right. The westbound interurban was on schedule. According to the timetable, he should reach Millburn College in ninety minutes. The distance wasn't great; most of the time was spent at intermediate stops.

Joel's stomach rumbled, but he didn't feel like eating the greasy fare offered near the station. Heartburn was merely annoying. It wouldn't distract him from his bad leg or his mosquito bites. And at that point, any distraction from his ailments would help him focus on the case at hand. Hopefully, the good people at the school would give him enough leads to satisfy Ms. Flaherty and anyone else concerned about the allegedly missing physicist.

When the train arrived, he flashed his badge and was given a seat at no charge. Public servants rode free, but they almost never rode in first class. Joel walked to a car near the middle of the train. Fortunately, he wasn't required to share the bench seat with anyone else, and as soon as the train pulled out of the station, he slumped sideways, rested his head against the window, and drifted in and out of sleep.

An hour and a half later the conductor announced his stop, and Joel lurched upright. A few awkward steps took him to the exit and back into the workaday world.

According to the station master, the school was within walking distance. Having learned long ago not to take such advice seriously, Joel hailed a cab which dropped him at a broad arch marking the school's main entrance. He squinted at a few of the multi-lingual phrases engraved on the iron span and then ignored it. Nothing to be learned there.

He decided that Millburn College came from the same cookie cutter used on all such institutions in northern New England. They consisted of ivy-covered buildings of uncertain vintage hidden behind towering hardwoods. Well-kept lawns covered the open spaces, while young people strolled innocently about with no apparent cares.

How lovely for them.

Such a traditional college had never been an option for him. He had the mental capacity, no one doubted that, but he lacked the social rank and the bank accounts required for entry.

Thus warmed to the environment, he inquired of a student where he might find the physics department and then headed straight for it. Once inside, signs directed visitors to the office of the department chair.

A woman he assumed to be Mrs. Flaherty met him at the door. As tall as Joel, but portly, she had a strip of light grey nestled between otherwise black hair running from back to front across the top of her head. "So, you're finally here."

The skunk-inspired coiffure startled him, but he recognized the voice instantly. "I'm managing quite well, thank you. And yourself?"

Mrs. Flaherty lowered her heavily plumed brows and waved him in. She marched around her desk and took up a position he felt sure was meant to intimidate students and provide a first line of defense for the chairman's door.

"Have you learned anything new?" she asked.

"I've only just arrived."

"Well, there's no time to waste. I've told you everything I know. It's time you spoke with the other staff members. Oh, and take this." She handed him an unsealed envelope. "I thought you could use a photo of Dr. Kerr and his daughter. Their home address is in there, too."

Joel accepted the offering, opened it, and quickly scanned the picture: a couple in beach attire on a summer day near the shore. The man appeared to be in his forties with dark hair, average height and features, and stood with his arm around a deeply tanned young woman with light brown hair. Her features were anything but average, especially her eyes, and Joel stared at her image until Mrs. Flaherty cleared her throat. He slipped the photo into his pocket.

She frowned when he remained in the room. Why he had that effect on people he didn't know.

While she glared, he lowered himself into a straight-backed wooden chair likely designed by Torquemada. Once settled, he massaged his bad leg. "I was hoping you could help me determine who, exactly, I should interview first." He didn't mention his relief that she actually remembered reporting someone missing. A repeat of the Smithers fiasco wouldn't sit well with headquarters. Assuming, of course, they ever read any of his reports.

Mrs. Flaherty crossed her arms like a cigar store Indian. "I'd begin with the history department. I'm sure that's where the trouble started."

"Trouble?"

"Intrigue. Politics. Career-bashing. Call it what you will."

"I sense you aren't enamored of the history department."

She stretched her neck and swiveled her sharp jaw from side to side like a turtle he'd seen while fishing. Her vertebrae thus aligned, she spoke. "Let's just say I believe in intellectual honesty. One doesn't have to agree with every notion simply because it's popular. Ideas should be examined on the basis of the strengths and weaknesses inherent therein."

An impressive credo, thought Joel. "Is that a quote?"

"Straight from Doctor Kerr himself," she said.

"Then I can imagine why you held him in such high regard." He paused for a moment. "You mentioned previously that you were unable to contact Miss Kerr. Have you heard anything from her since we last spoke?"

"Not a thing. And I'm more than a little worried. Their home isn't far. It's just off the campus and actually quite near the history buildings."

"There's more than one?"

"Obviously." Flaherty glanced toward the ceiling as if waiting for divine guidance or a dose of celestial patience. "Preparations are being made to host the Queen later today, something I wasn't aware of when we spoke on Friday. The entire department will be frantic with activity."

"Why?"

Another eye-roll. "Because the reception will be held in Chumley Hall, our history museum."

"That could prove interesting. People are often more talkative when they're eager to be rid of me. Seems an odd contradiction, don't you think?"

"I can't even imagine having an opinion on that," she said, then added, "While you're here, would you like to examine Dr. Kerr's office? Or, if you prefer, I can show you to his laboratory in the basement."

"I'll have a look at both, eventually," he said. "In the meantime, if I suspect foul play, I'll send an evidence specialist around." He stood up, only too happy to leave the chair and its Inquisition-inspired comforts, behind. "Well then, I'm off to visit the history department."

"You should start with Doctor Plouth. She's in charge over there."

"Thank you. I shall."

Mrs. Flaherty clearly did not envy him.

~*~

"Good morning," Raines said to the ever-ebullient Mrs. Cotswold, who met him in the dining room. "You wouldn't happen to know the Lancaster family, would you?"

"The Lancasters out by Worcester?"

"A little north of there, actually. Near Shrewsbury?"

Mrs. Cotswold set a steaming bowl of something Raines guessed might be porridge in front of him. "Oh yes, of course. Lovely people. And their estate... Well, a party there is not to be missed. Although, come to think of it, we haven't been invited to one in quite some time. But I can remember--"

Much to the physicist's relief, Gabriel entered the room. He looked quite somber.

"What's the matter?" Raines asked.

"It's nothing."

"Your face tells a different tale," Mrs. Cotswold said. "Out with it, now. Bad news is best served at daybreak."

Neither Raines nor the Cotswold's servant felt the need to point out that daybreak had long since past.

"Colonel Cotswold gave Master Smithers' horse to banker Armistead as payment for a debt."

Banker? "And why is that a problem?"

"It's not the Colonel's horse to give," Mrs. Cotswold said. "Although, I don't see that Master Smithers needs it any more."

"And Miss Chastity did say he had no family."

Things began to click in the time traveler's mind. As Gabriel had suggested, the Cotswolds were in financial trouble. Gabriel was not merely a part of Chastity's dowry, he *was* her dowry. Giving him to Smithers along with his daughter's hand would have--in the Colonel's mind--secured the girl's future. Raines wondered how far beyond that point the man had thought.

"We used to have a shop in town," Mrs. Cotswold said. "We built it with my husband's pension from his service in the Indian wars. The store did well until the rebellion began. The Colonel joined the Sons of Liberty and extended credit to many of the other members so they could afford to take up arms and fight. He said it was his duty since he was too old and fat to fight with them. I think he was embarrassed to admit his war wounds make him unfit. He felt guilty about it."

"He's clearly an honorable man," Raines said. "Why would he feel guilty?"

"Because many of those men were unable to pay him back. Quite a few died, and he lacked the heart to press their families for payment."

"I see."

Gabriel ended his silence. "I was going to hitch Master Smithers' horse to the wagon and take him to Master Lennox. Now we have no horses."

"Use the ox, then," Mrs. Cotswold said.

"I would, madam, but we ate the last of that fine animal in June."

"Oh. That's right."

Though the porridge lacked taste when he first tried it, what little flavor it had disappeared altogether. He pushed the bowl away. He had no idea they'd emptied their larder for him. "Perhaps I can be of some assistance," he said.

"I can't accept charity," Mrs. Cotswold said. "My husband wouldn't allow it."

"I'm not talking about charity. I have a business proposition for you."

"Then I must fetch the Colonel," she said. "Answers the Lord can't provide, I leave for him."

"I'll find him," Gabriel said.

"And be sure to come back *with* him," Raines said. "This involves you, too."

~*~

When Leah agreed to hear the colonials' proposal, she had no idea they would make her a prisoner--*in her own home*. But that wasn't quite true. She and her father had moved out weeks earlier in preparation for their Events. They had converted most of what they owned into cash and either thrown away or donated what was left to charity.

The lanky guerilla who'd met her on campus and brought her to the basement of her former home claimed she shouldn't have long to wait, although the man in charge was quite busy. She would just have to be patient. She never dreamed she'd have to remain patient all night.

The basement had never been well lighted, and the new occupants had made no effort to change that. The space under the house looked quite different without the Kerr's belongings in it.

"Why bring me here?" she'd asked.

The answer consisted of a shrug and a casual, "Why not? You aren't using it anymore."

In the morning--something she knew only from her watch since there were no windows--she asked, "Why can't you just tell me what you need from me? I have things to do. I can't waste time waiting for your mysterious general--"

"Captain."

"--whatever, to show up and discuss the issue. I need that note from my father. Right now."

"I can't imagine giving you that. What leverage would it leave us?"

"I can't imagine what you hope to accomplish

by blowing up the Queen! She's just a figurehead. She has no real authority. If you want to blow up someone important, go after the Prime Minister."

"I'd be fine with that," he said, "but I don't make those decisions."

"Who would've guessed?"

"You want something to eat?"

"Eggs would be lovely. With toast. And coffee. Cream *and* sugar."

"I was thinking more along the lines of pizza."

"We had that last night."

"And we've got some left over."

She eyed the box on the floor. "I'll pass."

He shrugged and helped himself to a slice. "I've had worse."

"You could be arrested for kidnapping, y'know."

He nodded, still chewing.

"That doesn't bother you?"

"In case you hadn't noticed, we're at war."

If you only knew what Daddy and I have in mind. But, of course, she couldn't say anything. Just because they had theorized a means to end the war didn't mean anyone else would want them to risk it. Not even the proposed victors. The plan had to remain a secret.

"How'd he do it?"

"What?"

"Get a message into that old jar."

She laughed. She'd been preparing for the question. "You *start* with an old jar. Wax you can get anywhere."

"And the parchment?"

"That was a little trickier," she said. "But people still make the stuff. Look hard enough, and you can find it." Though tempted to claim that she and her father had made it themselves, she knew that if pressed she couldn't come up with a plausible description of the process. Better to be vague.

"What I don't get," he said, finishing the cold pizza, "is why you went to the trouble. Why couldn't he just mail you a letter? Or call you on the phone?"

"It's hard to explain."

"I've got time, and nothin' else to do." He crossed his legs.

There were only two exits from the room: a cellar door leading up and out to the backyard, and a door at the top of a stairway leading to the kitchen. That door locked from the kitchen side, and she'd seen her captor set the lock before he marched her into the basement. The cellar door had a simple deadbolt in a heavy frame. The guard leaned his chair back against it.

He'd long since pocketed his switchblade and now cradled a pistol in his lap. She had little knowledge of handguns and couldn't have identified the weapon if her life depended on it. He, however, seemed quite comfortable with it.

"You'd really shoot me if I tried to leave?"

"'Fraid so. Orders."

She blinked and gave him a flash of her rarely used coquettish smile. "Surely you don't want to hurt me. Do you?"

"'Course not."

"Then maybe we can work something out." She hoped the bug bites and scratches she'd collected over the weekend wouldn't be too off-putting. "Deal?"

"Not likely."

She undid the top button of her blouse. "You're sure about that?"

He smiled. "There's nothing you could say to change my mind."

"I wasn't talking about... talking." She unfastened another button, then stopped. "You aren't gay, are you?"

"Hardly."

That much appeared evident in his gaze, if nowhere else. Leah wished she had worn something more provocative, but there'd been little need for anything like that recently. In fact, she didn't *own* anything that even came close.

"Straight? Good." Another button lost its job.

He cleared his throat. "You'd best stay where you are."

She took another step closer. He shifted in his chair and shoved his sleeves up above his elbows revealing a red and black tattoo on his forearm. "Please. Stop right there."

"But it's dark in here. You'll be able to see so much better if I get closer." She unfastened the belt around her walking shorts and let the loose ends dangle.

"Damn it," he said. "You're not being fair."

"Fair?" She couldn't keep from laughing. "Is it fair that you locked me up all night?" Though he'd been locked in with her, she wasn't under orders to stay awake. She hadn't slept well, but at least she'd slept *some*. Advantage: Leah. Now, if she could get just a little closer, a quick jab would take him out of the fight before it began.

"All I'm asking is that we make a fair deal," she said. "You get something; I get something."

"I can't let you go free."

"Sure you can." The last button came undone, and Leah held her blouse wide open. "What d'you think?"

"I think," said a voice from behind her, "you should put your clothes back on."

She whirled around to identify the voice.

"Captain!" the guard barked from behind her as he scrambled to his feet. She heard his chair clatter to the floor.

"I'm sorry to have kept you waiting, Miss Kerr," the rebel officer said.

Leah couldn't fasten her blouse fast enough. The captain kept his eyes on hers, however, which helped her maintain a shred of self-respect. She wished the light were better. His face remained in shadow.

"When you're ready, we can discuss our mutual needs."

"Of course," she said, turning her back to him as she tucked her blouse into her shorts and refastened her belt. The guard remained at the door, staring from her to the newly arrived officer and back. To the guard she mouthed the words, "Thanks, asshole."

"You can go now, Hanson," the captain said. "I'll take it from here."

Leah's guard righted his chair and executed a remarkably quick exit up the stairs to the kitchen.

Leah turned around once more.

At last, she and the man in charge of the colonial terrorists stood face to face in the same room.

~*~

Mrs. Flaherty's prediction proved correct-- the Millburn history department was in a state of chaos as they prepared for the arrival of the Queen. Joel stood and watched from the foyer of Chumley Hall. Lillian Plouth, Phd., directed her staff much like a conductor would lead an orchestra. He gave himself silent congratulations; he could not have picked a worse time, for her.

He smiled as he approached. Dr. Plouth appeared to have been designed on the Napoleon Bonaparte model: short in stature, but unquestionably in command. Though her minions towered over her, they deferred to her in everything. No one, it seemed, could be trusted to think for themselves.

"Good day, Doctor Plouth," Joel said to the woman's back. He held out his badge in anticipation of her turning to face him. When she didn't, he cleared his throat and introduced himself.

"I'm quite busy, Inspector, in case you hadn't noticed. Can you come back later in the week?"

"I'm afraid not. But this shouldn't take long. A few minutes at most."

"I don't *have* a few minutes," she said, her voice rising as she finally turned to look at him.

He stared into thick lenses which gave her

eyes an owlish look. He guessed her to be somewhere in her 50's, but he found it difficult to tell with extremely thin women. In his experience, they tended to look a bit older than their years, not that he'd ever expressed the observation to anyone. Doctor Plouth could have been anywhere within a twenty year range.

"I'm trying to locate Doctor Raines Kerr and his daughter, Leah. I'm told you know them both."

She exhaled mightily and put her hands on her diminutive hips. "I do. Though I haven't much use for either one."

"Why is that, exactly?"

"Raines is an idiot. Like all scientific types, he thinks the only important things in life begin and end in a test tube."

"I thought his field was physics, not chemistry."

She dismissed his comment with a wave. "I'm speaking metaphorically, not that I expect you to understand."

"My degree is in criminal justice," he said, "but I have a rudimentary command of grammar."

That earned him the tightest of smiles. "Indeed."

"And his daughter, Leah?"

"I know the name."

"She's a grad student in your department."

"My duties are quite extensive, Inspector. Are you suggesting that I should have personal knowledge of everyone and anyone who might have a notion to dabble in history?"

"If you've taken the time to read a thesis from

such a student, I would expect you to be familiar with her."

"I've read Miss Kerr's work. I know nothing about her personally, except that she's utterly lacking in scholarship. Her thesis, if one can call it that, is a sad, pointless joke. A travesty. She clearly has no idea what she's talking about. Her observations are not merely ridiculous, they're completely without merit."

"I see."

"I doubt it." She turned suddenly as a stoop-shouldered man passed by bearing a bulky cardboard box. He could barely see over the top of it. "Mister Bolland, would you be kind enough to join us?"

He slowed and turned in a wide arc. "Of course, Doctor Plouth." He lowered his burden to the floor and made a half-hearted attempt to stand up straight.

"This is Phillip Bolland, assistant professor of history. He is Miss Kerr's advisor. Isn't that right, Phillip?"

"Yes, ma'am."

"I'm sure Mister Bolland can fill you in on anything you wish to know about Miss Kerr and her, uhm, work. Now, if you'll excuse me, I have already wasted too much time on this nonsense."

"One last question," Joel said, stepping slightly to one side to prevent her from leaving. "When was the last time you saw or spoke to Doctor Kerr?"

"I have absolutely no idea," she said. "Possibly at the quarterly meeting of department heads, although he often failed to attend. It's no wonder his daughter is so undisciplined. Will there be anything else?"

"Not right now," Joel said.

"Thank God," she muttered with a shake of her head. She pushed past him and returned to the footstool someone had provided for her at ground zero. Once mounted thereon, she resumed her role as conductor of the Chumley Hall mayhem.

Joel eased the aging assistant professor off to one side of the room. "No need to be in the middle of things."

"Thank you," Bolland said, his voice breathy.

Joel smelled tobacco smoke on the man's clothing and wondered when someone might begin to suspect a link between smoking and respiratory ailments. He shrugged the thought aside. "I've only got a few questions."

"And you are?"

"Inspector Dawkins," Joel said. "Special Branch. I'm investigating a possible missing person, Raines Kerr."

"Doctor Kerr? Physics?"

"You know him?"

"Not well. But as Doctor Plouth mentioned, I've counseled his daughter, Leah."

"What's your impression of her?"

Bolland appeared distressed. "May I ask who might be privy to my remarks?"

"That depends entirely on whether or not Doctor Kerr, and possibly his daughter, turn out to be missing persons."

"Well, Leah Kerr certainly isn't missing,"

Bolland said. "I saw her in this very room just yesterday. She looked perfectly fine to me." He paused. "Well, that's not entirely true. She actually looked a bit agitated, but I have no idea why."

Joel made a note of Bolland's observation in his notebook. "I'm glad to hear that. I was hoping to talk to her."

"She had been standing around for a time, doing nothing for our preparations I might add, and then suddenly seemed to be in a great hurry."

Joel amended his note, then said, "If there's something you're not comfortable discussing here, we can go somewhere else."

"I just need to know if anything I say will get back to Doctor Plouth."

"In all honesty," Joel said, "it's not very likely. I can't promise you anything, but in most cases, no one ever reads my notes but me."

"Ah."

"Now, can you tell me what it is about Miss Kerr's work that has earned Doctor Plouth's ire? Is it really all that bad? I've been led to believe Miss Kerr is actually quite bright."

"She's a very clever young woman," Bolland said. "And her work, if examined objectively, is excellent."

"Doctor Plouth obviously disagrees. Why? What's the problem?"

"Miss Kerr's conclusions."

"I don't understand."

"She went to great lengths to trace the activities of the colonial era general, Benedict Arnold."

"The man who brought an end to the original rebellion?"

"The very same. When he switched sides and orchestrated the fall of the colonial's fort at West Point, New York, he ended any hopes the colonies had for winning their independence."

"That's what made him a hero."

"To England and the loyalists. Not to the colonials."

Joel shrugged. "Well, no, of course not."

"But he *had* been. They called him the Hannibal of the Rebellion. General Washington once considered him his most accomplished battlefield commander. His heroism was unquestioned."

"I always heard he'd simply chosen the wrong side in the beginning, and that once he came to his senses, he returned to fight for the Crown."

"That's how it's always been taught. But Miss Kerr looked deeper. She found that General Arnold's decision to change sides was driven by a bruised ego and the overpowering need to profit from his labors, whether on behalf of the colonies or the Crown."

"I still don't see why that's a problem," Joel said.

"Her theory is that if Arnold's defection had failed--if he *hadn't* been able to turn the fort at West Point over to our side--the war would have ended fairly soon afterwards, and it wouldn't have been a victory for us. The colonies would've won their independence outright."

"Rubbish."

Bolland shrugged. "I'm not so sure. We take a great deal of history for granted, since we know the final outcome. But only those who take the time to examine the historical details can determine how close such outcomes came to being in doubt. In her thesis, Miss Kerr suggests that once the colonies became aware of Arnold's treason, they would have risen up in righteous anger. Not only that, but if the plot to surrender the fort to the British had failed, General Washington would have remained in command of the continental army, and he would have overseen the eventual victory of the colonies."

"That's quite a supposition."

"Oh, indeed. And she went into great detail about how the plot could have been foiled. I'm actually quite amazed it succeeded."

"And that's what's got Doctor Plouth up in arms? The suggestion that the colonies could have won the war?"

"Yes, assuming someone we've long held in high esteem had actually not been able to commit his treason successfully."

"Thank you, professor."

"You're welcome." He shuffled his feet a bit. "You'll promise to guard my remarks."

"Absolutely," Joel said.

"That's a relief."

"Now, do you have any idea where I might catch up with Miss Kerr?"

Bolland took a long look around the room. "Sorry, Inspector. I have no clue."

And, sadly, neither do I.

~*~

Chapter Six

"History is a set of lies agreed upon."
                                    --Napoleon Bonaparte

Raines offered to help Mrs. Cotswold with the dishes, but her refusal came as a relief. He needed time to get his thoughts in order.

When he'd arrived in 1780, he had one goal: prevent Benedict Arnold from surrendering the colonial fort at West Point, New York, to the British. In order to do that, he needed Leah's help. They'd discussed their strategy at length and both had concluded her role was essential.

Now, however, he had become entangled in the lives of the Cotswolds and the earnest young slave, Gabriel. Raines couldn't imagine just leaving them, even if it meant a delay in his plans to save the rebellion from a catastrophic loss. He needed to figure out a way to help them and achieve his goals at the same time.

When Gabriel returned with the Colonel in tow, Raines met them at the door. The morning was mild and pleasant, and he waved them to seats on the front steps.

"What's this about a business proposition?" the Colonel asked once comfortably settled between his guest and his servant.

"It's fairly simple," Raines began. "I need help with a few chores, but I'm new to the area and don't know my way around. I'm not familiar with local customs, nor do I have any idea with whom I should trade."

"You'll not regret doing business with any of the Sons of Liberty."

Raines smiled. "I would prefer to patronize *only* those who support the rebellion. Alas, I don't know who those people are, and I fear that if I inquire, someone will think I'm up to something."

The Colonel furrowed his brow. "Mischief?"

"Prying for the Crown," Gabriel said.

"You're not some damned spy, are you?" the Colonel asked. "I'll shoot you myself!"

"Rest assured, he is not," Gabriel said.

The Colonel fixed the slave with a look of deep suspicion. "And how would you know?"

"I, uh--"

"I've no love for the Crown," Raines said quickly. "But I don't know how I could prove it. I swear to you, however, if successful, my plans could mean an early end to the war and guarantee independence for the colonies."

"That would truly be a miracle," the Colonel

said.

Gabriel looked at Raines in awe. "I knew it!"

Raines focused hard on ignoring him. "I have some funds with me, and will make arrangements to get more. In the meantime--"

"I'd dearly love to help," Cotswold said, "but my money is--"

"Your *contacts* are what I need," Raines said, "not your money. I've no doubt such introductions will be extremely valuable. I also need Gabriel's help, for running errands and helping me find my way."

"What are you proposing?"

"I have business to attend to in New York, and several important tasks to complete before I can begin my journey there. I need transportation, for one thing, and someone I can trust to accompany me. If you'll grant Gabriel his freedom, I'll pay you whatever you deem reasonable."

"But that's... I--"

"And I'll add a similar amount to replenish Miss Cotswold's dowry, though a young woman with her charm and breeding should have no trouble attracting a husband." He chose not to offer an opinion of the late Mr. Smithers.

"That doesn't seem fair," Cotswold said.

Raines felt the crush of disappointment. How could he have misjudged things so? "I assure you--"

"You're cheating yourself!" The Colonel rose to his feet and stepped away. "It wouldn't be right to profit from a man who means to advance the cause of liberty."

"Your help would be invaluable," Raines said. "A letter of introduction, for instance, from you to the Lancasters, would save me a great deal of time and effort."

"The Lancasters?" Cotswold squinted at him as if he'd suddenly gone fuzzy. "The *Shrewsbury* Lancasters?"

"Yes. I believe so." *Crap! What've I done now?*

"But, they're Tories!"

Up to that moment, Raines had enjoyed a feeling of growing pride. Suddenly, he felt as if he'd been wandering around, blissfully unaware that his pants were down around his ankles.

"What business could you possibly have with them?" the Colonel asked. He had tensed to the point of quivering.

"You're going to find this very hard to believe," Raines said, desperate to calm him, "but I need to see their Bible."

"I don't find that hard to believe, Master Kerr. Not in the least," Gabriel said brightly.

Bless you, Gabriel!

The Colonel put his hands behind his back and began pacing. Moments later, Mrs. Cotswold and Chastity joined them, standing close together on the porch.

"What's the matter, dear?" Mrs. Cotswold asked.

"Doctor Kerr wants me to write a letter of introduction for him."

"To the Lancasters," Raines said. "The family we discussed earlier."

"Lovely people," she said. "Dreadfully loyal to the King, of course, but they give such delightful parties. Or used to."

"Indeed," the Colonel said. "Looking back on it now, I believe most of their honored guests were traitors, too."

"Loyalists," Mrs. Cotswold corrected. "Everyone has the right to an opinion."

"I haven't been to a party in years," Chastity commented sadly, then looked expectantly at Raines. "Doctor Kerr? Would you take me to the party at the Lancasters?"

"There aren't going to be any parties!" the Colonel groused.

Chastity stuck out her lower lip. "Well, there should be."

"Surely someone we know is having a party," Mrs. Cotswold said. "It would be a splendid way for Chastity to meet eligible gentlemen."

"I'm sure there'll be a great celebration once the war's over," Raines said.

"Parties," grumbled the Colonel. "As everyone here knows--" he cast a wary eye at his wife and daughter "--most of the Tories in Massachusetts left when General Washington took the Dorchester Heights and chased the redcoats out of Boston. The Sons of Liberty, I can tell you, shed no tears upon their departure!"

"I see," Raines said, still stinging from his failure to know which side of the rebellion the Lancasters had taken. If Leah were there she might have steered him clear of such a blunder. She knew the history as if she'd lived it; he'd spent his time in a physics lab. Both roles were essential to the mission, but he needed her expertise more than ever.

"See here, Doctor Kerr," the Colonel said. "What's so damned important about the Lancaster's ruddy Bible?"

Gabriel's eyes grew wide at the blasphemy, but Cotswold ignored him and continued undaunted. "We've got a Bible, too. It's in the house, on the mantle. Gabriel has practically memorized it."

"That's true," the boy said. Deep pride seemed to have cancelled his anxiety.

"Where I come from," Raines hastily explained, "Bibles like the one the Lancasters own are considered great works of art. There's not another like it in all of Massachusetts, and I'd dearly love to see it before I leave for New York."

"I shall have to think on this," the Colonel said. "It's possible someone in Boston knows what happened to it. They may have put it in storage before they left Shrewsbury for the harbor. As I understand it, there were so many of the traitors clamoring to board the British warships, they had no room for their belongings. Good riddance to them, I say! But their Bible is still in Massachusetts. I'd bet my life on it."

"You'll do no such thing," Mrs. Cotswold interjected. "We do not wager in this house!"

Gabriel tugged the physicist's sleeve and whispered, "They've nothing left to wager *with*."

Raines nodded, then spoke to his hosts, "These are indeed strange and difficult times. And while I know it must seem trivial, finding that Bible is something I absolutely must do. I promised someone very dear to me that I would not just see it, but hold it in my hands."

"Seems like a waste of time, to me," Cotswold said.

Time is relevant, my friend. If you only knew how much! "Sadly, I have little to spare."

"You're not leaving, are you?" Chastity asked.

Raines tipped his head. "Duty calls."

She frowned. "But you don't have to answer."

~*~

Leah turned her back on the rebel Captain and marched to the chair left behind by her guard. She shoved it with her foot until it reached a spot roughly in the center of the room. A single light bulb overhead sent shadows pooling beneath her as she took a seat. "I'm ready for my interrogation."

"Don't be ridiculous. We're not the law. We're engaged in a military operation, and we need your help."

"Oh, silly me. I thought you were criminals using extortion to get what you want."

"Miss Kerr, I--"

"How is it you know my name, but I don't know yours?"

He paused as if to consider the question, then said, "You may call me Dwight. Captain Dwight."

"Is that your real name?"

"Does it matter?"

She shrugged. "I suppose not."

"We're not asking much. We just need a little help."

"To commit murder? My pleasure. Nothing like an assassination to start the day."

Dwight smiled. "I like you. You've got spirit."

"Well, just so we understand each other, I *don't* like you. And there's not a chance in hell that I'd help you kill anyone, let alone the Queen. Are you familiar with the expression, 'Fuck you'? Consider it expressed. You might as well let me go now and forget the whole thing."

His smile never faltered. "Wherever did you get the idea we wanted to kill the Queen?"

"From the genius who held me hostage all night."

"Ah. Hanson." He bobbed his head up and down as if saying the name explained everything. "He's a bit... reactionary. The war hasn't been easy on him."

"Unlike the way it's been on everyone else? Give me a bloody break. You people are insane."

"That's probably true," he said, which surprised her. "But it doesn't change anything. Not really."

"Lovely."

"Hear me out. We have no intention of killing the Queen. That *would be* insane. Killing her would provoke the great majority of New Englanders who are tired of the prolonged conflict. Killing a Royal would shake them so profoundly we'd never hear the end of their demands for vengeance. We'd never win our independence."

"So, what's this all about?"

"We merely want to demonstrate that we *could* kill her, if we wanted to." He motioned for her to stand up. "Come with me. I want to show you something." Without waiting, he turned and started up the stairs to the kitchen.

Though sorely tempted to bolt and escape via the cellar door, Leah stood and followed him. *Curiosity is such a bitch!*

"Are you coming?" he asked.

"I'm right behind you."

"Hurry then. I haven't got all day." He pushed open the door at the top of the stairs and waved her into the kitchen. Three more chairs, identical to the folding aluminum seat in the basement, were drawn close to a card table near the room's only window. When Leah was a child, her mother had served breakfast at a table in the same spot.

A potted flower arrangement sat in the middle of the cheap table.

"For me?" she asked. "You shouldn't have. Really."

"It's not for you."

"I'm crushed. I thought we had something."

"It's for the Queen."

Leah stared at the arrangement, but it was hard to keep her mind off the man in the room, and the door behind him which led to freedom.

"So, they're flowers."

"Not just flowers." He pointed to a wall which formerly held a large cork board on which Leah and her father had posted countless notes, printouts, passing thoughts and, occasionally, cartoons clipped from the local paper. Now, however, the wall was bare and marked by a huge green stain. It looked as if a can of spray paint had exploded next to it.

"*That's* what Johnson meant when he told you we wanted to blow up the Queen."

"You want to spray her with green paint?"

"Exactly."

"What on Earth for?"

"Simply to prove that we can." He made a fist and shoved the plant toward her with his knuckles. "Have a look."

Leah picked up the ceramic pot. It seemed heavier than it appeared. She poked her index finger into the potting soil. Buried just below the surface she found a metal cylinder as big around as her wrist. She looked closely at it and the nozzle attached to one end. "That's where the paint comes out?"

"It's dye," he said. "It's even washable."

"How thoughtful." She put the ceramic pot back on the table.

"We're not monsters, you know."

"No, you're not. You're kidnappers plotting to assault the Queen. There's a massive difference."

He gestured toward the basement door. "You don't have to help us. You're welcome to go back downstairs and wait until we're done."

"And what about the message from my father?"

"We'll keep that."

"It's not yours."

"True."

"I want it back."

"We're counting on that."

She stared at him. The light in the kitchen was much better than that in the basement, and she took the time to study his face. For reasons she couldn't quite fathom, it was important to her to catalog his features. Unfortunately, they were remarkably plain. He could have been a department store mannequin.

"If you want the letter back, all you have to do is provide a little cover for us."

"While you spray paint the Queen? You're out of your mind!"

"All we want you to do is carry a protest sign outside the building where she's scheduled to appear."

"Chumley Hall."

"Yes. Just march around and wave the sign. Protest! Isn't that what college students do?"

"Not Millburn students. I'd be arrested two seconds after I began."

"Rubbish. You'll be exercising your right of free speech."

"Millburn has a tradition of frowning on that sort of thing." She sighed in resignation. "What am I supposed to write on this protest sign?"

Captain Dwight walked from the room and returned almost immediately with a placard--white pasteboard tacked to a thin wooden handle. The hand-painted slogan read: "Freedom for all!"

She laughed at it. "I'd never carry a sign like this."

"Oh? What would yours say?"

"Remember West Point!"

He frowned. "I have no idea what that means."

"No," she said, "You wouldn't. Nor does it surprise me."

He glanced at his watch. "Time's running out.

Will you cooperate, or not?"

She eyed the sign, which he'd put on the table next to the potted plant. Both looked equally innocuous. *What could it hurt?* "Just carry the sign outside Chumley Hall?"

"That's all."

"And when do I get my father's letter back?"

"You can get it in the morning. We'll leave it right here on the table."

"I still think you're crazy," she said. "When do I have to show up with the sign?"

"Around five PM. The dinner is scheduled for seven."

"You seem to know an awful lot about this."

"Do we have a deal?" he asked.

"I suppose."

"Then you're free to go."

She walked quickly to the kitchen exit.

"Don't forget your sign," he said.

Gabriel and Raines walked to the home of the Cotswold's nearest neighbor, Lucas Benn, a widower several times over. Somewhere in his 70's, the man was bald as a boulder and missing most of his teeth, but his senses seemed as sharp as Gabriel's. He watched them approach with dark, deep-set eyes and never moved a single bone in his skeletal frame until they reached his house. When he finally spoke, his words seemed more grunt than greeting. He focused on Raines as Gabriel made the introduction, and the physicist felt as if the old codger meant to intimidate him, yet he only managed to piss him off.

Cotswold had written a note asking Benn for the use of a horse to deliver Smithers' corpse to its final resting place. Raines thought Benn must have read the note several times. Either that, or his reading skills were so poor that it took him that long to work his way through it. He could almost hear the gears whirling inside the septuagenarian's head as he plotted to take advantage of them.

"Ye want a horse, do ye?"

"Yes sir, Master Benn," said Gabriel.

Raines cut his eyes at the boy. His tone and attitude seemed far more servile than at any time since they'd met. Raines found it even more odd since he'd concluded his deal with the Colonel to buy Gabriel's freedom. Content to observe for a while longer, Raines kept silent.

"Tell me 'bout the Cotswold girl," Benn said. "She was gon' marry up wi' that Smithers fella, warn't she?"

"Yes sir, Master Benn."

The old man rubbed his stubbled jaw. "She's such a pretty thing. Any others come a callin'?"

"Only Doctor Raines."

Benn fixed the physicist with a suspicious glare. "And what, 'zactly, are yer intentions?"

"They're honorable, I assure you."

The older man laughed. "Ye think I'm a fool, do ye? I know what you want. Same's the rest of us. I ain't too old to leave my mark on such as thet."

Raines imagined what he meant and instantly regretted it. Wishing would not expunge that image any time soon.

"Cotswold's in trouble, ever'one knows it. He needs someone to take that bit o' fluff off'n his hands." He rubbed his own leathery paws, and his cackle made Raines shudder. "I could put 'er to work. Better still, I could work 'er m'self."

Though Gabriel remained quiet, Raines saw that Benn's words had cut him to the marrow. He took a cautionary grip on the boy's arm. "Easy, now," he whispered.

"Tell Cotswold I aim to come 'round. I 'spect the number of her gentlemen callers has been a might thin lately." Though he looked at Raines, he spoke to Gabriel. "They's mostly waitin' fer burial. She needs a man who's still alive. Like me!"

The teen managed only a stare.

"You hear me, boy?"

"We do," Raines said. "And we'll pass along your message. Miss Cotswold, I'm sure, will be thrilled to learn you wish to be a suitor. Now, about that horse?"

"I aim to do some ridin', too!" Benn laughed. "Oh, yes. Hee yah now. Gid'up!"

"The horse?" Raines said. "If we hurry, we can have it back before dark."

"In the stable." Benn waved at a dilapidated structure behind his house. "Don't have no saddle. Won't need one with Miss Chastity, neither!" He laughed again until he couldn't breathe, then bent forward with his hands on his knees and coughed.

"I'll kill him if he tries to touch her," Gabriel muttered.

"With his lungs the way they are, you probably won't have to."

"Can't you strike him down with righteous fire?"

"I was thinking more along the lines of a righteous boot up his ass."

"Mysterious ways," Gabriel said. "But I trust you know what you're doing."

They walked Benn's sway-backed mare to the Cotswold's home, and Gabriel quickly harnessed it to a buggy. They wrapped Smithers in an old blanket and loaded him into the back.

Raines regretted that it would be many years before anyone invented plastic bags big enough to accommodate a body. On the other hand, there was no reason he couldn't use his own knowledge to advance the technological timetable in his favor. Though not a chemist, he had some rudimentary skills, and he could imagine a bright future once the war ended. If Gabriel stayed with him, he would not only learn much, he'd likely amass a fortune.

They waved goodbye and left. Neither felt the need to mention to the Colonel Lucas Benn's intentions toward Chastity. Not only did they share a great degree of disgust for the old goat, they were eager to dispose of Smithers. Fortunately, they drove the buggy into a brisk headwind, and were thus spared the worst of the dead horse thief's ripening essence.

Raines couldn't get the thought of Lucas Benn out of his head, nor was the irony lost on him-- they'd borrowed a horse from one lecher to cart away the remains of another. He commented on it, knowing Gabriel fully agreed. The physicist was content to wait for the old man to join Smithers without their aid. Gabriel argued for a more direct approach.

"I would do it, and gladly. The world would be a better place without the likes of him. And surely God would not punish me, for my intentions are pure."

Raines shrugged. "You said it yourself: 'mysterious ways.' I'm not involved in the Almighty's decision-making process."

The conversation lasted all the way to the graveyard where they surrendered the corpse to Hiram Lennox.

Raines paid the carpenter/undertaker with a Spanish dollar dated 1753, one of many he and Leah had forged in his Millburn laboratory. Based on an authentic coin from the mint of Spain's Ferdinand VI, the fakes were quite good. They had the added benefit of being cast from real silver, and while they wouldn't have fooled a 21st century expert, no one in the cash-strapped colonies would refuse such hard currency, even if it was a bit too shiny. And, if anyone did question it, they'd find the silver in the fakes to be a bit more pure than that contained in the genuine article. Considering that the paper dollars printed by the continental congress held virtually no value, silver and gold were priceless. Mintmarks mattered little.

Lennox was delighted to accept the payment and assured Raines and Gabriel that Smithers would be properly interred. When he asked if there would be a service commemorating the man's passing, Gabriel said they'd already mourned the man enough. A formal service wasn't necessary.

At the physicist's request, Lennox sent them to a nearby stable where Raines parted with more of his bogus Spanish dollars, and when they eventually rode back to the Cotswold home, they had three horses in tow. Gabriel had assured Raines that he needed to purchase tack for only two of them, as the Colonel had been unable to part with his own gear when forced to sell his last mount.

The next purchase consisted of several laying hens, a pregnant sow, and a pair of sheep. The two "woolies" looked nothing like the animals he was used to. Gabriel solved the mystery when he pointed out that the English refused to export sheep in an effort to force the colonies to import wool and finished cloth. Raines had only seen purebred sheep in his former life. These were mongrels.

The menagerie would be delivered in a week's time, thus sparing the Colonel and his wife any embarrassment over Raines' largesse.

Since Gabriel's clothing was decidedly threadbare, and Kerr's period costume was intended for the stage rather than long-term use, the final purchase consisted of new clothing for both of them. Fortunately, they found a seamstress who was able to modify some men's apparel she already had available, since the man who ordered it never came back to get it. Ordinarily, she would have needed a least a week to finish just one outfit.

Raines tried to give her a tip as reward for all her effort, but she seemed suspicious of it. He waited until she was busy with Gabriel and left a few extra coins where she was sure to find them.

Proudly displaying his new wardrobe,

Gabriel rode with his chest inflated to the bursting point.

"You're a free man now, you know," Raines said.

"Thanks be to God," he said.

"I had a little hand in it."

Gabriel suddenly became sheepish. "Why, of course, sir. I apologize. Your charity overwhelms me. I can never repay you."

"Nonsense. You'll repay me, with interest."

Gabriel looked surprised. "But I have no--"

Raines laughed. "Relax, my young friend. You're now in my employ. I don't own you. No one does. You're going to earn your way in this world, and you're going to help me do the same. Together we'll both prosper. I'm sure of it."

"Mysterious ways," Gabriel said, shaking his head.

Someday, lad, if I get the chance, I'll tell you just how mysterious.

"When do we leave for New York?" the well-dressed ex-slave asked.

"Soon enough. I still have to see that Bible up in Shrewsbury."

"Assuming it's still there."

"Indeed."

"That confounds me yet," Gabriel said. "Surely you, of all God's creatures, have no need to see a Bible."

Raines smiled at him. "With you along, I certainly don't need a *printed* copy. But the Lancaster Bible is a different matter. I only need to see it for a moment. We can leave shortly thereafter.

By the way, you wouldn't happen to know a good fiddler, would you? I'm told one can't have a proper party without one."

"You're having a *party?*"

"I'm thinking about it. The man who sold me the livestock for the Cotswolds said he knows the fellow living in the Lancaster's home. A nephew, or a cousin, or an in-law. He wasn't sure of the exact connection, but the man fancies himself a lawyer and wants very much to un-tarnish the Lancaster name."

"I don't understand."

"Can you think of a better way to send a message of good will than by hosting a party?"

"But who's hosting this party, you or the Lancaster man?"

"If he agrees to my proposal, he'll host it. I'll pay for it."

The look on Gabriel's face made it plain he didn't understand.

"Not only will I be able to see the Lancaster Bible, I can repay the Cotswold's kindness by providing a party for Chastity."

Gabriel patted the physicist's arm. "And you claim not to be an angel! Who will believe that?"

~*~

Chapter Seven

"While we are sleeping, two-thirds of the world is plotting to do us in."

--Dean Rusk

As Joel walked away from Chumley Hall, he referenced the address Mrs. Flaherty had given him. He stopped a harried-looking female student to ask for directions. She stepped away warily until he flashed his badge then pointed to a cluster of homes just visible through the trees. He thanked her and headed in that direction.

Nearing the Kerr house, Joel spotted a strikingly attractive woman in her mid-20's leaving the building. Even at that distance he recognized her. Walking faster, he changed course to intercept her provided she didn't run. When she saw him staring at her, he feared that's exactly what she would do.

"Miss Kerr?" he yelled. "May I have a word with you?" He waved his badge and smiled, hoping to avoid the appearance of someone threatening.

"I'm in a hurry."

"I won't keep you long, I promise."

He quickly closed the gap between them, trying hard to ignore her beauty while objectively cataloging her general appearance: clothing wrinkled and slightly disheveled, hair in need of brushing (unlike in the photo), and minor bruising on her arms and legs. Her olive complexion may have camouflaged some of the discoloration. She held a placard, but it was turned away, and he couldn't read it.

He introduced himself and told her he was investigating a report of her father's disappearance. She displayed a look of concern at first, then gave him a disarming smile full of brilliant white teeth.

"Dad's away on personal business."

"Where?"

"He's... in the greater Boston area."

Not terribly specific, but Joel didn't think she was lying. Not exactly. "I'd like to talk to him."

"Me, too," she said with a laugh.

"Has he been away for a long time?"

She shrugged. "Not really. I just saw him on Friday."

"Here?"

"A short distance from here. At lunch. We had a picnic. There's a place we go fairly often. It's nice and quiet. Away from campus and all the crap that goes on here. He left right afterward."

Joel had worked with evasive witnesses

before. They often claimed to be too busy to talk, but their preoccupation was usually driven by the need to get away. He assumed as much of Leah Kerr.

"If you don't mind my asking," he said, "how'd you get so scratched and bruised? Been in a fight?"

She turned the sign so that he could read it. "Some people don't believe in ideas like this."

"'Freedom for all'? Seems reasonable to me. Who would object?"

She used the sign to point at Chumley Hall. "Just about anyone you're likely to meet over there."

He reached up to shade his eyes as he looked where she had pointed. The motion caused his sleeve to pull away from the tattoo on his forearm. Leah gave a little gasp when she saw it.

"What's wrong?"

"It's nothing."

He unbuttoned his cuff and extended his arm to display the red and black tattoo worn by so many of the men who had served in the Black Watch. "I got it a long time ago," he said. "Men do stupid things when they're young."

"Everyone does. Why should you be an exception?"

Her defiance failed to mask a general uneasiness. "What's the matter? Why did my tattoo give you such a start?"

"I'm just a little nervous about the protest. There are people around here who'd rather take swings at me than have a civilized discussion. You've seen the bruises I have to prove it."

"So, don't protest. Or figure out a safer way to

do it. Write a letter to the editor or something."

She shook her head. "I can't. It's hard to explain."

He crossed his arms. "I'm a good listener. Give it a try."

After a long pause, her shoulders slumped, and the defiance she'd shown before simply faded. "I may have made a mistake."

"About what?"

She pointed at his tattoo. "You said that was a Black Watch tattoo. That's a British regiment. Everyone knows that. I grew up hearing what great heroes they all are. How likely is it that a rebel would be wearing a tattoo that honors them?"

Joel laughed. "You'd have less trouble buying a winning sweepstakes ticket than finding a colonial with a tattoo like that."

"I feared as much." She looked at him solemnly. "I saw one this morning."

Joel suddenly felt exposed. He touched her lightly on the elbow and nodded toward a corner cafe. "It's already past lunchtime, and I haven't eaten. Let's grab a bite, and you can tell me about this man you saw."

"But, I--"

"Really," he said. "I need to get off this leg. I've been standing on it too long already."

Surprised, she glanced downward. "What's wrong with your leg?"

"If I tell you, will you level with me?"

That put a twist in her lip, but eventually she agreed and let him lead her across the street to one of three tables set up outside the little restaurant. He chose the one farthest from the cafe door. The others remained empty.

"Now, tell me about this person who was pretending to be a colonial."

"I don't know that to be true."

"Let's assume it is. After all, the Queen's in town. Where Royals are concerned, nothing is normal."

She acquiesced. "My father sent me a message, but the man I mentioned, or someone he works with, intercepted it."

"So, your father *is* alive and well?"

"Of course. And I've been waiting to hear from him."

Just then a waiter appeared. They ordered sandwiches and soft drinks without consulting a menu. When the waiter left, Joel told her to continue.

"They said they'd give me his message if I carried a protest sign outside Chumley Hall."

"The man with the tattoo said that?"

"No." She shook her head. "It was a colonial officer. A captain. Or so he claimed."

"Can you describe him?"

"Sure. As soon as you tell me about your leg."

He exhaled in mild exasperation. "I got shot."

"By a rebel?"

It would have been much easier to lie to her the way he lied to everyone else when asked about the wound. But at that moment, it didn't seem right. "No," he said. "My commanding officer did it."

"My God! Why?"

"Because I refused an order." He didn't feel the need to justify himself any further.

"That seems awfully harsh."

He shrugged. "War's funny that way. Now, tell me about this colonial captain. Did you hear his name?"

"White, I think. No. Wait. Dwight. That was it. Captain Dwight."

A lump suddenly formed in the pit of Joel's stomach. "You're sure?"

"Yes."

"And you saw his face? You can describe it?"

"There's not much to describe. Nothing really unusual except for his eyes."

Joel's hands knotted into fists. "What about them?"

"One was brown, and the other blue. Aside from that, he just looked... oh, I don't know... bland. Not handsome, but not ugly either. Just average."

Murchesson! Joel made a conscious effort to relax his hands. He took a deep breath while a tremor worked its way up his spine. He exerted his will to force it back down.

"What's wrong?" Leah asked, alarm written across her face. "What'd I say?"

"Your Captain Dwight is no colonial. His real name is Gerald Murchesson."

"You *know* him? How?"

"He was the one who shot me."

Leah was taken aback and clearly confused. "For... For refusing to follow orders?"

"For refusing to shoot an unarmed civilian." He looked deep into her eyes. "He wanted me to kill some poor kid whose only crime was being related to a rebel. Murchesson said we had to make an example of him. Show the colonials we meant business. But I wouldn't do it. I couldn't."

"And now he's working for them? Fighting with them?" she asked.

"Never. There's something else going on. There has to be. Did he say anything beyond that?"

"He claimed they had no intention of harming the Queen. They were just going to spray her with paint. 'Washable dye,' he said. He even showed me the table decoration they're planning to use."

"You actually saw it?"

"Up close. I picked it up and held it."

Joel's heart began to beat faster. "Did he touch it, or did anyone else?"

She shook her head. "Not that I recall. Why?"

"Was he wearing gloves?"

"No, but he pushed it toward me with his knuckles. I thought that was a bit odd. What's this all about?"

Joel exhaled in disgust. "I think he's trying to frame you."

"For a prank?"

"Murchesson isn't the sort of man who plays practical jokes--for political or any other purposes."

"You think they might actually try to harm the Queen? Why would he do that if he's on the Crown's side?"

Joel couldn't think of a valid reason, but that didn't calm his suspicions.

Leah broke his train of thought. "May I ask you something?"

"Sure."

"Why would you get a regimental tattoo if

your involvement was so... negative? Why honor the memory?"

"I got the tattoo long before I met Murchesson. I was fresh out of training. It's a tradition that goes back hundreds of years. I'm proud of the regiment, even though Murchesson, and people like him, sicken me."

He decided he'd said enough. There was no point in mentioning that his job with Special Branch came about as a result of the shooting. Murchesson had powerful patrons who made sure he wouldn't be punished for what he did to a lowly non-com. The gunshot which ended Joel's military career also made his law enforcement career possible.

And all he had to do was sell his soul.

"What are we going to do?" she asked.

"I don't know yet. Tell the Queen's security detail there's something going on even if I can't be sure exactly what it is. And as for you, I suggest you go somewhere safe. Away from Chumley Hall."

"But what about my father's message?"

"I seriously doubt Murchesson even bothered to keep it. It wouldn't pertain to him or whatever he's up to. If I'm right, and he intends for you to take the blame for whatever they're doing, he's probably already destroyed the note so it can't be tied back to him."

"But I haven't done anything!"

"I know," Joel said. "That won't stop him from placing the blame squarely on you."

"I'd deny it!"

"And I'll back you up to the extent that I can. But you won't be able to deny your fingerprints on the potted plant. Or on that protest sign."

She swallowed hard, unable to take her eyes off the placard.

"I'm sure I'll think of some way to disrupt this thing," Joel said. "For now, I need you to stay put somewhere. Preferably where Murchesson can't find you."

"I know a safe place," she said. "My father's lab. It's built like a vault. Nobody goes there, and I have a key."

He smiled. "If things go sideways, is there room for two?"

~*~

After returning Lucas Benn's horse and the Colonel's buggy, Raines asked Gabriel to help him seal a ceramic jar into which he'd placed a note for Leah. He aimed to keep the note light in tone, assuring her that he was well, and that the plan they'd devised was working out even better than he'd hoped. The only thing he wanted her to bring in addition to the supplies they'd accumulated, was a book on the chemistry of plastics. After dealing with Smithers' remains, the physicist had developed a much greater respect for the material, to say nothing of the profit potential in it once they'd completed their mission.

Leah had been far more altruistic in her view of the project, the successful completion of which would have served as her reward. Raines, however, took the view that if they were willing to give up everything for an adventure of unparalleled danger, there damned well better be a healthy bonus in it. Having a 232-year jump in knowing what technologies worked--and which would be the most popular--virtually guaranteed them a comfortable living once they trumped the historical wildcard that kept the colonies from winning the war in the first place.

Raines planned to "mail" his message while traveling to Shrewsbury to bargain with the Lancaster's house-sitter. Fortunately the Event site lay close to the route they'd be using. If another of the pre-arranged drop sites had been more convenient, he would have used it. The Lancaster Bible message was intended to put Leah's mind at ease. As long as she received it, she would know he had survived. But they also knew he might have trouble finding the Holy Book and jotting the drop site number in it. So, the plan called for Leah to check all the sites if the Lancaster Bible remained unmarked. If none of them yielded a message from him, she would presume the Event had killed him and would not attempt it herself.

He couldn't explain any of this to Gabriel, of course. But the young man seemed so intent on helping him, and so convinced that Raines had been dispatched directly from heaven, that he would happily subscribe to whatever fiction the physicist might concoct. Raines wasn't particularly proud of deceiving the lad, but he didn't want to run the risk of being seen as a lunatic either. It would be damned hard to put a stop to Benedict Arnold's treason if Raines was stuck in an asylum somewhere.

"You want me to dig a hole in the side of the

cliff?" Gabriel asked.

"Right under this stone slab," Raines said.

"Might I inquire why?"

"You might, but I fear you wouldn't understand the reasoning. It's... involved."

"Mysterious?"

"Oh, absolutely!"

Gabriel edged closer to the sharp side of the bank. "It's not all that far to the bottom."

Raines stood next to him and peered over the edge. "You're right, it's not too high. Lower than I remembered, actually. But, if you'd rather not assist me, I'm sure I can do it myself." He removed his topcoat and placed it on the ground, rolled up his sleeves, and removed a pick and a shovel from the buggy.

Gabriel relieved him of the tools before he'd covered half the distance. "I see you brought some rope. I'd be much obliged if you'd loop it about my waist and keep it taut while I work. I've no idea how deep the water is down there, nor how many snakes I might find if I fell in."

"Excellent idea," Raines said. "Let me anchor the rope before you go over the side."

The physicist's offer to do the digging himself had not been made frivolously. On the contrary, he would have been perfectly willing. But, there was no denying Gabriel's superior conditioning, better balance, and determination to be useful, all of which resulted in a much deeper hole in far less time than Raines would have managed. It was so deep, in fact, that he feared Leah might not be able to dig far enough into the cliff to find it.

"Don't bury it any deeper than the length of your arm," he told Gabriel.

"Why not?"

"Because I know who's going to dig it up, and I don't want her to have to work too hard."

"A *woman's* going to dig it up?"

"Yes. Why?"

"Miss Chastity could never dangle over the side of a cliff and dig a hole like this."

Raines nodded agreement. "The woman I have in mind is made of sterner stuff."

Gabriel stared at him for a long moment. "You have the most peculiar manner of speech. There are times when I have no idea what you mean, and at others your meaning is as clear as a winter sky."

"I have seen a great deal in my lifetime," Raines said, "and I've seen it in a great many different places. If you'll stay with me, I hope to share some of them with you."

"Here, on Earth, I hope!"

"Of course," Raines said, smiling. "Now, let's fill that hole and be on our way to Shrewsbury. I'd like to arrive before dark."

~*~

Leah had no idea what to make of Inspector Joel Dawkins--a man quite likable and yet every bit the copper he claimed to be. He and her father both projected an aura of protectiveness, as if they *needed* to shield her. In her father's case, he wanted to buffer her from the cruelty of a world that couldn't tolerate a dissenting view. In Dawkin's case, he wanted to safeguard her from a man who had no qualms about killing innocents merely to set "an example."

Without even realizing it, she dispensed with "Inspector" and "Dawkins," choosing instead to think of him simply as Joel. A knight with neither shining armor nor noble steed. He did, however, have a shield, though the letters on it proclaimed him a member of Special Branch rather than the Round Table.

Smiling at her own foolishness, Leah darted into an alleyway and carefully crammed the protest sign into a trash bin. Then, after a quick scan of the street, she hurried back across campus to the Jefferson Building. At that time of day, Mrs. Flaherty would still be stationed outside her father's office, protecting the lair of a man who'd never return from students who rarely saw him before he vanished into the past.

She would miss the old lady, despite her officious manner and her impatience with--it seemed to Leah--the rest of the world. Eventually poor Mrs. Flaherty would realize her boss would never come back, and the loss she was bound to feel would be enormous. As far as Leah knew, the woman had nothing else going for her. Fussing at Leah, and fussing after Leah's father, were major components of her life.

Though Leah had promised Joel she would go straight to her father's lab, she opted to make a short detour for a last few words with Francis Flaherty. Dodging a handful of students, Leah jogged through the halls and up the stairs to the office of the department chair. As always, she pushed the door open without knocking.

Mrs. Flaherty looked up at her through pince nez spectacles. She frowned at first, as she did at anyone who entered unannounced, and then relaxed with a huge smile.

"Leah! I was so worried. I've been trying to contact you and your father for days. Where have you been?"

Leah humped her shoulders in a classic college student shrug. "We should have left you a note. We've been traveling. It was a convenient time, and we've been putting it off for so--"

"And Dr. Kerr is all right?"

"Why, yes. Why wouldn't he be?"

The older woman seemed suddenly quite flustered. "Well, when I couldn't locate either of you, I began to worry. I checked around, and no one had seen either of you for days, possibly weeks. What was I to think? So I... I called the police and reported you missing."

"I'm sorry to have worried you," Leah said, "but I'm sure this sort of thing happens all the time."

"I wouldn't know, but the police are certainly taking it seriously. They've already sent two investigators."

Leah tried not to frown. "Two?"

"Yes, a nice young fellow from Boston named--" she paused to consult a notepad "--Dawkins."

"I've met him," Leah said. "Just a little while ago."

"Oh. And have you spoken to the other one?" She glanced once again at her notepad. "Inspector

Dwight. Not as pleasant as the first one, and older." She shook her head in dismay. "He had strange eyes, too. Odd colors. At least Dawkins looked like a detective. That Dwight fellow... I don't know."

Phantom fingers danced up Leah's back leaving shivers in their wake. She shook them off and came around the secretary's desk. Mrs. Flaherty rose to meet her, and the two hugged.

"I wasn't aware that there were two officers investigating us."

"Not you, dear," Mrs. Flaherty said, "your father." She tapped her lips with a knuckle as if she needed a bit of percussion to help her replay the moment in her memory. "That Dwight fellow wasn't interested in anyone else. When I mentioned your name, he grew very impatient with me, said his only concern was Raines Kerr, and he acted as if I knew where he'd gone. Naturally, I grew short with him, too, and pointed out that I was the one who reported him missing in the first place. He seemed surprised by that. What an odd man. I'd much rather deal with Inspector Dawkins."

"Me, too," Leah said. "When did all this happen?"

"Just this morning. Dawkins came first, then the other one, Dwight. And he acted like he didn't know Dawkins was already on the case!" She crossed her arms and frowned. "I can tell you, it certainly makes me wonder who's running the police department."

"I'm sorry for all the trouble you've been through. I'm afraid things will get even more hectic around here before long. But please, don't believe anything--she paused to find the right word--*unkind* you may hear about either me or Dad. It isn't true."

"Whatever are you talking about, Leah? Honestly, you're beginning to frighten me."

Leah laughed in an effort to put the older woman at ease, but it didn't seem to work. "I have to run. If I don't get the chance to tell you later, thanks for everything. That goes for Dad, too. He couldn't have survived without all you've done for him. For us, really."

"What are you up to?" Mrs. Flaherty said. She wore the reproachful look of a primary school headmaster.

"Gotta run!" Leah yelled over her shoulder as she hurried out of the office.

Gotta run like hell.

~*~

Raines had a mental image of the Lancaster home, but it was based on photos of the place as it looked in the 21st century. That building, though it lay mostly in ruin, occupied significantly more space than the house he and Gabriel found at the end of their journey to Shrewsbury. Still, compared to the other homes he'd seen, the Lancaster's house qualified as a mansion. Two stories tall, and surrounded by a high-ceilinged porch, it dwarfed the Cotswold's residence.

Gabriel was clearly impressed. Raines needed a little more time to process. Obviously the original building had been expanded by later generations, so the family had been successful in surviving the loyalist tag. Or, had they only been successful in the timeline he'd left behind, the one in which the Tories had been vindicated?

He had no desire to jump into another chicken vs. egg debate, especially not when he was the sole debater. They left their buggy in a shaded portion of the lane which passed close beside the house and walked toward the wide porch steps leading to the front entrance.

A man stepped outside and watched them approach. He didn't speak until they reached the base of the stairs. "May I help you?"

Raines stared up at him, but the man's face remained in shadow. Dressed in the manner of most colonials--a long-sleeved shirt, buttoned waistcoat, and breeches--he also carried a cocked hat and leather saddlebags. Raines tipped his head in a nominal bow. "I understand we have a mutual acquaintance in Boston. Samuel Harrow?"

"I know the man. He peddles livestock as I recall. What about him?"

"He suggested I have a chat with you."

"I can't imagine why."

Raines climbed the steps and offered his hand. "Raines Kerr," he said. "I hope you'll allow me to explain why I've come."

"I'm Anthony Lancaster," the man said, ignoring the proffered handshake with a look of disdain. "I'm in a bit of a rush, but you've piqued my interest."

"I'm told that because of the rebellion, the man who built this house decided to leave Massachusetts." Raines had mentally rehearsed his spiel, but doing that didn't guarantee a flawless delivery. Nor could he know how his audience would react.

"You make it sound so civilized," Lancaster said, not bothering to hide the bitterness in his voice. "The Sons of Liberty threatened to hang my uncle if he didn't leave when the British army sailed away from Boston. His wife and two daughters--my cousins Emily and Louisa--escaped with him. I'm the only Lancaster left in Massachusetts."

"You don't honestly believe the Sons of Liberty would have harmed women or children," Gabriel said.

Lancaster stared at the teen as if he'd just insulted the man's sainted grandmother. "I wasn't talking to you."

"No, but--"

Lancaster pushed him away with the back of his hand, as if he were swatting a fly. "When I want the opinion of a slave, I'll buy one and squeeze it out of him." He swiveled his head back toward Raines. "Really, Mr. *Kerr* is it? If you must bring servants, make sure they know their proper place."

"My name is *Doctor* Kerr, and Gabriel is a free man," Raines said, struggling to keep his voice even. "He's in my employ and earns a decent wage."

"How nice for him. Now, what do you want from me?"

The physicist had originally planned to pay Lancaster to host a party for the Cotswolds. By associating with the Colonel and his wife, Lancaster would be able to show that his family should no longer be castigated as Tories. But now that Raines had met him, he began to formulate a Plan B for getting his hand on the Lancaster Bible. Breaking and entering had suddenly become an option.

"May I be so bold as to inquire where you stand on the issue of independence?"

Lancaster pursed his lips as he pondered his response. After a long pause, he said, "I'm not a King's man, but I won't take up arms against him. I refuse to fight for either side, as I believe there is room for compromise, and some day the warring factions will realize it and come to their senses. What I cannot imagine is how my beliefs would influence any business we might have between us."

"I see," Raines said, not quite willing to abandon a late night visit to the Lancaster mansion while Lancaster himself was away on business. Unfortunately, he had no way of finding out when that might occur. "I have a proposition for you."

"Make it quickly then. I am a busy man."

"I'm sure you are," Raines said. "How would you like to throw a party?"

~*~

Chapter Eight

*"That's not a lie, it's a terminological inexactitude.
Also, a tactical misrepresentation."*
--Alexander Haig

Joel had considered calling headquarters with his suspicions before doing anything else, but he knew any such report would reach the ears of his "patron" before it could be forwarded to anyone connected with security for the Royals. And, considering the long-standing connection between Murchesson and the precinct supervisor, there was a good chance the report would be delayed if not completely lost in the crush of regular police business.

Murchesson, of all people, would have his flanks protected.

So Joel proceeded directly to Chumley Hall where he intended to alert a member of the on-site security team. The venue was already crowded when he arrived, and a police line prevented anyone from getting too close to the building.

He flashed his badge, but even that didn't gain him access. A uniformed officer merely pointed him in the direction of the "Mobile Command Center." Essentially a windowless cottage on wheels, the MCC had a roof festooned with radio antennas and cables linking it to the local telephone system. It had a single door in one end which was guarded by yet another uniformed officer.

Again, Joel flashed his credentials which he then had to surrender so that the uniform could run them past whoever occupied the MCC. After an interminable wait, his badge was returned, and a man stepped out to talk to him.

"I'm Clive Bicksley, Inspector. I'm told you have something to report?"

Try as he might, Joel couldn't place the accent, but since he'd never been outside the North American continent, he wasn't much of an expert. He knew enough, however, to be suspicious and therefore chose to proceed with caution. "I've heard some talk of a possible disturbance."

"Go on."

"This is going to sound bizarre, but I believe I've stumbled unto a plot to embarrass the Queen."

"How?"

"I think they're going to try and spray her with some sort of dye. Green, I think."

"Green dye."

Joel nodded.

"Why would anyone do that?" Bicksley asked.

"I presume these are colonials you're talking about?"

Now comes the sticky part. "Yes and no."

"Pick one. It wasn't a multiple choice question."

"Whoever is behind this wants you to think they're colonials."

"Simply because we've been at war with them for two hundred years?" Bicksley checked his watch. "Unless you've got some specifics for me, I have a great deal to do. The Queen will be sitting down to dinner in a matter of moments."

Joel looked at his own watch. "But it's early. I didn't think they would be eating until seven."

Bicksley frowned at him. "Nonsense. The schedule hasn't changed."

"Then you've got to stop her now!"

"Barge in on the Queen just as she sits down for a meal? What a lovely idea! I'll get on it right away."

"There's some sort of spray device hidden in the table decoration."

"Filled with green dye?"

"That's what I'm told, but it could be anything."

Bicksley digested the possibility, then grabbed Joel by the arm and dragged him toward Chumley Hall. Joel did his best to keep up, but his limp hampered Bicksley, and the security man was suddenly in too big a hurry to worry about Joel's comfort. The cordon around the building parted for them, and Bicksley headed straight for the main entrance. He deposited Joel with a pair of guards manning the door and told him to wait there while he went inside.

With a combination of glares and grunts, one of the guards positioned Joel in front of a window looking in on the dining area but well away from the building's entrance. He watched Bicksley work his way through first one pair of guards and then another as the Queen took a seat at the head table. Everyone else had been standing, of course, waiting for her.

As chairs throughout the room were scuttled back and forth, and formally dressed men and women took their seats, someone screamed.

Joel's gaze went immediately to the Queen who appeared wide-eyed and confused. She seemed unable to inhale, and her entire body began to shake violently. Those nearest to her began to suffer similar symptoms while the people slightly farther away drew back in horror.

Bicksley appeared as a blur as he raced to the Queen's side, but just before he got there, her body went rigid, and she pitched sideways to the floor.

Joel's heart raced as he watched, helpless, while several more party goers stiffened and fell. Moments later, Bicksley heaved himself back from the table while clutching at his own throat. The guards he had passed earlier backpedalled to keep their distance. Other diners ran toward the exits.

People were crowding the main door, some holding cloth napkins over their faces, others too frightened to do anything but run and scream.

The two guards at the main entrance briefly held the doors shut but were quickly overwhelmed by a stampede of terrified people. Joel moved with the mob as it dispersed on the grounds outside Chumley Hall. Several fell to the grass, coughing. None of them, however, went rigid.

Joel headed back toward the MCC to report what he'd just seen, although radio messages had doubtless been sent ahead. A man in a tweed jacket burst from the tiny building with a large black and white photo in his hand. Several other men swarmed around him, waiting for instructions which he dutifully barked. In the tumult, he never saw Joel, but there was no mistaking the two people in the photo the man clutched.

Anyone who'd ever met Leah Kerr was unlikely to forget a face that attractive. Joel's own mug was far less photogenic, but whoever had taken the picture of the two of them in front of the cafe an hour earlier had captured them perfectly.

~*~

General Fitzwilliam felt certain he'd made the right choice when he'd tapped Major Murchesson to handle the delicate matter of Phase One. That confidence hardly made the two days between decision and report easy on him. A slip-up would not only endanger the plan, it would mean the end of his career along with the lives and fortunes of all those who shared his dream of ending the war.

Murchesson had agreed to check in with him directly, bypassing all the intermediate levels of command and control. There were simply too many ways the truth could leak out, and that couldn't be allowed to happen. Murchesson's team consisted of three men, and the Major had been given carte blanche to recruit the two expendables working with him. Fitzwilliam wouldn't even learn their names until after they were dead, and he'd find out only so that he could accelerate the paperwork awarding them posthumous citations for bravery.

Missions of such importance almost always required sacrifices, knowingly or unknowingly. He felt a brief moment of sorrow for the two men Murchesson selected. God bless them. They would be honored as heroes even though their exploits could never be revealed.

The General had been sitting in his office, waiting for the call, for hours, and he'd gone through twice his normal allotment of tobacco and caffeine. He hadn't expected an early call, but he certainly didn't anticipate that it might be delayed. After all, there was no question about precisely when the Queen would take her seat at the Millburn College affair. Murchesson had already sent him a coded message to indicate everything stood ready for the critical moment.

Why the hell hadn't he called with the results?

The General began to fear he might have to wait and learn about it on broadcast radio like everybody else. Was that any way to run a bloody war? Maybe Murchesson had been the wrong choice after all.

Dear sweet Jesus, what have I done?

"Stop it!" he ordered himself. Take control. Be in command. Your entire life has pointed to this moment. There would be only one other that over-shadowed it, and one event could not succeed without the other.

Damn it! Why didn't he call?

Fitzwilliam stubbed out another cigar. Fine Cuban tobacco. None of that Virginia/Carolina crap. Everyone knew the damned colonials poisoned the stuff. Now *there* was a conspiracy! Who knew how many people sickened and died because of the toxins the bloody rebels sprayed on the tobacco fields? Surely someone was looking into that. And if not, they damned well should.

The phone rang.

Despite all the anxiety over the call's delay, it *still* came as a surprise.

He yanked the receiver from the cradle and held it to his head. "Yes?"

"It's done."

"What about--"

Click.

General Sir David Fitzwilliam, Chief of the Defense Staff and highest ranking officer in the whole Royal fucking Army, stared at the lifeless phone in his hand. Though he'd gripped it tightly before, he squeezed it even harder now. It quivered as an extension of his rage, but no matter what he did he couldn't squeeze any life back into it. He was no more successful than King Canute commanding the tides.

But, damn it, no one hung up on a general.

Certainly not *this* General.

No one.

Ever!

He took a deep, calming breath. He lit yet another cigar. Dominican, he thought. Or maybe

Honduran. *Who could tell these days?*

After looking at his empty coffee cup, he poured himself three fingers of 24-year old single malt scotch.

And then he turned on the radio.

The beginning of Phase Two could wait until he evaluated the reaction to Phase One. But it couldn't wait long. It had to begin before the coronation of the Queen's successor.

~*~

Anthony Lancaster surprised Raines by not instantly rejecting the idea of hosting a party. By offering to surreptitiously cover the costs, Raines insured that the attention of party-goers would be focused on Lancaster and Chastity Cotswold. Lancaster spent little time mulling over the offer.

"These are difficult times for the Revolution," he said. "There's been nothing but bad news all year long."

Raines wished he'd taken more time to memorize "current" events before he'd journeyed into the past. "I, uh... haven't seen a newspaper in quite a while."

"The incomparable General Gates lost his entire army at Camden, South Carolina. I've heard reports of up to 10,000 men and all their supplies."

Raines recalled hearing Leah discuss the disaster. She had nothing but disdain for Horatio Gates and insisted that General Washington shared the feeling. "As I heard it, General Gates didn't impress anyone with his skill."

"Certainly not with his skill *in battle*. But with the speed of his retreat?" Lancaster laughed. "Of all the colonials who broke and ran, he covered the greatest distance in the least amount of time. 170 miles in three days, or so the papers claim."

"I didn't realize that." *But I should have.* Once again he wished Leah had already arrived. He intended to make sure the party was scheduled so that she could attend. He needed her.

"Samuel Harrow," Raines said, "our mutual acquaintance, suggested you might like to build some good will with the faithful in the area."

"The faithful?" Lancaster looked dubious. "Faithful toward what?"

"The Revolution, of course. I can understand your feelings about those in the Sons of Liberty who made threats against your family, but there are men of honor among them, too. Men who would never punish women for the acts of their men."

"There is shame enough to go around, on both sides."

"War is ugly business," Raines said. "Surely we can find something to celebrate."

"I can't imagine what. The economy is in ruins. Neighbors who once were friends, now turn on each other to prove their hatred of the Tory label."

"I'm merely proposing a return to civility," Raines said. "People need an opportunity to forget the war for a time, to relax and enjoy life. And, I confess, I have an ulterior motive. I hope to introduce Colonel Cotswold's daughter to society. The war has robbed her of the chance to find a husband."

Lancaster gazed at him as if he'd lost his mind. "You'd bear all that expense just to satisfy some silly woman? She must be brutally ugly."

Gabriel had managed to keep silent since Lancaster rebuked him earlier, but the insult to his mistress was more than he could stand. He began a headlong charge up the stairs which Raines barely managed to arrest with a restraining arm. "Take that back, sir!" He shouted.

Lancaster ignored him.

"Miss Cotswold is a lovely young woman," Raines said calmly before ordering Gabriel to wait in the buggy.

"I demand satisfaction!" the young man groused.

Lancaster finally reacted. His smile stretched wide across his face. "You're challenging *me* to a duel?"

"I am!"

"Get in the cart, Gabriel," Raines said for the second time. "I'm serious."

"So am I," the ex-slave said.

Lancaster met his stare with one equally hard and devoid of apprehension. "I prefer pistols. Do you have one?"

"I can get one."

"Shut up, Gabriel, and get in the damned buggy!"

The expletive worked its way into the teen's brain, and he slowly backed down a few steps.

Lancaster eased by Raines and asked Gabriel, "Do you know how to use one?"

"I'll learn."

"One more word, Gabriel," Raines growled, "and I'll shoot you myself!"

Lancaster's chuckle lacked any trace of humor. "Don't think I've forgotten this, boy. I'll hold you to it."

"You'll do no such thing," Raines said.

"This doesn't concern you. The boy obviously doesn't know his place. I'm going to put him in it. Or in a grave. Either would suit me."

"Have I heard you correctly? You'd risk the powerful contacts you might make, and the goodwill you might earn, over such nonsense?"

Lancaster squinted at Raines. "Are you trying to link this party idea with my right to preserve my honor?"

Raines wanted to pummel Lancaster himself, and with the skills he and Leah had acquired, he could do it. He could kill him if he needed to, and the knowledge give him courage. "Don't be stupid," he said. "I forbid Gabriel to participate in anything as barbaric as a duel. If you force his hand, you can forget about my support for any efforts you might make to restore your family name."

"It's clearly a matter of honor."

"And you clearly don't have any."

The men stood a yard apart, and Raines could see nothing but smoldering anger in Lancaster's dark eyes.

"Perhaps I should challenge *you*," Lancaster said. "And once you're dead, I'll kill your nigger, too."

Gabriel hurtled up the stairs, his hands reaching for Lancaster's throat.

Raines pushed Lancaster away and stopped Gabriel's assault before the teen could reach his quarry. Propelled backwards, Lancaster tripped and fell to the porch floor. While Raines restrained Gabriel, Lancaster reached into his saddlebag and withdrew a pistol.

Raines and Gabriel stopped struggling when they heard the ominous click of the gun being cocked.

Unable to get a clear shot at the youth, Lancaster yelled, "Get out of the way!"

"Don't be an idiot," Raines said.

"Move, damn you!"

"No sir, I will not. Now, put the gun down."

"Move!"

"Put--"

Boom!

~*~

Leah's plans to leave the modern world had been scrambled the moment Dwight, or Murchesson, or whatever the hell he called himself had pulled her into his conspiracy. If Joel hadn't shown up when he did, she'd be out in front of Chumley Hall, prancing around with that stupid sign, and providing a perfect target for revenge. New Englanders took the Royals seriously, and anyone who attempted to embarrass one, let alone hurt one, could expect reprisals.

She had gotten enough of that just by having an opinion which ran counter to the doctrine of the brain dead administrators at Millburn. Though she didn't want to admit it, the mob attack had frightened her. Joel's revelations about Murchesson, however, *terrified* her.

She had to put an end to that. Clearly, it was time to go.

Running from the law--in the 21st century anyway--was something neither she nor her father had contemplated. She had resigned herself to the idea that she'd never see the note he sent via the jar, and only a concerted effort of will kept her from berating herself for not reading it the moment she found it. Fortunately, she realized nothing would be gained by self-flagellation, mental or otherwise. She would simply proceed with the original plan and set the temporal coordinates accordingly.

While waiting for Joel, she used the time to double-check that everything they felt they might need was packed and ready. When he left, her father had taken some non-historical reference materials and sundry odds and ends, but the bulk of his supplies consisted of hard currency. Her supplies varied little from his except that she would be bringing mostly gold, where he brought silver. The colonies were in such dire need of hard currency, she and her father would be able to buy anything they needed, provided it was available in the late 18th century.

That thought had caused her to double-up, and then *triple-up*, on an array of personal hygiene products. Then, realizing she'd never be able to bring a life-time supply, she collected recipes for everything from tooth paste to herbal remedies. All of it went into a thick leather satchel on a wooden base sporting a pair of small but sturdy wheels. A handle which could be folded down or locked in extended fashion made it easier to roll the heavy bag around.

Even before the mob had destroyed her bike, Leah had serious doubts about using it to haul her store of goods on the last trip to the Event site. She hoped to enlist Joel's help, though she wasn't quite sure how she'd manage it without giving any secrets away.

"Thanks for helping me drag my bag of gold a couple miles through the woods, Joel. You can go now. Have a nice life!"

Yeah, like that'd work.

Though tempted to leave and begin a solo trek to the Event site, she felt too guilty to actually do it. For reasons she couldn't explain, she felt the need to stick around and wait for the Special Branch inspector. For a little while, anyway.

She checked the wall clock. According to Captain Dwight--*no, make that Murchesson*--the Queen would soon sit down to dinner. With any luck, Joel would have managed to foil the attempt to humiliate her. And then Leah could go.

And if he failed? It didn't seem to make a great deal of difference. Either way, she had to leave, and there was only one place she knew of where they'd never be able to find her.

She had already changed into a colonial style shift, the underwear of choice for fashionable colonial ladies. Light and loose-fitting, the long, shirt-like garment could easily be gathered around her when she curled herself up to make the passage. Joel would question her about it, of course, but wearing it during the trip made more sense than trying to change in front of him.

Besides, I don't know him well enough to treat him to such a show!

Though tempted to bring walking shorts, T-shirts, and other familiar attire, she knew better than to do anything which would draw attention. Though not happy about it, she left all such 21st century trappings piled neatly on a corner of one shelf. The only exception were the running shoes. She'd wear those until the last moment.

She looked once again at the clock.

Where the hell was Joel?

~*~

The lead ball from Lancaster's pistol slammed into the physicist and spun him around. Gabriel grabbed him before he pitched face first down the stairs. The gunshot seemed to echo endlessly, while thick, acrid smoke veiled everything in clouds of dirty white.

Gabriel lowered him to the floor then lunged at Lancaster who had regained his footing and used his pistol like a club, smashing at the teen's head and arms. One such blow stunned the boy, and he staggered away as if drunk.

Raines stood, and despite a searing pain in his shoulder advanced on Lancaster.

"Leave now, and I'll let you live," Lancaster shouted, still brandishing the pistol.

Raines' mouth had gone dry, and he focused on one goal: disabling Lancaster. The man backed away until he bumped into the front door of the house. Raines closed the gap, and Lancaster threatened him with his makeshift club. Raines feinted to his left then jabbed Lancaster's Adam's apple with a knuckled hand. The blow landed squarely, and Lancaster dropped the pistol. Grabbing at his neck with both hands, he struggled to suck air through his damaged windpipe.

Raines briefly considered leaving Lancaster where he stood, then decided he might still be dangerous and kicked him in the groin. Hard. Though he had other options for immobilizing Lancaster, none of them offered the same degree of personal satisfaction.

It was short lived, however, because Raines then feared he might have struck Lancaster's throat too hard. The physicist's martial arts instructor had cautioned that while such a blow generally ended fights quickly, it carried significant risk. The laryngeal prominence could easily be crushed, and if the windpipe was blocked completely, the recipient of the punch would have little chance of survival.

Though Lancaster's attention was divided between his craw and his crotch, he seemed able to get *some* air. Enough, Raines imagined, to stay alive. He wasn't sure if that was a good thing or not, but reasoned that it would likely be best if Lancaster survived. Assuming the gunshot wound he'd just received didn't kill him, Raines would soon have his hands full dealing with Benedict Arnold. He certainly didn't need to be worrying about someone hunting him down for murder.

He reached down with his good arm and

grabbed Lancaster's vest--Leah would have called it a waistcoat--and dragged him clear of the door. Lancaster's eyes grew wide, but he made no effort to interfere. Raines turned toward Gabriel who had recovered enough to smile. The teen waved him off.

Neither of the two on the porch appeared ready to move anytime soon, so Raines left them both and went inside the house. A quick search turned up the family Bible on a sturdy wooden stand near a heavily curtained window. He pulled a ballpoint pen from his pocket and flipped the pages until he found Ecclesiastes, chapter 3, verse 15.

That which hath been is now...

He smiled as he wrote the number "1" and his initials in the margin, then closed the book and left it where he'd found it.

Glancing around at the interior, he realized the Lancaster home would have been a wonderful place to have a party. No doubt Chastity would have exemplified the expression "belle of the ball." But, suffering the presence of Anthony Lancaster was more than he could bear. He smiled thinking about how Leah might have reacted during the abbreviated fight. She not only wouldn't have pulled her punch, she'd have struck hard enough to smear Lancaster's larynx on the wall behind him. She had clearly inherited a warrior's spirit from her mother-- something they'd sorely need in the weeks to come.

Thinking of Beth, the woman he'd lost so long ago, almost demoralized him, but a vision of Leah snapped him back to reality. He had work to do. The damned clock was ticking, and he had already used his one chance to re-set it.

Quit sniveling and get to it!

Neither Lancaster nor Gabriel had moved in the short time before Raines returned to the porch. He leaned close to Lancaster's ear and whispered, "If you ever come near me, or Gabriel, or the Cotswolds, I'll finish the job. I'll rip out whatever's left of your throat and shove it up your ass. Do you understand?"

Lancaster nodded, his tear-clouded eyes still wide with fear.

Gabriel stood up as he approached. "You shouldn't be helping me," the teen said. "'Tis the other way 'round."

Until then, Raines had felt surprisingly able, except for the useless arm dangling from his shoulder like raw meat. But the moment Gabriel ducked under the physicist's good arm to support him, Raines felt lightheaded.

"I've got you," Gabriel said.

Raines mumbled, "Thank God."

Gabriel managed to get him down the steps and into the buggy. As he propped Raines in the seat, he kept muttering, "Mysterious, mysterious ways. My oh my, such mysterious ways."

He was still muttering when Raines passed out.

~*~

Chapter Nine

"Time travel used to be thought of as just science fiction, but Einstein's general theory of relativity allows for the possibility that we could warp space-time so much that you could go off in a rocket and return before you set out."

--Stephen J. Hawking

Joel had little trouble getting away from Chumley Hall. Word of the Queen's murder spread even faster than the dispersing crowd. A great deal of attention had been paid to the matter of keeping unwanted persons from entering the building; no one anticipated that they'd need to keep people from leaving it.

Relatively few in the crowd headed toward the physics building where Leah waited for him. He assumed he could find the basement and that Doctor Kerr's laboratory would be prominently marked. He got it half right.

A few emergency exit signs illuminated the windowless corridor in the basement of the Jefferson building. Joel saw a panel of electrical switches and raked his hand across them flooding the hallway with harsh light.

He pressed on, moving from door to door but only staying long enough to scan for names and titles. The portals bore either lengthy descriptions and multiple names or nothing. A blank door could open on a physics lab as easily as a broom closet, so he tried the doorknob on every unmarked entry. All of them were locked.

He started banging on the doors and yelling Leah's name, then quickly dropped his voice as he remembered the photo in the hand of the Queen's security chief. They could have reached the building as easily as he had. It wouldn't take them long to find and search the places associated with Leah. He assumed investigators were already ransacking his own flat, and he had little doubt that someone in Murchesson's employ had thoughtfully provided a damning bit of evidence tying Joel to the assassination.

One of the doors he had passed suddenly opened behind him, and he whirled around at the sound.

"In here!" Leah said as she stood with her back against the door. She was dressed in an odd sort of ankle-length shirt made of plain white linen. Though it may have been just his imagination, she seemed happy to see him. That lasted as long as it took for her to ask, "Is the Queen all right?"

Joel shook his head as he limped toward her. "They got her. It wasn't paint or dye, it was some sort of poison gas."

Leah gripped his arm as the color drained from her face. "No!"

"It was awful," Joel said. "She had no chance."

"You *saw* it happen?"

"Through a window. I got there in time to report the plot, but the man who went to investigate was killed by the same gas."

"What are we going to do?" Leah asked. "Shouldn't we report what we know?"

"Ordinarily I'd say yes, but Murchesson is way ahead of us. He's already set us up to take the blame."

"But we had nothing to do with it!"

"If claiming innocence worked, every copper in the world would be out of a job."

As he limped around the crowded laboratory, Joel explained about the photo and his suspicions that once Murchesson decided to blame them, he had the resources to fully implicate them both. While he spoke, something far less serious claimed his attention. He couldn't help but admire the way Leah's body moved beneath the thin dressing gown. The garment cried out for slippers, not running shoes. "Why are you dressed like that?"

"These are uh..." She shrugged. "Actually, they're traveling clothes."

"Charming, but not terribly practical. Anyone who sees you is going to stare. I'm finding it hard not to." Indeed, the white material contrasted deliciously with her dark complexion, and given the time, he'd be more than willing to continue staring.

"Doesn't matter," she said. "We've got to run. Both of us."

Joel patted his leg. "That's easier for some than others."

"Oh! I'm sorry... I didn't mean--"

"Forget it. Anyway, you're right. We can't stay around here. Do you have a car?"

She gave him a puzzled look. "A car? Good God, no. What would I do with a car?"

"It might be a handy way to get out of town."

"And go where?"

"I dunno. The midlands? You've got friends there, don't you?"

"No."

"Oh. Well, damn." He pried his eyes away from her and looked around Doctor Kerr's laboratory. It didn't match his notion of a lab. No beakers of bubbling chemicals, no tables crowded with exotic glassware. Instead, the room consisted of industrial shelving sporting clumps of electronics. Each assemblage sprouted wires, and these were bundled neatly despite frequent divergent cables running to other devices around the room. He shook his head as he tried to make sense of it. Some of the confusion resulted from Leah in the flimsy gown; the rest emanated from his investigative instincts. He struggled to square facts with reality.

One such fact was that Leah and her father had sold their family home and liquidated their assets. No one had seen Doctor Kerr in weeks. All of which suggested that Leah was a woman with "escape" not just on her mind, but at the top of her agenda. She claimed innocence, but if Murchesson hadn't pointed a photographic finger at Joel, he would have had some doubts.

"Tell me something," he said. "Where were you planning to go?"

She blinked, her lips twisting slightly before she responded. "You won't believe me."

"There's only one way to find out."

"I had planned to spend some time in the Boston area and meet up with my father. Then we planned to go to New York."

"The city?"

"Further north," she said. "On the Hudson River near West Point."

"Rather an odd destination, but not too hard to believe. When?"

"Ah. Well, that's where it gets a little strange."

"No," he said, "'strange' began two days ago with a guy named Smithers. I'll tell you about that sometime. But now? Things have gone way beyond strange. Now, they're bizarre."

She actually laughed. "It'll likely get worse."

He couldn't imagine how, especially since his ability to control his imagination began to fade as he watched Leah bend down to access a simple control panel on a low shelf. She carefully adjusted a dial and pressed a single button.

"There," she said. "We're all set. If you'll help me move my stuff, I'll explain on the way."

"On the way where?"

"Out of town."

~*~

Sensation returned to Raines' shoulder whenever the buggy hit a bump, and it returned with a vengeance.

He tried not to groan, or at least not too loudly, since Gabriel seemed to take his whimpering personally. But darting in and out of consciousness made processing difficult. He tried several times to engage Gabriel in conversation but found himself either babbling incoherently--even to himself--or drifting off. Eventually, Gabriel simply ignored him.

He awoke feeling multiple hands grabbing him, but he was too weak to struggle.

"Easy now," Gabriel told him, "we're just bringing you inside."

Oh, Christ, not to the bed. Not the teeny, tiny bed!

"Bring him into my room," the Colonel said.

"But, why?" Mrs. Cotswold asked.

"Because he's too damned tall for the guest bed!"

Grateful, Raines rolled his head to take in the crowd surrounding him. It felt like dozens of people, but there were only four: one black face and three white ones. And only one of them smiled at him. Chastity looked like the angel Gabriel thought him to be. Of the four, she seemed the most concerned by his condition, and he realized her smile was fabricated solely to buck up his spirits.

It worked. At least a little.

"I don't want to be a bother," he tried to say, but the words lacked precision. In fact, they lacked just about everything and came out as a string of disconnected syllables. In monotone. Chastity shushed him.

They managed to carry him into the house without banging his head on a door frame or jarring his wound too severely. Once he'd been stretched out on the Colonel and Mrs. Cotswold's bed, the two women went about removing his boots and breeches.

"What happened?" demanded the Colonel.

"Lancaster shot him."

"Whatever for?" asked Mrs. Cotswold.

"For standing up to him," Gabriel said. "He threatened to shoot us both."

"Bloody damned Tory," the Colonel muttered.

"Watch your language, dear," his wife said.

Chastity finally voiced the obvious. "He needs a doctor."

"Gabriel?" the Colonel said, "My horse is rested. Take him and summon Mrs. Bentley. You know the way?"

"Yes sir," he said as he ran from the house.

"You're going to be fine," Chastity whispered. She had moved so close that he could feel her breath on his cheek.

She gave him a kiss on the forehead just before he passed out again.

~*~

"I need a bit more to go on than just 'out of town.'" Joel said.

"I'll try to explain on the way." She reached for the wheeled bag and dragged it toward the door.

It seemed even heavier than she'd anticipated.

"May I help you with that?" he asked.

"Sure. But we'd better take turns. It's heavy."

Joel pulled on the handle and quickly discovered she hadn't exaggerated. "Good Lord! What have you got in here, lead?"

She chuckled. "Something like that."

"Where are we going?"

"To the spot I told you about, where Dad and I had lunch."

"Out in the woods? It'll be dark before long. How far is it?"

"Only a couple miles."

Joel suddenly looked depressed.

"What's wrong?"

He thumped his leg. "Normally, I'm good for a city block, maybe two if I've been drinking."

Without a word, Leah dropped down beside the heavily laden satchel and opened it. She rummaged around for a few moments before finding the bottle of painkillers she'd stowed there. "Take a couple of these," she said.

Joel looked at them dubiously.

"I'm not trying to poison you!"

He grimaced. "I've seen enough of that already, thank you."

She fetched him a glass of water, and he took a swig to wash the capsules down. "Sure hope they work."

"Me, too," she said. "I made 'em myself. They're mostly herbal but with a little chemical boost. Where I'm headed, I won't have too many choices when it comes to medicine."

"You make it sound like darkest Africa."

She frowned, then realized he didn't mean anything derogatory. "It *is* a little primitive. At least, compared with here and now."

He gave her a funny look, but didn't say anything.

Together they walked through the basement corridor, then took an elevator to the ground floor. The building seemed deserted, and at her insistence, they left through a door in the back.

As soon as they reached the lawn, the wheels under the heavily laden bag sank into the soft soil.

Joel gripped the handle with both hands and strained to drag it behind him. "This is more like plowing than pulling, and I'm not much of a horse."

Leah's heart sank. "This wasn't supposed to happen."

"I hear that a lot," Joel said.

"We can't pull this thing, not this way, for miles."

Joel cut his eyes at her. "You said it was only a couple."

"More or less. I've never measured it."

"How did you get there in the past?"

"I rode a bike or walked. It's an easy jog."

"I'm sure," he said.

"Sorry."

He waved the apology off.

She had no intention of abandoning her supplies. It was more than just a matter of her comfort. The freedom of the American colonies depended on it. She swallowed hard. "What are we going to do?"

~*~

General Sir David Fitzwilliam sat in his darkened Annapolis office, low on cigars, low on Scotch, and out of patience. He shifted in his over-stuffed chair and reached for the tuning knob on his radio. Hoping to find a station broadcasting facts rather than conjecture, he toured the frequency band for what must have been the tenth time. But all he found was the same old crap.

He paused briefly and listened to a commercial program called, of all things, "Rumor Has It." The show's host, obviously *not* a military man, took joy in heaping ridicule on callers who claimed to have knowledge of conspiracies. Though Fitzwilliam had never called in himself, he tried to keep tabs on the show in case someone mentioned his plans to attack the midlands. Thus far, no one had. He turned the radio off.

An aide had been in and out of his office with what he hopefully described as "updates." But the flimsies bore nothing beyond the bare details: the Queen had been assassinated by exposure to some kind of deadly gas.

The lab-coated boffins in the basement of the Home Office should have analyzed the gas cylinder by now, but no official findings had been released. He'd pressed all his contacts and subordinates for information, but none knew more than he did.

MI6 would undoubtedly be in an uproar; the Queen's Guards would be running around like insects suddenly exposed to light, and Parliament would be bristling with finger-pointers. All in all, pretty much what he expected.

What he *didn't* expect, was Murchesson keeping him uninformed. That could not be tolerated, and he looked forward to the moment when he could dress the young officer down.

At least the gas had worked. And it turned out to be every bit as efficient as he'd hoped. The news reports varied little about the total number of victims, which seemed to number about a half-dozen. Not bad considering how lightly concentrated the gas had been. When it came time to roll out the serious canisters, the concentration would be significantly more lethal.

~*~

A sharp sting in his shoulder brought Raines awake, or nearly so. He slapped at the hands fiddling with his shirt. "Who are you? Get away from me," he groused.

"This is Doctor Bentley," the Colonel said. "She's here to tend your wound."

Raines eyed the woman warily. She sat beside him on the bed seeming anything but professional. She looked and smelled as if she'd been working in a barn. "You're a doctor?"

"I'm a surgeon. I was working at a neighboring farm when Gabriel found me."

"Were you cleaning the stable?"

"I was with a patient."

"And you were burying him?"

"The patient was a goat, and I expect him to

survive. Now, you're my patient."

We'll see about that. Raines eyed her with suspicion. "Where'd you go to school?"

She sighed and gave her head a disdainful shake. "Just lie back, and let me tend to your shoulder."

"When was the last time you washed your hands?"

"He's delirious," she said.

"No, I'm not, and it was a reasonable question. I'd like an answer."

"Colonel, reach into my bag and get out the leather strap. He's going to need something to bite down on."

"I'll bite down on you if you don't answer me!" Raines said, his voice rising.

Gabriel appeared from the shadows holding an oil lamp. "She's only doing what's best for you."

"Nonsense! I'm more of a doctor than she is, and I'm not even a doctor. Not that kind, anyway." He pulled the soiled sheet over his wounded shoulder, ignoring the swarm of germs and bacteria it surely housed.

"You might want to listen to him," Gabriel said to the surgeon. "Though his ways are different, he has knowledge to which few men are privy."

Raines continued to glare at her. "Yeah. What he said."

She sat back and relaxed, but the look on her face told him she knew she was suffering a fool of the first order. "What would you have of me?"

"Where should I begin?" He took a deep breath. *Concentrate. Don't fight her; help her.* "I know this may sound odd, but where I come from, surgeons--and even doctors--wash their hands between patients. Always. In fact, it's a law."

She didn't look in the least bit convinced.

"That law is so closely adhered to that violators are taken out and shot."

She still didn't look convinced, but he'd gotten her attention.

"Not only that, they sterilize all their instruments before using them."

"Sterilize?"

"Clean them. Thoroughly. With soap and boiling water, and carbolic acid or something similar."

"Carbolic acid? What on Earth for?"

"To prevent infection! Dear sweet Jesus. How many people have you killed already?"

"I told you he was delirious," the woman said. "Carbolic acid? Whoever heard of such a thing! I need to bleed him right away, then I can try to dig out the ball."

"Bleed me?" Raines asked incredulously. "Are you completely insane? Can't you see how much blood I've already lost?"

"He's a big fellow," she said. "We'll have to strap him down."

Why wasn't anyone listening?

Raines watched as the woman bent down and stuck her filthy hands into a wooden case containing a variety of instruments, most of which would have looked more at home in a cabinetmaker's shop. But instead of producing something with which to bind him, she extracted a well worn book.

"Oh, thank God," he said. "She can read."

Her glare reminded him of an eagle fixated on a bunny. "This is Brown's *Elementa Medicinae*. I have studied it as thoroughly as anyone in the profession. I apprenticed under Horatio Grande, a graduate of Kings College in New York, and I have performed more surgeries than I can count. I know everything there is to know about patient care: bleeding, cupping, blistering, sweating, and amputation. I can prepare no less than a dozen different emetics and a like number of enemas. Does that satisfy you as to my qualifications?"

"Almost," he said. "I've just one more question. Do you *ever* wash your hands?"

Doctor Bentley stood up abruptly. "I came all this way at the Colonel's urging. I did not come here to be abused by a lunatic."

Raines stared straight at her. "I'm looking at the only lunatic in this room."

She wheeled toward the Cotswolds, then pushed past them. "I can't help him. He's in God's hands, and if you ask me, that's exactly where he belongs."

The Colonel rushed out the door after her. "Wait! Please!"

"Gabriel," Raines said, "before she goes, ask her for a pair of tongs. I saw them in her kit."

"Tongs?"

"Yes. We'll use them to dig out the bullet."

"Bullet, sir?"

"Lancaster's lead ball! The thing at the bottom of the hole in my shoulder--the one that's leaking blood all over Mrs. Cotswold's bed linens.

That bullet!"

"But wouldn't tongs be too big? There's a pair by the fireplace."

"Little tongs!" Raines' outburst required too much energy. He fell back on the bed. "Just ask her, son. Before she rides off into the bloody sunset."

"It's already dark, sir."

"Go. Please?" He never knew being an angel would be so much work. And just then, a real angel appeared at his side: Chastity. Her beauty all but took his breath away, and her obvious concern for him seemed to alleviate some of his pain.

"What will we do without a doctor?" she asked.

"I imagine we'll greatly improve my chances for survival." He forced himself to smile. "And as a bonus, you're going to get a lesson in modern medicine."

"I am?"

He nodded, then gazed into her green eyes. Looking at her gave him peace, something he realized he hadn't experienced since he lost Beth so long ago. Yet, this woman--a child really, likely in her late teens--shared the sort of strength he'd found in Leah's mother. Chastity's compassion and faith came from her parents, but something deeper emanated from her eyes. He couldn't identify it, couldn't explain it if he had to, but there was something there that gave him hope. More than that, it gave him confidence.

"As soon as I get better," he said, "we're going to have a party."

Her face lit up. "Really?"

"Absolutely."

"With music and dancing?"

"And food and wine and all the extras."

"I pray you're not toying with me, sir," she said.

Much as I'd love to toy with you, or whatever it's called in colonial Boston, I'm old enough to be your grandfather. "Consider it a promise."

"Will you dance with me?"

"Uh... sure." Leah had been his last dance partner, and she'd been just about ten years old. The college had sponsored a parent-child event, and she had begged him to take her. The memory brought a smile. Some of the lyrics had even stuck in his head:

> *You put your right hand in,*
> *You put your right hand out,*
> *You put your right hand in,*
> *And you shake it all about.*

"What kind of dancing are we talking about?" he asked. "I might need some lessons."

Great! Dance instruction. He and Leah plan a history-shattering rendezvous with the biggest traitor in New World history, and here he is dreaming about doing the hokey pokey with an 18th century ingénue turned practical nurse.

"I could teach you a few things," Chastity said.

I'll bet you could. He shook his head. *Dear Lord--I'm as bad as Lucas Benn!*

"Got 'em!" yelled Gabriel as he burst back into the room. He held a primitive pair of forceps in the air and waved them over his head.

"Excellent. What we need now," Raines said, "is some alcohol, some boiling water, and some clean bandages."

"The Colonel has some rum he was saving for a special occasion," Mrs. Cotswold said.

"That should do," Raines said.

"I'll have him fetch it. I can take care of the rest." Mrs. Cotswold motioned for Chastity to follow her. "Come along, now. You can help, too."

Chastity appeared torn between assisting her parents and staying with her patient. Gabriel, too, looked as if he needed someone to assign him a task.

"Give me a hand, you two," Raines said to the youngsters. "I fear it's going to be a long night."

~*~

Leah put her hands on Joel's shoulders. Though tempted to just sag into his arms and give up, that wasn't her style. And it certainly wasn't what either of her parents would have expected of her. "There's got to be a way around this."

Joel looked at her satchel, its wheels sunk in the soft ground almost to the axle. "Wider wheels would help."

"Where the hell are we going to get wider wheels?"

"I dunno. Hardware store? Bike shop?"

She crossed her arms and pouted, not that the tactic had ever worked before. Still, she and Joel were new to each other. Maybe he had a store of creative energy he didn't know about. Pouts could be powerful motivators, if used correctly.

"Stand by," he said as he turned away and started limping toward the corner of the building.

"Where are you going?"

"To find a bike."

She knew that wouldn't work. Her own bicycle had a broad basket on the front, and while it was suitable for hauling books to and from classes, it wasn't up to the task of supporting the weight of all she had crammed into the satchel. The overhead rack on a train might not have been stout enough for the job.

She waited for what seemed like hours, but in reality amounted to only a few minutes. In her current state, she couldn't tell the difference. And too, she didn't really know Joel all that well.

He could be looking for someone to come and arrest her.

He could tell them he had nothing to do with the plot to hurt the Queen. *His* fingerprints weren't all over the murder weapon.

He could be setting *her* up--just like Dwight, or Murchesson, or whatever he called himself.

Deep down inside, however, she didn't believe any of that. Anxiety, she knew, had a way of tinkering with one's ability to think rationally. Her father had taught her that, and it was a lesson with which she'd always struggled. But with Joel, she didn't have to struggle quite so much. There was something about him....

She heard the throaty rumble of a motorcycle. It grew louder as it approached the corner of the building.

Leah needed a place to hide, but for all the

trees on the bucolic campus, none of them stood close to the back of the Jefferson Physics Building. She wrapped both hands around the satchel handle and pulled for all she was worth, dragging the heavy bag toward the nearest tree which stood at least fifty feet from the building.

She'd never make it. Even without the ridiculously heavy "rolling" bag.

The rumble of the motorcycle grew louder.

Damn it--Joel had sold her out!

The bouncing headlight on the front of the big machine prevented her from identifying the driver, until he stopped the vehicle next to her and switched it off. The sudden silence surprised her.

"Can I offer you a ride somewhere, miss?"

Releasing the satchel, she rushed forward, threw her arms around his shoulders, and kissed him full on the mouth.

He sat back with a silly smile on his face, as if savoring the assault. "If I zipped around the building, and came right back, would you do that again?"

"Once is all you get," she said. She had to keep *something* in reserve. But for now, her store of confidence had grown a great deal.

"I don't want to put the kickstand down," he said. "I'm afraid it'll sink into the lawn. If the bike falls over, lifting it up again will be a pain."

"Where should we put the satchel?" A quick check of the police vehicle revealed neither basket nor saddle pouches. "Where did you get this thing?"

"From a mounted patrol officer."

"He just gave it to you?"

"Well, no, not exactly. I had to pull rank."

"You flashed your badge, and he gave it up?"

Joel looked sheepish. "I did flash my badge."

"And?"

"I told him I needed his vehicle."

"And?"

"He said I should do something that's not anatomically feasible. For me, anyway."

She grimaced. "So you stole the bike?"

"No. Actually, I hit him first, and *then* stole it."

"Merciful Mother Mary! You hit a constable?"

"And it hurt like hell. Bugger wore a helmet, and I got a piece of it when I went for his jaw."

"Did you knock him out?" she asked.

"Probably not for long."

"Lovely. What are we going to do with the satchel?"

He pondered the situation only briefly, then had her hold up the bike while he dragged the rolling bag to the rear of the two-wheeler and slipped the handle over the top of the tail light.

"You think that'll hold?" she asked.

"You said two miles, right?"

"More or less."

"It should last. Now, how much time will we need once we get there?"

Leah thought for a moment. "Twenty minutes, minimum."

"Climb on," he said, "and lean close. I want you to explain exactly where we're going and how it is our friend, Murchesson, won't be able to find us."

~*~

Chapter Ten

"Great occasions do not make heroes or cowards;
they simply unveil them to the eyes of men."
--Bishop Westcott

Raines imagined he knew how difficult the evening ahead would be. But despite an imagination capable of working through the complexities of time travel and the development of theories and applications beyond anything the realm of physics had previously accomplished, he came up well short of reality. The extraction of a projectile embedded in the human body, by a person with no training whatsoever, generated pain at a level inconsistent with consciousness.

In short, not only did Raines scream a lot, the only time he *didn't* scream was when he had passed out.

Getting to that point, however, wasn't too

bad.

"I'm going to need to drink a good deal of your rum," he said to the Colonel.

"I understand. I was wounded once myself, you know."

Raines took a huge gulp of the fiery liquid and nodded as if he actually understood. He would discover all too soon that he didn't, and the rum would have nothing to do with it.

"Gabriel, my friend, you must pay attention to Chastity. You'll be holding the lantern for her, and she's going to need all the light she can get. Do whatever she tells you."

"I will," he said, solemnly.

"Good." Raines took another swig. It still burned his throat, but less than before. *Prob'ly converted the lining of my esophagus to scar tissue.* "I'm counting on you, Gabe. And remember, I'm likely to say things I don't mean. Seriously ugly things. Just ignore 'em. Don't let anyone take offense." Another swig. "With any luck, I'm going to be looped pretty soon."

Gabriel just smiled. *What a nice kid.*

Another swig. He swished the rum in his mouth before swallowing it. He'd never much cared for rum before. Now, he wasn't so sure. He swallowed, and his throat sent the message that he'd just consumed a half cup of molten lava.

Good stuff. Oh yeah, damned good stuff.

When he stopped coughing, he managed to address the resident angel. "Chastity, you have the best eyesight and the steadiest hands. And, as far as I can tell, you actually washed yours." He smiled.

"Bless you."

She smiled back.

Mrs. Cotswold beamed, too.

"But you're going to have the toughest job." He forced himself to take yet another swig. It went down much easier. "You're going to have to dig out the bullet."

"He means the ball," Gabriel said.

Chastity ignored the former slave. "I don't want to hurt you."

Raines took another slug of rum. "You don't have much cheese. Er, choice. And besides, if I can get drunk enough, maybe I'll pash out."

She looked terribly concerned.

"Have you never been around someone who's utterly pissed? Not angry, love. God in heaven, not that. I mean, you know, legless. Boozed. Blotto. Boiled as an owl."

She looked at him as if he'd been invaded by evil spirits. Which, he realized, was quite true. "I'm hoping to get to the point where I won't feel it quite so bad."

"Feel what?" she asked.

"Feel you digging aroun' in my shoulder for that stupid piece of lead."

Another swig. His lips felt odd, as if he'd loaned them out to a stranger, and they'd come back a different size.

"I've got hot water and lye soap," Mrs. Cotswold said.

"Eggsalent. Innaminute, yer gonna wash my shoulder. Real good. You'll need to use clean rags. Okay?"

"Oh Kay?"

He giggled. "Just an expresshun. Don't give it a thought." He took another sip. "Clean rags. Clean th' wound. Get the nasty bits out--dried blood, dirt, anything else you find."

Mrs. Cotswold attacked the wound with soap, water, and vigor.

Raines responded with a piercing scream.

"Pull yourself together," the Colonel said. "I've seen men have their legs cut off that didn't raise such a fuss."

His words fell on unappreciative ears. Raines began to imagine removing the Colonel's appendages, one at a time, without benefit of anesthetic.

"It's bleeding freely," Mrs. Cotswold said.

"Thas prob'ly a good thing," Raines said when the worst of the pain subsided. "Helps wash out the wound." He took another sip of rum and rolled his eyes in the direction where he'd last seen Chastity. "It's your turn, darlin'. You got the tongs. Dig that little lead bastard outta there."

"*Doctor* Kerr!" Mrs. Cotswold said. "Your language."

"Colonel, it's likely to get a great deal worse. P'raps you should take Mrs. Cots--"

Just then, Chastity rammed the forceps into the hole in his shoulder, and the physicist rose from the mattress in a display of anti-gravitational skill he would never have thought possible. In retrospect, it may have been the sound he made which caused his body to levitate. Chastity, however, kept after the elusive slug with an unnerving single-mindedness that eventually turned the physicist's lights out.

He never heard her announce that she'd found the misshapen ferrous glob.

Gabriel poured some rum on the wound, and the stimulation of exposed nerves brought Raines back around. In dramatic fashion. He said some things which suggested a less than pleasant future for the lad, but to Gabriel's credit, he shrugged them off.

The Colonel offered to stitch up the wound, but Mrs. Cotswold laughed him from the room. While Chastity stared at the chunk of lead she still held clutched in the forceps, the ever-pleasant Mrs. Cotswold sewed the physicist's ragged wound shut.

Though he'd been tempted to express his eternal love and gratitude to them both, all Raines could manage was a prolonged grunt.

And then oblivion.

~*~

Though it had been years since Joel had last operated a motorcycle, the basics returned quickly. A preferred method of transportation for members of the Black Watch, bikes were as common as regimental tattoos.

Much more than the bike, he enjoyed having Leah Kerr pressed against his back. The combination of their thin clothing and her warm torso made it hard to focus on driving. Her breathy voice didn't help either, even though her directions were critically important. Without them, he'd never have found the remote location to which she guided him.

The growl of the motorcycle made conversation difficult, and while Leah overcame it by speaking directly into his ear, he had to raise his voice to be heard.

"So, you think we can just hide out once we reach your little picnic spot?"

"Of course not," she said. "That's our jumping off point."

"Jumping off?" The idea didn't sound appealing.

"Remember when I told you things were going to get really strange? I wasn't joking. We're going to a place my father picked out some years ago as the target for his Event Generator."

"I don't--"

"How 'bout you let me talk? I can barely hear you anyway, and I need to explain a few things in order to save time. We won't have much once we get to where we're going."

Joel nodded his approval.

"The Event Generator is my father's fancy name for a time machine."

"A *what?*"

"Hush! You agreed to listen. You can ask questions later."

He grumbled acquiescence but doubted she heard him. She just plowed on, occasionally directing him one way or another via hand gesture. He flipped on the headlamp as dusk shifted to night. Though he could have driven faster, he wasn't eager to lose the physical contact. Best of all, whenever Leah spoke, she hugged him and pressed herself even closer.

"Most of the equipment resides in his lab, but some of it had to be installed way out here to ensure that conditions would be the same at both ends of the transmission. If, for instance, there was a tree growing in the spot where someone materialized, both the tree and the arriving party would be obliterated. Dad said he had calculated the blast area, but it wouldn't matter to anyone at or near ground zero. 'Two things cannot occupy the same space.' Violate that law, and it gets ugly."

Joel nodded his head. He thought he understood that kind of ugly.

"Most of the gear Dad needed at the Event Site he installed underground. There is some focusing apparatus hidden nearby, too, but it's so well camouflaged I doubt anyone would ever see it, or figure out its function if they did."

"What about power?" Joel asked.

"What?"

"Power!" he shouted.

"Oh. He ran underground cables from the lab."

All too soon, she directed him to a clearing where he killed the engine. She dismounted and unhooked the "rolling" bag from the taillight, though it had acted more like a plow than a trailer. "If you turn the bike a bit, you can shine the headlamp right where we're going to need some light."

"Where's that, exactly?"

She walked away from him, sensuous in the thin shift, until she reached a spot overlooking a low cliff. Dense vegetation beyond absorbed the light from the bike. "Here," she said.

Joel maneuvered the vehicle into position and left the light on then joined her. He started to ask a question, but she put a finger to his lips. "Save it. We don't have much time. At least, not here."

Here?

She turned away and bumped her palm against what appeared to be a large stone. The top half of it rolled back on hinges to reveal a pair of toggle switches, one of which was mounted on a red background. She flipped the unmarked switch on, and Joel immediately heard a mechanical whirring.

"That sound is normal," Leah said as she dragged the rolling bag to the center of the smallest of two circles and collapsed the handle. "There are actually two focal points for the Events. The little one is for supplies, and it will operate first. If something goes wrong we'll have ten minutes to shut everything down before the second one fires."

"Fires?"

She shook her head. "Operates. Runs. Whatever. It makes a big popping noise. You'll see."

Seconds later, a thunderous pop shattered the stillness, and Leah's bag disappeared.

"Holy shit!" Joel shouted. "Where'd it go?"

"Into the past."

"Like last week?"

She smiled as she walked to the center of the larger circle and stopped. "A little further back than that. About 232 years further."

Joel could do little more than stare at her, his jaw slack.

"Listen carefully," she said. "This is terribly important."

He managed a nod.

"Is there any chance at all that you might want to come with me?"

"I uh... That is, I haven't--"

"See those two switches over there?" She pointed at the flip-top rock. "If you want to follow me, all you need to do is switch them both on. The unmarked one will reset itself to off as soon as I'm gone."

"Gone," he said. That didn't sound good at all. "Did you say *both* switches?"

"Yes. The red one is what Dad calls the Doomsday Switch."

That definitely didn't sound good.

"It will cause everything in his lab to melt down once the last Event takes place. If you're not coming with me, you need to flip that switch on right now."

"But, how will you get back?"

Her smile took on a wistful aspect. "That's the hard part. It's one-way. Each time the machine generates an Event, it records the settings and advances the timing so that no two transmissions end at the same moment. There has to be time to move out of the way before the next transmission begins."

"To avoid the ugly part?"

"Right," she said. Then she took off her wrist watch and her running shoes. She left them both on the ground a couple feet outside the circle. "There's only a couple minutes left. You need to decide."

"How can I make a decision like that at the drop of a hat?"

"It's terrible, I know. I've had years to think about it and prepare." She knelt down and gathered the edges of her shift around her. "The Event field is roughly spherical. Anything in it will be shifted back in time. Anything outside of it will be unaffected."

"What happens to anything that's half in and half out?"

She shrugged. "Half of it goes away. The rest stays right where it is. I'd curl up into a ball if I could, but I want to keep more of myself toward the center of the Event sphere."

Madness! "How do you even know you'll survive?"

"Because my Dad survived. He sent me a message."

"From the past? How?"

"How he did it isn't important. He did it. The machine works."

232 years into the past? Holy crap!

"Joel, think! Don't forget what that Murchesson character is trying to do. This is your chance to get away from him. If he's as bad as you say he is, do you really believe he'd let you go to trial?"

Joel shook his head. A trial wasn't likely, and the alternative clearly sucked.

"Can I ask you a question?"

She looked anything but confident and kept craning her neck to see her watch on the ground. "Of course, but do it quickly."

He took a deep breath. "Do you *want* me to come with you?"

Treason, Treason!

~*~

General Fitzwilliam had no reason to leave his office. No one waited for him at home. His wife had left him years earlier, and though he had always wanted a son who could follow him in the family tradition of military service, they remained childless. He always suspected the fault was hers, though she often voiced the exact opposite opinion.

There had been little point in even investigating alternatives. His grandfather had lost their ancestral home when he fled England rather than join the resistance. That host, mostly Scots who avoided the worst of the German invasion during the Great War, had been reduced to a ragtag band of guerillas. Unlike their New World brethren, the colonists in North America, they eventually gave up.

He had paintings and even a few photographs of the family's former holdings in rural England. As he understood it, the great stone buildings and surrounding grounds had been converted to some sort of school. No doubt German ingenuity had overcome the challenge of converting a nobleman's estate into something befitting commoners. The thought sickened him.

When the phone rang, he assumed it was the night shift aide checking in, something they did only on the rare occasions when he tarried in his office after hours. He'd all but given up hope of hearing from his covert agent.

"It's me," said a voice he almost didn't recognize.

"It's about bloody time! What's going on?"

"Someone suspects me," Murchesson said, a hint of panic in his voice. "I've got the authorities focusing on a pair of suspects--one male, one female--who allegedly masterminded the attack. But there's something else going on. A leak of some kind that I haven't tracked down yet. But I will."

"Leak? What kind of leak?"

"It has to do with a message we intercepted. I can't explain it yet. I'm still working on it."

The man was thorough, he had to give him that much. "Casualties?"

"The only one of note was the head of the history department. But, since she was the one who gave us the lead on our female suspect, we're well rid of her. The gas took out a few others in the hall as well. One of them was a police inspector."

Fitzwilliam grunted. Killing someone in law enforcement was always a bad idea. The police tended to be more diligent when investigating the deaths of their own. "And outside of the hall?"

"The two on my team of course. Oh, and an old woman in the physics department. A secretary. It was unavoidable. She may have had something to do with the leak I mentioned, but I couldn't get anything out of her. Still, she might have given the authorities more information than they need, so I put her down. On the plus side, I found one of the male suspect's business cards in her purse. I left it for the investigators to find."

"And do you know where these... uh, suspects, are now?"

"As a matter of fact, I've just been given a lead. I'll pursue it when we're done here."

"Good," said Fitzwilliam. "Carry on."

Click.

This time he didn't mind when Murchesson hung up on him.

~*~

Raines did not sleep well. The pain in his shoulder remained constant, and the addition of rum had more of an effect on his brain than on his wound. He tried getting out of bed and quickly discovered the folly of such efforts.

He looked out the window, but saw nothing save night sky. For at least the millionth time he wished he had kept his wristwatch even though he knew it would have raised countless questions. He had a hard enough time communicating without using phrases that sounded foreign to 18th century ears.

Thankfully, Gabriel took it all in stride. The Cotswolds were less easy to read. The Colonel gave him more sidelong looks than his wife or daughter, but they had their moments. He shuddered to think what he might have said while under the influence of demon rum and the colonial witchdoctor's rudimentary tweezers.

Hopefully, he had earned the Cotswolds' trust. He would certainly need it in the days to come. Especially now that he'd been shot, a possibility that had never been a part of the plan. Not at this stage, anyway.

Still fuzzy from the rum, he struggled to remember how much time remained before Leah arrived. A day? Two? Definitely less than a week.

What the hell day is it?

Working his way slowly and carefully from the bed to the door, Raines opened it and peered into the darkness beyond. Neither the banked coals in the fireplace nor the starlight coming through the windows relieved the varying shades of gray before him.

He listened intently, heard the sounds of breathing and moved toward them. Only at the last moment did he avoid tripping over Gabriel curled up in a thin blanket by the hearth. Raines put his hand on the back of a chair and lowered himself into it. Gabriel stirred.

"You shouldn't be up and about," the youth said.

"Couldn't sleep."

The boy yawned.

"I didn't mean to wake you," Raines said.

"I decided to sleep down here in case you needed my help. I can fetch the chamber pot if--"

"No, no. I'm fine. I just wondered... Do you know what day it is?"

He looked out the window then back at the physicist. "'Twill soon be Sunday morning. Do you think it wise to attend services so soon after being shot?"

"*Church* services? No. Good God, no. I'm not going to church." Then he scowled at his own vehemence. "Sorry. I didn't mean it that way."

"Myster--"

"Yes, aren't they? But what I need to know is the date. It must be--"

"July 30th," Gabriel said. "On the morrow."

"The 30th? Did I lose a day somewhere?"

"Most of one, I think. You took Master Lancaster's ball on Friday."

I wish he wouldn't say it like that. "Friday."

"Yes sir."

"And today is Sunday, the thirtieth."

"Of July." Gabriel smiled. "In the year of our Lord, seventeen hundred and eighty. That's it, exactly."

Raines smiled back at him. "I'm going to have a visitor this afternoon." Nor, he felt sure, could she have arrived at a better time.

"And who would that be?"

"My daughter, Leah."

Gabriel reacted quickly, a look of surprise spreading across his face.

"What?" Raines asked, suddenly uneasy.

"*You* have a daughter?"

"Yes."

"B-but you're an angel! And angels don't have... They can't... What I mean to say is... How is that possible?"

"Mysterious ways, Gabriel." Raines tried to lift his hands like Saint Francis welcoming doves, but he couldn't get his wounded shoulder to cooperate. He winced at the sudden sharp pain. "Trust me. Leah's my little girl. And she's much more of an angel than I'll ever be."

"And she's coming here?"

"Eventually, but she'll need help. She doesn't know where I am."

Gabriel looked confused.

"I want you to wait for her and then bring her here. She'll arrive at the same place I arrived, and in the same fashion."

"No lightning or trumpets for her either?"

Raines chuckled. "Correct. And she should show up right around noon. Can you be there?"

"I wouldn't miss it for the world."

~*~

The pop Leah warned Joel about felt louder than the one which apparently consumed her baggage, but it was no less effective. Before she could respond to his question about whether or not she wanted him to follow her, she disappeared.

He glanced quickly at the switches in the phony rock to reassure himself that the self-destruct mechanism remained off. He then inspected both of the circles carved into the rock. Neither gave a clue about what had just transpired. Nor did they show any apparent wear, although the spot Leah had most recently occupied was unquestionably warmer.

What the hell was he supposed to do now? Leah's comments about Murchesson were spot on. The only thing that bastard could be counted on doing was *undoing* Joel.

Decision time.

Could he really leave everything he knew? *Everything?*

The annoying truth was, his "everything" didn't amount to much. He had some friends. At least, he thought they were friends. They greeted him with smiles when he entered the Small Arms.

Other than that, what did he have? The guys at the precinct? Sergeant Billings?

He wandered closer to the bogus rock and stared at the toggle switches. *Throw 'em both and then curl up on circle two.* What could be easier?

But 232 bloody years?

"Dawkins!" shouted a voice from the dark. "As I live and breathe."

Murchesson!

Joel froze. *How the hell had he gotten here so fast?* Moving as little as possible, Joel flipped both switches then closed the faux rock. He turned around slowly. "I can't see you."

A dark shape stepped between Joel and the headlamp on the motorcycle. "Is this better?"

"Not really."

"Put your hands up, Dawkins."

"I'm not armed."

"Do I sound like I care?"

Always the sweetheart. He raised his arms-- "This okay?"--and stepped sideways.

"Quit moving!"

"I still can't see you. The headlight is blinding me." Joel moved again. The center of the larger circle was only two steps away.

"I said stop, Dawkins. I meant it."

"Or what? You'll shoot me?"

"Probably," Murchesson said. "Can't have you talkin' to the Queen's Guard, or whoever's taken their place."

Joel bent down to massage his leg. "I can't stand still. Gotta keep movin'. Thanks to you."

"Oh, yes. I remember. It was nothing. My

pleasure, really." Murchesson moved, too. They managed an outlandish dance, both circular and constricting.

The angle had improved, and Joel could make out his former commander and the gun in his hand: an Mk 1 N, chambered for the .455 Webley automatic. A double-action revolver--old and noisy, but effective. Dodging, especially for someone lame, was not an option.

"How did you find me?" Joel asked.

Murchesson smirked. "You were always too soft. You never should have left that copper alive after you stole his bike, and you sure as hell shouldn't have left a trail a blind man could follow. You're an idiot."

Joel nodded his head as if he'd been complimented, but otherwise didn't respond.

"What's that whirring sound?"

"I dunno. Insects?"

"Bullshit."

"Okay, it's bullshit."

"Where's the equipment that's making that noise, and what's it doing?"

Joel lowered his arms, but kept them in plain sight. "Would you believe I don't know the answer to either question?"

"Not for a minute."

Murchesson stood fairly close to the first circle, his weapon pointed at Joel's midsection. "I heard a loud pop a while ago. Couldn't tell what it was, but you know, don't you?" He raised his gun.

"I'm a cop, not a lab rat. I honestly don't have any idea what's making that noise. But I'll tell you this much: I'm intrigued by it."

"Just what I need: more bullshit. Where's the girl? And how much does her father know?"

"What girl?"

"Don't be an ass. You were seen with her earlier today."

"Ah yes, the photo. I thought that might've been your handiwork," Joel said. "Good composition, but the lighting was a bit off."

"You know I'm going to kill you, right?"

"I figured as much."

"You don't seem worried. A few years ago, you were very worried. Even more so when I put a bullet in your knee."

Joel worked up a smile. "I've matured. Assholes don't scare me as much as they used to, and I imagine by now you've risen to the rank of asshole king. Am I right?" *Gotta keep him talking.*

"I've just had an inspiration," Murchesson said. "I'm going to shoot you in your good knee."

"Oh, that's brilliant! And so thoughtful."

"We'll see how cheeky you are when that joint's turned to boiled cabbage."

"I can't wait," Joel said. "May I ask you something first?"

"What?"

"How did it feel when you killed the Queen? Did it make you feel manly? I mean, how much courage did it require to squirt poison gas into the face an old woman? You must be so proud."

"Maybe I won't shoot you in the knee. Maybe I'll just shoot you in the head and be done with it."

Joel smiled. "That's the man I know! Ever

willing to fire at someone who isn't armed. My God in heaven, what a stout heart you have! The regiment would be so proud."

"Shut up!" Murchesson screamed. "Shut the fu--"

Pop!

Doctor Kerr's amazing machine finally kicked into gear, and the Event sphere promptly eviscerated the unsuspecting Murchesson. The gun, most of his arm, part of a leg, and a huge sliver of his torso departed to rural Boston circa 1780. The rest of him, now literally *and* figuratively disarmed, crumpled to the ground while he screamed.

Joel stayed within the second circle, but watched Murchesson writhing on the turf. Arterial blood had sprayed his blue eye, yet he kept blinking the brown one.

"You've gotta help me," Murchesson wheezed.

"Oh, really? Why?" Joel removed his wristwatch and checked the time. Based on what Leah told him, he had just under ten minutes to take off, or fade out, or whatever it was. He leaned down and placed the timepiece just outside the circle.

"I'll make it worth your while," Murchesson said as he struggled to wrap his belt around the stump of his arm as a tourniquet. It kept slipping off before he could tighten it. "Help me, please! I'll pay anything."

"Even if I wanted to, which I don't, you couldn't afford to bribe me. Not by a long shot. So, just face it, King Asshole, you're going to die. Right here, beside this shitty little creek."

"Come on, Dawkins! Give me a chance. You owe me that much."

"I do?" Joel said. "Hm. Let me think about that for a few minutes."

"I don't *have* a few minutes!"

"Shut up," Joel said. "I'm thinking."

"Right. Fine. I'll shut up. But, please. Hurry."

Hurry up and wait? Whatever.

Joel's crappy knee kept him from crouching in a tight ball, but he managed as best he could to retract his arms and one good leg to occupy the center of what Leah had called the Event sphere.

"What the hell are you doing?"

"Taking a little trip."

"Dear God, Dawkins," Murchesson screamed, "Don't leave me like this!"

Then something turned out all the lights. Including the stars.

~*~

~ Part II ~

Excerpt from the *Boston Globe & Mail*:

Conspirator Names Released

Millburn, Mass., Tues., May 22, 2012--Sources close to the inquiry released new details in the hunt for two suspects in the assassination of Queen Elizabeth II: Leah LeCroix Kerr, 25, a graduate student at Millburn College, and Joel Denard Dawkins, 33, an investigator with the Boston Police Department's Special Branch.

Kerr was last seen carrying a protest sign near Chumley Hall where the Queen was murdered in a poison gas attack on Monday afternoon. Experts say self-styled "patriots" from the midlands executed the raid, and that Kerr hid a poison gas dispenser in a table decoration.

Dawkins reportedly assaulted a motorcycle patrol officer, and escaped on his vehicle. Investigators released a photo of the conspirators. While neither Kerr nor Dawkins is believed armed, both are extremely dangerous.

The attack left five dead in addition to the Queen. Four were members of the Millburn College faculty; the fifth was a police officer assigned to the Queen's security detail. Fourteen others at the dinner are hospitalized in critical condition. Names have not been released.

Chapter Eleven

"[America is] a rebellious nation. Our whole history is treason; our blood was attained before we were born; our creeds were infidelity to the mother church; our constitution treason to our fatherland."
--Theodore Parker

If there was anything in Benedict Arnold's world which could take his mind off the destruction of his leg, it was his second wife, Peggy. At 20--slightly more than half his age--she had become not merely the shining light in his world, but very nearly the only bright spot.

This had been especially true for the past year or so since they'd wed. Peggy had been his salvation, rescuing him after all the abuse he'd suffered at the hands of the Continental Congress. Never in the history of mankind had God allowed such a staggering collection of blind, arrogant, and incompetent men to oversee anything.

Scoundrels, all of them!

Not content to let bunglers like Horatio Gates and Joseph Reed--no greater fools had ever worn uniforms--steal the credit for his military accomplishments, congress had passed him over for promotion, declined to reimburse his costs and even charged him with petty crimes. And when they couldn't convict him of anything, they claimed *he owed them* for war expenses!

Peggy, however, had shown him the love and respect that congress couldn't muster. She had won his heart while they had earned his enmity.

It had taken nearly three years to recover from the musket ball that shattered his left leg in the second battle of Saratoga, a colonial victory he'd won almost single-handedly. Thanks to the fates--as feckless as the backstabbers in Philadelphia--all three of the serious wounds he had received over the years were visited on the same limb. But, by God, he'd shown the world what he was made of, and when the surgeons came to remove his leg, he'd shown them the door. Gangrene be damned! He still had the leg, even though it was two inches shorter than it had been at the start of the war.

More importantly, he had Peggy. She had convinced him that he'd given enough to the cause--in fact, more than enough. His future lay with the Crown. And if he was clever, patient, and careful, he would enjoy the life of ease and luxury he'd already paid for in valor and blood.

Given a choice, Benedict would have remained with Peggy in their Philadelphia quarters, the occupied home of Richard Penn at Fifth and Market Streets, which had also been the military headquarters of General Howe prior to the British withdrawal. Now, however, he was forced to wait near Stony Point, New York, for the arrival of the Commander in Chief, his mentor and former friend, General George Washington.

Benedict prayed that the fates would give him a better hearing this time around.

~*~

Leah felt like someone had stuffed her head with cotton. She could move easily enough, but she felt disconnected from those movements, as if she were operating her body by remote control, and a two-second delay separated her from every command.

Someone, somewhere at the edge of her awareness, called her name. She closed her eyes and concentrated on the voice. It had to be someone who knew her, but it certainly wasn't Joel. He was still back in 2012.

Back?

Geez.

No, Joel couldn't be talking to her. It had to be... Dad?

Not a chance. She knew his voice, and whoever was calling her definitely wasn't Raines Kerr, PhD. So, who the hell was it?

She opened her eyes.

A young black male watched her from a safe distance. He appeared slightly nervous and stood beside a nondescript horse harnessed to a utilitarian buggy.

"Miss Leah?" he said.

Not yet willing to trust her voice, she gave him a nod.

"Your father sent me."

If she wasn't already on the ground, she would have collapsed with relief. "Thank God."

The black youth clearly appreciated her response, and she began to feel more comfortable with his presence.

"May I help you up?" he asked.

"Yes," she said. "Please."

The transition from horizontal sprawl to vertical stagger went smoothly, but once she had her head well above her feet, she swooned. The teen caught her before she fell.

"I have to move out of the circle," she said, waving a marginally compliant index finger at the unmarked stone on which she'd arrived.

Hadn't daddy cut circles into that rock? And then she realized it would be many, many years before he could.

"I'm Gabriel," the teen said.

"Of course you are."

Stop it, you twit! Be civil. He's only trying to help. "I'm sorry," she said. "I didn't mean to sound..." She couldn't think of a word he was likely to understand, and let the sentence die.

"I hope you won't mind. I put your bag in the buggy."

She gave him a huge smile. Guys loved smiles. She assumed *that* hadn't changed since men abandoned caves for grass huts. "Thank you, Gabriel."

"I consider it an honor," he said. "But if you'll excuse me for being bold, shouldn't you put some clothes on?"

"Hm?" She looked down at the shirt-like undergarment she wore.

"Yes, ma'am. I would feel much more comfortable if you were fully dressed. People might get the wrong idea."

"About what?"

"Please," he said. "I know it's unlikely that anyone would come along and find us, but even so, I'd rather you put some clothes on." He seemed to be shuffling his feet.

Who shuffled their damned feet these days?

He continued, "I know you're not used to living among... well, us. And you're probably more comfortable dressed the way you are. Like an--" he swallowed "--an angel. But it might be best for everyone if you covered up."

Reality somehow managed to insinuate itself in her consciousness, and she realized--quite suddenly--she was but one small step removed from total nudity. At least as far as the lad was concerned, and he clearly wasn't comfortable with the idea.

Duh!

"Hand me my bag, please," she said.

He looked dubious.

"Oh, right. Never mind." Even if he could have "handed" it to her, she'd have collapsed under its weight like a feather under a fist. Instead, she gingerly negotiated the short distance between the Event site and the back of the buggy. She opened the satchel and unpacked the clothing she had prepared for her arrival in 1780.

Through her studies, she knew what the well-dressed woman of the 18th century wore. Unfortunately, for historical accuracy if not for comfort, she couldn't fit either whalebone stays or a hooped petticoat into her satchel. Instead, she slipped into a long-sleeved gown and bodice combination, then buttoned in a triangular shaped insert called a stomacher, and topped it all off with an apron and a lace neck kerchief.

"It's rather sunny," Gabriel said. "Do you have a hat?"

"I'm afraid not." That wouldn't fit in her bag either. Sadly, three-suiters weren't available for time travel.

He nodded with what seemed like a great deal of smugness.

"What?"

"Nothing," he said. "Who needs a hat when they've worn a halo?"

She tried not to stare at him as if he'd just swallowed an ostrich, whole.

"We need to be moving," Gabriel said. "It's quite a long ride to the Cotswolds'."

"The Cotswolds." *Where in hell was that, Britain?* Leah shook her head. "It'll have to wait. At least a little while."

"Your father is anxious to see you."

The mere mention of him helped her focus. "Daddy? He's... safe, right? And well?"

When Gabriel's mouth twisted, Leah's heart lurched.

"What's wrong? What's happened to him?"

Gabriel continued to shuffle, and Leah wanted to shake him. "Tell me!"

"He's been shot, Miss Leah."

Steel talons clamped down upon her heart. "Shot? Is he all right? Is he--"

Gabriel shrugged. "He refused to let the doctor work on him. Said something about her not washing her hands. I didn't understand. Anyway, she left without doing anything."

"You mean no one removed the bullet?"

"No! Miss Chastity got it. And Mrs. Cotswold stitched him up, good as new, but when I left this morning, he had a fever. He was talking, but he wasn't making sense."

Leah found herself swimming in a sea of unfamiliar names and nonsensical locations. Her father would be fine. He had to be. She couldn't afford to do anything she hadn't fully considered. That meant waiting for Joel, even though the chances of his following her seemed thin. Desperately so.

Forcing her concerns aside, Leah removed her white tennis socks and pulled a pair of period costume shoes from her bag. She stuffed the socks into the bag and slipped the shoes on, grateful that she'd taken the time to break them in before she left the 21st century.

"How long must we wait?" Gabriel asked.

Leah's father had confided in her that "aiming" the Event generator was--by his standards anyway--dicey, and without the experimentation he would have preferred to conduct, hitting a specific time was less likely than hitting a specific day. More than once he'd complained that he might not even hit the right decade. But if that had been the case, he would certainly have made note of it in the message he'd sent her in the ceramic jar.

Swell. Thank you Mr. Murchesson.

"Gabriel? You wouldn't happen to know anything about a jar my father buried near here, would you?"

He beamed. "Yes, ma'am! Buried it myself, just over the edge, there." He pointed to the low cliff overlooking the turgid creek.

"I don't suppose you know what he put in there?"

"No, ma'am," he said, unconvincingly.

"Are you sure?"

He stammered a bit, then confessed. "It was just a note. That's all."

"Did you read it? You can tell me. I promise I won't get angry."

"I'm afraid I couldn't help myself," he said. "I did peek at the note, but I didn't get a good look at it, and I couldn't understand some of the words he used."

"When was this?"

"Just a few days ago. I'm sure it's still there. Want me to dig it up?"

"No! It's fine right where it is," she said.

And then she started thinking.

~*~

Waiting had never been easy for Benedict, whether for promotion, battle, or the attentions of a woman. His natural inclination was to pace, but his leg made that difficult and at times, impossible. To get his mind off his physical condition, he turned toward an issue about which he might actually be able to do something.

His darling Peggy had made it possible for him to communicate with John Andre', a major in the British army, with whom she had dallied before meeting Benedict. Andre' had been one of many suitors, and despite being--according to all reports--handsome, ten years younger, and exceedingly fit, he had failed to win the girl's heart.

Even when it came to romance, Benedict was driven by pragmatism. Peggy was now his, and whatever she might have done with Andre' prior to Benedict's courtship was immaterial. And even if that weren't the case, he would never have mistaken Major Andre's value. The man became his direct link to General Sir Henry Clinton, the British Commander-in-Chief in North America.

For over a year, Benedict had used Andre' to forward assessments of American troop strength and deployments. When such information wasn't readily available, he passed along details about supply depots and shipments of military equipment.

In compensation, Benedict had asked Clinton to pay him 10,000 pounds, exactly what the execrable Continental Congress had given General Charles Lee, the miserable failure who once rivaled George Washington for control of the entire Continental Army.

Lately, however, Benedict realized he could earn vastly more. Since the war began, General

Clinton had dreamed of controlling the Hudson River Valley. Not only did the Hudson provide a natural waterway between the British strongholds in Canada and the port of New York City, it also separated the manufacturing centers of the northern colonies from the agricultural bounty of those in the Mid-Atlantic. Considering how much of the men and material used in the war effort came from Massachusetts and her sister colonies, it was easy to see how control of the river valley could end the war.

The key to it all was the geographical oddity of West Point, something General Washington recognized from the start. Not surprisingly, the idiots in congress completely mishandled the task of fortifying the crucial spot. West Point overlooked a narrow switchback in the river and provided an ideal defensive position. The river thinned there to its narrowest point; the ebb tide could be treacherous; and wind patterns, so critical for sailing ships, were unpredictable. Ships would crawl through the choke point while eager cannoneers trained their weapons on them from 300-foot tall cliffs.

Except the blundering politicians ignored West Point and fortified less desirable locations, and did so poorly. As a result, three years earlier, General Clinton had been able to seize those fortifications in a campaign lasting mere days.

Benedict himself salvaged victory from the disaster when he crushed Burgoyne at Saratoga, leaving Clinton stranded in the Highlands. Clinton withdrew, and Washington took direct control of the problem, ordering the construction of a fortress at West Point. He was so grateful to Benedict, in fact, that he named it in his honor: Fort Arnold.

For General Clinton, the door to the Hudson River Valley had been slammed shut. But, if Benedict's meeting with his former friend, George Washington, went as he hoped, Benedict would soon hold the key to that door.

Besides, he had grown weary of Philadelphia, of keeping secrets, and of writing hidden messages in code or invisible ink. He had not earned his reputation as America's greatest warrior by plotting treachery and lurking in the shadows.

And yet, now his future depended on precisely that.

~*~

Leah had resigned herself to waiting no later than sundown for Joel to arrive. She owed him that much for making her escape possible. If her father had not been wounded, she would have been willing to wait a full twenty-four hours. Still, it didn't seem too likely that he would make the trip.

She tried to look at it from his viewpoint, something at which she'd gained some proficiency while trying to understand what had driven Benedict Arnold to turn on his country. *Had driven? Make that: was driving.* How long would it be before she fully realized she had left the 21st century forever?

"Miss Leah?" Gabriel asked. "You look a little lost."

"I am," she replied. "I'm thinking of many different things, and not the least of them is your offer to dig up my father's jar. Are you really willing to do that for me?"

"Oh, yes ma'am," he said.

She found the word "ma'am" more than a little disconcerting.

"Now that I work for Doctor Kerr, I suppose I work for you, too. Since he's not here."

Leah made a mental note to ask him how he and her father had managed to develop such a strong relationship so quickly.

Or, had it been quickly?

"Gabriel, this is the 30th of July, isn't it?"

"That it is," he said. "It's Sunday, and normally I would be in church, but Doctor Kerr insisted that I meet you here since he couldn't meet you himself. I hope that's all right."

"Absolutely!"

"So, do you want me to dig up the jar?"

"Yes. If nothing else, it'll help to pass the time. But let me know if you get tired. I'm more than willing to do my share of the work."

Muttering something about a "mystery," the teen went to the buggy to get a shovel. He left his topcoat on the seat and rolled up his sleeves, then went about retrieving the ceramic container.

Obviously, there wasn't anything she could do for her father in response to his note. She had a healthy curiosity about it, but beyond that the whole issue was out of her control. On the other hand, she knew who *would* read the note, and there was certainly something she could do with *that* knowledge.

She would only have one opportunity to say something to the man who murdered--no, *would* murder--the Queen of New England. What, she wondered, would he least like to discover when reading the note in the jar? Something vaguely threatening would do, but nothing specific enough to reveal who, exactly, had written it. The prospect made her smile.

"Gabriel," she called, "did my father leave any extra parchment lying around?"

"He didn't have his own. He borrowed some from Colonel Cotswold."

Ah, the elusive Cotswolds. The only ones she'd ever heard of weren't even people, they were a range of hills somewhere in old England.

She wandered closer to the edge of the low cliff where Gabriel was hard at work. "How are you doing?"

"Very well," he said. "The ground is much softer than the last time."

Her memory had been quite different, but then he hadn't had to wait 232 years between interment and exhumation. And, he was able to dig straight to the spot where he'd left it, while she'd had to dig practically from one side to the other.

"Got it!" he said as he scrambled up to level ground. He handed her the familiar jar and dusted off his clothing.

"If I open it here, how will we reseal it?"

"Why reseal it? The jar's for you, isn't it? That's what Doctor Kerr said, but I confess, I didn't understand him. He does some very odd things.

Now, it seems, you do, too."

"I want to replace the message and leave it for someone else," she said.

"The seal is made of wax."

She examined it as if to confirm the statement. "Yes. And...."

"And so you just save the wax, and we melt it down again to reseal it." He cleared his throat. "Things must be very different where you come from."

She just laughed and carefully broke the seal. The cork came loose with little resistance, and she unfolded a sheet of parchment on which her father had scrawled a typically short note.

Leah,

My dear, you're a genius! You thought of nearly everything. My entry into Colonial life was nothing like I imagined, and was in fact, much better. I am well and have connected with a fine family of patriots. Can't wait to introduce you to them. I know you'll have a safe journey, and I promise to be there when you arrive.

All my love,

Dad

PS: See if you can find a book on the chemistry of plastics and bring it along if there's room in your bag.

She was still laughing when she reached the end of the note. It reminded her of messages he'd scrawled on memo paper and stuffed in her lunch bag when she was a child. "On your way home, kindly pick up a loaf of bread and a primer on subatomic particles by that German fellow. Einberg, Einstern--whatever his name is."

Dear daddy, I hope you never change.

Gabriel approached with a much larger piece of crockery.

"Water, miss?"

She accepted it gratefully and took a sip. Gabriel had barely raised a sweat while digging. She hoped it went as well when he returned the jar to its hiding place. "Why don't you rest for a bit while I write a new note?"

He needed no further urging and retreated to the shade of a nearby tree. Meanwhile, Leah tore her father's note from the parchment. He'd only used about a third of the space, leaving more than enough for her message. She dug a pen from her bag, and after a moment's concentration, began to write. She worked slowly and used block letters like her father did, in hopes of hiding her authorship.

Greetings, Captain Dwight! Or is it Murchesson?

I will keep this short because I know you have much to do. But understand, I absolutely do not condone what you are attempting. The authorities have already been alerted, and it

*is my fervent hope that when they arrest you--
and they will--you will be hanged without a
trial and buried without a marker or a
prayer.*

She left the note unsigned. The conspirators would assume her father had written it. And, while it was a complete bluff, there was always a chance they'd be frightened out of trying to assassinate the Queen.

Once again, the oddities of time travel left her confused about the consequences of practical jokes played across the centuries. Her note would either work, or not. Either way, she would never know.

She offered to replace the jar in the hole Gabriel had already dug, but he insisted on doing it for her, and then promptly filled it in with dirt. As he washed his hands with water from the jug he'd brought, they heard an astonishingly loud pop.

Both of them whirled toward the sound which was followed quickly by the thump of a disembodied arm falling to the ground. A gun fell from the dead hand and rattled across the stone surface.

"Oh, my heavens," Gabriel said, his voice strained and low.

Leah crept forward, her eyes riveted to the gruesome body parts littering the smaller of the two Event sites. She narrowed her gaze as if to focus more closely on the arm without touching it.

"What happened?" Gabriel asked. "Is this who we've been waiting for?"

Leah prayed that it wasn't, but she couldn't

be sure. She didn't think Joel had been carrying a weapon of any kind.

She picked up the gun, surprised at its weight, and used it to roll the dead limb over. Near the middle of the forearm, just where she feared it might be, was the regimental tattoo of the Black Watch.

Her breath caught so fast, she began to choke, and Gabriel rushed to her side. "What's going on? Please, Miss Leah, tell me!"

"I can't say for sure." She turned away and hurried to the buggy where she slipped the gun into her satchel. She hoped her father would know how to use it well enough to teach her.

Gabriel was rapidly approaching panic. "Where's the rest of him?"

"I don't--"

"I see part of a leg and some scraps of cloth. And, oh-- Oh, what's *this*?"

"It's part of a body," she said, forcing calm into her voice. "Leave it alone. There's a good chance we'll get some answers very soon." Then inspiration struck, but she couldn't see the remains with Gabriel in the way. He seemed intent on shielding her from the sight.

"Is it a left or a right leg?"

"Huh?"

"The leg! Is it a left or a right?"

"Right," he said.

"Look at the knee. Does it have a big scar?"

Gabriel bent down and poked at the raw meat on the ground. "I don't believe so. No."

Leah felt relief bathe over her as if she'd

dropped into a pool of spring water. The body parts weren't Joel's. And just as suddenly, she felt empty again.

The only logical explanation she could find was that Murchesson or one of his henchmen had followed them and had been accidentally--and brutally--bisected by the Event sphere. Clearly, the wound was not the sort that someone could shrug off. Whoever suffered it would have bled out very quickly. She couldn't even begin to imagine how painful it would be. And, if it was Murchesson, then Joel no longer had anything to fear from him. Would he still risk everything to follow her?

Even though she'd been expecting it, the second pop startled her nearly as much as the first. She was facing away from the larger Event site, afraid to turn around and find the spot empty. What if he chose not to join her? What if--

Don't be such a ninny! Just look.

Chewing her bottom lip, Leah took a deep breath and pivoted slowly around.

Joel lay on the ground in front of her.

Intact.

"Who's this?" Gabriel asked.

"A friend," Leah said, surprised to find a tear trickling down her cheek.

Gabriel walked close to Joel, then knelt beside him. After a brief inspection he looked up at Leah. "Where on Earth did he get clothes like these? I've never seen their like."

"Hm? Oh." Leah pondered the question for a moment. "Harrods, I think. The quality seems about right."

"I've never heard of it. Where is it?"

"A long way from here." She smiled. "A very long way."

~*~

Excerpt from the *Hartford Courier*:

New Clues in Queen's Murder

Millburn, Mass., Wed., May 23, 2012--
Sources close to the Queen's Guard, the agency
investigating Monday's assassination of Queen
Elizabeth, claim enigmatic new clues have been
found in the hunt for Leah LeCroix Kerr and Joel
Denard Dawkins, prime suspects in a crime which
has infuriated the nation.

The new evidence includes a pair of shoes,
the partial remains of an unidentified man, and a
police motorcycle. Investigators can't explain how
the odd elements relate to each other. Police
believe the shoes were worn by Kerr, the female
suspect. The motorcycle has been positively
identified as the one stolen by Dawkins, Kerr's co-
conspirator.

Authorities hope dental records will reveal
who the dead man is, but have made little
progress. The body, which was missing parts of an
arm and a leg, was found about two miles from the
Millburn College campus where the Queen was
murdered.

Chapter Twelve

"It is not necessary to change. Survival is not mandatory."
-- W. Edwards Deming

Joel couldn't remember falling down, but he'd been on the ground often enough to recognize the condition even if the bulk of his senses refused to report the obvious. He reached toward his right knee to give it a rub, as he normally did upon awakening, but for some reason the faulty limb wasn't sending him the usual ration of pain signals. And then he remembered the homegrown pain medication Leah had given him.

Wha'dya know? Sometimes a guy could *catch a break.*

"Joel? Can you hear me?"

"Yes, Mum."

Another voice, youthful and male, said, "Mum? You're his *mother?* But he's-- You're--"

"Hush, Gabriel. He's delirious, that's all. It'll pass in a few minutes."

"But--"

"And I'm definitely *not* his mother."

Joel opened his eyes. Leah and a black kid in a Paul Revere costume stared down at him while something sharp dug into his spine. He shifted to relieve the pressure and discovered a stone which had caused the problem.

"Unless someone else is coming," Leah said, "you're better off right where you are. You just need to rest."

Completely ignoring her advice, Joel pushed himself to a sitting position with his bad leg straight out in front. "Am I-- Are *we* where you said we'd be?"

"Yes."

He took a good long while to scan their surroundings. "I guess I expected something different. Other than your clothes, I mean."

"Nature hasn't changed all that much," she said, "but you'll see big differences soon enough." She knelt beside him. "Want to try standing up?"

"Only if you make me."

"If we leave now, Miss Leah, we can reach home before dark."

Joel looked at the teen. "Home?"

"We'll be staying with the Cotswold family. They're friends of my father."

"Do we need to stop somewhere and grab a bottle of wine?"

She and Gabriel helped him to his feet. "You really are out of it, aren't you?"

"Okay, I guess we skip the wine."

He looked toward the smaller Event site

where he'd last seen Murchesson. Dark red blood covered the stone slab, and portions of the killer lay scattered on the ground attracting flies. It seemed fitting. "I guess it's true what they say about travel these days. It really does cost an arm and a leg."

Leah winced, but the teen didn't seem interested. Instead, he kept staring at Joel's clothing. Admittedly, he didn't have his jacket cleaned as often as he should, and though he'd bought top quality, the garment was definitely showing some wear. He'd likely drop it in the collection bin at the Anglican Church fairly soon. And then it occurred to him that if what Leah said was true, the church probably didn't exist, yet.

He turned his attention back to the juvenile. "I'm sorry if my clothes bother you, mate, but when I got up this morning, I didn't know I was going to the ball, much less what costume to wear."

Gabriel gave Leah an exasperated look. "Does he always talk this way? I fear I shall never understand."

"We all have a lot to learn," she said. "I just wish we had more time in which to learn it."

Gabriel pointed at Murchesson's remains. "What should we do with that?"

"Leave it where it is," Joel said. "Let the animals have it."

Leah suddenly looked concerned. "Animals?"

"Sure. Bears, wolves. God knows what else."

"Gabriel? Are there bears in these woods?"

"Probably," he said, without fear. "I'm more worried about Indians."

"I think it's time to go," she said.

"Hold on. What's beyond the ledge?" Joel asked.

Gabriel briefly puckered his lips. "Nothing, really. A marsh."

"Perfect!"

Joel took a couple steps toward what was left of Murchesson and paused. He waited for the spinning to stop, then continued at a slower pace. Neither Leah nor Gabriel offered to help, so he picked up the body parts, carried them to the cliff's edge, and dumped them into the soup where they sank from sight.

"Adios, asshole," Joel said.

Gabriel appeared stricken. "Shouldn't you show a little respect?"

"I showed him as little as possible, but it was still more than he deserved."

Leah was shaking her head. At him.

"What?"

"The first thing we need to do is blend in," she said. "That means we--but mostly *you*--need to pay attention to what you say and how you say it."

"Why?"

"Because unless you adopt the idioms of the period, and abandon those you grew up with, my father and I will be the only people on Earth who can understand you."

"Oh." Though still feeling a bit foggy from the Event passage, Joel knew she was right. She was, after all, the expert. "Fair enough. I'll try to do better."

They piled into the buggy, and Joel quickly determined the seat had been intended for either smaller bottoms or fewer passengers. Fortunately, Gabriel was as willing as Joel to let Leah squeeze between them. The feel of her warm thigh pressed against his bad leg acted like a tonic--an addictive one.

"We need to get Joel some clothes," Leah said as Gabriel turned the buggy away from the sun, which had already begun to work its way toward the horizon.

"That will be difficult on a Sunday," Gabriel said.

"Any chance we can steal some?" Joel asked.

The teen fired another sidelong glance toward Leah. "Aren't you supposed to abide by the commandments? Especially since you're... you know."

Leah and Joel exchanged puzzled looks.

"You should be able to wear some of my dad's things," she said, "even though he's a little bigger than you. But as soon as we can find a tailor, I'll have new clothes made for both of us."

He lowered his voice for her. "Can't we just buy something off the rack?"

Leah chuckled. "Off the rack? Not for a long, long time. Everything's made by hand. In fact, the colonies import cloth more than any other product. We won't have any trouble finding a tailor."

At that, Gabriel seemed to be on firmer footing. He even smiled as he slapped the horse with the reins.

I'm going to have to learn how to do that, Joel thought. *But if the kid can do it, I can, too.*

Leah leaned close and put her lips near Joel's

ear. "I'm glad you came."

"Me, too. But to be honest, I didn't have many choices. I'm sure there's a manhunt underway. You know, back... when."

Leah pondered the nearing darkness for a long while. "The Queen really is dead?"

"I'm afraid so."

A moment later, she smiled.

"What?" he asked.

"It's 1780."

"So?"

"The Queen hasn't been born yet."

~*~

The buggy ride proved tiresome from the beginning. The springs on the vehicle, assuming it had any, did almost nothing to spare them from the uneven surfaces they traveled over. At first Leah hadn't minded being packed so tightly into the hard seat, but hours later, she felt differently. Only half the perspiration on her legs belonged to her. Despite the discomfort, the ride devolved still further into boredom.

Joel didn't seem to mind when she leaned against him and nodded off. Several times she had jerked awake muttering apologies, until he put his arm around her and pulled her close.

"If you think you can sleep, for God's sake, go ahead and do it."

She didn't have to be told twice.

Suddenly, or so it seemed, Gabriel's low voice woke her as he brought the buggy to a halt in front of a plain, two-story house. "This is it," he said. "I'm sure everyone inside has gone to bed."

"It can't be that late," Joel said.

Leah yawned. "What? You thought they'd gone to the cinema?" *See? You aren't the only smart ass in the game.*

Gabriel had quit paying attention to them during the ride unless they asked him a direct question or made it plain they weren't talking to each other in some kind of code.

"Wait here," he said as they climbed down from the buggy and stretched their arms and legs. "I'll stable the horse and then show you to your room."

"It's a much bigger house than I anticipated," Leah said as Gabriel drove off.

"Guess they had bigger families way back when."

"They certainly didn't have contraceptives."

Joel chuckled. "I knew I forgot something."

"Don't get your hopes up."

He frowned.

"Yet," she said.

To which, he smiled.

When Gabriel returned, they followed him up the front stairs. Before Gabriel could open it, the door swung wide, and a sleepy young woman peered out at them. Slender, blonde, and hardly older than their guide, she spoke in a pleasant alto. "Gabriel? Miss Kerr?"

"I'm sorry we're so late," Gabriel said. "Doctor Kerr's daughter didn't arrive alone." He gestured toward her. "This is Miss Leah, and her friend is Master Joel... Uh..."

"Dawkins," Joel said.

Leah couldn't help but notice his appreciation for the girl's natural beauty. *Men!*

"Charmed," said the girl. "I'm Chastity Cotswold," though she muffled her last name with a yawn. "Excuse me! Please, come in." She held a lighted candlestick at shoulder level and backed away into the dark interior. They followed. Gabriel lowered Leah's bag to the floor and rubbed the muscles of his arm.

"Thank you, Gabriel," Leah said, trying not to look at Joel. "You're a true gentleman."

"I'll take it from here," Joel said. He tested the weight of the bag and groaned just loud enough for Leah to hear.

"I'd like to see my father," she said. "How is he?"

Chastity looked uncertain. "He's sleeping. It's been a difficult day for him."

"But he's all right?"

"I hope so, yet he has a fever. In such cases I've always heard a good bleeding is in order. But... I presume Gabriel told you he sent the doctor away?"

Leah wasn't surprised. "May I see him?"

"Of course." Chastity led the way, a small procession following a single flickering candle through the darkness. She stopped, opened a door, and whispered, "I really think you should let him sleep."

"I will," Leah whispered back, then slipped inside. Her father lay face up and shirtless, his left shoulder swaddled in linen strips. A dark stain marked the location of his wound.

Leah bent forward and lightly kissed his forehead, pleased that he didn't wake but worried about the perspiration and the heat of his brow. She backed quietly out of the room and closed the door.

"I put his things in the room with him," Chastity said. "That's where my parents usually sleep, but they're in my room now. I'm sleeping on the settee. You and Mr. Dawkins may use the attic."

Leah and Joel looked at each other uncertainly.

"It's quite comfortable up there and has a big bed," Chastity added. "My sisters and I slept there when we were children." She paused and broke into a slow smile. "And we have a bundling board."

"I'm sure we'll be fine," Leah said. "I'm too tired to think straight."

"In that case I'll definitely have Gabriel install the board."

"A bundling board?" Joel frowned, but only briefly. "I, uh... Oh. I'm sure that won't be necessary."

Chastity waved off the objection. "It's no trouble. And besides, my father would not look kindly on any other arrangement."

"Certainly not," Leah said. She gave Joel a short but hopefully menacing glare.

They followed the girl up two flights of stairs. The second set, leading to the attic, groaned under every step. The stairway ended within the room. Chastity lit a candle on a nightstand, bid them good night, and left.

Joel lurched forward with the satchel and left it beside a big feather bed.

Leah lowered herself onto the bed and let out a sigh she'd been holding since seeing her father's wounded shoulder. "Now comes the hard part."

Joel's expression told her he didn't understand.

"The hard part," she continued, "is figuring out whether or not my dad can play the role I expected him to play."

"What role? What are you talking about?"

"There's a reason we went to all the trouble to come here--to this exact time and place."

"I figured you didn't intend it as a vacation."

"I probably shouldn't say anything more until I know for sure what condition Dad's in," she said.

"Swell. That way I can stay awake all night trying to guess what you're up to."

She patted his cheek. "You might not like the idea, but I'm trusting that you won't try to stop us."

"We'll see," Joel said. "But I think I already know what you've got in mind. I talked to your advisor in the history department at Millburn."

"Mr. Bolland?" She gave her head a sad shake. "He's a luv, but such an odd duck. What did he tell you?"

"We discussed your thesis."

"Ah. Well, so much for confidentiality. Not that it matters any more."

"According to Professor Boland, you think Benedict Arnold's treason kept the colonies from winning their independence."

She instantly felt energized, but also threatened. The years she'd spent defending her views made her testy. "I don't just think it, I'm certain of it. He's the sole reason they captured General Washington. That alone would have been enough to end it, but he didn't stop there. Oh, no. Because of him, they rounded up and hanged almost the entire Continental Congress, too."

"I get it," Joel said. "You mean to stop that from happening."

"Damned right I do! And I'd hate to think you might try to interfere."

"There's no reason for dramatics," he said, turning away from her and walking toward a gabled window. "But we probably ought to talk this through a little more. Like you said, you've had a long time to think about it, but all this is new to me. And don't forget, I spent nearly four years in the army--the Royal one. I've been shot at by the blokes you've come to help. Well, not *them*, exactly, but their descendants."

When he had his back to her, she reached into the satchel and retrieved Murchesson's gun. Joel stopped at the window then pivoted to face her.

She pointed the weapon squarely at his chest and held it with both hands.

"That's not a toy," he said.

"And this isn't a game. I'm deadly serious."

~*~

The morning of Monday, July 31, 1780 dawned clear and bright on the Hudson river near Stony Point. Benedict Arnold looked out across the river to the British position on the high ground. Though the Americans had stormed that fort the previous summer and won an astonishing victory, they soon retreated, and General Clinton retook the fort, doubling the size of the garrison stationed there.

Benedict paced on the American side, at Verplank's Point, while waiting for the arrival of George Washington. If everything went as Benedict hoped, the American Commander-in-Chief would put Benedict in charge of Fort Arnold on West Point, roughly a dozen miles up river.

He had made his case to Washington over the course of two months. In a variety of letters and through the offices of two New York representatives to the Continental Congress, Benedict had made what he believed to be an unassailable argument for such a posting.

Washington arrived amid a cadre of aides who, along with Benedict's own subordinates, moved a discreet distance away, leaving the two generals to confer privately.

"You certainly look well," Washington said as he pumped the hand of his valorous warrior. Both men wore the blue and buff of the Continental army, but Washington, standing six feet tall, towered over Benedict by eight full inches. Benedict's shortened left leg made the difference even greater, at least to him. Washington seemed not to notice.

They traded niceties for some time before Washington addressed Benedict directly. "I cannot express how badly I need you--how badly the country needs you. We both know this has been a difficult year. The losses we've sustained have been... profound."

Benedict couldn't help but smirk. "Ah, yes. Gates." Sent by the Congress in response to the British capture of Charleston, General Horatio Gates, one of Benedict's worst tormentors, had blundered away an army of four thousand.

Washington remained silent, his face wooden. Congress had not consulted him about Gates' mission, and Benedict had no doubt things would have been different if they had.

The mere mention of Gates' name came as a slap in the face to Benedict's commanding officer, one he absorbed with nothing more than a tightening of his lips and silence. Before long, however, he switched to a topic which clearly fired his enthusiasm.

"We shall soon have an opportunity to strike back in a meaningful way," Washington said. "Rochambeau and his French forces are in Rhode Island waiting for us to commit to a campaign. It's not the army we'd hoped for, but in light of our losses this year, it's the kind of support we desperately need. If we use them properly, and demonstrate our own resolve, we can achieve wonders. A combined army--and most of them well-trained and armed. Can you imagine? I've been able to think of little else."

"It would be a miracle," Benedict said, wondering if General Clinton knew of Washington's intent.

"With the French at our side, I know we can rally the militia. And with good planning and a bit of luck, we might even re-take New York City."

"I'm certain of it, General," Benedict said.

"And I hope that I may be of service in some small way. Have you thought of anything I might do?"

"Oh, indeed I have."

Benedict held his breath.

"You shall have a post of honor and serve directly under me."

West Point was his!

"You will command the left wing of the army. I have no doubt there will be a monumental struggle, but nothing you haven't managed before--and with magnificent result. I need my greatest warrior now more than ever. Stand with me, Benedict. We will make history together."

Where he had merely held his breath before, Benedict suddenly found he *couldn't* breathe at all. Washington gave him a rare smile, but that look disappeared quickly in light of Benedict's response.

"What is it, man? What's wrong?"

Benedict shook his head, too stunned to speak.

Washington called for the aides, and they came running. Richard Varick and David Franks, the two assigned to Benedict, rushed to his side. Feeling truly faint, he allowed the two officers to hold him upright.

"Take him to my quarters," Washington said. "See how flushed he is? Get him out of the heat." He patted Benedict on the shoulder. "Get some rest, old friend. We'll talk over the details later. You have my promise."

With Varick and Franks supporting him, Benedict shuffled away. No matter where he looked, the view had been supplanted by a vision of complete disaster, and all of it his own.

~*~

"I still can't believe you pulled a gun on me," Joel said while staring up at the raw underside of the Cotswold's roof. He lay on one side of the bundling board, Leah on the other. "If Gabriel hadn't walked in when he did, I don't know what would have happened."

"I felt like I needed to get your attention."

"Well, you certainly accomplished that!"

"I'm sorry," she said. "But you clearly didn't appreciate my reasoning for this whole thing."

"I probably still don't." He sat up so he could see her. "But next time, give me a chance to think it over before you shoot me."

"I didn't shoot you!"

"No, but you scared me shitless." He grinned. "That and your snoring kept me awake all night."

Leah sat upright. "I do *not* snore!"

"Ask Gabriel, I'm sure he heard you, too."

"He's been gone since sun up," she said. "I think we took his bed."

Joel ran his fingers through his hair and looked slowly around their attic quarters. Not even his army barracks had been this Spartan. "Poor bugger must've slept on the floor."

"I wonder what time it is," Leah said.

"Time for a shower and coffee. Maybe a sweet roll."

"You're so funny," she said, frowning. She eased her legs over the side of the bed and gathered up her clothes. "Turn around while I get dressed."

"Aren't you going to put that gown thingy on over your nighty?"

"It's a shift, not a nighty. And yes, I am. It's the only one I have, for now."

"Well then, why do I have to look away? It's not like I'll see you naked."

"A gentleman would turn his head. Perhaps you'd like me to ask that we make other sleeping arrangements?"

Joel turned away. "I'm not ready to switch places with Gabriel."

"I was talking about finding you a spot in the barn."

"Okay! I'm not looking. Geez." He stood up, still facing away, and put on the clothes Gabriel had left for him. They belonged to Leah's father, who was taller and weighed a good deal more than Joel.

"I feel stupid in this outfit."

"You'll get used to it."

He doubted that. "Maybe if I had clothes that fit, I'd feel better."

"Help me with my plan, and I'll take you to a tailor. Fair enough?"

"I don't have a farthing to my name. No job, and as far as I know, in this world I have no skills. How the hell am I supposed to pay for a tailor?"

She sniffed at the objection. "I'll pay for it. And everything else. Will you help me?"

"That depends on what you want me to do. I refuse to murder anybody."

"Who said anything about murder?" Leah fussed through the final adjustments to her outfit.

Despite covering every inch of her athletic frame, she still looked as desirable as ever.

"My options seem a bit limited."

She nodded, and her smile appeared both sincere and sympathetic. "Maybe not. I suspect I'm going to need your help. Especially if my father can't carry out his part of the plan."

"To kill Benedict Arnold, right?"

"Kill him? No. Absolutely not."

"Then what?"

"To reveal his treachery before it causes any real harm. Once the country learns what he intended, I'm hoping it will not only anger them, but reinvigorate them. There's still time to win this war, but only if everyone pulls together."

Joel scratched his head. "Seems like it'd be a lot easier just to shoot the bastard."

"I agree, but right now the man is a hero. Next to George Washington, he's probably the best known soldier in the Continental Army. He's certainly one of the most respected. Men have died for him."

"Then why would he turn traitor?"

Leah looked straight into his eyes. "Vanity."

"*Vanity?* You're kidding, right?"

"It's the only explanation I can find. Several times during his career, lesser men either took credit for his accomplishments or were simply given credit for them by jealous types who couldn't abide his arrogance. The Continental Congress repeatedly passed him over for promotions--even when General Washington recommended him for them."

"Bloody politicians."

"He spent a great deal of his own money on supplies for his missions. He even sacrificed a merchant ship he owned to win a battle. But when he approached Congress for compensation, they denied him. Later, they claimed *he owed them*."

"I'm still not sure 'vanity' is the right word for it," Joel said. "Sounds to me like the rebel congress brought this upon itself."

"There's a lot of truth in that," she said. "No one could question Benedict Arnold's bravery or resolve. He was wounded often, but usually managed to fight on. He took musket balls to his left leg three times over three years. The last one was at Saratoga in the fall of '77. Though relieved of field command by General Gates, he ignored the prohibition and rallied the American troops to victory. His actions led directly to the surrender of General Burgoyne. It was a huge blow to the British."

"That definitely doesn't sound like vanity."

"In tribute, Congress restored his rank and seniority, but they never apologized. They never admitted being wrong about him. He felt they were acting out of sympathy because, in his own words, he'd become a 'cripple.'"

"How do you know all this?" Joel asked.

"I'm an historian," she responded, laughing. "It's my job. Or ought to have been. I've studied the man for years. I've read his letters and every document I could find that might have had anything to do with him."

"So, you're obsessed by him. Wait! Oh my god, you're a stalker--of the historical persuasion, sure, but a stalker just the same."

She shrugged. "I suppose so. My mother was, too. She got me started. And my father was so madly in love with her, that when he jokingly suggested we go back in time and make things right, she challenged him to do exactly that."

"And now you're here."

"And half my team may not be able to pull their own weight."

"Which is where I come in, right?"

"Assuming I can talk you into it." She grinned. "You're pretty smart for a copper."

~*~

Excerpt from the *Philadelphia Record*:

Assassination Protest Riots Paralyze New England

New York, New York, Fri., May 25, 2012--A second day of riots battered cities throughout New England. The massive response to the assassination of the Queen caused the closure of schools and businesses across the country.

Mass demonstrations and civilian gangs searching for suspected "colonials" have authorities considering martial law. General Sir David Fitzwilliam, Chief of the Defense Staff and acting Chief of the General Staff, promised swift reaction to lawless acts. "We are a civilized people," he said in a radio address Thursday evening from Royal Army Headquarters in Annapolis, Maryland, "unlike the terrorists who murdered the Queen. Rest assured they will be punished. Meanwhile, we ask the country to stand ready to support our troops in the upcoming hostilities."

General Fitzwilliam, the country's highest ranking military officer, had no comment when asked for specifics about the "upcoming hostilities." He also denied rumors that the unidentified body found recently with evidence left behind by the assassins, had ties to the Royal Army.

Chapter Thirteen

*"The biggest conspiracy has always been the fact there is
no conspiracy. Nobody's out to get you. Nobody gives a shit
whether you live or die. There, you feel better now?"*
-- Dennis Miller

For three miserable days Benedict had been
forced to put on a show. When Washington's
General Orders were posted on the first of August,
they confirmed Benedict's worst fears. He had been
given command of the left wing of the army. There
had been no mention of Fort Arnold or West Point.

Once the orders had been made public, he
began a campaign meant to show his incapacity for
field leadership, in the American army, if not for the
British. He limped around in plain sight of both
Washington's aides and his own, muttering that his
mangled leg caused him such pain that he couldn't
stay in a saddle long enough to fulfill his duties.

As he had promised, Washington came to him
to discuss the issue. "I'm told you've been up and
about. That's good news."

"I'm up as much as I'm able." Benedict slapped his shortened and misshapen leg. "I can't do much with this."

Washington searched his old friend's face, clearly hoping to find some sign that the old warrior yet lived.

Benedict took it as his cue. "The truth is, General, I'm too crippled to fight. How can I maintain the confidence of my men if I can't sit a saddle long enough to lead a charge? I'm done, sir. In fact, the only place where I might be of any use is a stationary posting. I have told you often enough how I feel about West Point."

Washington tried to be reassuring and obviously assumed Benedict had lost his confidence. The Commander-in-Chief said as much right to his face adding, "You're surely more capable than you imagine yourself to be. Get back up on the horse, man! It's been three years since you were wounded. No Hessian musket ball can keep our American Hannibal off the battlefield!"

Benedict had wanted to shout that he wasn't afraid of battle, he was afraid of being in the wrong one. But of course, he could say nothing. At least, not directly. And so he continued limping and muttering, and even summoned a doctor to whom he complained that his pain had increased dramatically within the last few days.

On Thursday, August 3, 1780, a new set of General Orders came out which contained the directive that "Major General Arnold will take command of the garrison at West Point."

Benedict's spirits, along with his leg,

improved instantly, and he began preparations for the move to his final posting with the Continental Army.

~*~

Raines had been delighted to see his daughter. When Leah entered his room, it seemed as though she brought the sunshine with her. But when he learned that he'd been feverish for three days instead of one, it seemed as though the clouds had returned even darker than before.

"I think your fever is going down," she told him as she mopped his forehead with a cold cloth. "That's a good sign."

"Let's hope so. I just wish I could move my damned shoulder." He had tried, as often as he'd come awake, but the joint and all its attendant sinews refused to cooperate. "I'm afraid I've already ruined our timetable."

"I can revise it," she said.

He shook his head. "Not with me in it. I'd only slow you down. I can't play my part. I want to, with all my heart--believe me--but I won't put you in danger. That means I'd have to be healthy. And sweetheart, I'm not."

"What's he talking about?" Chastity asked. "If he means the party, I'm in no hurry at all. It can wait 'til next spring for all I care."

Raines smiled at her, then looked back at Leah. "What can we do? We never even considered that something like this might happen."

"Chastity, would you be a dear and fetch Joel,

please? The three of us need to talk."

"Of course," the girl said, rising lightly to her feet and floating to the door.

Raines smiled as he watched her go.

"She's a little young for you, isn't she?" Leah asked. "If she were a boy, she'd be a little young for me!"

"What? Oh." He felt sheepish. "I could be her grandfather." He paused as an impish smile lit his face. "Technically speaking though, she's older than me by a good two hundred years."

"Oh, please!"

"But seriously, I can't help it if she sees me as something more than I am."

"I don't know about that," Joel said as he joined them. "I think she sees you as a meal ticket. Potentially, anyway, and a damned good one."

"Do I detect a hint of jealousy?" Leah asked.

"From moi?" Joel feigned a superior air. "Just because she's young and lovely? Please. Girls like that flock to me all the time. It's embarrassing. I can afford to leave one in play for someone else."

Raines smiled at that. He had met Dawkins earlier, during an apparently rare moment of lucidity. Leah had given him her assessment of the former police inspector who, she believed, might be willing to help them despite his former ties to British rule of North America. But that was in a 2012 which might never even happen. "Leah says she's already told you about our plan."

"Some of it."

"And what do you think?"

Joel exhaled heavily. "I think you're mad, both

of you. The whole enterprise is one great, gigantic fantasy. It's utterly impossible--a dream built on a foundation of hope, rather than reality."

"That's a bit dire, isn't it?" Leah said. "Why not tell us what you really think?"

"I just did. You're crazy."

"That's probably just what you were thinking when I told you I was about to go back in time."

He nodded.

"And that didn't turn out to be crazy, did it?"

"No."

"Well then?"

"It's like a turtle that manages to cross a road without being run over. That doesn't mean he'll make it every time."

Raines smiled. "We only need to make it one more time. And believe me, getting *here* was by far the hardest part."

"I've got a better analogy," Leah said. "We've already crossed the road. All we've got left to cross is the shoulder. But we need your help to do that."

"You want me to be a traitor to the Crown so you can stop someone *else* from being a traitor to the colonies? Is that about right?"

Raines and Leah exchanged looks.

"I would never have said it quite that way," Raines admitted, "but yes, that's what we're asking."

"No it's not!" Leah said. "It's much, much more than that. Everything which follows will be different. Think about this, Joel, if England didn't need to split its forces between North America and Europe when the Great War broke out, do you honestly believe the Germans would have won?"

239

"Well...."

"Of course not! We're not asking you to be a traitor to the Crown, we're asking you to make it possible for the Crown to save the homeland."

Not bad, daughter. Your Mum would be so proud.

"I hadn't thought about it that way," Joel said, "certainly not that aspect of it. Lately, my thoughts about the future have been more... immediate. More along the lines of my own survival, not England's."

"Then you'll work with us?"

"I'll listen to what you have in mind, and if I think it's reasonable, then... maybe."

"Fair enough," Leah said.

Joel looked from one to the other. "But I will not commit murder."

"That's a restriction we can live with," Raines said, turning to Leah. "Isn't it?"

"Absolutely," she said.

"Then I guess you'd better fill me in on the details."

"All right then," Leah said. "Come with me."

~*~

Anthony Lancaster sat in a rocking chair on the front porch of his home outside Shrewsbury as the squat physician he'd summoned to examine him clucked like a hen. He would have preferred a male doctor, but they'd become scarce owing to the surplus of medical business resulting from the rebellion.

"Will I heal?" he asked, his voice so raspy as

to be unrecognizable.

"How did this happen?" she asked, ignoring his question.

"Attacked," he said. Verbal communication had become painful, extremely so, and accordingly, Lancaster scaled back his use of words.

"By whom?"

"Cotswold," he growled.

The name shocked her. "Harry Cotswold? The Colonel?"

Lancaster shook his head. "Friend."

"A friend of Cotswold's?" Her face registered a hint of recognition.

When he nodded, she become excited. "A big, tall man? About my age? Highly opinionated?"

Lancaster shrugged. Hardly an appropriate response, but easier than forming words.

"Try whispering," Bentley said. "It shouldn't hurt too much. Requires less air I suppose. If that's too painful, just mouth the words, and I'll try to figure out what you're saying."

Lancaster nodded again.

"By any chance did the man who attacked you call himself a doctor?"

"Yes!"

"I know him," she said, and then she scowled. "Did *you* shoot him?"

Lancaster mouthed the words, "self defense," but Bentley couldn't understand him. He tried whispering, and that hurt nearly as much as talking. The effort left him short of breath, but she got his meaning.

"Well, for what it's worth," she said, "you

winged him good. That shoulder of his will never be right, assuming he survives. And I'm not sure of that by any means. He wouldn't allow me to treat him. Raved about the strangest things, too. Claimed he came from a place where people are shot for not washing their hands. Can you imagine?"

Lancaster shook his head.

"I couldn't, either." She closed her medical bag. "I don't think bleeding you will do anything for your throat. Truth to tell, there's nothing anyone can do to help that. It will feel better over time, and you'll have to learn to live with a raspy voice and a little less air. You won't be singing anymore."

He made a face.

"Cheer up. You're lucky to be alive."

Lancaster felt anything but "lucky."

"For now, you need to rest. Get your strength back. Don't exert yourself, and if you can avoid it, don't talk."

He snorted. At least that didn't hurt.

"I will be back out this way in a month. I'll stop by and look in on you."

He nodded.

"That'll be two shillings," she said. "In coin. I know that seems high, but these are hard times."

He handed her the money and watched her amble down the steps to her wagon.

God cures, and the physician accepts the fee. He'd heard the phrase often enough growing up. Now he understood the truth of it.

He had two items on his agenda. The first was recovering from the assault he'd suffered at the hands of Colonel Cotswold's fine friend. The second involved finding a way to pay Colonel Cotswold's fine friend back.

~*~

Rather than move into the building normally used as the West Point commander's residence, Benedict chose to live some distance away. For his purposes, the best choice was the former home of Colonel Beverly Robinson, a loyalist serving with the British army in New York City. Located a couple miles south of his namesake fort, the house was quite large and stood less than a mile from the east bank of the Hudson, and therefore closer to the British lines.

His aides, Lieutenant Colonel Richard Varick and Major David Franks tried to dissuade him citing security issues, but Benedict wouldn't listen. "When my wife arrives, she's not going to want to live in such a hostile environment. She's a city woman, born and bred in Philadelphia. She deserves a fine country home, and I aim to give it to her."

Varick and Franks had been with him long enough to know he could not be dissuaded. Major Franks had served under him while he lived in Philadelphia, the largest city in the colonies. Rather than let them continue badgering him about his choice of living quarters, he set them to work almost immediately on tasks he had been thinking about for some time.

He needed to prepare West Point and its various fortifications for the coming battle. Despite being a bit run-down, the Point's strategic position made it formidable. If General Clinton hoped to take it, Benedict had to make it more vulnerable. That would take time and effort, especially since he had to make it look like he was doing exactly the opposite.

Therefore, he gave out a series of orders to be executed immediately. These included a stiff increase in the number of guards on duty at all times. In addition, he required that every sentry be inspected, every night, by field grade officers.

After assigning a new chief engineer to do a hurried inspection of all the works, he made up a preliminary list of repairs and ordered that they be finished as quickly as possible. When the engineer's report came back, he ordered that work begin on virtually every recommendation--at the same time.

On his orders, watercraft would no longer be managed informally. Hospital patients would be treated differently from then on. Nothing lay beyond his purview, and in the minds of his subordinates, anything that didn't need fixing, needed changing. Benedict ignored any and all complaints.

As the construction teams launched into the repairs, he raided their ranks to fill out work parties cutting wood, clearing shoreline, and tackling other projects that slowed, and sometimes halted, the progress on the fortifications.

Benedict felt quite proud of himself. No one could accuse him of dereliction. All anyone had to do was look around, as long as they didn't look too closely. Meanwhile, he had other work to do.

Though eager to relocate Peggy and his infant son who were still in Philadelphia, that would have to wait for at least a little while. She provided his only reliable means to exchange messages with General Clinton. Even though the process was convoluted, they both knew it worked. Now that he was stationed at West Point, he needed to find a new way to stay in touch with the British general.

Unfortunately, he had no idea to whom he might turn.

~*~

Leah found it increasingly difficult to concentrate on the mission. Her father's shoulder showed no signs of improvement, but at least his fever had finally broken. Though he had somehow managed to avoid a major infection, the wound looked dreadful to her untrained eye. Joel assured her, however, that a severe infection would be painfully obvious. He never mentioned the possibility of gangrene, but the idea lingered in her mind.

As did the possibility that Joel might not be willing to work with her. She had discussed it with her father who urged her to recruit him. "Either he works with us, or we give up before we've even started."

"I'll never give up," she'd said. "Even if I have to track down George Washington all by myself and convince him that his favorite general is a traitor."

She knew he shared her passion, but he was pragmatic enough to realize such a direct approach would never work. "Recruit Joel," he'd said. "He's our best chance."

She had reluctantly agreed. Coaxing him to join in their counter-conspiracy conspiracy added yet another dimension they hadn't considered.

"Our basic plan is to sabotage the saboteur," she said when they settled into the privacy of the Cotswold's attic. "Right about now, Arnold is at work on West Point. He's trying to weaken it before General Clinton attacks."

She spread out a map of the Hudson River and indicated the location of West Point.

Joel pointed south, to New York City. "Clinton's here?"

"Yes. With about 15,000 soldiers. That includes redcoats and loyalists."

"That's *all*?"

"That's more than we have on our side," she said, "even counting the militia."

"What have you got against the militia?"

"Nothing. But they aren't 'real' soldiers. They've had little training, and the men who command them are as ill-prepared as the men serving under them. So they tend to desert in large numbers, and those who stick around are more likely to run when the bullets start flying."

He gave her a long look. "You've never been in battle, have you?"

"No."

"Then don't criticize the poor bastards who have."

"I'm being realistic, Joel, not critical. And I readily admit it's based on research, not personal experience. We can't win this war without the militias. I know that. But they have limitations, and we'd be foolish to ignore them."

"I suppose."

"Okay, so Arnold's in West Point. General Clinton is in New York, and Arnold's wife is in Philadelphia. When she leaves to join him, he's going to lose his ability to communicate with Clinton. She's been coordinating his messages to the British since before they were married."

"So, that's a good thing."

"Yes, because it forces Arnold to look for other ways to communicate. He has to find a loyalist who'll work with him, and he needs to find a place for clandestine meetings. That's where we'll fit in."

Joel didn't look wildly excited by the prospect. "I don't think I've ever heard anyone use the word 'clandestine' in normal conversation."

"This is hardly a normal conversation."

"No kidding. And just what, exactly, are we supposed to fit *into*?"

"The home of Joshua Hett Smith. He's a loyalist with ties to Colonel Beverly Robinson, another Tory who's working with General Clinton. It's Robinson's home that Arnold's living in. Robinson will set up a meeting between Arnold and a British spy that will seal the fate of West Point."

"And the meeting takes place at Smith's house?"

"No, but a lot of planning takes place there. Arnold can't do much from inside American lines. Too many aides and soldiers wandering around. Smith's house is in a sort of no-man's land. It's located between the areas held by the two sides. That's where we need to be."

"We'll just pop in and introduce ourselves?"

"Of course not. We'll have to figure out a plausible reason for being there. Dad and I had planned to present ourselves as distant relatives of Smith caught up in the chaos of the rebellion. We've got enough money to make it worth Smith's while to put us up for a few weeks. What could be more innocent than a concerned father trying to take care of his only daughter?"

"We could be husband and wife," Joel said. "Of course, you'd have to be a lot more submissive. For the sake of realism. We wouldn't want to raise suspicions."

"I see. So, for instance, no more bundling boards?"

"Exactly!"

She wanted to slap him. "Is that all you can think about? I'm talking about something incredibly serious, and you're too horny to pay attention? What's the matter with you?"

Joel didn't even blink. "You brought up the sleeping arrangements, not me."

"I--"

"Let's get back to this Smith character and his house. Why are they so important?"

She growled at him and then let it go. "Because of who Smith knows and where he lives. He knows Robinson, and he lives on neutral turf. We have to figure out how to get Joshua Smith, and his family, out of the way so--"

"No murder!" Joel said.

Leah shook her head vigorously. "Of course not. We already agreed on that. We need the Smith home as a base of operations, but more importantly, we need it so we can spy on Arnold."

"And you really think Smith will fall for the long-lost relative story?"

"Hopefully, yes," Leah said. "I thought we could work out the details while we travel to Haverstraw."

"Where the hell is Haverstraw?"

She reached for the map and pointed to a spot just south of Stony Point. "It's about fourteen miles downriver from West Point."

He stared at the map. "There's nothing there."

"Nothing but a few farmhouses," she said. "The whole Hudson River Valley is thinly settled because there's not much good farmland."

Joel sighed. "This has got to be the screwiest plan I've ever heard of."

She put her hand on his arm and looked into his eyes. "Trust me, we can make this work. I know it."

He clearly wasn't convinced.

"Once we're close to where everything takes place, we can make any adjustments needed," she said. "For now, we have to get to Smith and earn his trust so that we can be there when Arnold makes his plans."

"Because we're going to sabotage them."

"Hopefully, yes."

"And you're confident you know everything he's going to do?"

"Well," she said, "up to a point."

"What d'you mean 'up to a point'?"

"We'll be acting out history--literally--and

that's something I know better than anyone, especially here and now. But once we stop Arnold from planning the fort's surrender, we go off-script. The history I know won't apply anymore."

"Why not?"

"Because back where we came from--*our* version of 2012--Benedict Arnold was successful right out of the gate. He met with a British major named Andre', and they worked out all the details. A few days later, West Point fell. General Washington was captured, and hanged, and Arnold led the force which eventually rounded up and executed the Continental Congress."

"I never knew that. Not all of it."

She smiled at him. "You said you wouldn't commit murder, even if the target was a traitor. How do you feel about preventing the deaths of non-traitors?"

He took a long time working up his answer, then said, "What the hell, it's not like I have anything better to do."

And then she kissed him.

~*~

Colonel John Lamb, who fought with Benedict at Quebec and Danbury, and now commanded the central portion of West Point, marched into Benedict's offices unannounced. Both of Benedict's aides, Colonel Varick and Major Franks, rose to greet him. Benedict remained seated with his bad leg propped on a pillow atop a milking stool.

"This madness must stop," Lamb roared. If

Benedict had not known the man, his badly disfigured face might have frightened him. The livid scars contorted even Lamb's most gentle expressions into something fierce. When he was upset, as he was now, the visage grew even worse.

"What are you talking about?" Major Franks asked.

Lamb addressed Benedict directly. "You've got men working everywhere, but nothing's being accomplished. You order work started, and then send the men away to do something else. We shall neither be able to finish the works that are incomplete nor be in a situation to defend those that are."

"Calm down, Colonel," Benedict said. "I know what I'm doing."

Lamb fixed him with a baleful glare. "Are you, sir? Really? I'm not so certain."

"Remember your place, Colonel," Benedict warned.

"I understand his concern, General," Colonel Varick said, easing himself between Lamb and their commanding officer. "I couldn't help but notice how much you've concerned yourself with the most minor elements of post life."

"Such as?"

Varick swallowed. The man rarely showed signs of nerves, but lately he'd been on the verge of making critical remarks. Benedict had little patience either for him or his criticism.

"Well sir, one cannot help but wonder why you would concern yourself with how we bake our bread."

"I like bread," Benedict said.

"Of course, sir. We all do, but--"

"And if I want to specify precisely how it is to be baked, that is my right."

Lamb rolled his eyes toward the ceiling, the whites showing clearly, and disturbingly, within the ruin of his face.

"Could we switch to a topic of slightly more importance than bread?" Lamb asked, his voice evidencing strain.

"And what would that be?" Benedict asked.

"We don't have enough men to do everything that needs doing."

"Then get some more!"

Lamb grimaced. "And where would you have me find them?"

Benedict faced him down. "I suggest you try the militia."

"I can't imagine they would be of much help," Varick interjected. "We've tried to work with a few from around here, but--"

"I don't want excuses, gentlemen," Benedict said. "I want results. Quit wasting my time with complaints and get something done!"

Lamb's face may have reflected more anger than he actually felt, but Benedict didn't care. It wouldn't be long before he'd have nothing further to do with any of them, and that day couldn't come soon enough.

He shoved himself upright and dismissed both Varick and Franks, then followed them to the door and closed it.

The three men stood in quiet conversation

outside, but he could still hear them, especially Varick and Lamb.

"He seems even more irritable than usual," the scar-faced Colonel said.

Varick responded, "He's under great pressure. It would go easier on all of us if we could collect his wife and bring her here."

"I suppose so," Lamb said. "But he's not the man I used to know."

~*~

Excerpt from the *New York de Journal*:

Death Toll Mounts From Assassination Conspiracy

New York, New York, Fri., May 30, 2012--The remains of an apparent murder victim were located today in a wooded area of the Millburn College campus. The body was identified as that of Francis Flaherty, a 62-year-old Millburn College secretary. Police made the discovery while investigating an anonymous tip.

Flaherty worked for Dr. Raines Kerr, Chair of the Millburn Physics department. His daughter, Leah Kerr, is wanted in connection with the assassination of Queen Elizabeth II on May 21.

Details of the crime are being withheld. Sources say Mrs. Flaherty reported Dr. Kerr missing three weeks prior to the murder of the Queen and five others.

Dr. Kerr was last seen in early May. His behavior in the months prior was reportedly "suspicious." Not only did he leave no forwarding address, he liquidated all his assets before disappearing. Further, his laboratory was burned in an electrical fire. The blaze ruined experimental gear, the function of which has yet to be determined.

Chapter Fourteen

"You can't stay in your corner of the forest waiting for others to come to you. You have to go to them sometimes."
--Winnie the Pooh (A.A. Milne)

Despite the constant pain in his shoulder, Raines Kerr felt better than he had in nearly two weeks. Saying goodbye to Leah had been an emotional low point, of course, but knowing she had Joel riding beside her--and willing to assist her--made a huge difference. It gave him hope. And more importantly, her success might fulfill the dream his wife had instilled in them: independence for America.

Leah and Joel had been gone for over a week, and Raines had done everything he could think of to reassure himself that they would be fine. But constantly assessing the positives and negatives of the venture yielded only anxiety. Chastity had commented on it, but Raines wasn't ready to share the goal of their mission. At least, not yet.

"Mrs. Cotswold and I will be going into town today," the Colonel announced over breakfast. He looked directly at Raines and said, "I look forward to the day when you feel well enough to accompany us."

"As do I," Raines said.

"Is there anything you need?"

Raines smiled at Chastity. "Dancing lessons?"

"You're not still talking about that party nonsense, are you?"

"Why shouldn't he?" Mrs. Cotswold asked. "He's mentioned it often enough."

"Only while feverish," the Colonel pointed out. "Surely that doesn't count."

"I'm still very interested in having a party," Raines said. "It would give me a chance to reward my lovely nurse."

Chastity blushed.

"And perhaps it would be a good way to meet some of your friends in the Sons of Liberty."

"Are you thinking of joining?" the Colonel asked.

"Perhaps," said Raines. "If they'll have me." *And if I'm still here.* It wouldn't hurt to give some thought to the future, and knowing a few leading citizens might come in handy. While Leah's mind was focused on a traitor, there was no reason why he couldn't focus on a patriot or two.

"Being shot by a loyalist should provide ample evidence of your sympathies."

Raines laughed, something he had rarely done since the incident at Lancaster's house. "I hope the typical requirements for membership are less painful."

"Usually," the Colonel said with a chuckle. "There are a couple gentlemen I'd like you to meet. But they may still be in Philadelphia."

"Doing what?"

"The usual--scrambling for funds to pay for the war. Or trying to figure out how to get Maryland to ratify the Articles."

"The Articles of Confederation?"

"Indeed. If one can believe Samuel Adams, and I certainly do, our future depends on the colonies agreeing to a single set of rules for everyone."

Raines nodded his head. "Seems reasonable."

"Twelve of the colonies think so."

"But not Maryland?"

"Not yet, anyway."

~*~

Benedict's efforts to make West Point vulnerable, while *appearing* intent on hardening it, proved not only difficult but tiresome. His subordinates, Colonel Lamb in particular, were quick to voice their apprehension if not outright disagreement with his policies and plans. Overruling Lamb had become an annoyance, but one he had to temper since the man had the respect of nearly everyone on the post. *If only Peggy were here.* Benedict longed to see her, for she knew better than anyone how to calm him and restore his spirits. Unfortunately, it would be weeks before she arrived.

Meanwhile, the work had to continue. In

addition to weakening the fortifications, he needed to open a new line of communication with General Clinton in New York. This proved to be a delicate task, as Colonel Varick and Major Franks, his aides, both wanted to be involved in any efforts to establish *sub rosa* channels of information. For the time being, neither seemed to suspect his true intent, and he had to exercise extreme care to keep it that way.

The answer to his communications dilemma came from a most unlikely direction--the renowned Colonel Elisha Sheldon, whose 2nd Continental Light Dragoons ranked among the most celebrated units in the American army. His troops safeguarded a sizeable portion of southern Connecticut and New York from roving bands of loyalists who preyed upon the local citizenry. "Sheldon's Horse," as his dragoons were commonly known, also raided British army supply efforts and provided security for General Washington.

What truly interested Benedict was the discovery that Sheldon also operated a network of spies, men and women who freely crossed the lines of both sides. Surely he could find among them someone willing to do his bidding, in effect to be a double agent--precisely what he needed to pass messages to Clinton.

As soon as he learned of Sheldon's resources, he set about taking advantage of them. The timetable, he felt certain, had just been advanced.

~*~

At Colonel Cotswold's insistence, Leah and Joel had taken the busiest of the three Boston Post Roads leading to New York. The so-called Upper Post Road ran west and slightly south to Springfield, then turned directly south through Connecticut until it joined the Lower Post Road in New Haven. It continued along the coast into New York. They would travel overland once they got closer to the Hudson. Though not the most direct route, Colonel Cotswold insisted it offered the best selection of taverns and accommodations for travelers.

The Colonel had suggested that they take Gabriel with them, but they declined thinking Leah's father might be in greater need of his assistance. After packing spare clothes, plenty of cash, and a few other odds and ends from the Kerr's limited cache of 21st century goods, they had taken their leave.

Joel announced a discovery: he had neither the temperament nor the physique needed for prolonged horseback riding. They discussed it over supper in a tavern near Shrewsbury after their first day in the saddle.

"I'm dying," he said.

"That's a bit dramatic, isn't it?"

"Seriously. I can't go on. My spine will never be the same."

"How's your leg?"

"I don't know. I can't feel anything below my navel."

Leah giggled.

"What? No sympathy?"

"I rode right beside you," she said. "I'm a little sore, too. We'll feel better after a good night's sleep."

"A long hot bath might help."

She looked around the rustic, candlelit room. "We'll be lucky if they even have rooms with beds."

"I can't believe I'm doing this," he said.

"You just have to be patient. Once you get used to it, riding won't be so bad."

"Maybe we should have driven the buggy."

She shook her head adamantly. "At some point we may need to go in different directions, and I don't think either of us wants to walk."

She couldn't remember saying anything like that to her father.

"Do you remember that pain pill you gave me back at the school?" Joel asked. "I could use another. Maybe a handful."

"I have some," she said reaching into the saddlebags she'd brought into the tavern with them. Palming the plastic vial so only he could see it, she handed it to him across the table. "Don't be obvious about it. Pills aren't exactly common in this era. Wash 'em down with your beer."

He took the homemade meds and nodded his thanks.

"How is the beer, by the way?"

"Terrible," he said sliding his drink toward her. "Tastes like it aged in someone's boot."

She took a sip, made a face, and pushed the red clay mug away.

"How's your cider?" he asked.

"About like your beer. Wanna taste?"

He shook his head. "How much more of this do we have to look forward to?"

"Depends on whether or not we can pick up

the pace without hurting the horses. They can only go so far so fast, y'know. I'd like to be in Haverstraw right now, but I suspect it's going to take a couple weeks."

Joel let out a groan. "Any chance I could talk you into shooting me in my sleep?"

"Would you rather walk?"

He reached reflexively for his bad leg. "I dunno. Maybe. How far is it?"

"A couple hundred miles, at least. Maybe two fifty."

"Then you definitely need to shoot me in my sleep."

"Not unless you recruit your replacement first. Know anybody reliable from the 21st century who doesn't have anything to do right now?"

"Don't expect *me* to be reliable after two weeks in the bloody saddle."

"Oh, poor baby." She made pouty lips at him.

As they finished their meal of roasted potatoes and brown bread, a man approached their table. Dressed in a dark topcoat, green waistcoat and beige breeches, he carried a cocked hat under his arm and bowed from the neck. When he spoke, he kept his voice low. That, and its raspy quality, made him hard to understand.

He seemed to be choosing his words not just carefully, but sparingly. "Traveling through?"

Something in the man's manner put Leah instantly on guard, but Joel didn't seem concerned. Instead, he smiled and offered a greeting. "We're on our way to New York. I've always wanted to go there."

"From Boston?" the man asked, ignoring Joel.

Leah nodded. She felt as if he was undressing her with his eyes, but as a woman in male attire she had already drawn looks from everyone else in the tavern. As she had explained to the Cotswolds when they objected to the idea, women's fashions weren't terribly practical for extended horseback rides.

That sparked a commentary on deportment from Mrs. Cotswold which Leah endured and then ignored.

"It's been a long day," she said, rising to her feet. She matched the newcomer's height and looked him eye-to-eye. Joel followed suit.

The man pursed his lips. "Your accent is... unusual."

"Oh, really?"

"But familiar."

~*~

Raines napped for a while after the Colonel and his wife departed. The windows were open, and a late summer breeze fluffed the curtains like the sails on a schooner. He woke when the door creaked open. Chastity floated in and sat beside him on the bed. She put her palm against his cheek and asked, "Did you really mean what you said earlier about a dance?"

Raines looked into her emerald eyes and felt his pulse quicken. The girl's pale complexion and honey blonde hair complimented a flawless face. He had to clear his throat before he found his voice. "Sure I did. Of course."

She rewarded him with a smile that broke upon her lips like a sunrise.

"I take it you like the idea," he said.

"I can't begin to tell you how much." She leaned over him, careful not to touch his damaged shoulder, and kissed his forehead.

He placed his hand on her side as if to support her. The warmth of her torso radiated through her gown as she kissed him again, this time on the nose.

What are you up to, girl?

"I don't know how well I'll ever be able to dance. It's going to be tricky holding a partner with only one arm."

She kissed him on the ear. "There are many different ways to dance."

Raines cleared his throat again. "That's... Uh, comforting."

He felt her palms on both his cheeks as she gently tilted his head back and kissed him full on the mouth. The sounds of their breathing and the rustling of the sheets grew symphonic. Running his hand across her back and up toward her shoulders, he pressed her closer. She melted into him and responded with the tiniest of moans. Raines shifted slightly to hide a burgeoning erection.

When she leaned away from him and pushed a loose strand of straw-colored hair back into place he could do nothing but glory in her smile.

"You, sir," she said, in a voice too sultry for her years, "need a shave."

And a bath. And a condom. Maybe several. And some vitamins!

"Don't move," she said.

"I wouldn't even if I could."

She left the room on cat's feet, leaving him with the biological equivalent of a tent pole and a conscience overflowing with self-reproach.

He wondered if Gabriel had accompanied the Cotswolds into town, alternately hoping he had and then that he hadn't. While his guilt operated with all the subtlety of a blinking neon sign, Chastity returned.

She slid a three-legged stool close to the head of his bed and deposited upon it a bowl of hot water, a towel, and the colonial version of a straight razor.

Raines swallowed, and the tent collapsed.

"Are you sure you know what you're doing?" he asked.

She smiled confidently. "I've shaved my father's face for years. My mother taught me. Daddy always cuts himself. The trick is a sharp blade. Gabriel sharpens ours and does it better than anyone." She brandished the tool with its finely honed edge. "When Doctor Bentley was here I saw she had a razor in her bag, but it didn't look nearly as nice, or as sharp, as this one."

Raines thought back to the handful of blades he'd brought for his safety razor. Thus far, only Gabriel had seen him use it, and he had respected the physicist's request that he not mention the mysterious device to anyone else. Someday, Raines knew, he'd have to learn to wield one of the ungainly instruments Chastity waved in front of his face.

"It would be easier if you sat up," she said.

He complied, and she loosened the collar of

his all-purpose shirt which, under the covers, had bunched up around his waist. He had no underwear.

Her hands were feather light, her touch soft as she tilted his head one way and another. Yet when she applied the razor to his stubbled cheeks, she did so with confidence and precision, completing the process in short order. She held the bowl while he dipped one end of the towel in it and rinsed his face, an operation a two-handed man could complete with ease, but one which challenged him.

"Oh, dear," she murmured, examining his garment. "You've gotten it all wet."

Indeed he had, despite feeling smug about not spilling the entire bowl.

"Off with your shirt," she said. "I'll get you a clean, dry one."

He wondered how he might accomplish the task with only one arm.

"Oh! How silly," she chuckled, "you can't do it by yourself. Let me help."

Sitting sidesaddle on the bed she tackled the job but made little progress.

Raines shifted, trying to free his good arm. "Maybe if we do one side at a time...."

Chastity frowned as he struggled with the long-sleeved shift, then hiked up her skirt and straddled him, settling lightly on his outstretched legs with her knees on either side of his hips. He could feel the warmth of her thighs through the thin blanket that separated them.

"Now pull your arm in," she said as she held the end of his sleeve steady.

With one arm free, she carefully worked the

linen up his torso and over his head, steadily moving toward the injured arm.

Raines smelled the cloth as it passed his nose. Neither he nor the shirt had been washed since the day he was shot.

Chastity exercised extreme care in freeing his shoulder from the shirt and then tossed it on the floor.

"There," she said with evident pride.

"Thank you."

She put her palms on his chest and leaned forward, kissing him once again. "Much better," she said.

Raines was afraid to say anything for fear the moment might end, but then grew more fearful that his silence might end it even sooner. "Maybe you should check again."

She leaned forward once more, slid her arms under his, and pressed herself into his bare chest. Then she rocked her pelvis in a motion as seductive as anything Bathsheba ever attempted. His entire mind began operating on the neon light principle, flashing alternate thoughts of *Dear God, don't stop!* with *Where in hell did you learn this?*

He sought her mouth with his own, and she responded with a soft, wet kiss that left his heart hammering. He slipped his one good hand beneath the bunched material of her gown, past the thin shift under that, and found the soft smooth flesh of her leg. He explored further, testing the swell of her bottom.

She squirmed again, moaning lightly as she pressed her cheek against his and breathed into his ear, "Will you dance with me?"

"Dance? *Now?*" he asked, not catching her meaning at first.

She eased away and clawed the blanket from between them, allowing him to point at the ceiling without using his hands.

"I, uh--"

"Shh," she said, "I told you, there are many ways to dance."

And slowly she lowered herself onto him.

Raines leaned back and responded vigorously, oblivious to the wrongness of what he was doing, unable to think in terms of age differences, cultural mismatches, or birth control. Lust had taken over and drove them both in a mindless search for release.

Ragged breaths replaced words, and desire displaced thought. Passion triumphed over reason as they rocked and thrust and groaned. Somehow, no doubt through the intervention of a benevolent God, Chastity finished first and hugged Raines fiercely as he spent himself.

They remained where they were, arms wrapped around each other, taking deep breaths between self-conscious giggles. Eventually Raines opened his eyes.

And saw Gabriel standing in the doorway staring back at him.

~*~

Joel walked Leah to their tiny room on the tavern's upper floor. It housed a pair of narrow beds and a low stool beneath the only window. Other than a pair of cast iron coat hooks, the room had no other furniture. Leah set the tavern's candle lamp on the stool while Joel piled their saddlebags on the floor between the beds.

He eyed the rough linens and wondered when they'd last been washed, if ever. Leah seemed to be entertaining similar thoughts. He decided to change the subject. "What do you make of that guy who stopped at our table to chat?"

"He's shifty," she said. "I wouldn't trust him for a moment, and his comment about my accent set me to wondering."

"About what?"

"Well," she said, "this *is* Shrewsbury, where according to Gabriel, someone in the Lancaster family shot my dad."

"Did Gabriel say anything else to you about it? I couldn't get a detail out of him with a pry bar."

"No," she said. "No one would talk about it. The only thing that mattered, the Cotswolds said, was getting Dad well. When I asked if the authorities were looking into it, the Colonel mentioned something about it being a matter for the Sons of Liberty."

"They're vigilantes, aren't they? I think that's what it says in the history books."

"In *British* history books."

"Whatever. That guy downstairs seemed awfully interested in you."

She dismissed the remark with a shake of her head. "He was interested in *both* of us."

Joel stepped closer. "But I can easily

understand why someone would be interested in you." She did, after all, do breathtaking things for her tight breeches--something that had no chance of escaping his notice, nor that of any other male they encountered.

Smiling, she gave him a gentle shove backwards. "Right now, all I'm interested in is sleep."

"How 'bout a bath?"

"A bath would be lovely, but if I can only have two or three a year, I'll save mine until we get where we're going."

Joel felt his jaw drop. "Two or three *a year?*"

"If we're lucky. Our best bet will be to take a dip in a stream somewhere along the way between here and the Hudson. Face it, Joel, for the next couple weeks we're going to smell like horse blankets."

"Charming."

"At least it's still August," she said. "The water in the smaller streams shouldn't be too cold. Yet."

A cold bath and a filthy bed. Who could ask for anything more?

"I've been giving some thought to our timetable," she said. "Remember when I said we might be riding for a couple weeks?"

"Try as I might, I *can't* forget."

"Well, today is August 11th, so we've got exactly a month to get settled in Haverstraw and do whatever is necessary to disrupt our treasonous friend, Benedict Arnold."

"What happens in a month?"

"On September 11th, he's going to hop in a boat manned by eight American soldiers, and they're going to row him downstream from Haverstraw to a place called Dobb's Ferry. Redcoats control the eastern side of it. That's where our boy is going to meet with Major Andre' and pass over all the information the British need to take West Point."

"And just how are we going to stop him?"

"I have no earthly idea. Maybe bore holes in his boat? I was hoping you might think of something."

"Oh, sure. No problem. Need me to quell a riot or drain a swamp while I'm at it?" He rubbed his temples. "Do you remember the pain medicine you gave me?"

"Of course."

"Have you got anything to treat crazy? Nothing extreme--like for utter insanity or head-banging depravity--just a little something to cure a touch of madness."

Leah ignored him, folded her topcoat inside out and used it for a pillow. Leaving her boots by the saddlebags, she stretched out on the bed, fully clothed.

"This is going to be a long two weeks, isn't it?" he said.

"Yeah."

She waited while he followed her example with his boots and jacket, then blew out the candle. "Joel?"

"Hm?"

"Thank you for coming with me."

With those few words, his attitude about the

coming weeks improved dramatically.

~*~

Anthony Lancaster finished his beer and set the reddish brown pottery mug on the rough hewn log table. All in all, it had been an interesting evening. He'd come to the tavern for the cockfights, as usual, only this time he'd lost money on nearly every contest. The blood and noise were as amusing as ever, and he never tired of watching the fools who bet more than they could afford to lose. But he had never become accustomed to losing--at anything-- and his losses that night only added to the ill humor he'd been harboring since Raines Kerr came to call.

Luckily for him, curiosity had tempered his mood through the appearance of a woman with fair hair and a dark complexion. Her beauty had drawn his attention at first, as it had every other man in the place, for even though she dressed like a man, no one could mistake her femininity. Intrigued, Lancaster had moved close enough to her table to eavesdrop, a skill he'd developed in his service to King George.

The woman in the dining room, and her companion, had the same peculiar accent as the man who attacked him. Much of what they said meant little, which suggested either their vocabulary was quite foreign, or they spoke in some sort of code. Either way, they deserved further observation.

He engaged them politely, as a stranger ought, but managed to glean only one thin bit of intelligence, their destination: New York. He wished he knew more specifically where in New York they were headed, but they didn't say.

They carried their belongings with them. No surprise there. Taverns traded with brigands as often as honest men, and in a time of war, the two looked quite the same.

However, the appearance of the fetching young woman and her crippled friend fascinated him. Following them wouldn't be difficult, but it could be tiresome. He needed more time to evaluate them and discover their weaknesses. With any luck he might be able to talk his way into their confidence and fully ascertain their intentions.

He handed the innkeeper's daughter a coin. Though slow-witted, the girl was pleasant and didn't smell too bad. For an extra farthing she would warm his bed. He considered the option but rejected it knowing he would have to rise early to observe the mysterious couple on their way to New York.

Sometimes he surprised himself with his devotion to duty.

~*~

Treason, Treason!

Excerpt from the *Providence Times*:

Military May Call Up Reserves

Annapolis, Maryland, Thurs., June 7, 2012--Wide-spread rumors about a call-up of ground force reserves have been swirling around the military capital. No official announcements have been made, but sources close to the Royal Army command have hinted that plans are already underway to expand the draft of active duty personnel.

The speculation among well-informed observers is that some sort of armed campaign is being planned in response to last month's assassination of Queen Elizabeth II. The *Times* cannot verify or deny the reliability of such rumors.

Chapter Fifteen

*"An army of asses led by a lion is better
than an army of lions led by an ass."*
--George Washington

The constant headache Benedict had suffered since assuming command at West Point always grew worse whenever John Lamb came calling. The man had but one attitude: anger, and his sole means of expressing it was through confrontation.

"What is it *today*?" Benedict asked as the hideously disfigured Colonel burst through the door of his office. Both of Benedict's aides, Varick and Franks were on their feet as if in salute.

"It's the damned militia, again," Lamb roared.

Benedict closed his eyes and willed his headache to subside, which, of course, it didn't. "Is there something in particular about the militia you wished to bring to my attention, Colonel?"

"Aside from their refusal to follow orders?"

"That's an issue I have already discussed with

their officers. They're aware of the problems and have agreed to resolve them."

Lamb's disturbing countenance grew even more fearsome. Benedict could only imagine what the man's subordinates said about him--at least those who hadn't already been frightened to death.

"I'm not talking about the damned pigs running loose everywhere. At least those we can kill and eat. And I'm not talking about the way they look, either, as more often than not we can distinguish between them and the pigs."

"Colonel, I will not have you making disparaging remarks about the troops."

"Troops? You call them *troops?* Sometimes I wonder whose side they're on! Do you know what they've done this week? To the chain? Do you?"

Benedict shook his head. "I have no idea what you're talking about. The chain is where it always is, stretched across the Hudson."

"No," said Lamb, "it's stretched across the *bottom* of the Hudson."

"Well, yes, of course. We can't prevent civilian passage on the river. Much of our own needs are supplied by boat."

"Indeed, and what do we do if we suspect British ships are trying to work their way through the narrows?"

"Must we be pedantic?" Benedict said. "We both know the chain will be raised."

"A feat accomplished by great logs upon which the chain rests. We float the logs, and the chain rises." Lamb rocked back and forth on his heels with his hands clenched behind his back.

"Correct?"

"Yes, of course! So what?"

"Your God damned militia has taken it upon themselves to chop up those great logs for firewood!"

"I would caution you about your language, sir," Benedict said. "You know how General Washington feels about profanity."

"I also know how he feels about the chain!" Lamb roared. "Shall we also allow these mindless militiamen to dismantle our fortifications to provide stones on which to balance their cooking pots?"

Benedict turned away from Lamb and calmly addressed Major Franks. "Have the logs replaced, Major. Issue orders for an immediate work party. And use regulars."

"Sir, the regulars have already been assigned to other tasks," Franks said.

"Then re-assign them!" Benedict barked. "Must I do all your thinking for you?"

Franks gave him a hurried bow and left the room. A quick glance at Varick told him what his senior aide thought of the episode, but the man knew better than to say anything.

Lamb, however, fairly shook with anger. "You would reassign regulars when those backwoods louts could just as easily cut new logs? You're mad! If the British should learn who we're relying on to man these fortifications, they'd attack us overnight. And they'd win."

"Your concerns have been noted, Colonel," Benedict said.

"Then note this too, General, I cannot spare a

single man from the 2nd Artillery to go foraging, or catch roving pigs, or plant God damned daisies! They will either man their posts, or fortify them. When the redcoats come, we'll be ready for them."

Lamb whirled around and left the building without waiting for Benedict to either respond or dismiss him.

"That man tests the limits of my patience," Benedict observed to Varick.

"But only recently. You've known him for years," Varick said. "And his men love him."

"I'm sure of it, but that does not give him leave to be insubordinate."

While the massive iron chain was invulnerable, its management was delicate. The device was far too valuable to impair, and would be crucial in controlling river traffic for whichever side used it. Benedict had already written a note about it, sent via Peggy, to General Clinton in New York. When the British fleet sailed up river, the chain must not be available to interfere. Any ships stalled by the chain would be shelled mercilessly by Colonel Lamb's cannons.

Bother!

He desperately wished Peggy were with him. But until he could be sure of his ability to communicate with Clinton via his contacts in Colonel Sheldon's command, that would have to wait.

But it couldn't wait much longer.

~*~

Raines spent most of the day, and all of the night, alone. The Colonel and Mrs. Cotswold did not return, and Chastity said they were probably staying with friends in town as they often did in years past.

"There's no need for them to rush home," she said, "not while I have you and Gabriel to protect me."

He doubted she could have found less comforting words for him to hear. His mind had nothing to do but wander as he sat around the Cotswold's home, too weak to do anything productive, but too well to stay in bed. When he wasn't mentally reviewing his tryst with Chastity, he worried about the encounter he would eventually have with Gabriel.

He couldn't blame the youth if he told the Colonel what he had seen. And it wouldn't matter in the least--to anyone whose opinion mattered--that Chastity had been the architect of their assignation. But could he say that to Gabriel?

The lad chose not to join them for any meals, but whether he fixed something for himself or just went hungry, Raines didn't know. Near the dinner hour of the following day, Raines tracked him down in the Cotswold's stable where he was busy mucking out the stalls.

"We need to talk."

Gabriel responded with a blank expression and silence.

"C'mon, Gabe. We've been through a lot together. Can't we have a simple discussion?"

"It's *Gabriel*," he said bluntly. "I'm named after an angel. I used to believe that was something

279

to be proud of."

"It still is."

"Not based on what I've seen thus far."

Raines exhaled heavily. "Listen, son--"

"I'm not your son."

"Right. I'm sorry. The thing is, you have some ideas in your head that I should have set straight long before now."

Gabriel rested his arms on the end of his shovel handle and looked directly into the physicist's eyes. "What ideas?"

"This whole business of you thinking I'm some sort of angel. I'm not. I told you that the day we met, but you didn't believe me, and... Well, it was easier just to let you go on believing it."

"You couldn't possibly be an angel," Gabriel said. "I was a fool to think so."

"Good. I'm glad we've got that cleared up."

"Now I'm of the mind that you're the opposite of an angel. The kind of creature who would take advantage of a girl's weakness or a boy's trust."

Raines felt like the stuff Gabriel was shoveling. "What I did with Chastity was wrong. I know that. I could have stopped it, but I didn't. It was a moment of weakness. Total weakness. I'm not an angel, but neither am I some kind of devil."

"How can I know that?"

"Did I not take a bullet meant for you?"

Gabriel pursed his lips in thought.

"Have I not promised to help you prosper and enjoy your freedom?"

The boy shrugged.

"That hasn't changed."

"It will if I tell the Colonel and Mrs. Cotswold what I saw."

Raines shook his head. "No, Gabriel, it won't. Unless you want it that way. I don't want to hurt the Cotswolds, or Chastity, or you. If you feel you need to tell them, then go ahead. As long as the Colonel doesn't shoot me, I'll make sure you all have a prosperous future once the war's over. No matter what, I'll do my part to insure the bounty to come."

"Do you love Chastity?" Gabriel asked.

"I believe so."

"Will you marry her and care for her?"

Raines was taken aback. He'd lost Beth long ago but had never seriously considered marrying anyone else, let alone courting anyone.

"She's young enough to be my daughter!"

"That didn't seem to matter much to you the other day. You're as bad as Master Smithers."

And Lucas Benn, the ancient lecher who loaned us the horse to haul Smithers to his grave.

"I would be honored to make Chastity my wife," Raines said. "But I'd be stunned if she would want me."

"She fears for her future," Gabriel said. "She told me when I asked her why she'd even consider the likes of Elihu Smithers."

"She'd marry for *security?* That's a terrible reason!"

"I wouldn't know. It's never been an option for me."

"It is now," Raines said. "That's a promise. I hope you won't say anything to the Cotswolds, because I wouldn't want them to think badly of

Chastity. Or me, for that matter. But if you must, it won't change anything between us. I guarantee it. And I also promise to talk to Chastity about the future. As much as I would like to see her find and fall in love with someone her own age, if she would rather be my wife, then I shall do my utmost to make her happy."

"I can live with that," Gabriel said. "But know this: I will hold you to your word."

"I would expect nothing else."

"Good. And don't be surprised if Chastity tells the Colonel what you two were doing while they were away."

Oh? Oh. Damn.

~*~

Anthony Lancaster was not normally an early riser, but then he rarely slept well unless he occupied his own bed. The one he used at the tavern in Shrewsbury was better than sleeping on the ground, but only marginally, even if the innkeeper charged more for the room based on its size and features. The fireplace and chamber pot were a definite plus, especially on chilly nights.

He splashed cold water on his face, dried himself off and then dressed for travel. Stopping by the scullery on his way out, he helped himself to a biscuit and a slab of cheese, enough to see him through the morning. His primary goal was the fenced area where guest's horses were pastured for the night. His own mare was hobbled near a tack shed. He lingered there, breaking his fast, while he waited for the couple he'd seen in the taproom the night before.

They arrived shortly after he did and appeared neither well rested, nor pleased to have spent the night together. Lancaster found that quite odd. Why else come all this way for food and lodging when neither was worth the price charged? They had to be involved in something more than sex, and he seriously doubted it had anything to do with pleasure travel.

He watched while they attempted to prepare their mounts, a process obviously foreign to them both. Seeing them flounder about trying to catch and harness their horses proved almost painful. Though tempted to volunteer assistance, he wasn't quite ready to adopt the role of friend.

Eventually they gained control of their animals, got them saddled and mounted, and then looked quite lost about which way to go. At that point, he decided to follow them wherever they went.

"New York?" he asked, waiting until he was close enough to speak without having to raise his voice.

The woman nodded, and he pointed away from the rising sun. "West," he said, still not used to the rasp in his voice. He doubted he ever would get used to it.

"Thanks," said the woman's companion, and they turned in that direction. The horses broke into a trot that set both of them bouncing painfully down the rutted road. It was almost enough to make him feel sorry for the horses.

He waited until they were out of sight before saddling his own horse and hurrying after them. Catching up to them didn't take long.

"Good day!" he called as he rode up alongside them and slowed his horse to a walk. They did the same and looked relieved at having an excuse not to endure a trot without posting. Teaching them to ride, however, was not on his agenda.

The woman's companion tipped his hat, a clumsy gesture which suggested he was as unused to wearing one as Lancaster was to speaking in a harsh whisper. The woman merely nodded.

"I failed to introduce myself last night," he said. "I don't know what caused me to be so impolite. I apologize. The name's Anthony Balfour." It was a name he'd used before when unsure of his company.

"Joel Dawkins," said the man.

The name meant nothing. But when the woman introduced herself, he had to struggle to keep from reacting. *Leah Kerr?* Could she be any relation to the man who'd attacked him?

But then, how could she not be related to him? They had the same accent and obviously had not grown up around here. It wouldn't be wise to make it known that he had shot Doctor Kerr, even if it was in self defense.

"When you mentioned last night that you were headed to New York, I thought how fortunate I was to find someone else traveling in the same direction."

Dawkins looked anything but pleased.

"These are dangerous times," Lancaster went

on. "The road can be unkind to those not used to such travel. I have encountered my share of thieves, to say nothing of Indians."

"On this road, Mister Balfour?" the woman asked.

"This one and others like it." He wanted desperately to fire up his pipe, but ever since Kerr hit him in the throat, smoking gave him more pain than pleasure.

"What are the Indians around here like?" Dawkins asked.

"I imagine they're like savages anywhere," he responded. "In truth, it's been quite a long time since I saw any. The rebellion may have something to do with that. Cutthroats and thieves are another matter, and the worst of them are militiamen."

"Is that so?" said the woman.

"Can't blame them, really. They leave their homes to fight a war they can't possibly win. They'll likely catch the pox. They're rarely paid, and most of them live off the land. Stealing comes naturally to them, especially the ones from the Crown lands."

Dawkins looked confused. The woman turned to him and explained, "the Crown lands are west of the Appalachians and were supposedly reserved for the Indians years ago, but the colonies claimed the land, too. It's sparsely settled."

"Not so sparse any more, and the white population continues to grow," Lancaster said. "As long as the red men don't kill them off. But that's none of our concern, is it?"

"Not yet, anyway," Dawkins said. Lancaster decided he didn't like him, and if given the chance, wouldn't hesitate to see that he never reached his destination. The woman, however, was an entirely different proposition. Stunning despite her dark skin, she would undoubtedly come in handy. Either the two of them would provide him with information he could pass along to the proper authorities, or she would serve to help him exact his revenge on Raines Kerr. Whichever way it went, riding with them would be worth his while.

~*~

Knowing Balfour's name didn't alter Leah's feelings about him. He still struck her as shifty, and it had become increasingly apparent that Joel felt the same way. And for good reason. Balfour--assuming that was his real name--was a complete ass. She had seen his kind often enough on campus: supercilious blowhards who expected to be treated as experts, when all they had done was memorize and regurgitate the same old drivel. New ideas were as foreign to them as horseback riding was to Leah.

She and her father had often discussed the need for equestrian training since riding and walking were the primary means of transportation in 1780. But in the back of their minds, they both assumed it couldn't be too hard a skill to acquire and thus kept putting it off until it was too late to do anything about it.

Joel had a worse time of it than she did, and she assumed that was because of his leg. But aside from some theatrical complaints and a few off-color, if amusing remarks, he'd been a boon companion.

Perhaps more importantly, he felt comfortable in the woods. His time in the army, he claimed, had been spent largely in wilderness conditions.

At first, Leah assumed Balfour would quickly tire of them and ride on. She had no intention of having a conversation with him, and her responses were meant merely to be polite. Joel was more willing to engage him, but she suspected he had an ulterior motive. After all, hadn't he been a police inspector for a good decade? He wasn't just another pretty face.

She smiled to herself. Not only was Joel a decent looking fellow, as far as she could tell, he hailed from a similar reading group. That, according to one of her college professors, should be a prime consideration when selecting a mate.

If only she could figure out a way to get rid of the troublesome Balfour.

~*~

Joel wondered if Balfour might not be an ancestor of Gerald Murchesson. They shared a number of traits, though multiple eye colors wasn't one of them. He had assured himself of that when the man rode up and invited himself to join them. Very Murchesson-like. Unfortunately, he couldn't count on an Event sphere coming along at a convenient moment to dismember Balfour. A pity.

Knowing that Murchesson's gun was safely stowed in Leah's saddlebag gave Joel a measure of confidence. Despite his other shortcomings, Joel could rightfully lay claim to the title of marksman. At close range and with a decent sidearm, he could be as deadly as anyone. And that included members of the vaunted Special Air Service. What separated him from them was a bad leg, and a conscience.

Even so, his conscience had limits. Murchesson had stepped beyond them, and he'd paid the price. The same would apply to Balfour if he went too far.

Joel had smelled deceit the moment the swaggering little snot approached their table in the tavern. His initial reading of Balfour hadn't changed even though the man's attitude from the previous evening, had. Joel didn't trust him. And he was glad to know Leah felt the same way.

He decided to give him some time to reveal his true intent. Joel had worked with undercover operators before, and he was always surprised at how thin their facades were. He found a chance to warn Leah about him when they stopped to water their horses, and Balfour excused himself to answer nature's call.

"He's up to something," Joel said.

She nodded agreement. "But what?"

"I dunno. Yet. But if I think of something, just play along. All right?"

"Certainly."

"Good."

"And Joel?"

"Yes?"

"If you feel the need, go ahead and shoot him."

Joel's head snapped around as if spring-loaded. "*Shoot him?*"

"I'm kidding," she said, her amazing smile spread wide.

"Sometimes you scare me."

"Good. That means you're paying attention."

He swatted her lightly on the bottom as she climbed back on her horse, but she didn't seem to mind.

He waited until Balfour came back out of the woods before he mounted up, and they rode on in silence for most of the afternoon.

When they reached Brookfield, Joel declared he'd had enough.

"I'm sure we can reach Palmer before dark if we press on."

"No," said Leah. "If there's a decent place to stay in Brookfield, I want to stop. I've had enough, too."

They found a tavern near the town commons on which grazed a variety of livestock from local farms. Balfour tried to talk them into looking for another inn, but they weren't interested.

"Ever been here before?" Joel asked.

Balfour shook his head and took his leave to secure rooms.

"What d'you suppose he's got in mind?" Leah asked as they entered the tavern's surprisingly large taproom.

Joel shrugged. "I didn't get much out of him during the ride."

"Me, either. But then, I was content to look at the scenery. I counted it a blessing when he kept his mouth shut. You still think he's a spy?"

"I never said that."

"You didn't have to. The man's as subtle as an erection."

Joel winced.

"What?"

"Never mind. But you're right, I think he's a spy. The only time he wanted to talk was when he was pumping me for information about where we're going and what we're going to do when we get there."

"We should tell him something to throw him off the track."

"Actually, I've got an idea about that, and I'll need you to play along. If he's any good at what he does, it'll help us. If not, we'll be no worse off than before."

"Joel?" Leah said, drawing out his name as if it had a dozen syllables.

"Yeah?"

"Do whatever you think best. I trust you. But be careful, all right?"

Just then, Balfour returned. He held three mugs of beer and set them on the table nearest Joel and Leah. "Good news," he said, his voice as rough as sandpaper.

"What's that?" Leah asked.

"There's goat left over from Sunday."

"Yum," Joel said looking askance at Leah.

"*Goat?* That's... splendid," Leah said.

Joel picked up his beer mug and clinked it against Balfour's. "I'm afraid I haven't been entirely honest with you."

"You don't like goat? It's stew. Not as tough."

Joel tried not to roll his eyes. "What I mean is,

we haven't been forthcoming about our trip."

He shrugged. "Not my business."

"No, but there's a chance you might be able to help us."

Leah looked concerned but remained silent. She took a sip of her beer, made a face, and returned her mug to the table.

Balfour was paying close attention to Joel, for once, and ignored Leah. "Help?"

"We feel we can confide in you," Joel said, leaning closer and lowering his voice. "These are perilous times. You said so yourself. We believe the future of the colonies will be brighter if they remain dependent on the Crown."

"I see," Balfour said. He looked casually around the tavern, but at that hour, few others occupied the room. "Tories aren't welcome here."

Joel nodded solemnly. "We know. But we're not foolish enough to think we alone can stop this... thing from happening."

"What *thing*?" Balfour's voice softened on the final word.

"A weapon of some kind. Doctor Franklin had a hand in its development, and we're told the invention will completely change naval warfare."

"*Benjamin* Franklin built a weapon?"

Joel thought he remembered reading that Franklin was an inventor. He hoped he hadn't made that up, too. "Actually, no," he said. "The French built it, but it's based on his design. It's small enough to fit in a longboat but supposedly can sink anything on the water."

When Balfour's expression didn't change, Joel

continued, "I have no idea what it looks like or how it works. But I do know this, if the rebels are allowed the freedom to install the device, they will completely control the river. In time they will build more, float them down the Hudson to New York Harbor and destroy the entire British fleet."

Balfour shook his head. "That can't be true!"

Joel shrugged. "For now, they have only one such contraption, and they need to see how well it works. If it's destroyed before it proves itself, they may not be willing to pay for another."

"And you think *I* can stop it?" His voice had grown even more raspy.

"Possibly, if your contacts are better than ours. That's not the point. It doesn't matter who delivers the message as long as it's delivered--and soon. On September 12th, the information becomes worthless."

"Why trust me with this?"

Joel crossed his arms. "It's too important not to take a chance. We've spent some time with you. I understand your feelings about the war and the people fighting it. I'm a good judge of character, and I believe I know where you stand."

Balfour leaned back in his chair and took a long draught of his beer. He returned the mug to the table with a belch. "How did you learn all this?"

"He didn't," Leah said. "I did."

Her eagerness to add her voice to the story surprised Joel.

Balfour narrowed his eyes at her as she explained, "I met an officer who wears the buff and blue of a continental."

"In Boston?"

"Yes. He thought to impress me with his knowledge of military affairs."

"A braggart then?"

Her smile grew playful. "He's a handsome fellow, and he made good on his other boasts, so I have no reason to doubt him. But I suppose he could have lied. He obviously wanted to impress me with how close he is to the highest levels of command."

"Does he have a name?"

"Well, of course. But he's not such a fool that he'd share it with me. He didn't come to brag; he came for..." She paused to consider her words, then blinked her lashes. "He came for the pleasure of my company."

Oh, really? Joel looked the question at Leah.

Balfour's eyes widened briefly before he returned to the topic. "What's significant about the twelfth of September?"

"Nothing. But on the *eleventh*, a rebel officer and his crew will install the weapon. My friend tried to explain, but I confess, my talents lie in a different area." She channeled innocence.

If Joel hadn't known she was lying through her teeth, he would have taken every word she said as Gospel.

"But," she murmured, "he claims the device, whatever it is, will give his side a hellish advantage. In future battles no British ship will be safe."

"Why would they wait to install it?"

Joel responded, "Because the French haven't delivered it yet. General Washington is also relying on the French troops the fleet carries. By the eleventh of September, all the pieces will be in place. If Washington knocks out the British fleet, or ties them up on the Hudson, he and the French will attack New York City."

"That's preposterous," Balfour said.

"Is it?" Joel asked.

Leah added, "Without their navy, the British can't hold New York."

"Ridiculous."

"That's not for us to decide," she said.

Balfour didn't look convinced. But then, what Balfour thought didn't matter as long as he took the bait.

~*~

Treason, Treason!

Excerpt from the *Richmond Intelligencer*:

Power Spikes Remain Mystery

Hampton, Virginia, Sun., June 10, 2012--A resource management consultant for the national power grid, Henrietta Childers, has flatly denied reports that the system barely survived a half dozen demand spikes during the month of May.

"While the system had never experienced such large and unexplained surges in demand, few customers were inconvenienced," she said. "Though spikes hurt portions of the grid in Massachusetts, the rest of the system continued to work admirably."

Investigators are working around the clock to find the source of the power draw which by-passed usual metering. "When we finally learn the identity of the person responsible," Childers said, "they'll have a consumer utility bill of epic proportions."

Chapter Sixteen

*"A murderer is less loathsome to us than a spy. The
murderer may have acted on a sudden mad impulse; he
may be penitent and amend; but a spy is always a spy,
night and day, in bed, at table, as he walks abroad;
his vileness pervades every moment of his life."*
--Honoré de Balzac

Raines found Gabriel hard at work making
repairs to his old clothing. Though it was quite likely
a skill common among colonial youth, the physicist
admire the lad for taking care of his belongings,
meager as they were. It reminded him of a college
friend he hadn't thought of in years.

"I once had a friend," he mused, "who swore
he could repair almost anything given sufficient
quantities of duct tape and paper clips."

"Duck tape and... *what?*" Gabriel waved off his
response. "No. Don't bother to explain. It's clear you
enjoy tormenting me."

Raines groaned at his *faux pas*.

Yet, Gabriel's eyes never left his, and he kept

his own counsel for a long moment, then said, "I can't stand it. What's a 'duck tape'? And that other thing you mentioned as well."

Raines had no idea how to convey the concept of tape, and so tackled the less complicated invention. "Forget tape. Let's focus on something easier. He reached into his bag and rooted around for some of the notes he'd brought with him from the 21st century. They were conveniently grouped by topic and held together with paper clips. He removed a sample and handed it to Gabriel.

"It's a piece of wire," the ex-slave said. "That's it? That's all it is?"

Raines smiled. "The point is not that it's simple. The point is it's simple *and useful*."

"For what?"

Raines demonstrated by clipping two pages of his notes together, then unclipping them.

"Fancy that," Gabriel said, echoing apathy.

"Concentrate! Imagine the potential. It's all about organization. There's not a business anywhere in the colonies, or the world for that matter, which couldn't use a thousand of these things, or more. Governments, too. A paper clip won't change anyone's life, but it'll make it easier. Trust me when I say that once people see them, they'll all want them."

The boy nodded like he barely understood, but then slowly began to smile as he unbent the thin looped wire before bending it back into shape. "And you know how to make them?"

"Well," Raines said, surprised by Gabriel's interest, "I'm sure I can figure it out. The design's simple, and--"

"Then, let's make some! And start selling them in Boston. We can print particulars in the newspapers. We'll make a fortune!"

Raines laughed. "My boy, once this damned war is over, you and I are definitely going to go into business together. One way or another." He offered his hand. "Let's shake on it."

The teen accepted the proffered hand hesitantly. "I've seen you do this before," he said. "Is this the custom in heav-- I mean, in the place you came from?"

"It is," Raines said. "It's an old custom, I think, to show that both parties are unarmed."

"But we already know that," Gabriel said, withdrawing his hand. "Here in Massachusetts we bow. It's considered polite. And for those in my station, a deep bow shows respect for my betters."

"What betters?"

"Basically anyone who isn't a slave."

The physicist shook his head. "That's just nonsense."

"You needn't convince me," Gabriel said. "Just the rest of the colonies. And Europe. And pretty much any other place I can think of."

"Like our business plans, that's a job for the future."

Gabriel appeared crestfallen. "You mean, we have to wait?"

"I'm afraid so."

"Why?"

"Because I'm finally fit enough to travel, and I'm going to Philadelphia to see some of the

Colonel's friends. I have some information to share. My only fear is that I won't arrive in time."

"When are you leaving?"

Raines tried once again to move his arm, but the effort proved futile. On the plus side, he had all but forgotten the pain. *That* only kicked in when someone moved the arm for him. Chastity's efforts came immediately to mind, along with her other "therapeutic" endeavors, and those continued to be the most amazingly restorative exercises he could imagine. If Gabriel truly sought to find an angel, he need look no further than that young woman.

"Will you come with me?" Raines asked. "I'm going to need plenty of help until this stupid arm of mine starts working again."

"If the Colonel doesn't mind, I'd like to." He paused before continuing. "What about Miss Chastity?"

"Let's get a couple things straight here. For one, you are your own man. What the Colonel thinks or doesn't think isn't important. The only thing that should matter to you, is what *you* think. Got that?"

"Yes sir."

"And as for Miss Chastity..." he let his voice trail off. "She's the only reason I didn't leave sooner. I am going to miss her terribly."

"Does she know?"

He shook his head. "I thought I'd tell her later today if you agreed to go with me."

Gabriel narrowed his brows. "And if I don't?"

"Then I might have to ask Chastity to accompany me. It's a long, long journey, and to be perfectly honest, I would rather spend twelve hours a day in a coach with her than with you."

"Then why are you even asking me?"

Raines went silent. It was a question he had already asked himself many times. The answer, of course, was that the Colonel and Mrs. Cotswold would never approve of their unmarried daughter traveling so far from home without them.

He not only needed to marry her, he wanted to. But how would he get word to Leah? She and Joel had already been gone for over a week.

"Well?" Gabriel said.

Raines stared at him.

"That's a dam-- a profoundly good question."

~*~

Lancaster, his mind aswirl with conflict, remained in the tavern's taproom long after his newfound "friends" retired for the night. On the face of it, the couple's talk of the rebel's strange new weapon seemed outrageous. But then, the French had proven themselves a race of inventive folk even if their motives were devious.

If their claim was true, he had no choice but to report it. Once he'd done that, the problem would no longer be in his hands. But if their story turned out to be nonsense, he could become the object of ridicule for failing to quash it at the outset. When it came to ridicule, Lancaster had always been the one *dispensing* it. He couldn't let something like this ruin his reputation.

The fact that neither Kerr nor Dawkins could give him any specifics put the whole idea of "strange, new weapon" completely into the realm of his imagination. And he would be the first to admit his imagination suffered from a lack of scope.

And, as if to top all that off, the goat stew hadn't set well. He'd been to the necessary twice since he'd eaten it and assumed at least one more visit would be required. Possibly several. Not a pleasant prospect in any locale, and even less so at a run-down roadside tavern. He wished he'd gone with egg and potato as Kerr and Dawkins had done.

What, he wondered, if those two pitiful amateurs were actually telling the truth? If he ignored them, loyalists and their British comrades could suffer. Yet, if he brought it to the attention of his superiors, they still might not be able to prevent its use. And just how might they stop it? Dawkins suggested sinking the rebel's boat as they rowed the device into position. Didn't the navy already have orders to attack rebel traffic on the Hudson? Of course! So, acting on his report would require nothing more than added vigilance. If the weapon proved to be the nonsense he suspected it to be, and the Royal Navy sank it anyway, who would know? And since the pathetic Continental Congress had so little money, it seemed unlikely they would spend any on a second gamble.

The more he labored over the decision the clearer it became that he had to report what he'd learned. Only the narrowest of circumstances could result in negative consequences for him.

With his mind at ease about his decision, he had only to say farewell to his traveling companions. He hated to forego a chance to experience the intimate skills Miss Kerr advertised. He would undoubtedly dream about them, but dabbling would have to wait, as would the disposal of Dawkins and the man who was, in all likelihood, Miss Kerr's father. But there was no hurry; time had always been his ally.

Lancaster paid the tavern keeper and went to bed. The hard riding would commence at dawn.

~*~

Leah and Joel sat at a communal breakfast table. Balfour chose not to sit among strangers and helped himself to an apple and a handful of bread, both of which he stuffed into a cloth bag hanging from his shoulder.

"We'd better eat fast," Leah said, eyeing the rest of the diners at the table, all of whom were male, and none of whom appeared to have missed many meals.

"I would," Joel said, grabbing a pair of hot rolls from a pile on a platter, "but there's not much here I feel comfortable eating."

Leah snatched two apples from a bowl and a hunk of cheese. The latter gave off a questionable odor, and she promptly returned it to the table.

Balfour seemed amused by their reaction to the food, but he didn't comment on it. Whatever happened to his voice box seemed to drive his speech patterns. He avoided long sentences and didn't mince words. Ever. Of course, that was to be expected of an asshole, and he had proven himself more than worthy of the title.

"I'm going to take my leave," he said.

"Pushing on to New York alone?" Joel asked.

He nodded. "I have some... news to deliver."

"I imagine you do," Leah said.

Though he smiled at her, Leah wished he hadn't. She had endured a tiresome conversation with Joel about her efforts to dazzle Balfour with her sexuality. Joel didn't like it. And when she pointed out that she didn't really give a damn, he hadn't taken the news well. Once again, they'd woken up in the same bed, but frowning.

Joel was a decent guy, and aside from her father, was probably the only man in the world who had any hope of understanding her. But that didn't give him the right to monitor the way she acted. Somewhere in the back of her mind she had harbored the idea that once he embraced that concept they could engage in a little make-up sex, and all would be well. But the hard-headed copper just couldn't get past the fact that Leah had no problem using her sexuality to gain her objectives.

What the hell was wrong with him? Just because they were living in the 18th century didn't mean he had to think like someone who'd grown up in that era.

"God speed," Joel said.

Huh?

"Thank you," Balfour said. "I hope you also fare well."

Leah couldn't think of anything that might sound appropriate, so she smiled and nodded her head like the kid who ate white glue in Sunday school when she was a child.

"Nice," Joel said.

She gave him a hand signal which conveyed a timeless message.

That, at least, got him smiling.

"Ready to go?" he asked.

She rose from the table with an apple in each hand. Every male eye at the table focused on her. Leah hefted the fruit as sensually as she could, and the gesture left most of her audience ready to drool. A sidelong glance at Joel confirmed the value of her effort. If he was pissed, she was pleased.

How stupid was that?

"Are you finished?" he asked.

"Yeah."

His "Thank God" was voiced sotto voce, and she followed him from the room. Balfour was not in sight.

"Have you paid for the room?" Joel asked.

"No," she said. "The innkeeper was busy when we came down to eat." She spotted him leaning against a wall in the dining room and tried not to react to his clothing which sported bits of everything that had passed through the kitchen in the previous year. She waved a coin at him, and he quickly covered the open space between them.

"You slept well?" he asked.

She suppressed a shudder at the memory of the bedding and the smell of the room. "It was... lovely."

"Then you'll stay here on your return trip?"

"Oh, absolutely," she said, *when pigs grow propellers.* "But when we return, we won't be traveling with Mr. Balfour."

"Who?"

"Balfour," Joel said. "Anthony Balfour. We came in together."

"I don't know any Balfours," the proprietor said. "But I'd know Anthony Lancaster anywhere. He's stayed here often enough."

She stared at him. "Did you say Lancaster?"

Joel put his hand on her shoulder.

"I most certainly did," the innkeeper said. "Is there a problem?"

"No," Joel said. "No problem at all."

Leah paid for their food and lodging with a coin.

"Thank you," he said. "Real money is scarce these days. I won't take paper anymore."

Still stunned by the revelation about Balfour, Leah mumbled something to the innkeeper as they walked out to saddle their horses. "I can't believe we spent all that time with the man who shot my dad! Do you think we can catch up with him?"

"Why?"

"So I can shoot him."

"Let him do his job, first," Joel said.

"And *then* I can shoot him?"

"We'll see."

"Damn it, Joel, you're no fun!"

~*~

Nearly two weeks had passed since Colonel Lamb marched into Benedict's office complaining about the Great Chain. In the interim, new logs had been secured to float the barrier, but there weren't enough, and the work caused an additional slowdown in fortification repairs. Benedict considered it a reasonable trade, as he had no intention of allowing the chain to be used to block Clinton's ships when they sailed up river.

The smile on his face didn't come as a result of the chain incident. It was a byproduct of his success in reconnecting with an acquaintance from Philadelphia, Joshua Hett Smith. Not only was Smith one of Colonel Sheldon's agents, he was a friend of Beverly Robinson, the loyalist whose home Benedict had commandeered for his private residence while running West Point.

Benedict had sent a few messages to Major Andre', General Clinton's spymaster, using Sheldon's network, but he never knew who was actually carrying the messages until very recently. But now that he had a grasp of the players at his disposal, Peggy could join him for the final stage of his payback to the country which turned its back on him.

"Major Franks," he called to his junior aide. "I have a mission for you."

Franks approached his desk and gave Benedict his full attention.

"I want you to take a detachment into Philadelphia and escort my family here."

"Do you think that's wise, sir?" Franks asked. "There have been rumors of an upcoming battle here in the Highlands. Perhaps it would be wiser--"

Benedict's cold, angry stare muzzled the major. "When I want your advice on what's best for my family, I'll ask for it."

"Of course. How large a detachment shall I take?"

"Ten men should suffice. Use your best judgment in choosing a route. The safety of my wife and son will obviously be your foremost concern."

"We'll leave as soon as the men can be ready," Franks said.

"And Major?"

"Yes sir?"

"Take only regulars with you on this trip, no militia. I won't have that riffraff near my family."

~*~

"Chastity said you wished to talk to me." Colonel Cotswold stood with his hands on his wide hips, rocking back and forth on his heels. Raines had seen the nervous gesture before, but couldn't understand why the man might be hesitant to talk to him. It should have been the other way around.

"Yes sir," Raines said. "Pardon me if I find this... awkward."

"No sense beating about the bush, sir. Have out with it."

"I intend to travel to Philadelphia and make contact with Sam Adams, among others."

"Splendid. I will be happy to give you a letter of introduction."

"Thank you," Raines said. "That would be very helpful."

"I don't suppose you'd care to tell me why you need to speak with Adams."

Actually, no. This probably isn't a good time to

say I've come from the future to call one of the nation's greatest heroes a traitor.

"As much as I'd like to, this isn't the right moment."

Cotswold kept rocking.

"There is something else," Raines said. "I'd like your daughter to accompany me."

"To Philadelphia?"

"Yes sir."

"What on Earth for?"

Here it comes.

"For a couple reasons. First she's taken such good care of me, that I'm hesitant to travel such a great distance without her, in case my wound reopens."

"And the second reason?"

"I believe she would enjoy seeing the biggest city in the New World. If I can make that possible, it may begin to repay her kindness."

What followed was a long, uncomfortable silence during which Cotswold continued to rock, and Raines began to perspire.

Eventually, the Colonel spoke. "If someone my age asked you for permission to take *your* daughter on a long and possibly dangerous journey, what would you say?"

"I suppose I'd want to know all the circumstances. But the question isn't germane. My daughter is older than yours."

"And I'm older than you," Cotswold said. "What's the difference?"

"Leah is quite capable of taking care of herself."

"And that should give me confidence in you?"

Rather than make continued eye contact, Raines inspected the tops of his shoes. "I, uh--"

"I presume you would stay in taverns along the way. Would you sleep in separate rooms?"

"Well, no, for the sake of security--"

"So, you'd share a room?"

"I suppose so, yes."

"Would you share a bed?"

"That might... I mean, I don't think... You see, if we--"

Cotswold crossed his arms on his belly and continued to rock. "I'm sure you can appreciate the awkwardness of traveling as an unmarried couple."

"Indeed," Raines said. Though he never truly believed Cotswold would go along with the trip idea, he felt he had to make the effort.

"What if we all made the trip together?"

"The *four* of us?"

"Five. Don't forget Gabriel."

"I honestly hadn't considered that," Raines said. The round trip could take a month or more. That meant a very great deal of time spent with the Cotswolds. And likely no private time with Chastity.

"On the other hand," the Colonel said, "if you two were married, there would be nothing I could say about it."

Had he talked to Gabriel?

"That would be up to her, of course," Raines said. "It's not something we've discussed. And in any event, I would never mention such an idea to her unless I had your blessing, and that of Mrs. Cotswold, too, of course."

"Of course."

He waited for the Colonel to continue, but suddenly he didn't seem talkative.

"How would you feel about that?" Raines asked.

"About giving you our blessing?"

"Yes."

"I'd have to discuss it with Mrs. Cotswold, but we rarely disagree."

Raines nodded. "I understand. And I realize our age difference may be a problem, but--"

"We're far more concerned with our daughter's security than with the age of her husband. A man of substance is what she needs, first and foremost." Cotswold squinted at him. "You seem to be such a man, even if your background remains a mystery. If you're to be my son-in-law, I should like to know a good deal more about you. I failed to make proper inquiries in that regard when Master Smithers approached me about Chastity. I shan't make that mistake again."

Great. A background check.

"Timing may be a problem," Raines said. "It's imperative that I reach Philadelphia very soon. I have information which could alter the course of the rebellion, but it will be worthless if not delivered on time."

"So a marriage would have to be arranged quickly?"

"Yes," Raines said. "Almost immediately."

Cotswold had stopped rocking during the give and take, but resumed the mannerism with intensity. "I shall have to talk to Nora."

Raines assumed the Colonel had been rattled by his proposal. He'd never heard the man refer to his wife by her first name.

~*~

After several days on the dirt track everyone claimed was a "road," Joel had come to terms with his discomfort. Leah's homegrown pain remedy had continued to provide more relief than the drugs he tried "back" in the 21st century. They were even better than the whiskey he'd become accustomed to at the Small Arms. He wondered if his old mates wondered what had become of him. But, of course, he knew. Murchesson had taken care of that.

Not that it mattered anymore. He'd never be bothered with the pitfalls of his old existence. His days were now consumed with a different kind of monotony--the endless ride to Haverstraw and an encounter with Joshua Hett Smith, man of mystery and Tory to the stars.

"What're we gonna tell him when we get there?" Leah asked for what must have been the tenth time that day.

"How 'bout, 'We're poor little lambs who've lost our way?'"

"Bah."

"Cute."

"Seriously, have you thought of anything?"

"Tell me again," he said, "what do we know about this chap?"

"Bits and pieces, mostly. His father was a well-respected judge, and the British offered to make him the chief justice of the province. That was back in, hell, I don't remember exactly, but it was well before the revolution started. Anyway, he said no, which pleased the people intent on breaking away from England. But the loyalists never trusted him after that. *His* son, William junior, took the job instead."

"William Smith junior was Joshua's Smith's brother?"

"He *is* Joshua Smith's brother. It's 1780, remember?"

"Right. And he's a judge."

Leah nodded. "And for what it's worth Joshua is a lawyer."

"Swell. And they're both Tories?"

"Yes, but we need to focus on Joshua, because based on my research, he's playing both sides for his own advantage."

"Imagine that--a lawyer working angles."

Joel let his mind wander as they continued riding. He'd hoped to find some sort of mental zone where he could stash his discomfort and anxiety. Sadly, that hadn't happened yet, although the ponderous gait of his horse, combined with a bit of daydreaming about Leah, came close.

"Joel?"

"Hm?

"You drifted off."

"Sorry. I was thinking--" *About you, actually.* He shook his head to clear it. "What do we really need from Smith?"

"His house. We know he's passing messages from Arnold to the British, and we know his house is

313

conveniently located away from both armies. And that's where we want to be--in the thick of things."

"So, how do we make him think he needs us? How do we make it worth his while?"

"I wish I knew," Leah said. "But none of the work I've done to prepare for this addressed that. I was relying on--" she twisted her mouth "--instinct, I suppose."

"What if we keep using the 'secret weapon' angle? We claim that Arnold isn't really switching sides. His real intent is to draw the British fleet into a trap where he can use the secret weapon on them."

"What's in it for Smith?"

"He can be a hero by stopping Arnold. If Balfour--I mean, Lancaster--bought the idea, why wouldn't Smith? Of course, if Lancaster gets the message through, we may not have to do anything. The Brits will simply blow Arnold out of the water."

Joel paused. He wasn't happy about the possibility that Arnold and the men rowing his boat might be killed. He felt especially guilty about the men.

Leah responded as if she'd read his mind, "It is a war, after all. There are casualties. It's not murder."

"I hope you're right," he said.

They rode on in silence for some time until Leah announced the need for a break. They hobbled their horses near a stream and after walking around to stretch their sore limbs, sat down for a bite of lunch. While Leah unpacked their apples, cheese, and hard bread, Joel walked a short distance upstream to fetch water. As he knelt to fill their cups, he heard voices and hurried back to investigate.

Three armed men stood over Leah. Joel smelled them almost before he saw them, but his arrival, once they determined he was unarmed, had little effect. "What can we do for you?" he asked.

"What are *you* doin' in these parts?" asked the senior member of the trio, none of whom appeared less than forty. All were lean, weathered, and in need of new clothing. Joel guessed they had done most of the patching themselves. They seemed more interested in Joel and Leah's attire than in the travelers themselves.

"We're just passing through," Leah said, still holding an apple from the tavern and a knife Gabriel had given them.

"From where to where?"

"What business is it of yours?" Joel asked, stepping toward them.

All three turned to face him. "Unless you're on the King's business, whatever mischief you have in mind ends today."

~*~

Excerpt from the *Trenton Tattler*:

Father Of Accused Assassin Obsessed With Time Travel

Long Island, New York, Tue., June 12, 2012-- A friend of Dr. Raines Kerr, father of the woman sought in the murder of Queen Elizabeth II, claims the physicist holds some unorthodox views, but none are political.

Abelard Greeley, PhD, a physics professor at King's College said Monday he's known Kerr since college days. "The last time I saw him, we talked about his favorite topic: time travel. He's obsessed by it. I warned him that if he didn't muzzle himself, such talk would ruin his career."

Greeley introduced Kerr to Elisabeth LeCroix, an exchange student from French Colonial Africa. "They had absolutely nothing in common. Beth was dark-skinned, of course, and athletic. Raines was big, but bookish. She studied social science, not physics. Yet, they married within a year."

Greeley was interviewed as part of the inquiry into the Queen's murder. Sources report very little progress.

When asked about their last conversation, Greeley said, "We argued. Raines claimed the physical world would adapt to changes made in a revisited past, and do it in such a way that few would realize it. History would conform to what he called a 'new reality.' But of course, time travel is impossible, so his theory is pure rubbish. I told him so."

Chapter Seventeen

"When I was younger, I could remember anything,
whether it had happened or not."
--Mark Twain

"Of course I'll marry you!" Chastity exclaimed as she wrapped her arms around Raines and sent a thousand-volt spike of agony through his shoulder and into his brain.

He managed to hug her back and hoped she wouldn't notice how tightly he had clenched his jaws waiting for the jolt to subside. Eventually he managed to speak. "I don't even have a wedding ring for you yet. But I promise I'll find one."

"I know someone who can help you with that," the Colonel said from across the room. He and Mrs. Cotswold had asked that they be allowed to view his proposal to their daughter. "Fellow named Revere. A good man and loyal to the cause."

Raines smiled his thanks, wondering if Leah knew anything about him.

"I know this is sudden," Raines said, "but I'd rather we didn't wait. I'd like to take you to Philadelphia for our honeymoon."

"But you'll wed right here," the Colonel said.

Raines mused that if Mrs. Cotswold smiled any wider she might hurt herself. "We already sent Gabriel to fetch the minister," she said.

"Oh, Mother," Chastity cried, "what shall I wear?"

"I'm sure we can find something," Mrs. Cotswold said. "We'd best begin packing your things now, before the preacher arrives."

Raines, occupying center stage, felt distinctly unemployed. The Colonel came to his rescue with the remains of his rum.

"You didn't leave much," he said.

"I promise to replace it."

The Colonel grinned. "And I'll hold you to that pledge." He poured two stiff shots in pewter cups Raines had not seen before.

"Bottoms up!"

Raines couldn't keep his imagination from running wild, right up until he recalled that Leah knew nothing about his whirlwind affair.

"What's the matter?" asked the Colonel.

"I was just thinking about my daughter. I've got to get word to her."

"All in good time, sir. All in good time."

He closed his eyes in a brief prayer to his long lost Beth. *I hope you don't mind, love.*

"Looks like we've got enough for one more round," the Colonel said.

Raines held out his cup. "Why not?"

"Indeed. I'd rather share it with you than the preacher. And he'll be here soon."

"Really?"

"Unless he's off burying someone."

They both chuckled at the Colonel's dark humor and finished the rum. "There's something important I need your help with," Raines told his future father-in-law. "It can wait until after the ceremony, but once we're on our way to Philadelphia, I'd like you and Gabriel to get started."

"What would you have us do?"

"I've written instructions. It's not difficult, but it's going to be time-consuming."

"It sounds mysterious," the Colonel said.

Raines chuckled. "Gabriel said that, too."

~*~

The loyalist militiaman nearest Leah pushed her to the ground with his foot. She went limp. Joel saw a look on her face he might have interpreted as fear, which is the way the man standing over her took it. Joel, however, knew better.

"I wouldn't do that if I were you," he warned.

"Shut up and bring us the saddlebags," the trio's leader said. "Then take off your clothes."

Joel squinted at him. "I don't think so."

"You can keep anything that doesn't fit us."

"How thoughtful."

The third member of the trio, a man whose shoes were so badly worn he would have done better without them, raised his musket and pulled back the hammer. Joel found that to be a convincing argument and turned away to retrieve their gear.

He untied the bags from his own saddle first, then moved on to get Leah's.

Which side held Murchesson's gun?

But he knew something was wrong the moment he felt the second set of leather pouches. Slipping his hand inside he felt for the cold steel grip of the pistol. What he found instead was a plastic object somewhat larger than a cigarette packet. Unable to investigate further, he had no idea what it was. What in God's name had she done? He walked even slower as he approached the men then stopped, looked up at the sky, and screamed, "Damn it, Leah!"

While the three men stared at him, Leah attacked. She moved so suddenly Joel had no time to react, nor did the three men.

She lashed out with her knife and sliced deeply into the inside of one man's thigh, then jammed her blade into the leader's groin. Both men went down in a tangle of muskets, groans, and squirting blood.

The third man raised his gun over his head to club Leah, but Joel knocked him to the ground before he could strike. While the two struggled for the weapon, Leah stabbed the loyalist's neck, rolling to one side to avoid arterial spray.

"Watch out!" she screamed as the first man she'd attacked swung his flintlock toward Joel, its bore black and cavernous.

There was nowhere to go.

Aw shit!

The loyalist grinned. At such close range, he

didn't need to aim. Still amused, he slowly squeezed the trigger.

The hammer smashed down and produced a spray of hot red sparks.

Something sizzled, and a wisp of thin gray smoke drifted from the powder pan which must have been all but emptied in the brawl.

The look on the loyalist's face shifted from taunting to terrified. Joel clubbed him in the forehead with the butt of the musket he'd just claimed, leaving the militiaman unconscious while his severed femoral artery spilled his life into the dirt.

Leah pushed the remaining weapons away from the reach of the patrol's leader who had curled into a ball and was trying to staunch his bleeding crotch with both hands.

"What'll we do with him?" Joel asked.

Leah shrugged. "It's not like we can take prisoners."

"But we can't leave him like that."

"Why not? Once he'd helped himself to our stuff, do you think he'd care if we survived or not?"

He knew she was right.

"This is war, Joel."

"I know that, damn it. I've played the game before. I just didn't ever want to play it again."

Making matters worse, the man on the ground moaned, his face contorted.

Joel looked at the other two men lying dead on the ground. Leah had yet to react, but he knew that would come soon enough.

"Joel!" she cried.

The wounded loyalist had pulled a knife from his boot. Though weak, he could still attack.

"Shit," Joel muttered as he cocked the musket and shot the man in the head. He could barely see the body crumple for all the smoke.

Leah scrambled to her feet and rushed to Joel's side. The trembling began almost immediately. "I-- I've never ki-- I've never done anything like that before."

"I know," he said. "It sucks. And what's worse, I used to be on *their* side."

As the smoke cleared he worried about other loyalists nearby. The sound of gunfire could carry a long way. "We need to get moving," he said.

Leah groaned, "I'm covered in blood."

"I see that, but are you hurt?"

She shook her head, no. "But I'm a mess. I can't be seen this way. The questions...."

"We'll take care of it, I promise," he said. "Grab our gear while I do something with these three. Once we've put a little distance between us and them we can stop and clean up. Right now we've got to get away from here."

Leah's movements, so quick and sure only moments ago, had become labored and deliberate. Her hands shook and tears streamed down her face. He'd seen the reaction before, and not just in a mirror.

Some remorse is good; too much can paralyze.

He wanted to hold and comfort her, but there wasn't time. Not here, and not now. But soon.

She brought the horses and stood nearby while he piled brush over the dead bodies. When finished he gave her a quick hug and helped her into the saddle. He followed suit, and they kicked their horses into a run, something the two novice riders had done only rarely before.

If he hadn't just killed a man, Joel might have been exhilarated by the ride. Instead, all he could think about was getting as far away as possible--just like any other murderer.

~*~

"My God, man," said Colonel Varick as the courier stepped into General Benedict's West Point headquarters, "did you swim across the Hudson?"

"No, sir," the man said. "I came from the west, from Pennsylvania."

Benedict lurched up from behind his desk, knocking maps and other documents to the floor. "From Philadelphia?"

"Yes, sir. I have private correspondence for you, and some dispatches from the Continental Congress."

"I'll take the letter," Benedict said, nodding at Varick. "Give the rest to him."

"See that this man is fed and cared for, Colonel. His horse, too. If he needs clothing or anything else, provide it. I don't care how."

"Thank you, General!" the courier said.

But Benedict's mind was locked on the letter in his hand. Not only was he oblivious of the courier, his senses had dulled to the stormy weather outside. Not even when hail the size of musket balls crashed down on the roof, did he look up from the envelope in his hand. He tore off the wax seal and unfolded the note inside. Just seeing Peggy's handwriting made his heart race. How he missed her!

"General, if I may--"

"What is it, Varick?" Benedict bellowed, "Can't you see I'm busy?"

"Of course, sir. My apologies. We'll talk later."

Benedict waved him away and returned to the letter. It was dated a month earlier, and he paused only long enough to curse the inevitable delays in deliveries. He then read through the missive at breakneck speed, soaking in Peggy's endearments. But all along he knew it contained something far more important--a coded message from Major Andre, General Clinton's spy chief.

Benedict looked up to see Varick in conversation with the courier. They chatted while looking through a window at the storm. The hail had stopped, replaced by sheets of hard, slanting rain. Lightning flashed while thunder rattled the building.

"Did you not hear me?" Benedict groused. "Get that man some food. Now!"

Hurriedly donning his hat and cape, Varick led the courier back outside and hustled him toward the mess.

Finally, Benedict was alone and free to decipher the secret message.

The work went slowly, but easily, as he'd done it often before. Peggy's words blended with those of his British conspirators into a message of profit and joy. General Clinton had agreed to virtually everything! If West Point fell as promised, and the British captured the three thousand men stationed thereabout, along with artillery and supplies, Benedict would earn twenty thousand pounds sterling, exactly what he'd asked for. And in the event the attack yielded somewhat less, Clinton assured him that his compensation would be just and fair.

Benedict could barely restrain himself. After more than a year of secrecy and deceit, his efforts were about to yield a most bountiful reward--a fortune in cash to either roll in or roll over into business ventures beyond anything he'd ever imagined.

The only disturbing element was Clinton's insistence that he meet with the General's representative prior to the attack to finalize details. How was he supposed to manage that, when he had no way to communicate with him directly?

~*~

Anthony Lancaster rolled into New York City in what was, for him, record time. But since his journey resulted from a chance encounter, he wasn't fully prepared for the costs involved. Surely Major Andre', who headed General Clinton's spy ring, would see that he was reimbursed for his expenses. Unfortunately, he had yet to connect with the major, and his prospects for doing so immediately didn't look good.

Lancaster found accommodations he could afford in a rough part of the city. The boarding house was run by a widow, Maude Grint, whose monumental size and poisonous disposition precluded any activity he might have deemed enjoyable. Smoking, gaming, and drinking were strictly forbidden by her edict. He assumed smiling, laughing, and having a good time were likewise frowned upon.

On the other hand, Madam Grint provided edible food and a room he wouldn't have to share. Until Major Andre' saw fit to cover his expenses, Grint House would be his house.

After his initial failure to meet with Andre', Lancaster treated himself to a day of recuperation. The September 11th deadline was still two weeks away, so he felt no urgency. Instead, he experienced a growing sense of uneasiness about his failure to secure any real details about the rebel's new weapon, whatever it was.

Hence, the rub. It had no name, nor could he describe what it could do. He had mentally reviewed his encounter with Kerr and Dawkins, searching for details, but in the end, he had to admit, details simply didn't exist.

He felt all but certain they had fed him false information. But why? What could they possibly have gained by it?

Perhaps Andre' knew. Lancaster certainly didn't.

On the third day following his arrival in New York City, Lancaster breached the inner sanctum of General Clinton's headquarters. A man dressed in a uniform rich with the red and white of the Royal Army waved him to a chair in the antechamber of several busy offices. Lancaster could not determine the man's rank but assumed he had to be an officer since the crown would never leave anything as important as spy craft to a commoner.

"Major Andre' is away on... business," the man said.

"I need to speak with him, Captain."

"Don't we all?" He gave Lancaster a disdainful look. "And I'm not an officer, I'm a sergeant-major."

Lancaster scowled back at him, but the man acted as if he hadn't noticed.

"I have information the Major will find of the utmost interest."

The sergeant nodded. "I will be happy to pass that along to him when he returns."

"When will that be?"

"Very soon, I'm sure. Now then, about this information...."

"I'd rather not share it with anyone else," Lancaster said.

I didn't ride my ass off just to speak with a lackey.

"I understand," the soldier said. "But I can't tell you when the Major will be available. He's very busy."

"So am I, damn it! And I've accrued hideous debt just to deliver this bit of news."

"I'm sure we can advance you some cash for your trouble," the sergeant said, "but you'll have to share *something* with me, or I'll have no reason to authorize a payment."

Sheer madness!

"How do I know I can trust you?" Lancaster demanded.

"Obviously, you can't. But what choice do you

have? There's no one else here. Either you give the information to me, and I pass it along, or you leave." He spread a sheet of paper on his desk and dipped his quill into an inkwell. With his pen poised to record Lancaster's remarks, he nodded for the spy to begin.

"I can't believe I'm doing this," Lancaster said.

"So says *every* virgin," quipped the soldier.

"I met with two agents outside of Boston who claimed to have information about a new type of weapon the rebels will obtain from the French."

The man wrote furiously for a short while then looked up at him. "Can you describe this weapon?"

"No," Lancaster said. "The French built it, but Benjamin Franklin designed it."

After still more pen scratching, the soldier bid Lancaster to continue.

"It's small enough to fit in a longboat."

The man nodded and added another note.

"And it's designed to sink ships--anything that floats."

The redcoat looked up at Lancaster. "How, exactly?"

"I don't know."

He put his pen down and leaned back in his chair.

"You don't believe me," Lancaster said.

"It doesn't matter whether or not I believe you. What matters is that you give me information we can act upon."

Lancaster waved his hat at the room. "Then

act upon this: it will be installed in the Hudson River on September 11th."

"Anywhere in particular?"

"Near King's Ferry, I believe."

"Why there?"

Lancaster stared at him. "Because it's logical! The rebels don't want the British to sail up the Hudson to West Point."

"I see," the soldier said. "And where did you say you got this information?"

"From a reliable source."

"Does this reliable source have a name?"

"Of course she has a bloody name! Everyone has a name. You have one. I have one. What difference does it make?"

The sergeant calmly rested his pen on a blotter. "Sometimes, Major Andre' likes to verify information from different sources before he takes action."

Lancaster slapped his palm on the soldier's desk. "Listen to me! The weapon will be on a boat, in the river, on September the eleventh. Just see that someone sinks the damned thing. How difficult is that?"

Utterly nonplussed, the soldier made an additional note, then looked up into Lancaster's eyes. "Is there anything else?"

"Money," he said. "I'm nearly destitute."

Smirking, the soldier reached into a bottom drawer of his desk and withdrew a ledger and a strongbox. He opened the latter and counted out forty shillings, in coin, which he stacked on the desk and pushed toward Lancaster. He then made a note in the ledger and returned both book and box to the drawer.

"What's that?" the spy asked.

"Two guineas. That's all I'm allowed to pay," the soldier said. "Unless Major Andre' authorizes more."

"And he's away on business."

"Indeed." The sergeant cracked his knuckles. "Unless you'd accept payment in Continentals." He pointed at a pair of wooden chests stacked against a wall. "They're both full; help yourself. The lads back home have been printing them as fast as the rebels. The idiots can't tell ours from theirs."

Lancaster scooped the coins from the desk and put them in a pouch inside his waist coat. "Keep the paper money," he said. "No one wants it."

"Suit yourself."

Lancaster shook his head in disgust. "You know, we're going to lose this stupid war."

~*~

The Cotswolds insisted on traveling with Raines and his new bride to the "Ox and Sparrow," a tavern on the Lower Post Road where they would catch the stage wagon to Providence, the first leg of their journey to Philadelphia.

"I can't believe you've never taken a coach ride," Chastity said.

Raines tried to phrase his answer so that it wasn't technically a lie. "I haven't traveled much." But he still wasn't quite sure what to expect.

His plan had been to take a letter of

introduction from Colonel Cotswold to Samuel Adams. Once he made contact, he could alert the statesman about Benedict Arnold's impending treason. He hoped to make other contacts as well.

He and Leah had discussed the option when planning their mission, but discarded it thinking they would go to West Point together to disrupt Arnold's plans. Lancaster's bullet changed all that. Raines maintained hope that Leah and Joel could do the job without him, but he hated the idea of not taking direct action himself.

"The stage wagons are amazingly fast," Chastity said. "They simply fly down the road. Mum says they have to change horses every ten miles or so. The poor beasts get tired so quickly."

"I suspect I would tire quickly, too, if I had to gallop all that way."

"Good Lord," the Colonel interjected. "No one could expect a team to gallop such a distance. They trot. The pace isn't quite as frantic as she would have you believe. After all, this is her first trip, too."

It seemed as if Chastity hadn't let go of Raines' good arm since the wedding, a novelty he enjoyed, though it proved a bit cumbersome.

When the coach arrived, Raines paid their fare to Providence with two phony Spanish dollars, which the driver gleefully accepted. He even helped them into the vehicle and ordered two passengers already seated to exchange places so the newlyweds could have seats with back support. After some grumbling and the exchange of dark looks, everyone settled in. With a crack of a whip they were off.

The Colonel had assured him they would

arrive in Providence the same day despite a distance of over fifty miles, but Raines had no real idea what the trip would be like. He quickly found out.

The stage wagon had no springs, and the road had no smooth surfaces. The padding on the seats had been packed down from the weight of countless riders, and the vehicle tossed the occupants around like gravel in a tin. By the time they reached their first stop, Raines was quite willing to surrender the colonies to British rule forever if only he could be spared another moment in the "coach."

Chastity pointed out that it could have been much worse, due to the rain. If Raines hadn't been willing to pay extra for "inside" seats, they'd likely have drowned sitting atop the bone rattling death wagon. Despite the discomforts, she retained her enthusiasm and convinced Raines to keep going.

Fortunately, they made several stops en route to Providence, and the passengers were welcome to do whatever they pleased to prepare themselves to continue. Raines contemplated the profit potential of providing massage therapy at each intermediate point, but his fellow travelers seemed better suited to the rigors of travel. Their complaints were muted compared to his, a point Chastity made more than once, to his chagrin.

Eventually, however, they reached their first overnight destination. The midday meal they'd taken along the way had been overpriced and undercooked, but the physicist ate it anyway, just like everyone else. Somehow, it stayed down, for which he offered abundant thanks.

Much in need of a nightcap, Raines took his

bride into the taproom of the inn where they would bed down. The innkeeper frowned at him, looked hard at Chastity, and motioned toward another room. Raines didn't understand and told the man so.

"Ladies usually stay in the parlor," he said. "We have rough sorts in here from time to time, and I can't always be here to see that female guests are not offended."

"I'll take care of that," Raines said. "We've only just been married, and we don't wish to be separated."

The barman muttered something as he turned away, and the bride and groom took seats at the only empty table. The room smelled of tobacco, but it wasn't overpowering. The innkeeper brought them rum and left them alone. Chastity, Raines saw, had no trouble consuming the demon beverage.

"I'm hardly new to it," she said. "Papa's kept rum in the house for years. He says it's for special occasions."

"Like Christmas?"

"More like: It's Tuesday. Let's celebrate!"

They were well into their second round when the man who'd driven the stage wagon asked if he could join them. Raines waved him to a seat hoping he wouldn't stay long. The man ordered beer, two mugs at a time, and downed the first before he said another word.

"Did I hear you say you were going all the way to Philadelphia?"

"That's our plan," Raines said, not nearly drunk enough to say more.

"Unfortunately," the driver continued, "you

may have trouble in New York. There are loyalists everywhere, and they often stop coaches to question travelers. There have been incidents."

"What kinds of incidents?" Chastity asked.

"Avoid politics in the company of Tories," he said. "I've heard of arrests for no reason at all."

Raines took a sip of his rum. It wasn't nearly as good as the stuff the Colonel shared with him before the wedding. "So, we should just smile, and nod, and praise King George?"

"You don't have to like it," the driver said. "But it's better than spending the night in a redcoat jail." He tilted his head toward Chastity. "You have a very pretty passenger in this one. You don't want to do anything that'll cause her distress."

Raines had been reconsidering his decision to travel to Philadelphia ever since the wheels of the stage wagon began to turn. He had even more reason to doubt the wisdom of his decision now.

~*~

Treason, Treason!

Excerpt from the *Savannah Sentinel*:

Government Spokesman On Port Closure: No Comment

Savannah, Georgia, Thurs., June 14, 2012--Royal Army personnel arrived shortly before dawn Wednesday and closed the Port of Savannah to non-military traffic. The closure caught commercial shippers by surprise.

In a brief press conference, Clive Clarke-Mitchell, a spokesman for the Port Authority, said: "The Port of Savannah is one of the largest shipping terminals in all of New England, and disruptions here will be felt far beyond the borders of the province."

Neither the Royal Army nor anyone in the national government has commented on the mysterious activity at the port.

Chapter Eighteen

"To love someone deeply gives you strength.
Being loved by someone deeply gives you courage."
--Lao Tzu

Benedict's first attempt to respond to General Clinton came in the guise of a Continental soldier named William Heron who asked that he be allowed to travel to New York City on personal business. To the evident dismay of Lieutenant Colonel Varick, Benedict granted the request, with the provision that Heron deliver a note to an associate of Benedict's, "John Anderson," the code name for Clinton's spy chief, John Andre'.

A full week had passed since then, but Benedict heard nothing and assumed his message had gone astray. While disappointing, it wasn't terribly unusual. Besides, he had been able to connect with one of Colonel Sheldon's spies who had agreed to ferry a message for him. That message was virtually identical to the one he'd sent by way of Heron and was carried by a woman named Mary

McCarthy, a refugee from Quebec. When she arrived in New York, she was accompanied by a 9-man squad of uniformed Continentals.

There was no doubt in Benedict's mind that his second message had gotten through. He was musing on the situation when Varick burst into their shared offices with a message from General Washington. Breathless, he turned the dispatch over to his commander and waited while Benedict read the document, then passed it back.

Varick read the most relevant passage out loud: "There will be an attack on the main army or an attempt on the post in the Highlands. I wish you therefore to put the latter in the most defensible state which is possible."

"We aren't ready, General," Varick said. "Not by any means."

"Nonsense," Benedict replied. "Things are by no means bleak." To be completely truthful, he would have had to add the words, "for you." But he wasn't fool enough to make that kind of mistake.

~*~

Leah and Joel rode their horses hard until they felt certain they'd put enough distance between themselves and the dead loyalist militiamen. They were several miles west of Bridgeport, Connecticut, when they found a stream crossing the cart path they'd been following since they left the Post Road.

Joel went first, tracking the waterway for a while until the stream appeared both deeper and wider. There he stopped and helped Leah down from her horse. She held onto him longer than usual.

"Are you all right?" he asked.

"I will be. Just now, I need to get my mind off what happened with those men--with what I did."

"I understand."

She undressed quickly then and waded into the cold water with her blood-stained clothing in hand. Joel smiled at her from his perch atop a boulder. He acted as if he'd been appointed to make her feel better.

"You're just going to sit there and watch me?" she asked.

"Well, yes. The view is... breathtaking."

She splashed water at him, but it barely reached the toes of his boots.

"You look a bit cold," he said.

"Really, how could you possibly tell?"

"Because your nipples look like test tubes and you're shaking like a Chihuahua on an iceberg."

"What a gent you are. C'mon! Give me a hand. I'm freezing. Besides, the last time I was downwind of you, it was obvious you need a bath, too."

He relented, stripped, and waded slowly into the water with his clothes in his arms.

"I thought you were going to help *me!*"

"How would it look if we walked into a tavern and only one of us was completely wet? If we're going to be miserable, we should do it together."

She kissed him on the cheek. "Just don't get any ideas."

"In this water?" He glanced below his waist and laughed. "You've nothing to worry about."

They each scrubbed their own clothes, but

Leah's bore the heaviest stains. Working together they got the worst of them out, although her white shirt and light brown breeches both had a pinkish tint they couldn't eliminate.

After a final rinse, they scrambled up the rocky bank, shivering. The sun would set before long, and they had nothing with which to dry off.

"I'd rather not drop in at a way station dressed like this," he said.

Leah's teeth chattered too intensely for her to answer clearly. "Fire" was the only word she could articulate.

Joel took the hint and soon had a small blaze going. Leah stood beside it, still shivering, while he went in search of branches on which to hang their wet clothes.

Once they'd arranged their laundry to dry, Joel put his arm around her and they both huddled by the flames. At some point her teeth stopped clattering, and he asked her the question she'd been expecting since their encounter with the loyalist militiamen earlier in the day.

"What did you do with Murchesson's gun?"

"I gave it to my father," she said.

Joel remained silent for a long while, then said, "You might have mentioned it. I was planning to use it on the three charmers we ran into earlier."

"I thought so. That's why I attacked them when I did."

"I should have known."

She put her hand on his arm, but when he still didn't look at her, she reached for his cheek with her palm and turned his face toward hers. "I'm sorry. It was stupid of me. I should have said something. But I just couldn't leave Dad without some sort of weapon."

"Oh, I get it. I do. You were worried about ol' Raines stuck there just outside of Boston, hundreds of miles from the nearest redcoat. And we mustn't forget Chastity, lurking in the dark, ready to jump on him at any moment."

"You don't know Dad like I do," she said.

"Granted."

"I have no doubt he'll cook up something to be of help."

"Bully for him," Joel said.

"It's just that he's not terribly well prepared to live in this era."

"And *we are?*" That set him to chuckling, but it didn't last long. "You know what? It doesn't matter. If I had Murchesson's gun, I'd probably just kill some more people, and I'm having enough trouble getting over the one I murdered today."

"It *wasn't* murder. Not at all."

"Well, that certainly makes me feel better." He crossed his arms to rub his shoulders. With the sun down, the temperature dropped. "What else is in the saddlebag? I didn't have time to look at it when I went after the gun."

"It's just one of the odds and ends I brought along. Definitely not a weapon. It wouldn't have been of any use against the loyalists. She hugged herself and looked away. "Can we talk about something else? Or better still, about nothing at all?"

"Yeah, sure." He put his arm back around her shoulders and pressed her close. "Just so you know, I really like the way you feel when you're naked."

"Oh? Then, how 'bout this?" She put her head on his shoulder, careful to let her long, wet hair drip down his arms and chest.

"Tell me one thing," he said, wiping away the frigid runoff, "does your *Dad* know he has the gun?"

"Absolutely," she said.

"And can he manage it with one hand?"

"You think he'd do better with a musket?"

Joel conceded the point. Sometime later he asked, "Do you want to just camp out here for the night? It might be easier than packing everything up and wandering around in the dark for hours."

She looked around and decided *everything* didn't amount to much. "Fine," she said, "But on one condition. You must promise to keep me warm."

"*All* night?"

"Of course."

He sighed. "Slave driver."

~*~

Raines and Chastity were both exhausted by the time they settled into bed. Raines wondered if he even had the strength to make love to his new bride, but she curled up next to him and went to sleep before it became an issue.

In the dark, with Chastity snuggled warm and close, he felt much as he had years before with Beth. He felt a growing sense of guilt, as if he'd betrayed them both merely by thinking of the other, a dilemma from which he'd never escape. It seemed only fitting that past and future had managed to get all mixed up, again.

Eventually he drifted off and dreamed about a graduation ceremony at which Leah received her PhD in history. Beth handed her the diploma, but it was Chastity who shook Leah's hand.

The next morning they got an early start on the next leg of the journey. There would be a total of five legs to reach the halfway point--New York--if the weather didn't turn too ugly. Road conditions along the coast were alleged to be better than those inland. Raines decided that wouldn't take much.

He purchased two feather pillows from the inn so they'd have at least some cushioning as they rattled on through Rhode Island and Connecticut. And after thinking about his chat with the driver, he shifted the gun Leah had given him from their trunk to a valise which he kept at his side. It also held a magazine he'd brought from his office at Millburn and some other materials he thought might come in handy. He'd left a larger selection of such papers in Boston with instructions for Gabriel and the Colonel.

For the next few days he would concentrate on his approach to Sam Adams, to regaining some use of his damaged arm, and to keeping his new wife happy--three very tall, and very general, orders.

~*~

Joshua Hett Smith arrived at Benedict's headquarters office on September 9th, in the company of two armed guards from Colonel Sheldon's command. Smith was clearly peeved by their insistence that he stay within arm's reach while inside the fortifications.

"Colonel Sheldon sends his regards," said a soldier wearing a stripe of green cloth on his right shoulder denoting his rank.

"Please thank him for me, Corporal," Benedict said. "You may stand down. Get something to eat while I have a chat with Mister Smith."

"Begging the General's pardon, but Colonel Sheldon ordered us to keep him in sight," the corporal said.

Though tempted to shout at him, Benedict chose a softer approach. "I think I can manage that. We'll only need a few minutes anyway. If you're not hungry, then go outside and light a pipe. Colonel Varick has tobacco if you need some."

Both the corporal and the private who accompanied him appeared pleased by his suggestion and were quick to take their leave.

Benedict addressed his visitor in a low voice. "Have something for me?"

Smith gave him a conspiratorial smile. "I have a letter addressed to 'Mr. G.' Do you know anyone by that name?"

Benedict snatched the envelope from his hand and then looked to see if Varick was watching. Fortunately, he was engrossed in paperwork. Benedict had come up with an endless array of things for him to requisition from Congress, though both men knew very little would ever be supplied.

With Varick thus occupied, Benedict opened the letter and read the contents. Cast as a business proposal, it simply stated that at noon on September 11, Mister John Anderson would be available on the

British side of Dobb's Ferry to meet with Mister Gustavus, both oft-used code names.

The letter further stated, "Should I not be able to go, the officer who is to command the escort, between whom and myself no distinction need be made, can speak on the affair."

This tortured phrase merely meant that Andre' could not attend the meeting in civilian attire since if caught by the Americans, he would be treated as a spy. He would therefore bring someone else along pretending to be the fictitious Mister Anderson, so that Andre' could attend the meeting in uniform.

The proposal sent a chill through Benedict's blood. The meeting was only two days away! But how could he possibly attend? If he went dressed in the buff and blue of a Continental, he'd be arrested on the spot. And if he went dressed as a civilian, he could be treated as a spy himself.

What was Andre' thinking?

He immediately wrote a response suggesting they meet at Colonel Sheldon's headquarters and promising that "Mr. Anderson's" safety would be absolutely guaranteed. He signed the letter "Gustavus" with a flourish, sealed it, and gave it to Smith.

"It's imperative that this is delivered overnight. I cannot stress the urgency enough."

Smith looked doubtful in the extreme, and Benedict knew why. It had taken six days for Andre's letter to reach West Point--*with a military escort*. Reducing that timeframe to a single day, or even two, was unimaginable.

"It can't be done," Smith said.

"Then at least get it in British hands."

Smith agreed. Yet, Benedict had no choice but to attend the meeting on the 11th.

~*~

Anthony Lancaster paid Mrs. Grint for three additional nights lodging. He could have relocated to more agreeable quarters, but that would have cost more, and he had to save something for his return trip to Massachusetts if, as seemed probable, he would be unable to secure additional funds from Major Andre'. Indeed, just meeting with the spy master grew more unlikely every day.

He took a long walk to escape the squalor of Mrs. Grint's neighborhood and eventually made his way to the tip of Manhattan from which he could see sails on both the Hudson and the East rivers. What interested him the most, however, was the arrival of a great number of ships, all flying the British flag.

Over a dozen heavy warships dotted the harbor, while many smaller ones floated in-between.

The vessels seemed in no hurry to dock, which he realized was the heart of the problem. Including the commercial vessels, there were just too many to be given wharf space all at once. The sight of so many ships called to mind the warnings he'd carried from Kerr and Dawkins. How many of these same ships would soon be sailing north, up the Hudson, to a rendezvous with a secret weapon that could destroy them?

A nearby tavern caught his attention when

the door was thrust open by two sailors and a female practitioner of commercial affection. The three of them cackled and screeched like seagulls as they headed for a dark and secluded alleyway.

Lancaster shook his head in disgust. Sensible men waited 'til later in the day, but no one ever said sailors were sensible men. Besides, if those poor bastards were fated to cruise up the Hudson and die tomorrow, who was he to deny them some creature comforts today?

He had already done what he could in service to King and country. It was time for a drink. Without another thought, he entered the tavern and made himself comfortable.

~*~

Despite his earlier misgivings, Joel had finally reached a point where the thought of climbing aboard his horse and spending a day in the saddle no longer intimidated him. He hardly considered himself a skilled horseman, nor did Leah, but the prospect of riding was no longer a source of concern for either of them.

The only problem he still had was dealing with his bad leg. Mounting proved cumbersome and dismounting painful. Anything in between he handled with relative ease.

Since their encounter with the loyalist militiamen, they had avoided further trouble. Between Leah's map and his compass skills, rusty though they were, he got them to Dobb's Ferry. There they passed themselves off as "foreigners"--

and simple ones at that--owing largely to Leah's skill at speaking a form of Pig Latin she learned from a Swedish nanny after her mother died.

Leah had used it on Joel several times leaving him mystified by what she said. The technique involved inserting the letters "A" and "G" after vowels in English words; both letters were given a hard pronunciation.

She maintained a few other "grammatical" rules, but the basics were simple, and to the untrained ear, the result was undecipherable. "How are you," for instance, came out: "Hay-gow ay-gar yay-goo." Longer words sounded almost painful-- "honeymoon" became "hay-go-nay-gee-may-goon." But when it flowed, as fast and seamless as it did from Leah's lips, it passed for a genuine foreign tongue.

Though she urged him to practice so that they might share a secret language, he found the concept childish and made only a half-hearted attempt to learn it. But at the ferry crossing, she'd left both American and British troops scratching their heads over her rapid fire yet incomprehensible commentary. After that, he vowed to knuckle down and become proficient.

Once they reached the east side of the Hudson, passed safely through the British checkpoint, and traveled up river a short distance, Leah called a halt. She pointed at the crossing they'd just made. "That's where it'll happen. Benedict Arnold will float down the river and dock right there. He'll meet with John Andre', and the two of them will work out the details. Arnold will surrender West Point and murder liberty in North America."

"You make it sound so dramatic."

She stared at him with a rare intensity. "Did you really just say that?"

"I-- uh...."

"Forget it. If we're going to prevent that meeting--"

"You don't think Lancaster raised an alarm?"

"I wouldn't bet tuppence on the man, let alone the future of the country."

Joel both understood and agreed.

"So," she said, "We can't do anything from here. Our best bet is to keep going north until we reach West Point."

"And then what?"

Her confidence visibly sagged. "I'm not sure. Do something to his boat, maybe?"

"Like drill holes in it?"

"That'd work."

"How much time do we have left?"

"A day," she said. "Say, another thirty miles to ride before we get there."

"And let's not forget, we need to beg, borrow, or steal a drill."

~*~

The coach Raines and Chastity boarded just outside New York to begin the next phase of their journey to Philadelphia appeared much newer than any of their previous vehicles. Even the driver seemed younger, though his demeanor matched that of the others they'd encountered: tough and trustworthy men who took their jobs seriously.

Their driver met them at breakfast in the inn where they'd spent the night. After collecting their fare, he pulled Raines aside.

"I'm worried for yer lady friend," he said.

"She's my wife."

"Ah. Even worse."

Raines felt himself tighten. "Why?"

"The redcoats watch the King's Road to catch anyone doin' business at the State House."

"Where Congress meets?"

"For a fact, sir."

Raines shrugged. "We have nothing they'd be interested in."

The driver cast a quick glance at Chastity. "I wish t'were so, but yer wife's a fine 'n sturdy lass. I fear the men what guard the road will take liberties with her, if you get my meanin'."

"I most certainly do *not*," Raines growled.

The driver exhaled wearily. "Them redcoats ain't yer genteel types. One of 'em's had his way wi' several ladies. Now, I'd like to protect yer little dove, but they got muskets; I don't. The odds don't favor me. Not alone."

"I'll be there, too."

He stared at Raines's useless arm, suspended in a sling. "I'm sure ye' mean well, but in a pinch, you ain't the kinda help I'd need."

"Then, let's take some other road."

"What other road?"

"Right. Can we hide her somewhere in the coach?"

The man remained adamant. Chastity would be in danger, and if either of the men intervened, they'd all be in trouble.

"I've a thought," the driver said. "Fella I know from the Post Road says one o' his fares tricked the guards what blocked his route. Lady claimed she had the pox when the redcoats came near, and they backed off, quick like. I don't own the particulars, but I trust the man what told me."

Raines didn't know what smallpox looked like, but the ruse might work. He had no other ideas.

He thanked the driver and returned to Chastity to discuss it.

"I've seen smallpox," she said, "but from a distance. It's horrible. It starts with little red blisters that grow into welts the size of peas, and they sprout everywhere. The scars they leave behind are uglier than you can imagine." She shuddered. "I'd rather not discuss it."

"I'm not saying you should get the disease," Raines said. "I'm just wondering if we can make it *look* like you've got it. To scare the redcoats."

"I understand. But that doesn't mean I know how to do it."

Raines ground his teeth. "How 'bout make-up? Surely you have some rouge or something. No one has rosy cheeks like you all the time."

She looked hurt. "You don't like my cheeks?"

"I *love* your cheeks." *All of 'em!* "But that's not the point. I don't want anything bad to happen to them." He reached for her with his good arm. He needed to hold her tight and know she was safe--*feel* she was safe. But all the while he cursed the fact he couldn't use both arms to ensure it.

"No, damn it," he said at last. "It's not worth it. I won't take the chance."

"What are you talking about?"

"We're going back to Boston."

She stared at him as if he'd done something monumentally stupid. "No."

He stepped back in surprise. *"No?"*

"You must've had a reason for going to Philadelphia, and not just to please me. I won't let you stop simply because someone, somewhere, *might* try to hurt me. I'm a Cotswold, sir, and as my father will be only too happy to point out, we don't run from threats. Ever. He didn't, and I won't."

"This is more than just a threat, sweetheart," he said.

"And I'm more than a mush-headed child."

No kidding.

"All right then, but let's at least try the driver's idea. Have you got some rouge, or whatever it is the stuff is called?"

Chastity lowered her brows. "Rouge?"

"Yes. Something to make your cheeks red."

She chewed her lip. "Well...."

"What?"

"Promise you won't laugh and think me silly?"

"Of course!"

"Mum gave me a paste that puts a bit of color in my cheeks."

Raines bit his own lip. "Yes? Go on."

"Well, perhaps if I put it on in dabs and splotches it might give the appearance of the pox."

"Yes!" he said. "Do it! Now, before the driver signals it's time to go."

"But everyone in here will see me!"

"Do it in the coach, darlin'. I'll stand guard if you'd like."

"What will the other passengers think?"

He tried to make his smile reassuring. "We'll use them as a test. If they think you look like you've got smallpox, they won't board."

"That's terrible!"

"No. That's common sense."

She and Raines applied the makeup, and it definitely turned her complexion ugly. Unfortunately, for testing purposes, there weren't any other passengers--no one to confirm their efforts. The driver checked on them before their departure and smiled at Chastity. "You don't look so good, ma'am."

Raines tipped his cocked hat. "Thanks. How far away is the roadblock?"

"Not far enough," the driver said. "Settle back, now."

The coach shifted as the driver climbed into his seat. He cracked his whip and the vehicle lurched toward Philadelphia. As feared, they reached the roadblock all too soon.

Raines looked out the coach window as a single redcoat approached. He held a musket across his chest, but showed only an officially required degree of interest in their vehicle.

"What's the matter?" Raines asked, his voice loud in the confines of the coach.

"No cause for alarm," the soldier said. "Just

seeing who passes this way."

"Report, Dawkins!" yelled someone Raines couldn't see. The voice came from a low stone-sided building beside the road.

Dawkins? Like Joel Dawkins? No, it couldn't be.

"Two, sir," the recoat yelled back. "Father and daughter, looks like."

"Husband and wife," Raines grumbled.

"Is she fair?" the voice demanded.

"Can't tell, sir. It's dark in there."

"Damn it, man! Must I do everything?" The speaker exited the roadside structure looking nothing like an officer or a gentleman. With his white wig askew and his waistcoat open, he made no attempt to look presentable as he trudged forward with his saber drawn and a dark scowl on his unshaven face.

"Get out, everyone!"

"I must warn you," Raines said. "My wife may have smallpox."

"Fancy that," the man said. "Now climb out."

Raines struggled to keep his muttering to a minimum. Before leaving the coach he slipped Murchesson's pistol inside his sling. It nestled close and heavy against his ribs. "We'd better do as they say," he said to his bride who exited first and then helped him disembark.

"What have we here?" the redcoat officer said when he got a better look at Chastity. He reached for her face, gripping her cheeks with one hand.

"Let go of her," Raines growled, but he was ignored.

"Looks like the pox to me, Lieutenant," the

soldier said.

"Really?" The officer examined the smeared make-up on Chastity's face and the same red color on his fingers. He held his hand to his nose and sniffed. "Since when does smallpox smell like fruit? You're an imbecile, Dawkins," he exclaimed. "Stay here with the old man while I... uh, *question* the girl."

"Very well," Dawkins said.

The officer glowered. "Very well, *what?*"

"Very well, *Leftenant* Fitzwilliam," said the soldier, though his manner suggested he cared as little for the order as for the man who gave it.

Fitzwilliam used his saber to herd Chastity into the stone building, and Dawkins told Raines to "stand easy."

"While that prig has my wife?"

"Please, sir. It'll go much easier that way. For both of you."

"I see. He does what he wants, and you do nothing?"

"I've no choice," he said, sounding almost anguished. "Fitzwilliam's father is a member of the House of Lords."

"So what?"

"So if I interfere, he could have me hanged."

And if you don't, I'll shoot you. Son, you're screwed either way.

~*~

355

Excerpt from the *Carolina Crier*:

Army Prepares For Possible Midlands Offensive

Greensboro, North Carolina, Sat., June 16, 2012--Reliable sources claim military tanker trucks have been dispatched from ports and military bases throughout New England and are generally headed west. Speculation is rife that the vehicles will be used as part of a broad assault on population centers throughout the midlands.

General Sir David Fitzwilliam, Chief of the Defense Staff, declined to comment on reports of a massive attack aimed at ending hostilities between the Crown and the self-styled Colonial Army of Independence, or CAI.

Rumors that the CAI planned and executed the plot to assassinate Queen Elizabeth have caused observers to keep ever-watchful eyes on top military brass. Since the tragedy in May, parliament and the armed forces have been criticized for failing to protect the Queen, and for not ending the war. Experts agree that frustration over the government's inability to apprehend those responsible for the Queen's murder has left the entire country in turmoil despite the imposition of Martial Law throughout the land.

Chapter Nineteen

"History can be well written only in a free country."
--Francois-Marie Arouet (Voltaire)

Knowing they had a long way to go, Joel and Leah pushed their horses hard on the ride to West Point. But they'd covered less than half the distance when it became obvious the pace was too much, and they were forced to let the animals rest. Hoping to make use of the time, they stopped at a farmhouse and inquired about the residence of Joshua Smith.

"He lives in the Judge's house," said a female householder who cast a suspicious eye at Leah's traveling attire. The woman made a show of squinting and staring at Leah's waistcoat and tight breeches, then at her own gown spread wide by a hooped petticoat.

"'Tis up on a hill," she added after concluding her inspection. "Keep the river close and ye'll stub yer toes on it."

She closed the door on them before they

could thank her or say farewell. Leah chuckled over it, but the incident made Joel think even harder about what they'd say and who they might pretend to be when they reached Smith's house, assuming they'd have to.

"Maybe you should change clothes. It might help if you looked a little more ladylike."

She managed a quick pirouette before lightly taking a seat astride her horse. "I thought you liked the way I look. As I recall, you couldn't take your eyes off me while I did my laundry in the creek."

"Those were uhm... special circumstances," he said, not admitting how often he had replayed the scene in his head. "But I'm troubled by how we'll be received if you're dressed like just one of the lads."

"Who knows? Maybe it'll work to our advantage."

Joel hoped she was right, and they rode on without discussing it further.

They found a tavern near Stony Point and ate while the horses rested. Afterwards they made their way to the local smithy and purchased an auger with a 2-inch bit.

"Is that the biggest one he had?" Leah asked.

"No. It's the *only* one he had."

Joel slipped the tool, shaped like a huge, T-handled corkscrew, through a strap on the back of his saddle. The iron shaft bounced against the side of the horse, but she didn't seem to mind. A rather contrary animal, her non-reaction came as a pleasant surprise.

They rode on through the afternoon, hoping to reach West Point before sunset. Neither of them had any idea what they'd find when they arrived, but figured stumbling around in the dark near an armed camp would not be a good idea.

They reached a point on the eastern shore of the Hudson, just below West Point, at dusk. Much to their chagrin, several boats were pulled up on the rocks a good distance from the water.

"Great," Joel said, counting the potential targets, "eight of 'em."

Leah shook her head and pointed out on the water at a boat approaching shore. "Nine."

Three men occupied the boat, and none of them looked like soldiers, for either side. If anything, they looked like fisherman, and spoke in excited shouts and expletives.

"Lend a hand, will ye' lad?" asked one of the men as he tossed a line to shore.

Joel gave his horse's reins to Leah and grabbed the rope. The fishermen didn't seem in the least concerned about who was pulling their craft in, they were too busy laughing and congratulating themselves. Joel and Leah soon saw why.

In the bottom of the boat lay a fish the likes of which neither of them had ever seen before. Easily ten feet long, it appeared to be a prehistoric shark. A row of bony, armor-like plates ran the length of its back and sides, and its huge pale eyes looked distinctly sinister.

"What the hell is that?" Joel asked.

"Dinner," quipped one of the fisherman.

"Albany beef," said another.

The first man out of the boat, the one who'd thrown the rope, helped Joel drag the bow out of the water. "'Tis just a sturgeon, lad. But I wager it'll take all five of us to haul 'er up the hill."

"Five?"

The man tipped his head toward Leah. "He can lend a hand, too, can't he?"

Joel chuckled. "Leah, dear. Would you like to help us carry this big fish up to the fort?"

"*Dear?*" The fisherman squinted at Leah, then smiled. "My, aren't you a sight! But ye'll give us a bit o' help, won't ye' lass?"

By then the other two fisherman had scrambled out of the boat, and all three turned their attention to off-loading the aquatic monster.

"How long will it take to cook?" Leah asked after she'd secured the horses and taken her place between Joel and the man who seemed to be in charge.

"A good long while, I'd warrant. But I just catches 'em, missy. Another crew does the cookin'."

"Hold on," said one of the other anglers. "There's a cart over 'ere. This way!"

They all shuffled sideways until they reached a stout, two-wheeled cart and dumped their burden into it.

"Ye'll be joinin' us, then?"

"We'd love to," Leah said, "but we've got work to do. I can't imagine what Albany beef tastes like."

"Veal, mostly, if it's done right. But that's not too likely 'ere."

Eager to be on their way, the other two fishermen cajoled their leader into leaving, and all three labored at moving the cart up the steep, stone slope.

"Now what?" Joel asked once the others were gone. "Do we bore holes in all these boats? That could take all night."

"There's no point," she said, her voice reflecting defeat. "Everything I've read says Arnold sailed down river to Dobb's Ferry in a barge rowed by eight men. Do you see any boats here that fit that description?"

"It wouldn't be the first time an historian got the details wrong."

She gave him a weary look. "Then they must've all gotten it wrong."

He waited while she paced about, deep in thought. Eventually she returned to his side. "There's nothing we can do," she said. "We could probably try shouting a warning to the men rowing him to the meeting, but I can't imagine they'd pay any attention to us. He's a damned hero!"

"Odd phrase."

"Well, it's true. He gets away with murder simply because of his record."

Joel put his arm around her. "More often than not, that's a good thing."

"Let's go," she said. "I can't bear to stay here and see that bastard sell out his country."

"There's still a chance that Lancaster got someone's ear and passed off that nonsense about a secret weapon." He tried to look hopeful.

But she didn't.

~*~

Monday, September 11, 1780, dawned clear and bright. Benedict, however, felt anything but carefree. He focused solely on his meeting with John Andre'. Everything depended on it, and yet the planning could not have been more haphazard.

The biggest issue, and the one he had yet to resolve, was how he might engage a British officer while still wearing a Continental uniform. He carried a flag of parlay, and hoped to get close enough to the British side of Dobb's Ferry that he could at least hail Andre' and meet with him privately in the middle of the river. Stranger things had been known to happen.

Beyond that, he had no other options.

After a hearty breakfast at the home of Joshua Smith, where he and his men had spent the night, his barge was pushed back into the water by the eight men who would row it. Sturdy, disciplined soldiers, they knew the return trip--against the current--would be difficult, but they'd done it before.

Benedict boarded and signaled for the men to get under way. The trip south down the Hudson to Dobbs Ferry would take quite a while, despite currents in their favor, and he contented himself by observing the scenery along the way. If nothing else, it kept his mind off the likelihood that his treachery would be revealed.

Steep cliffs and heavy foliage marked the route, with only occasional farms to break the pattern. It would not be long before the bright colors of autumn burst upon the scene. Peggy would love that, he felt sure, but the opportunity for a leisurely float upon the Hudson with her was remote at best.

Two hours later, as the men began to grumble about a mid-day meal, Dobbs Ferry came into view in the distance.

~*~

Raines waited a few minutes longer, but then Chastity screamed. He'd taken two steps toward the stone building when Dawkins barked an order for him to halt. Raines whirled on him. "What kind of man would shoot someone for protecting his wife?"

"I-- Uh...."

Raines ignored him and ran toward the guard house. When the driver also yelled for him to stop, Raines waved him off. Dawkins again yelled for him to come back, but the effort was lackluster.

Using his good shoulder, Raines smashed the door open, staggering inside to keep his balance. Fitzwilliam's sword clattered across the floor when Raines stumbled into it. A snarl escaped his lips when he spied Chastity, stretched face down over a narrow trestle table. She struggled against a pair of soldiers holding her arms to keep her pinned down. Fitzwilliam stood behind her, his hands busy with her gown and undergarment, his breeches bunched around his ankles.

Raines pulled the gun from his sling and yelled, "Stop it!"

Fitzwilliam, his face bland, turned his head casually, as if bored. "Jones, Digby--one of you--shut that peasant up. I need to concentrate."

"I said stop." Raines held the gun on Fitzwilliam. "Or I shoot. In fact, I'm looking forward to it."

Fitzwilliam, though now facing Raines full on, ignored him and spoke over his shoulder to his subordinates. "Jones? I'm waiting!"

Raines thumbed back the hammer on the double-action revolver. He had checked to ensure all six rounds were fresh before they left Boston. He needed only to pull the trigger. "Last chance," he said.

"Kill him!" Fitzwilliam bellowed.

Raines swung the gun toward the soldier trying to follow the Lieutenant's orders and fired without aiming. The bullet caught him in the chest, and he dropped to the floor with an astonished look on his dying face.

Chastity's screams had tapered off to deep, wracking sobs. Raines swiveled the gun back toward Fitzwilliam.

"Grab him, Digby," Fitzwilliam cried. "He can't stop you now!"

Raines fired again, and the bullet tore into Fitzwilliam's thigh.

"Bastard!" he roared. "You've crippled me!"

"Pity," Raines said, "I meant to hit your other leg, the tiny one in the middle."

Digby released Chastity and stared in awe at the gun in the physicist's hand. "You fired *twice!* But... How?"

Raines kept the gun on Fitzwilliam. "It's magic. I pull the trigger and: Bang!"

"Get him!" squealed the lieutenant. "That's an order!"

"Don't even blink, Digby," Raines said, not

bothering to move his gun.

Dawkins pushed open the door and peered in.

"I'll see you hang," Fitzwilliam groaned. "You, too, Dawkins."

Raines shook his head. "I doubt it."

Chastity screamed again, only this time she raised her voice in a war cry as she rushed past Raines and drove Fitzwilliam's sabre into his belly. She met resistance at some point and used both hands to ram the blade in to the hilt.

She staggered back away until she bumped into Raines, then grabbed him around the waist and held on.

Digby and Dawkins seemed paralyzed as they stared, open-mouthed, at the two men on the floor. Jones was already dead and drawing flies; Fitzwilliam would be joining him soon. The lieutenant tried to give one last command, but the words died on his lips, and his bowel emptied in a final gesture worthy of his character.

Slowly, Dawkins shifted his gaze to look at the physicist.

The adrenaline that fueled his attack left Raines shaky. He raised the gun again, trying to center it on Dawkins' chest. He didn't trust himself to hit anything smaller.

~*~

"I'll see to it you all get a decent meal after this day's effort," Benedict said. He felt it was the least he could do for them, under the circumstances.

When all was said and done, every one of them would likely be in chains.

"How close should we approach, sir?" one of the men asked.

"Close enough to hail shore." Benedict held up a speaking horn. He'd never used one but had been given hurried instructions by the subaltern who'd assembled his crew. He felt ready. The time had come to put the final plan together and ensure the surrender of the fort.

His thoughts drifted toward the future and what he might do with the 20,000 pounds General Clinton promised him. The possibilities were astounding!

"Sir?" the lead rower said.

"What?"

"There's a boat coming this way."

Benedict needed no spyglass to confirm the report. A British gunboat was headed directly toward them.

Andre' must've organized this. I certainly hope he's arranged to release the crew so I can return to the Point without drawing even more attention.

"Steady," he said. "No reason to panic."

"Sir! They're turning."

"I can see that," Benedict said. "I imagine they'll drift close enough that we can parlay." He had just put the speaking horn to his lips when the gunboat fired its first round. It hit the water twenty feet from the bow of the barge, and the accompanying splash doused Benedict and half the rowers.

"Are you mad?" he screamed, shaking his fist

at the British ship.

Three more cannons fired in quick succession, and the balls threw up huge gouts of water on both sides of the barge.

"Row!" Benedict screamed. "Pull! Hard! Now!"

The men leaned into their oars, rowing for their lives. The barge leaped shoreward in response, knocking Benedict off his unsteady legs. Someone in the back of the boat began shouting a rowing cadence which gave the bulky little craft a bit more speed.

Benedict could do nothing but hang on and curse. He cursed Andre'; he cursed cannons, and he cursed small boats. But mostly he cursed the British spy master for failing to secure Benedict's safety.

With canon balls splashing all around them, Benedict yelled encouragement to his men as they toiled to get away from the gunship and make their way back up river.

The gunship stayed close despite an opposing wind, tacking to advance and firing repeatedly.

"Row!" Benedict yelled again, though it wasn't necessary. The men were pulling as hard as they possibly could.

As soon as they touched the western shore, everyone scrambled out and turned to watch as the British ship eased back into the center of the river and dropped anchor.

Stalemate.

Benedict paced. Andre', he felt sure, was on the opposite shore doing the exact same things: pacing, cursing, and waiting, separated by a mile of river, and a gunboat flying King George III's colors.

As dusk slipped quietly across the water, Benedict had his men launch the boat once again, and they began the long, muscle-rending chore of rowing back upriver. Though it was late at night before he arrived home, Benedict fired off a letter to Colonel Lamb at West Point. He ordered him to send two heavy pieces of artillery to the patriot side of Dobb's Ferry.

"The enemy's boats come up almost every day and insult the post," he wrote.

Though he vented his anger at Lamb, it was Andre' who deserved the brunt of it. Sending cannon to Dobb's Ferry was mere window dressing. The British controlled enough of the river to force Lamb to haul the heavy guns overland. That could take weeks, and with any luck, Benedict would be wearing the uniform of a British brigadier general by then.

As he mulled over alternatives to another disastrous encounter with the King's cannoneers, Joshua Smith's residence quickly came to mind.

~*~

Joel and Leah rode in silence toward Haverstraw Bay, their destination: "the Judge's House" where Joshua Smith lived.

"It's over," she said, "I just know it. Arnold and Andre' met and made their little plans, and now the colonies are doomed."

"The British haven't attacked West Point yet," Joel pointed out. "There still might be time to do something."

"Like what?"

"I don't know. Alert General Washington? Ride back up to West Point and tell everyone we meet that General Arnold is a traitor? Hell, you're the historian. You tell me what's feasible."

"That's just it!" she yelled, her frustration getting the best of her. "I don't *know* what else to do. Everyone trusts the bastard. It wouldn't matter who we tried to tell, they wouldn't believe us."

Joel remained silent for a time, and Leah wracked her brain to think of a solution. Unfortunately, the only one she kept coming up with--the only one that had any chance of being successful--was the one he had already vowed *not* to participate in.

"What're you thinking?" he asked.

"Oh, nothing."

Joel chuckled. "I've been around women long enough to know that 'nothing' usually means just the opposite. What aren't you telling me?"

"I'm just trying to figure out where we need to go to avoid being killed in the coming battles. It's not going to be easy."

"Do tell."

"Our best bet would probably be to head west, through Pennsylvania, to the far frontier."

"Indian country."

"Yep."

"And we'll be better off there than here?"

"Probably."

He looked off into the distance, brooding silently.

"What?"

"We're doomed, y'know. We're too soft to survive in the wilderness. I've got a game leg and a pathetically underdeveloped survival sense. You'll likely be grabbed by wild Indians, raped senseless, and left to die in some dreadful way."

"What about you?"

"Oh, they'll kill me right at the start. Boom! Dead. Just like that."

She punched his shoulder. "They probably don't even *have* guns. Yet."

"Great, then they'll whack me with clubs or stone knives. What fun! I can't wait. By the way, what colors do Conestoga wagons come in?"

"Any color you'd like, I suppose. But you'd have to paint it yourself."

She enjoyed the back and forth Joel offered. His world view was radically different from her own, and his responses never failed to delight her. When the time came to act on her plans, or whatever one might label what she intended, it would be damned difficult to do without implicating Joel.

"Listen," he said, "I know you're upset because we couldn't keep Arnold from meeting with Andre', but it's foolish to think the game's over. It's not. There have to be things we can still do."

"I suppose," she said, but her answer lacked conviction.

She knew what would happen once they talked their way into Smith's house in Haverstraw. In three days, on September 14, Arnold would intercept his wife, Peggy, at Smith's house to plan their escape once West Point fell. That's where Leah would have to do it. That's where she and Joel would likely part company forever.

That's where she'd have to murder Benedict Arnold. All by herself.

~*~

"What are you doing?" Chastity asked. She put her hand on Raines' arm and pressed down. The gun in his hand slowly eased toward the floor. "He's not trying to hurt anyone."

"We just killed two soldiers," Raines said. "Redcoats. These two can't just let us walk away."

"But that one--" Chastity lightly kicked the foot of the dead lieutenant. "--tried to rape me."

"You were right to shoot him," Dawkins said.

"And that one--" Chastity pointed at Jones. "--held me down for him."

"Given the chance," Dawkins said, "he'd have taken a turn after the lieutenant."

"Then they both deserved what they got," Raines said.

Digby was still mesmerized by the physicist's gun. "Where did you get that?"

Once again the name "Dawkins" came to mind as Raines recalled where the gun came from. Nor could he get past it while he tried to figure out what to do with the remaining soldiers. Killing them would be the easiest course, obviously, but the repercussions could be dramatic, and irreversible. And that only applied to how the British would react to losing a detail headed by the son of a Lord.

Lord!

His bigger concern was the man named Dawkins. What if Joel was his direct descendant? Killing him could cause Joel to disappear. Is that truly what would happen? His theories cried YES, and his heart urged him not to take the chance.

Besides, Leah had feelings for the ex-cop. No doubt about it. Raines saw it the moment she introduced him, despite the fog of his recovery from Lancaster's bullet. And even more obvious were his feelings for her. Why else would he have abandoned his entire world to follow her on a venture so fraught with risk? No, it was inconceivable to him that Joel felt anything less than full bore, head on, no holds barred l-o-v-e for Leah.

So how in hell could he take a chance on letting the universe dissolve any trace of the only guy his daughter ever loved?

"What do we do now?" he asked as he lowered the gun to his side.

"We'll say a band of rebels attacked us," Dawkins said.

Digby snorted. "With guns that shoot as often as one pulls the trigger?"

"Of course not!" Dawkins said. "Who would believe *that?*" He turned toward Raines and Chastity. "I apologize for what the leftenant tried to do. No man has that right. And no one'll miss 'im. At least, no one around here."

"Then, you won't try to keep us here?"

"No, sir. When asked, we'll say we were overrun. Jones and Leftenant Fitzwilliam went down in the battle. As for Digby and me, we're lucky to have lived through it."

"Digby?" Raines called.

"Sir?"

"Can you live with that?"

"I can, sir. I'm obliged you haven't killed us."

Raines scratched his head with the gun. "Think nothing of it."

"Husband?"

He looked into Chastity's intense green eyes. "Yes?"

"Take me to Philadelphia."

"But--"

"Now."

"Yes, dear," he said. "No problem."

~*~

Excerpt from the *Susquehanna Shopper*:

Radio Show Host Claims Government Cover-up

Scranton, Pennsylvania, Tues., June 19, 2012--Bradley Nettles, host of the nationally broadcast radio show "Rumor Has It," claims he can prove that a massive cover-up is underway to hide the disappearance of David Fitzwilliam, whom Nettles says was a top military official.

Nettles, whose celebrity status has swollen since his program first aired on a single station in 2009, says that while most conspiracy theories can be debunked, this one has too much supporting evidence to be ignored.

"He wasn't just some unknown Royal Army recruit," Nettles said in a Monday broadcast, "he was the biggest of the big guns, Chief of the Defense Staff. And suddenly, no one's ever heard of him?"

General Sir Malcom Nash, the current Chief of the Defense Staff, had no comment other than to say he doesn't "...have time for commercial radio programs."

Chapter Twenty

"While you here do snoring lie, Open-eyed conspiracy
His time doth take."
--William Shakespeare, *The Tempest*

Still infuriated by the shelling he'd received trying to rendezvous with Major Andre', Benedict retained enough self-discipline to ignore the incident and plan another meeting. He still could not understand why General Clinton insisted on a face-to-face encounter with his spy chief since Benedict had been supplying accurate, pertinent, actionable intelligence for nearly a year and a half.

But none of that mattered. His reward, his commission in the Royal Army, his entire future--all hinged on the fall of West Point. That wouldn't happen unless he met with Andre' in person.

An attempt behind the lines of either side remained out of the question since neither man could risk being out of uniform if disaster struck and they were apprehended. Spies were hanged. Always.

Therefore they had to find middle ground, and the only realistic place Benedict could think of was the home of Joshua Smith.

Though Benedict's aides, and others in command roles at West Point, suspected Smith of duplicity, none of them could prove he was a double agent. Benedict knew he was playing both sides for his own gain, but as long as the country lawyer got Benedict's coded communiqués into the hands of the British, he didn't care how much extra money he picked up in the process.

And then it dawned on him. Even if the Americans didn't realize Smith was a double agent, the British almost certainly did. That would explain Clinton's otherwise irrational demand for Benedict to risk showing up for a meeting. It would prove conclusively that the Americans weren't intercepting his messages or that they hadn't dreamt up the whole thing to trick Clinton into making a foolish move--like attacking West Point when it was heavily defended.

For his purposes, Smith's house would be perfect. He would need Smith to vacate the premises during his meeting with Andre', of course, but he didn't anticipate any difficulty in persuading the man to cooperate. Smith's hunger for acceptance in some enterprise of great importance made him quite vulnerable. Benedict could therefore play upon at least two flavors of Smith's greed, one of which was sure to net the circumstances Benedict desired.

Best of all, he would be able to see Peggy a day or so in advance of her planned arrival at the Robinson's house. If Major Franks maintained his travel schedule, Peggy and her escort would arrive at Smith's house on Haverstraw Bay on September 14th, a mere two days away.

It was enough to put a smile on his face and dampen the memory of British cannon fire.

~*~

"Let's think about this for a minute," Joel said as he and Leah rode south from West Point to the "Judge's House" where Joshua Smith lived. "We need some sort of cover story that'll get us close to Smith without making us suspicious to Arnold, right?"

"Yeah."

"So, why don't we use a variation of the story we told Balfour, or Lancaster. Whatever the hell he calls himself."

"Okay, go on," she said, uncertainly.

"We claim we're working for a third entity-- we aren't members of either spy ring Smith knows about."

Leah rubbed her temples. "You're givin' me a headache."

"C'mon, it's not that complicated. Hear me out. We tell him we're on a special assignment, ordered by King George himself, or Parliament or whoever. We say we're investigating reports that the rebels have some sort of secret naval weapon that could wipe out the British fleet."

"How does that help us?"

"We tell Smith we suspect that Arnold is only pretending to help the British, in order to lure the fleet into a trap."

"In hopes that Smith will turn the British against Arnold?"

"Yes."

Leah rode on in stunned silence, then turned to him and said, "You know, that's really quite--"

"Brilliant?" He wore his best Cheshire Cat smile.

"Actually, I was going to say 'devious.' But the more I think about it, the more I believe it has a chance. Not a very good one, mind you, but better than anything else we've come up with."

He slumped down in his saddle. "You're way too kind."

"No, I mean it," she said, completely missing his sarcasm, "I think we could make it work. If...."

"If what?"

"If we can be utterly convincing. We can't say anything to raise his suspicions."

Joel laughed. "Raising suspicions is *all* we'll be doing!"

"I know. I meant we can't raise his suspicions about our authenticity."

"You think he'll compare us with *other* spies he knows on special assignment from the King?"

She arched her back until it cracked. "I see your point."

"I would appreciate it, however, if you didn't use your uhm... feminine wiles on him. Or anybody else, for that matter."

"What in hell does that mean?"

He squirmed. "It's just that sometimes you give the impression you're a little... you know. Easy."

"As in pleasant?"

"As in *available*."

"Available for what, exactly?"

He tried to extricate his foot from his mouth by mumbling, but she refused to let his comment escape scrutiny. "Sorry, I missed that. Define 'available'."

The scenery along the Hudson suddenly seemed quite dazzling.

"*Joel?*"

"All right, here's the thing. Sometimes, when you need to get something from a bloke, you're pretty quick to unbutton your blouse or... or wiggle your bottom. Whether you're trying to attract or distract doesn't really matter. I... It's just--"

"Effective?"

"Well, yeah. It's that, in spades. But I wonder how often it happens in real life. I mean, do female spies really act that way?"

"This one does." She reached out and gently patted his cheek. "It doesn't mean anything, sweetie. Don't take it personally. You've been to the theater. Think of it as part of an opera or a play. Just imagine I'm an actress in a love scene on stage. It's illusion, but it has to look real to be effective."

"Oh."

Hey, wait--she called me "sweetie!"

"But it makes me feel good to know you're a little jealous."

"I, uh...."

"Remember that when the time comes, and I need a jealous boyfriend to get me out of trouble."

"That assumes I don't get you *into* trouble first."

She was still chuckling when the Smith residence came into view atop a hill overlooking Haverstraw Bay.

~*~

Raines enjoyed the second half of the journey to Philadelphia far more than the first. Not only was he more relaxed, but Chastity seemed to have undergone a more profound change. When they left Boston, her actions were typical of a young bride. Excitement and adventure put color in her cheeks, and she smiled and laughed almost constantly despite the rigors of their traveling conditions.

After the near-rape, however, she seemed more content to sit close to him without being obvious about it. When she rested her head upon his one good shoulder, it meant she was weary rather than passionate. Their overnights at inns along the route became more sober and, to his regret, more chaste.

He feared their actions in the melee' at the redcoat roadblock had wrought some psychological damage with which he had no way to cope, much less repair. But he had to do something.

"You amaze me," he said. "You know that?"

She aimed her green eyes at his. "Why?"

"Because you're resilient and resourceful."

"And a killer?"

"And *courageous*. You did what had to be done."

She looked away. "I killed a man who was already wounded. He couldn't hurt me anymore. He lay on the floor, helpless, and I killed him."

"Do you recall what he tried to do to you?"

"Yes."

"So why do you care? That wasn't a man you killed. It was an animal--a sick, loathsome *thing* that didn't deserve to live."

She stared out the window. They would reach Trenton soon, and he looked forward to getting up and walking around when the driver changed horses. He hoped they would have time for lunch, or "dinner" as it was more commonly known. The thought made him realize his young bride had not eaten anything since they left the roadblock.

"I had no right to kill him," Chastity said.

"On the contrary," Raines said, softly. "You had every right. Think of how many women will be free from him! There's no telling how many he violated in the past. You put an end to that."

"But--"

"If you hadn't done it, I would have." He tipped her head up and kissed her lightly on the lips. "I promise you, I won't be losing any sleep over it. You shouldn't either."

She shrugged and let him put his arm around her shoulder.

"It must've hurt terribly when I stabbed him."

"I certainly hope so."

"You shouldn't say that!"

He shifted so that he could look straight at her. "Listen to me, please. When someone commits a crime like rape--when they do something horrific to satisfy their own sick desires--they show themselves unworthy of consideration, or mercy. If you ask me,

I'd say it wasn't you who killed that man. It was God acting *through* you to protect others."

"Do you honestly believe that?"

"Completely." *And if saying I believe in the Easter Bunny will make you feel better, I'll gladly sign up for that, too.*

"Thank you, husband," she said, beginning to looking relieved.

"You're welcome, wife."

A short while later she reached for a button on his waistcoat and began playing with it. "May I ask you a question?"

"Of course," he said.

"Will you teach me how to handle your amazing pistol?"

Raines bit his tongue.

~*~

The front door of Smith's house opened quickly at their knock, and a small-statured woman stared out at them. Wearing a dark gown and an apron of similarly muted colors, she appeared crestfallen at the arrival of unannounced visitors.

"Yer early," she said.

Joel and Leah exchanged a quick look, then Leah spoke. "We're here to see Mister Smith. Can you tell us where to find him?"

"Ah. Then, yer not part of Missus Arnold's escort?"

"No, ma'am," Joel said.

"What's this about?"

"Nothing much," the former Special Branch

officer said. "We have mutual friends and some business to discuss."

"But ye don't need lodging?"

"Well," Leah began, "that depends on our talk with Mister Smith."

The woman sighed heavily and pointed at a barn some distance from the white stone house. "Joshua was yonder last I looked, but 'e moves about, constant like. Never lets on who'll join us at table, or 'ow many beds'll be full from one night t' the next. My own two lads never know where they'll lay their 'eads." She continued to mutter as Joel and Leah backed away and started for the barn.

"Happy as a hangman, that one," Leah said.

"Can you blame her?"

"Prob'ly not. We'll know better once we've dealt with Smith. You ready?"

He raised his palms in a familiar gesture, then waved her toward the barn. "After you, madam."

She made an extra effort to swing her hips as she went by, and Joel swatted her lightly on the behind. With only a modest effort she managed to keep him from seeing her smile.

Joshua Smith was smoking a pipe when they found him in his barn. There were no animals in it, but the building was rife with the aroma of their recent presence. Either it had no effect on Smith, or the smoke from his pipe blocked the worst of it.

After a round of introductions, Leah asked that they move outside, it being too nice a day to waste indoors. Smith seemed amenable, and more so when Leah pretended to slip on the waste-strewn ground and grabbed him to steady herself. He offered his arm for the rest of the walk which she accepted with more gratitude than necessary.

"We've come a long way," Joel said, "just to meet you."

"Indeed? How do you know me?"

"Strictly from reports," Leah purred. "But I must say, you have quite a reputation. When Lord North summoned us to--"

"*Lord North?* The Prime Minister?"

"Yes, of course. Or if you prefer, Frederick North, second Earl of Guilford."

"Lord North knows *my* name?"

"Intimately," she said in a low voice. "Or at least, as intimately as one can be known by their accomplishments."

Smith preened. "And what would the Prime Minister have of me?"

"Your help," Joel said.

Leah patted his arm and smiled. "Allow me to explain. We know you've been instrumental in getting messages to and from a General in the rebel army. We don't need to mention his name, but we both know to whom I refer."

"Of a certainty!" Smith said, his head bobbing up and down. "Gustavus."

"Which is merely one of his pseudonyms."

"There are more?"

"Oh, indeed. But here's the rub. We believe he may not be as sincere in his efforts to assist the Crown as he would have our people in New York City believe."

Smith looked surprised.

"He could be planning something sinister,"

Joel said. "Unfortunately, I can't share the details."

Leah pushed him lightly on the shoulder. "Don't be ridiculous. This is Joshua Smith! If he can't be trusted, no one can. Tell him."

Joel cast about for a moment, then relented. "As you wish." He looked closely at Smith. "Surely you've heard of Doctor Benjamin Franklin, the man who's representing the rebels in France?"

"Everyone knows that name," Smith snarled. "May he rot in hell."

Leah squeezed his arm as Joel continued. "Despite what we may think of him, the man is quite brilliant. And he's put his intellect to use for the colonial cause in more ways than one. You will recall, he's not merely an ambassador, he's a scientist and inventor."

"And," Leah said, "our agents in Paris say he's designed a device that will change naval warfare forever."

Smith stared at them, enthralled.

"The French constructed one such machine and conveyed it to Rhode Island. It is on its way here, to the Hudson, even as we speak. We believe General Arn-- er, Gustavus wants to install it somewhere close by."

"What on Earth for?"

"The plan--we think--requires him to lure a portion of the British fleet up river where it can be destroyed. Such an event would prove the worth of Franklin's invention and would be a convincing argument for the construction of more such weapons. Once deployed, and used against us, the greatest navy known to man would soon be lost."

Smith looked drained. "I-- I had no idea."

"Of course not," Joel said. "How could you?"

"What do you need me to do? Perhaps we could lure him--"

Leah put a finger to his lips. "It's all taken care of. Gustavus will be here tomorrow."

"Are you certain? I only know his wife is on the way. She'll likely spend the night in Goshen. But Arn--"

"Gustavus," Leah said. "He'll be here, too. Trust me."

"He'll have troops with him," Smith said. "He never travels alone."

They hadn't fully considered that, but she tried to sound reassuring. "We'll deal with them if we have to."

"You can hide out here, if you like."

In the bloody, stinking barn? Leah looked to Joel for a way out.

"We're tired," he said. "We've traveled a long way to see you. Why not introduce us as relatives? Distant relatives, perhaps. We'll play our parts."

"And staying close to Gustavus may give us an opportunity to learn more about his plans."

"Mrs. Smith can move the children. You shall have the room next to the one Gustavus will use."

"You're everything we read about and hoped for," Leah said, giving him a quick hug. "Your king and country thank you."

Smith could barely contain himself. "You'll stay for supper?"

"We'd be honored."

"Bring your things up to the house," he said,

"I'll go tell Mrs. Smith."

~*~

Though he tried not to be overly curt, Benedict allowed himself the luxury of a few additional grumbles. It had been weeks since he'd last seen Peggy, and the absence had operated on him like an infected tooth. The ache was constant, and nothing he could do would lessen it. The only solution was being reunited with his young bride, and he was up early to begin the short journey from the Robinson house to that of his message bearer, Joshua Smith.

Yet, an early departure was not to be. Colonel Varick hailed him from mid-river as his own men eased his barge into the water. Varick stood in one of the sad little boats that represented the Colonial Navy.

"General, a word!"

"I've already posted passwords today, Colonel. I will return tomorrow."

"Very good, sir, but--"

"It will have to wait, Colonel. I'm in a hurry in case you hadn't noticed."

With that he urged his rowers to apply themselves and take advantage of the current. While his craft moved swiftly downstream, Varick sat in his boat as two men labored to return him to shore.

Would they never leave him alone?

Benedict mulled over his options for meeting Andre', but they hadn't evolved in any appreciable way. He still had to meet face to face, and he had to do it soon. Operating on the assumption that all would go well, he turned his attention to providing a safe exodus for Peggy and their son. At some point, Washington or whoever succeeded him, would realize what Benedict had done. He could not allow them to take out their revenge on his wife and child. Washington certainly wouldn't, but Lamb? He couldn't count on that man to do anything reasonable.

His best option, he supposed, would be to make it appear that Peggy had absolutely no knowledge of his intentions. Any hint of participation on her part had to be eliminated *before* he surrendered West Point. Fortunately, he would be able to discuss contingencies with her before the fateful day. A day which, as far as he was concerned, couldn't come soon enough.

They arrived at Smith's home with time to spare, and once the men had pulled the barge on shore, Benedict dismissed them. Mrs. Smith would arrange to feed them in the afternoon, but beyond that, they were on their own.

Benedict strolled up the steep steps to the front door. How, he wondered, did a country lawyer obtain a house of such proportions? Stone it was, carefully cut and fitted by masons who knew what they were about. If he ever wanted a country manor, this would be the style he'd choose and the craftsmanship he'd expect.

Smith welcomed him in with unusual enthusiasm. His attitude in the past had been far more subdued. But perhaps he sensed Benedict's anticipation of Peggy's arrival.

"Come in, come in!" Smith said making a grand gesture toward the interior of his home. A couple he didn't know rose to greet him. Smith introduced them as Mr. and Mrs. Dawkins. Benedict did his best to suppress his annoyance at Smith for inviting strangers to his reunion with Peggy. Smith explained that Dawkins was some sort of cousin who'd brought his dark-skinned wife north after the recent conflict in the Carolinas.

Benedict looked right past Dawkins, obviously a man of little consequence, and focused on his wife. Tall enough to look directly over his head, the woman possessed a regal bearing and stunningly good looks. Her light brown hair gave her complexion a deeply tanned appearance which might have camouflaged her heritage. But he wasn't fooled.

Neither of them had an accent he recognized, despite his travels. But then, he hadn't been everywhere. Yet. Once he ended the war he'd have the means to go anywhere he liked, and he'd do it in style. If he wanted to bring along someone like Mrs. Dawkins, there'd be no one to stop him. And that included Peggy. She'd be home with the children.

Dinner was served later than usual in order to accommodate her arrival. Peggy swept into his arms with her usual flair. In most cases, she drew the eyes of every male in attendance, but this time she had competition. Major Franks, for instance, never even looked up from his conversation with Mrs. Dawkins when Peggy entered the room. Neither woman seemed aware of the other's presence until Smith made a formal introduction. If not for that, there might have been some awkward moments. Benedict had no doubt Peggy could acquit herself well in a verbal exchange, but no one could deny the sheer animal magnetism of Mrs. Dawkins. It begged the question of what she saw in her husband. Such musing paid little dividends, and Benedict quickly abandoned it.

The mid-day meal was less lavish than usual, for which Smith apologized. He explained that the demands on his larder had been higher than usual of late, a thinly veiled attempt to extort funds directly from Benedict rather than from his handlers. Still, the company treated Benedict with the respect due a warrior. That inspired him to comment on the shelling he'd recently undergone.

Peggy became upset and demanded to know what he was doing in such a dangerous situation.

"As I informed General Washington," he said, "I went to Dobbs Ferry because it's so close to enemy lines. I wished to establish signals by which movements of British sail could be reported to me at West Point."

In their bedroom after the meal, he told her he really wrote to Washington and offered the signal story to explain his presence at Dobbs Ferry.

"If you care anything for me, and for our son," she said, "you won't put yourself in danger that way." She gripped his hands tightly. "What would we do without you?"

"Would you rather I had told Washington my intent was to meet with Major Andre' to arrange the surrender of my command?"

"Of course not, but the risk--"

He raised her hands to his lips and kissed them. "Risks don't frighten me, my dear. Ask anyone who's fought beside me. But I understand your fears about this enterprise, and I promise, as much as I am able, to shift such dangers to those receiving the benefit of my actions. If Andre' wants my help, *he'll* have to take the risks to get it."

He unfolded a sheet of paper. "I've already written a letter to him for Smith to have delivered." He quoted from it: "I will send a person in whom you may confide, by water, to meet you at Dobb's Ferry on Wednesday the 20th instant between 11 and 12 o'clock at night, who will conduct you to a place of safety where I will meet you."

"So you'll put Major Andre' at risk?"

"No, no. Here, let me finish. 'You may rest assured that if there is no danger in passing your lines, you will be perfectly safe where I propose the meeting.' You see? This way we both avoid danger."

He knew the Dobbs Ferry meeting point presented problems, but he had no intention of pointing them out to Peggy. She seemed satisfied, and that was enough.

The rest of the afternoon and evening passed with only one incident. The three couples plus Major Franks were taking brandy after supper. They sat under the veranda on the wide front porch. Smith and Franks smoked their pipes while Benedict and Dawkins occupied opposite ends of the open space.

Small talk had been the order of the day, something at which Peggy excelled. She moved casually but continually among the assemblage, a skill she'd acquired entertaining her father's business associates in Philadelphia. A side benefit of her ability to move so easily in social circles was a knack for overhearing muted conversations.

As she and Benedict prepared for bed later, Peggy commented on something odd she'd picked up between Dawkins and his dark bride.

"What was it?" he asked, more to be polite than out of curiosity.

"She seemed the tiniest bit put out with him, so I paid closer attention. You know how husbands and wives can sometimes say as much with looks and gestures as they can with words."

He nodded, trying not to appear impatient. "And?"

"She began whispering, and in a manner that completely defied understanding."

"How do you mean?"

"I thought she may have been speaking some African language, but evidently it wasn't one with which Mr. Dawkins was overly familiar. He grew impatient with her and demanded that she just tell him what was on her mind."

"What did she say?"

"That she wished he hadn't said they were husband and wife."

~*~

Treason, Treason!

Excerpt from the *Newport News News*:

Parliament Wonders Who's In Charge Of The Royal Army

Hampton Roads, Virginia, Wed., June 20, 2012--Top army officials have yet to address Parliamentary concerns about various issues relating to military activities and preparedness. Rumors of a shake-up in command have left observers wondering who is really in charge.

No official announcements have yet been made in response to queries from elected officials about why they weren't consulted prior to the recent expansion in military manpower. A second line of investigation was opened Tuesday when reports surfaced that military convoys currently stalled in the west are carrying tanks of highly concentrated nerve gas.

Speaking off the record, a source close to the office of the Chief of the Defense Staff suggested the toxic material may have been en route to disposal facilities. No official word has been posted to confirm this.

Chapter Twenty-one

"The only winner in the War of 1812 was Tchaikovsky."
                                                    --Solomon Short

Mrs. Smith's mood remained unchanged from the first moment Joel and Leah met her. Two days of feeding guests she hardly knew, and an abundance of semi-uniformed Continental soldiers with whom they traveled, had clearly left the woman on the brink of collapse. Leah insisted they do something for her, even though she couldn't think of anything specific just then.

"We'll look into it later," Joel said, wondering how the poor woman would react to a kindness from such an unexpected source. "Right now we need to talk to her husband."

"I'm sure Arnold is up to something," Leah said. "Especially after his revelation about being shelled by a British gunship."

"How did he put it? Something about a great commotion as their cannon 'stirred the waters' around his barge."

"I can only imagine how his crew reacted to being a target for redcoat artillery."

"Arnold seemed pretty calm about it."

Leah sniffed. "He's a general. Who's going to suggest he wet his pants when the cannons went off? Certainly none of the poor slobs rowing his boat. And besides, his wife was sitting right there at the table. He had to put on a convincing show for her."

"I suppose."

"She's known for her hysterics, Joel. I read an account of her reaction when she thought Arnold would be serving in the front lines rather than at West Point."

"A bit dramatic?"

"Award worthy."

"So, she's in on it, too?"

Leah nodded. "I've always thought so. And now that I've actually met her, and had a chance to see her in action..." She paused to look Joel in the eye. "Did you notice the way she cruised around eavesdropping while we were all out on the porch last night?"

"Actually," he said, grinning, "I was more interested in looking at you."

"Listen to you! But little Peggy was trolling for information. I wonder what she picked up."

"By the way," Joel said, "I noticed you got up after we went to bed. With all the troops camping out around the house I wasn't comfortable with you going out to the necessary all by yourself."

"You *followed* me?"

"Only a short distance. I stopped when I saw

you weren't going to leave the front porch. Who were you talking to out there?"

She gave him a puzzled look.

"I could hear you speaking, quietly, calling to someone. But I couldn't tell who."

At length her smile returned. "I thought there was a guard standing nearby. I didn't want to startle him at night for fear of being shot. We've had enough of that in my family lately."

Joel thought the explanation a bit lame but didn't pursue it.

Standing on the elevated front porch, Leah leaned against a column supporting the broad roof and surveyed the scene on the grounds below. Major Franks had assembled Peggy Arnold's entourage, though she would no longer be a part of it. Peggy's place had been claimed by the major himself. He and the driver would ride together in a two-wheeled carriage which Leah speculated had been provided by Peggy's wealthy father. It put the Cotswold's buggy to shame.

Peggy and Arnold would travel via barge, but whether that was for her comfort or to ease her mind about the stability of the flat-bottomed boat, Joel couldn't tell. It may just have been an easier way for them to reach the Robinson house which stood on the opposite side of the Hudson from West Point. Smith stood near them on the dock, chatting amiably until Arnold climbed awkwardly aboard, and signaled for his men to shove off.

Smith had a fresh bowl of pipe tobacco going by the time he topped the steps to join them.

"Any idea what Arnold's up to?" Joel asked.

Smith looked smug. "Seems 'e needs me to deliver a letter."

"May I see it?" Leah asked.

Smith surrendered it agreeably. "What'll I tell him when he finds it's gone missing?"

"I'll tell you in a moment. I have to decode this first," Leah said. "Shouldn't take long. The worst part is his sloppy handwriting." She turned away from them and concentrated on the document.

Joel and Smith made small talk while she worked, and she finished the translation quickly. "Looks like he may have shot himself in the foot."

Smith looked stunned. "I heard no gunfire!"

Leah groaned. "It's an expression, like 'hoist with his own petard.'"

"Ah."

"Go on," Joel said.

"He's proposing to meet Andre' at Dobbs Ferry just before Midnight on the 20th. It's good timing, though. Washington's on his way." She refolded the letter and gave it back to Smith. "Handle this the way you normally do."

Clearly surprised, the lawyer said, "But surely we can't let him arrange for the fleet's destruction!"

"Until we catch him red-handed, he can deny everything."

Smith brightened. "Red-handed! I know that one. It means with blood on his hands. An old Scots saying."

Leah nodded appreciatively. "I had no idea you were so cultured."

"It helps, Madame. My father left us with a modest library, but he bade us read every title."

"You'd best get moving if you're going to send that note to 'Mister Anderson,'" Leah said. "We don't want to keep 'Gustavus' waiting."

Smith started down the stairs until Joel called after him.

"Is there anyone nearby we might hire to give Mrs. Smith a hand?"

"With what?"

"Anything," Leah said. "She looks... fatigued."

Smith appeared less than enthusiastic about the idea. "T'would be a cost I hadn't anticipated."

"Mrs. Dawkins and I will cover it," Joel said. "You can tell her it's from Lord North."

"Or from yourself," Leah suggested.

"She'd never believe it came from me," he said, laughing. "But, there's a woman on a tenant farm nearby who might be interested." He waved vaguely to the south. "Name's Cahoon. Talk to her. But you'd best have a coin or two handy."

When Smith was out of earshot, Joel looked through the front door of the house, but found no sign of Mrs. Smith. He asked Leah, "You said Washington was on his way. How could you possibly know that?"

She grinned. "I've told you. I studied this stuff--memorized much of it. But now things are off script. Arnold should have met with Andre' three days ago. He didn't, and now he's going to scramble to work things out. Reinforcements for the British fleet have already arrived in New York Harbor, and the French fleet is in Rhode Island."

Joel tried to put the relative facts into a mental map. "Okay."

"Washington wants to retake New York City, and he's hoping to combine forces with the French to do it. Meanwhile, General Clinton intends to trap Washington and the French on Long Island while he sends a smaller force to take West Point."

"Compliments of Arnold."

"Exactly."

"What happens when we've moved completely away from the history books?"

She frowned. "I don't know. On one hand, if we prevent Arnold's treachery, the outlook for the colonies should improve. On the other hand, what I've memorized about our history--the one we grew up with--won't help us once we've altered things."

He couldn't help but smile.

She put her hands on her hips and tilted her head a bit. "What?"

"That'll make us equals."

"Hm. I'd prefer being partners."

~*~

Benedict saw Colonel Varick waiting for him on shore as they prepared to pull in by the road that led to the Robinson house. He had no way of knowing how long the officer had been waiting, nor did he care.

"Good afternoon, General," Varick said as Benedict's men dragged the prow of the barge clear of the water.

Benedict returned the greeting without enthusiasm.

"Good day, Mrs. Arnold," the Colonel added.

He steadied Peggy's elbow as she disembarked with their infant son in her arms. Benedict clambered after.

"I'm going to be busy helping Mrs. Arnold settle into our quarters," Benedict advised Varick. "Surely anything you have for me can wait until the morrow."

"Everything but this," he said, handing his commander a message from General Washington. "This is what I tried to give you before you left yesterday."

Benedict bristled at the casual admonishment but quickly put it out of his head as he read the note from Washington:

> *I shall be at Peekskill on Sunday evening, on my way to Hartford to meet the French Admiral and General. You will be pleased to send down a guard of a captain and fifty at that time, and direct the quartermaster to endeavor to have a night's forage for about forty horses. You will keep this to yourself, as I want to make my journey a secret.*

Rochambeau and his French troops had landed two months earlier, and Benedict had been wondering when Washington would meet with them. Suddenly he was faced with the arrival of his commanding officer three days before his planned meeting with Andre'. He had a great deal to do to get ready, not the least of which was to pen a coded message to General Clinton about Washington's travel plans.

~*~

Somewhere between their encounter with the British roadblock and the outskirts of Philadelphia, Raines Kerr noticed that he could actually move his wounded arm a few inches without suffering too much discomfort. He had been working the arm consistently since leaving Boston, mostly because Chastity urged him to, and by the time the first rough buildings outside colonial America's largest city came into view, he was able to hold lightweight objects in his hand.

"It won't be long before you can put both arms around me," Chastity whispered in his ear. Such encouragement had been missing from his life for far too long.

They had picked up a pair of passengers in Trenton for the final leg of their journey. The two men, both older than Raines, spent most of their time in guarded conversation. Though they were courteous, neither evidenced any interest in engaging their fellow travelers.

Raines didn't mind in the least. He found it refreshing just to gaze out at the slowly passing countryside, enjoy the company of his young bride, and give some thought to what he would say to Sam Adams once he found him.

An idea had been brewing in the back of his mind ever since his arrival in 1780, and his chance meeting with young Gabriel played a huge part in it. Though he'd only been able to discuss the topic in the sketchiest terms with Leah, she supported him completely, and they had modified their earlier plans accordingly. At the time she felt reasonably confident that she could rely on Joel, and when the time came, she would bring him up to speed on the plan.

For now, connecting with Samuel Adams came first.

"Where will we stay?" Chastity asked.

"That's a splendid question. I've never been to Philadelphia, but I imagine we'll be able to find lodging easily enough. And I'm sure the coachman can make a suggestion or two." He glanced at the two men sitting opposite them. "Perhaps one of these gentlemen could suggest a suitable place."

His comment landed during a moment of silence in their discussions, but neither seemed motivated to respond.

"Come, come," Raines said, "surely one of you can recommend a reputable place where Mrs. Kerr and I can stay."

"I'd say much depends on your business in the city," one of the men said.

Raines wondered briefly if name-dropping would be a bad idea, but before he could respond, Chastity said, "My family has long been friends with Lawyer Adams--Samuel, not John. He's here now, and we intend to meet with him. We'll need lodging as close to the State House as we can get."

"Then it's City Tavern you want," he said. "You can't get a glass of Madeira there without tripping over a politician."

"Philadelphia has more public houses than

churches," said the second man. "You won't have trouble finding lodging. And, from what I hear, there are no end of loyalist houses standing empty. You could have one of those for a song."

"Thank you," Raines said. "We'll look into it."

"You may find a room at City Tavern difficult to obtain," said the first man. "But be careful. There are scoundrels about."

Raines had no doubt of that, and when the coach finally stopped, and the four passengers debarked, they stood directly in front of the tavern in question.

Their two fellow travelers quickly walked away with neither a "farewell" nor a "by your leave."

The driver agreed to haul their trunk to the side door before he left, and Raines rewarded him with a generous tip. He grinned knowing what a bargain he'd just gotten compared to what the man's 21st century counterparts would have expected.

Arm in arm, Raines and Chastity prepared to enter the front door of City Tavern, Philadelphia's most celebrated congressional watering hole.

Unfortunately, two men blocked their path. Though they dressed marginally better than frontiersmen, they displayed an air of hostility Raines associated with biker gangs, or in contemporary terms, buccaneers. Both appeared intensely interested in Chastity and not the least concerned by his presence.

He couldn't help but wonder what he'd been thinking when he left the gun in his valise for the driver to deliver with their trunk.

Treason, Treason!

~*~

On Sunday, September 17th, Benedict hosted a gathering early in the day to celebrate Peggy's arrival. He left the afternoon open in order to meet General Washington when he crossed the Hudson on his way to Hartford. His many guests would surely understand.

The Smith family, plus the enigmatic Dawkins couple, Benedict's aides, Colonel Lamb and a few other officers from West Point, all attended the soiree at the Robinson estate. A messenger arrived during the meal with a message.

What now, I wonder.

He opened the missive while still at the table and struggled to maintain his composure while he read it. At that very moment the loyalist Colonel, Beverly Robinson, was aboard the 14-gun British sloop, *Vulture*--with a business associate named Anderson--requesting a meeting with the "current occupant" of his home, ostensibly to determine the physical condition of the building and grounds.

Benedict kept a straight face as he turned to his guests and apologized for the interruption. "It's a note from our host," he said, causing several of his guests to dip their brows in confusion.

He gestured with both hands to the well-appointed home they occupied. "Colonel Robinson has requested an interview."

Colonel Lamb coughed. "*Beverly* Robinson, the Tory swine? That Robinson?" His face grew redder with every word, and the combination of his scowl and his scars caused Peggy to gasp.

"He wants to know if we're taking proper care of his house," Benedict said.

"You'd be a fool to have anything to do with him," Lamb growled.

Neither Varick nor Franks said anything. Nor did they need to. With the exception of Benedict himself, everyone else in uniform held a low opinion of loyalists. The fact Robinson held a commission in the British army only made it worse.

"You'll see Washington later today," Lamb said, still angry. "He needs to be aware of such improper correspondence. If Robinson wants an interview, let the devil grant it in hell."

Benedict admonished the Colonel, reminding him there were ladies present.

Lamb nodded to the three women, then gave Smith a disdainful glare. "I suspect most people at this table would share my sentiments."

"I'm sure they do," Benedict said, putting Andre's note in his pocket. "I will be sure to show it to General Washington. And, if I don't wish to be late, I must leave now for that very rendezvous."

Varick and Franks were on their feet as Benedict rose from his chair. He set them in motion with a glance to the door. They would have his barge ready in moments, and he'd be on his way.

~*~

Soon after Arnold and his aides departed, everyone else left the dining room. Mrs. Smith stood beside the long table eyeing the dishes and food left behind.

Leah put a hand on her shoulder. "You don't have to clean up this time."

The woman looked up, bewildered, and Leah pointed to a pair of soldiers who had already begun to clear off the table. No doubt there were many who would volunteer for such duty as they would be able to avail themselves of leftovers.

Mrs. Smith just nodded and walked unsteadily out of the room.

"I'm worried about that woman," Leah told Joel. "She's not stable."

"That's a given, considering who she's married to, and what she puts up with."

They walked outside and observed Colonel Lamb and the rest of the patriot troops preparing to return to their posts.

"That Colonel Lamb is--" Joel hesitated "--really something."

"He's served with Arnold from the start," Leah said. "Got wounded in a couple of the same battles, in fact. But he never lost sight of what the fighting was for. I'm not sure Arnold ever had it. He wanted glory, and the power of command. But I doubt he ever gave a damn about freedom for folks at the bottom of the food chain."

"Like Mrs. Smith?"

"And millions more." She leaned close, and he put his arms around her. It felt incredibly good to have someone like Joel to depend on, and she was tempted to tell him about the next phase of the plan. But it would have to wait.

"I wish we could have gone with Arnold to meet Washington," she said. "I can't imagine what that would be like."

"Probably not very pleasant," Joel said. "Especially if your goal is to point out that his most heroic general is really a turncoat."

She acknowledged the point, then added, "That's not the only thing I need to talk to him about."

"Oh? What else is there?"

Me and my big mouth!

"I'll tell you... later."

~*~

"Pardon us, gentlemen," Raines said, attempting to ease his way between the two men blocking the entrance to City Tavern.

Neither of them moved.

Raines stepped back. "We'd like to pass."

Neither of them spoke.

"So much for 'brotherly love,'" Raines said. He reached for Chastity to guide her away, but she shook free.

"We're going inside," she said staring up at the taller of the two.

His lips spread out in a parody of a smile, but his teeth were so bad the result was revolting. "We'd rather take you somewhere else," he said, though Raines had difficulty understanding him.

Instead of backing away, Chastity moved closer, and Raines' heart rate kicked up several notches. "We don't want any trouble," he said.

"It's no trouble," said the tall, dentally handicapped one. He stood with hands on hips and legs wide, his chest mere inches from Chastity's.

Raines was contemplating how to deliver two, quick, incident-ending punches before either man could retaliate, but Chastity was in the way.

"Let's go," he said reaching once again for her arm.

The tall man's eyes suddenly went wide in surprise, but his expression quickly changed from anticipation to dread. He tipped his head forward and looked down. Raines watched his Adam's apple bob as Chastity grabbed his belt with her free hand and reduced the distance between them still more.

"You got whut I think you got?" the man asked, his breath potent.

"Would you like to find out?"

He tried to back away, but she moved with him, her arm pressed between them.

"What's she doin'?" the second man asked, belatedly aware that their subtle attack plans were rapidly lurching sideways. "Hey now!" He started to reach for Chastity when his comrade screamed at him to stop.

"*Whut?*"

"She's put a knife t' me bollocks!"

"No, sir," she said, "it's a razor. Ever so much sharper."

Raines began to smile. "Move back," he cautioned the shorter man.

He resisted, barking, "Or whut?"

No longer concerned about Chastity, Raines relieved his pent-up hostility on the shorter man, striking him with a palm to the nose. The resulting crunch tore the taller man's eyes away from the girl threatening to geld him.

"Ah'm sorry, ma'am. We'll jes' go now," he mumbled as his companion lay moaning on the wooden walkway.

Chastity applied upward pressure with the weapon in her hand causing the remaining assailant to rise up on his toes, his face a Greek tragedy mask. "Don' cut me, ma'am. Please!"

The downed man shifted a hand from his ruined nose to the ground to stand up. Raines stepped on the hand, pinning it in place, which generated still more moaning.

"Stay there," Raines growled. "And be nice."

"Please, we'll trouble ye' n'more," the tall man said.

Raines stepped off the downed man's hand and settled himself for another strike in case his taller friend tried to retaliate. Fortunately for all of them, he didn't.

Instead, he helped his friend to his feet, and the two of them skulked away.

Chastity's bravado crumbled as soon as their assailants were gone.

Raines hugged her as well as he could with one arm while she choked back tears. "I can't believe you brought your father's razor! Where have you been hiding it?"

She looked up at him and smiled through a sniff and a tear. "I don't have a razor."

"You what? But I saw--"

She eased back far enough to reveal a collapsible fan. "That's why I had to stay so close to him. I couldn't let him see what I was really holding."

Raines shook his head in wonder. "You're amazing, you know that?"

"No," she said, "you are! I've never seen anyone strike such a blow. He went down like you'd struck him with a mallet."

He gave her an "aw shucks" grin. "I have to keep fights short. I'm not quick enough to get in more than a punch or two. Gotta make 'em count."

She kissed him on the cheek. "I'm hungry."

"Me, too," he said. "Beating up street toughs is hard work."

"Maybe after we eat we can inquire about Master Adams."

"Excellent," he said.

They entered City Tavern arm in arm. Fearless.

~*~

The current on the Hudson made Benedict's ten mile trip downriver to Stony Point reasonably quick. Had they traveled a mile or two farther, they would have reached Smith's great stone house. As previously agreed, the Smiths would stay with Peggy and leave their riverside mansion available for him to meet with Andre'.

Washington's party arrived at King's Ferry a short time later. The total contingent numbered four dozen rather than the three and a half he'd mentioned in his letter. Not surprisingly, every man in the company was uniformed, and while some of their clothes bore patches and stitch work, they looked every bit the military professionals Benedict knew them to be. Whatever else Washington's men might lack, they had a store of pride unequaled anywhere.

Watching that entourage, and remembering what it felt like to have the trust of the man leading it, brought Arnold to an uncharacteristic moment of indecision. Could he really go through with it? Could he really turn on this company of gallants, and walk away from everything for which he'd fought so hard?

But as Benedict observed Washington interact with his cadre, he envisioned one man who *wasn't* there--Joseph Reed--the Commander-in-Chief's former aide-de-camp and personal secretary. And with that memory came a hardening of Benedict's resolve. Reed, currently serving as President of Pennsylvania, had been the worst of all the thorns in Benedict's hide. Of all the people who'd rankled and belittled him, Reed topped the list.

The bitter general was still musing on his younger rival when Washington called him over. Benedict shook off his memories and hurried to meet his superior.

Washington welcomed him warmly and ushered him aboard the ferryboat for the crossing. Large enough to accommodate two freight wagons and a dozen horses, the huge, flat, floating platform offered no seats or any protection from the elements. Fortunately, the weather remained fair and visibility excellent.

Benedict shared with Washington the letter he received from Robinson, knowing the loyalist was once a dear friend of the commanding general. He even referenced Colonel Lamb's thoughts on the matter. Washington read the note and quietly returned it. He stood looking toward the south end of Haverstraw Bay where the British warship, *Vulture*, rocked in the gentle river swells. After a while he requested a telescope with which he surveyed the distant vessel, never once revealing his thoughts.

Finally, he put Benedict's restless mind at ease, telling him to follow Colonel Lamb's advice and ignore Robinson's request.

Feeling he'd demonstrated sufficient faithfulness, Benedict reported on the status of the repairs to West Point and the surrounding fortifications. He tried to give the impression that considerable progress had been made. But Washington couldn't be fooled, and if Benedict ever doubted that the General had his own eyes and ears in the area, his orders to Benedict confirmed it.

"It must be shored up. Clinton has received reinforcements, and he desires battle in the worst way. You must prepare. I will return from Hartford on Saturday, the 23rd. Do not wait for my return to restore the fortifications to readiness."

"I will do my best, sir," Benedict replied.

"I will order a shift in forces," Washington said, "and have patriots directed to the highlands."

Benedict bid the General farewell and prepared to return to Peggy and his other guests at the Robinson house. The curtain had finally begun to rise on the final act.

~*~

Excerpt from the *Susquehanna Shopper*:

Host Suspended In Media Flap

Scranton, Pennsylvania, Fri., June 22, 2012-- Fans of the nationally broadcast radio program, "Rumor Has It," are upset over the suspension of the show's popular host, Bradley Nettles.

A spokesperson for the program's home station said the often prickly on-air personality had been given time off to recover from an "undisclosed illness." Listeners were quick to challenge the station's claim saying Nettles had been silenced after asserting that the government was involved in a cover-up meant to hide the disappearance of a top military official.

In a nation-wide broadcast earlier in the week, Nettles claimed that someone named David Fitzwilliam, supposedly a descendant of Sir William Fitzwilliam, a member of the House of Lords in the late 18th century, had gone missing. The alleged missing man supposedly held a leadership position in the Office of the Defense Staff.

A careful search of peerage records reveals that Nettles' claim has no merit. Sir William Fitzwilliam had but one heir, and he died during the North American Colonial Rebellion in 1780.

Chapter Twenty-two

"If Moses had been paid newspaper rates for the Ten Commandments, he might have written Two Thousand Commandments."

--Isaac Bashevis Singer

By inviting Smith to stay at the Robinson house, Benedict effectively removed him from the game, at least as far as conveying messages. That was not entirely a bad thing, as Benedict had begun to have doubts about whether or not his notes were getting through to Andre' without first being intercepted by spies for the colonists. Double agents, while quite helpful, could never be fully trusted. Smith lacked the subtlety of a good spy, but he had yet to do anything to make Benedict overly suspicious.

With such thoughts in mind, Benedict contracted a different agent to deliver his next letter. Completely disregarding Washington's advice to ignore Robinson, Benedict wrote back on Monday, September 18th, saying he would "send a person to

Dobb's Ferry, or on board the *Vulture*, Wednesday night the 20th," and suggested it would "be advisable for the *Vulture* to remain where she is until the time mentioned."

Based on Robinson's note, Benedict knew Andre' was with him. Benedict counted on Andre' to realize it would be easier for everyone if the *Vulture* remained where she was, near Teller's Point, since it was so close to Smith's house on Haverstraw Bay. Dobb's Ferry, on the other hand, lay three times farther away to the south.

Smith had already agreed to let Benedict meet Andre' at his house on the Hudson, so Benedict felt confident Smith would agree to make the trip to the *Vulture* to collect the British officer and deliver him to the meeting. It was a minor point but still open on Benedict's agenda. He would tackle it as soon as he finished his official business: ordering that "no person whatever" would be allowed to cross the river without a pass.

When Benedict returned home to the Robinson house late that day, Smith and the Dawkins couple were engaged in spirited conversation. Mrs. Smith sat nearby, but they may have been speaking Mandarin for all the attention she paid them.

Benedict called Smith aside, and they walked casually out of earshot. As the weather had turned cool, they stayed in the dying sunlight to keep warm.

"I need your help once again, my friend," Benedict said. "It's a mission of great importance."

"You know you can count on me," Smith replied.

Benedict filled him in on the particulars, stressing the importance of meeting his agent on board the *Vulture* at the appointed hour--midnight, two days hence. Though it required considerably more than the usual level of inducement, Smith agreed.

Finally, Benedict gave him safe conduct papers for himself, two servants, and John Anderson "to pass and re-pass the guards near King's Ferry at all times."

Rather than walk back with Smith and waste time with the man's relatives, he entered the house through the back and went immediately in search of Peggy. They had some planning of their own to do.

~*~

Samuel Adams, Raines quickly discovered, was adept at staying out of sight when he wasn't engaged in affairs of the Continental Congress. According to one of his legislative colleagues who maintained a regular weekly table at City Tavern, Adams was too driven by his work to join in social affairs. Another associate pulled Raines aside and confided that Adams lacked the means to join them. He was, in fact, a poor man despite being possessed of a rich mind.

Raines smiled at such a characterization and offered to buy his new found acquaintances a round of Madeira to thank them for their candor. It was after the third such round that one of them divulged Adams' Philadelphia address.

Wasting no time to find the man, Raines hired

a buggy to take them directly there. "But t'will soon be dark," Chastity protested.

"If needs be, I'll procure a lamp," Raines said, wondering when he'd begun using colloquial speech patterns. "He'll be back in the State House by morning, and we'll never get in to see him there. Maybe we can buy him a meal or something, and I can present my case."

Chastity patted his arm and settled in for the remainder of the ride. Somewhat later she asked, "What did you mean the other day when you said, 'so much for brotherly love'?"

"'Philadelphia' is Greek for 'brotherly love.'"

"Of course. You were speaking in jest."

"Absolutely."

She hugged his good arm. "Promise me you won't keep me pregnant and stupid."

Pregnant?

He looked at her in consternation. "I-- What?"

"I took the liberty of looking through your things while you slept."

Oh, hell....

He closed his eyes, dreading what might come next.

"It puzzled me that whenever Gabriel mentioned you, he talked about 'mysterious ways,' but I never knew quite what he meant. Now, after seeing the things in your valise..." She looked at him in awe. "I can't describe them. They're wondrous."

"The gun--"

"Not just that. I'm talking about the printed papers. The illustrations are astounding! They're so... so *real*. And your tools! I've never seen such things."

"Tools?" He said, keeping his voice low, and hoping she would do the same. "What tools? And more importantly, what about pregnancy?"

"I'm not pregnant," she said. "At least, I don't think so. I meant I want more from life than having babies. I want them, too, of course, but there's so much more. So much to learn. And I want to start with the things in your valise."

She went on to recount what she'd seen, finally describing what could only have been the radio. He and Chastity had been together constantly since leaving Boston; he hadn't had a chance to test it. "I wish you hadn't done that," he said.

"What?"

"Poked around in my things."

She looked disappointed. "But-- Was I wrong in that? I meant no harm. And as husband and wife, we shouldn't keep secrets from one another."

Oh? Then where did you learn the "dance" moves you used to seduce me, you little vixen?

"What is it?" she asked.

He rubbed his forehead. "I-- I suppose this is as good a time as any to level with you."

"Level with me?" She appeared completely adrift. "Whatever do you mean?"

"Here we are, sir!" the driver said, his voice loud in the growing darkness.

Saved by the bell?

"Can you stay here awhile?" he asked the driver. "I've no idea if the man we're looking for is at home."

"I kin stay th' night if need be." He looked at

Chastity. "Ah'm sure the lady and me kin find some'at to discuss."

Though hardly excited by the idea of leaving Chastity alone, she'd shown herself to be more than just merely resourceful. She had courage to back up her instincts. And, she had the gun. Raines nodded to the driver. "I'll be right back."

He walked to the door of the boarding house where Samuel Adams supposedly lived. Adams was arguably one of the two most despised men on Earth, as far as the British were concerned. Leah had been adamant about the distinction. The other was Alexander Hamilton, the only two men *not* covered by a blanket amnesty issued by King George III.

How was Raines going to tell such a man he'd come calling from more than two hundred years in the future, especially when he had yet to explain that little detail to his own wife?

He took a deep breath, exhaled, and knocked on the great man's door.

When Joshua Smith returned to the front porch, Joel and Leah were waiting for him. Smith's wife, sitting in a rocker with her head tilted back, had dozed off. Smith ignored her and walked straight to them.

Leah addressed him directly, "Well?"

"He paid me to row out to the *Vulture*, collect a passenger, and bring him back to my house," Smith said. "He didn't say who or why he needed to meet with him."

"There could be a dozen reasons," Joel said.

Smith looked confused. "I didn't let on that I know about his strange device--"

"Thank God!" Leah whispered harshly. "You must never give him *any* reason to think you know such a thing! There's no telling how he might react."

"Oh, I know," Joel said. "He'd kill you on the spot and think nothing of it."

Smith swallowed hard.

"I know it's unsettling," Leah said. "But you must be strong. For your wife and children if not for yourself."

Smith's wife snorted, then murmured something in her sleep.

"I wish there were some way to protect you," Joel said. "In case something goes wrong, and Arnold's contact decides he can't leave any witnesses."

Leah shuddered. "He'd put you over the side in an instant."

"You really think there could be treachery?"

"*Think?*" Joel laughed. "I'd be amazed if there weren't."

Visibly shaken, Smith lowered himself into a chair. "Surely they wouldn't do anything rash. I'm merely providing transportation. I'm not actually involved in--"

"Oh, you're involved all right," Leah said. "I just hope you're not in over your head." She grimaced. "Sorry! When I said 'over your head,' I didn't mean in water over your head, or that you'd be drowned." She waved her hand in front of her face. "There I go speaking out of turn. I'm so sorry. I don't mean to alarm you."

Joel took a firm grip on Smith's shoulder. "We're merely trying to help. You can't go into this blind. You must be aware of the consequences."

Smith gave his head a shake. "I- I won't do it! I'll tell him I've other business, or that I'm ill, or--"

"That would be worse," Leah said. "He'd suspect you changed your mind for some other reason. I doubt he'd believe any excuse you offered."

"Th-then I'll run!"

"In case you've forgotten, he has an entire army he can devote to finding you," Leah said.

"I'm done for."

Leah smiled encouragingly. "Maybe not."

Smith reached for her as if he were drowning. "What are you thinking?"

"Perhaps one of us could go with you."

"Yes, yes--that's it! When I told him I lacked the strength to do so much rowing by myself, he told me to hire tenant farmers to man the oars. One of you could do it instead."

Joel shook his head. "It's too risky. Arnold knows us, and he only tolerates us because he thinks we're related to you."

Smith's voice had a plaintive tone. "B-but Arnold wouldn't have to know you're coming along! I wouldn't tell him. You'd just be there. He wouldn't find out until we delivered whoever it is he wants to meet. By then it would be too late for him to say or do anything about it. If he complains, I'll tell him I was merely being thrifty, and you were trying to repay me for providing a roof in your hour of need."

Joel rubbed his chin, but tried not to be

overly dramatic. Though he'd never sailed anything larger than a canoe--and that had been long ago--he doubted rowing would be very difficult.

Leah made a show of considering Smith's proposal. "It might just work," she said at length. "In fact, we could both go with you."

Have you lost your mind, Leah?

Overcome by relief, Smith wilted in his chair. "Oh, yes! It will be so much better this way. Safer for everyone."

Joel tried to make eye contact with Leah in hopes of discouraging her, but she wouldn't cooperate. He had no idea how she intended to make herself look like a tenant farmer instead of a runway model.

They continued to discuss the mission, careful to keep their voices low. By the time the soldier assigned to cook for General Arnold announced that the evening meal was ready, Smith's spirits had been restored.

Joel's were headed in the opposite direction.

Later that evening, as the household quieted for the night, Leah slipped out of the room she shared with Joel and walked out onto the front porch. It had taken forever for Joel to go to sleep, especially after they'd had words about her intention to help him row Smith's boat out to the *Vulture*. He tried to talk her out of it, but she prevailed. She knew he only meant to protect her, and his efforts moved her. He cared for her, deeply.

And if she allowed herself, she could easily feel the same way. But a greater need drove her, as it had from the beginning, and she couldn't let her feelings get in the way.

The late September night was quite cool, and she wore her topcoat over the thin undergarment that doubled as both nightshirt and blouse. It didn't help much.

A guard sat on the bottom step with a musket across his lap. He neither moved nor spoke when she left the house, appearing all but invisible in the darkness.

"I beg your pardon," she said in a low voice, but the guard didn't react.

She walked down a few steps and gave the man a closer look. Though she couldn't see his face, he didn't appear too old. She cleared her throat, but he still didn't respond, so she reached out and touched him lightly on the shoulder.

He raised his head, slowly at first, and when she spoke again he yelped as he leapt from the step. He looked as if she'd tried to set him on fire.

Startled, she sat down hard on the steps with her hands above her head. "Don't shoot!"

Blinking rapidly, the young soldier swept his musket in a broad arc between them.

"I didn't mean to startle you," she said. "I had no idea you were asleep."

"No, ma'am," he said, "t'warn't sleepin'."

"Of course not. You were probably just going over your orders in your mind."

He frowned. "Ah don't-- It's--"

"It's all right," she said, smiling. "Everything's

fine. I imagine it's about time to make your rounds, or trade off with someone else, right?"

"Ah'll be here all night. Keepin' the Gen'ral safe. Them's orders."

"I see. Well, don't let me bother you."

He yawned. "'Tis no bother. But now that I think on it, maybe I should walk aroun' some."

She watched him meander into the dark and listened intently until she could no longer hear him, then she removed the radio from the pocket of her coat and thumbed it on.

Her earlier attempts to reach her father had gone unanswered, but she wasn't surprised. Considering that neither of them had a good watch, and both had companions who knew nothing about the radios, timing their efforts would be difficult.

She thumbed the transmit button. "Dad?"

After a prolonged silence, she tried again. "Daddy? Are you there?"

"Leah?"

Joel's voice made her freeze.

"Is that what I think it is?"

She turned to face him. "It's a radio."

He pursed his lips. "Probably the smallest one I've ever seen." He crossed his arms. "In fact, I'll bet it's the smallest one in the whole world."

"There's no need to be sarcastic," she said. "Dad has one just like it."

"And you expect to reach him in Boston with it? *From here?*"

"Actually, he should be in Philadelphia by now. It's a little closer."

Joel stepped back and leaned against the

door. "You're just full of news tonight, aren't you?"

"I was going to tell you in the morning."

"Sure you were," he said. "But why bother? A toy like that is only good for a mile or two, tops."

She switched it off to conserve power. "Dad figured out a way to amplify both the power and the signal when he was working on his time travel device."

"Great. Did he build anything else? A death ray maybe? Or a perpetual motion machine?"

"Stop it, Joel. What d'you want?"

"I want you to quit lying to me!"

"I never lied to you," she said. "I just didn't tell you everything."

"That's a distinction I never much cared for. Heard it way too often as a cop."

"So now I'm a criminal?"

He shook his head. "No. But you're not doing much to keep my trust. I thought we were on the same side."

"We are!"

"Then, why the secrets?"

She stood and climbed up the steps to get closer. "You have to understand, all my life it's just been Daddy and me. I didn't have many friends, and when I got to college, the few I did have didn't like my politics. They didn't stick around long. Not one of them. I taught myself not to care, to live within myself."

"I get that. Most of my life I've been alone, too. Can't remember the last time I spent Christmas with someone who wasn't in uniform, or jail."

"I'm sorry," she said. "I mean it."

He shrugged. "So, tell me about the radio."

"I've been trying to reach Dad."

"Obviously. And that's what you were doing the other night, at Smith's place?"

"Yeah. I should've told you then."

"No," he said. "You should've told me back in Boston!"

"All right! I screwed up." She chewed her lip. "I'm sorry."

"So tell me the rest of it."

"The rest of what?"

"What you hope to accomplish with the bloody radio!"

"I need to tell Dad when we stop Arnold."

"That's it?"

She nodded.

"Damn it, Leah! Stop playing games and tell me the rest of it."

A westerly breeze wafted across the porch, and she tried to withdraw deeper into her jacket. Joel looked impatient rather than sympathetic.

"It's kinda theoretical."

"I kinda don't give a shit," he said.

"It won't change anything we have to do." She reached for him, but he didn't respond. "We're a team, Joel. No--we're more than that. We're a *great* team. We're great together!"

"Woohoo. Makes me wanna run out on the field and score a goddamn goal. Yay team!"

"Sometimes you can be a real asshole."

"True," he said. "But I can be a pretty decent guy, too. And maybe, if given the chance, I could be the most important guy in your life."

"Joel, I--"

He reached for her with both hands and gripped her upper arms. "Look at me, damn it! This is all there is--all I am, and all I've got. If you want me to take a bullet for you, just say so. I'll do it. Seriously! I don't care. I don't have anything else to live for. But for God's sake, don't bullshit me anymore. I may not deserve much, but I deserve that, at least."

She melted into his arms, holding him tight, as if by sheer will they could merge their bodies where they stood.

"The truth is," she said, "I don't know what's going to happen."

"What's going to happen... *when?*"

"When we're successful. Assuming we stop Arnold."

He eased back far enough to look into her eyes. "I thought the whole idea was that if we're successful, the world becomes a better place."

"That's right," she said. "And that's the truly important part."

He frowned, his confusion evident. "And what does that mean, exactly?"

"It's pretty simple, really. If we're successful, the world changes. But... we might change, too."

"How?"

"That's the part that sucks. Dad and I talked about it a lot. He's got a ton of theories--some good, some not so good."

"And?"

"And the truth is, we don't know what'll happen."

"So we could what, I dunno, disappear?"

She looked directly into his eyes and spoke from her heart. "Yes. That's a distinct possibility."

~*~

As he usually did, Benedict brought a flask with him to his headquarters office in West Point the next morning. He paid a premium for good whiskey, and he appreciated its palliative effects on his ruined leg. Varick and Franks, to their credit, had sense enough to make no mention of it, despite the obvious odor on Benedict's breath.

Still, Benedict made a mighty effort to exhale *away* from his aides when they approached his desk. But when a message from Robinson arrived, he dropped all such pretenses. The only thing that mattered was the note, which he promptly decoded.

Surely God smiled on the enterprise! Robinson advised that the *Vulture* would remain precisely where she was, and that Mister Anderson would be pleased to meet the General "at any place you please."

Nothing could be more clear: Andre' would accept the ride from Smith to a midnight rendezvous with Benedict at Smith's house.

When he left his office that afternoon and headed home, Benedict had but one thing in mind: make sure Smith understood what was being asked of him--row out to the *Vulture*, pick up a passenger, and deliver him to his own house where Benedict would be waiting.

It was so simple nothing could possibly go

wrong.

~*~

The man who responded to Raines' knock was short, stout, and unpleasant.

"What?" he growled, from the shadow of his compartment.

"Mr. Adams?"

"What do you want? It's late. I'm tired. Who are you? Never mind. Go away!"

Slam!

Raines stared at the door a few inches from his nose. And then he grew angry. He hadn't spent a week in a rolling deathtrap just to have a door slammed in his face. He used the flat of his hand to pound on the politician's door.

It flew open, and the short, red-faced Bostonian glared at him like a demon from the fiery depths.

"I'm sorry to disturb you," Raines said.

"You most certainly are!"

"But we must talk." He shoved his letter of introduction from Colonel Cotswold toward the aggrieved legislator.

"What's this?"

"My introduction," Raines said. "May I come in?"

"No!" Adams said. "Stay where you are. Let me find my spectacles. Have you any idea how outrageous this is? To bother a member of congress at this late hour?"

"Of course I do," Raines said, not bothering to

disguise his irritation. "If there were some other way to reach you, I'd have chosen it."

Adams stood with a candle lamp in one hand and Cotswold's letter in the other. He read quickly, then looked up as he returned the letter. "You have one minute."

"For what?"

"To state your case. After which I'm going to close the door and go to bed. Now, speak your peace."

Raines swallowed his anger as best he could. "What I have to say I'm sure you'll find difficult to believe." He handed Adams a copy of *Applied Physics Quarterly*, the periodical he'd brought with him from the 21st century. "But it may save time if you'll simply thumb through that."

Adams peered at the cover of the thin magazine. Beneath the masthead lay a full-page, full-color illustration of an exploding star. Information bullets touted a variety of esoteric articles within. "What is it?"

"A souvenir from the 21st century."

Adams looked deep into his eyes. "You're not here to kill me, are you?"

Raines shook his head and smiled. "Of course not."

"Then, why *are* you here?"

"Both to offer help, and ask for it."

Adams returned his gaze to the magazine. He set the candle lamp on a dresser just inside the door and used both hands to flip through the pages. "This is remarkable. It's unlike anything I've ever seen."

"And yet it's commonplace in my world,"

Raines said.

Adams returned the publication. "I admire the pretty pictures. It's a handsome periodical, and I'm sure you'll earn great sums for its publication, provided you don't go bankrupt first. The cost must be exorbitant. Now, if you'll excuse me--"

"How would you like to talk to General Washington?" Raines asked.

"What?"

"General George Washington. Would you like to talk to him?"

"We've spoken many times."

Raines kept his foot beside the door to prevent Adams from closing it prematurely. "What if I told you I could make it possible for you to speak with him while he's in New York?"

"I'd say you were mad."

"Possibly," Raines said, still forcing himself to maintain a smile. "But play along with me for just a moment more. If I could make it possible for you to speak with the Commander-in-Chief of the Continental Army, at any time of the day or night, no matter where in the world either of you happened to be, would that be of some value?"

"Don't be ridiculous! Such a thing simply isn't possible."

"But if it were?"

Adams exhaled in monumental fashion, then said, "If such a thing were possible, which I don't believe for an instant, then of course I'd be interested."

"That's precisely what I wanted to hear. If you'll grant me some time to arrange a private demonstration, I'll put you in direct communication with General Washington."

"Here? In Philadelphia?"

"You'll be here," Raines said. "General Washington will still be in New York."

"But--"

"I hope, by the time we meet again, that he'll have apprehended a traitor."

"*Now* what are you talking about?"

"One of Washington's subordinates, also a general, will attempt to betray this country. My own daughter is going to stop him, *and* make it possible for you to discuss the case with General Washington himself."

"This is preposterous."

"I know it's hard for you to believe. But if I'm nothing more than a charlatan, you'll have lost only a little time. On the other hand, if I'm telling the truth? What then?"

"If only a portion of what you claim is true, then you'll have my ear any time you want it."

"Thank you, sir," Raines said. "I hoped as much. I'll contact you again, right here if you wish, when I have established the connection with General Washington."

Adams continued to stare at him as if he'd dropped naked from the sky, painted purple, and playing a xylophone with his willie.

"Good night," Raines said. "And sweet dreams."

~*~

Excerpt from the *Baltimore Ledger*:

Government Can't Explain Poison Gas Scandal

Philadelphia, Pennsylvania, Tues., June 26, 2012--Parliament remains in an uproar over the scandal involving military transports and vast quantities of a deadly nerve agent said to have been readied for use against rebels in the Midlands.

Sources close to the Ministry of Defense claim that records for the procurement of the intensely concentrated toxic gas have either been misplaced or destroyed. The poison, reportedly of German origin, is an exact chemical match for the toxin used to assassinate the Queen in May.

Though martial law was declared ten days ago, enforcement efforts have fallen well short of expectations. "Rioting," according to Prime Minister Nathan Shelcroft, "has become the new national pastime."

Chapter Twenty-three

"It is hard to imagine a more stupid or more dangerous way of making decisions than by putting those decisions in the hands of people who pay no price for being wrong."
--Thomas Sowell

"I still haven't gotten through to my father," Leah said. "I need more time."

He hated to say "I told you so," especially knowing how prickly Leah got when someone helped her up after she tripped over her own pride, but Joel couldn't help himself. "As I recall, you were the one who insisted on coming along."

"I know, I know. But I thought I'd be able to connect with Dad before now."

"I presume he hasn't told Gabriel about the radio either."

Leah shook her head. "I doubt it. But he told me he's got great faith in that kid, and Chastity, too."

Joel smiled thinking of Chastity. He wondered what else Raines had in her besides "faith."

"What are you grinning about?" Leah asked.

Josh Langston

"Nothing."

"Oh, right."

Time to get back on track.

"I've got an idea for stretching things out," he said. "Instead of using the boat Arnold left for us, let's take the horses. By the time we get to Smith's place, it'll be too late to row across the Hudson. That'll give you an extra day to radio your Dad."

Leah agreed. "Smith should go for it, especially since Arnold's already on his way downriver. He won't be able to stop us."

"Are you going to get into your disguise now or later?" Joel asked.

"My tenant farmer costume? I'll wear parts of it and bring the rest."

They easily managed to avoid Peggy, who stayed busy with her baby, while they prepared for a long, leisurely ride to Smith's house.

The trip was uneventful except for a brief moment as they passed through Stony Point some two miles north of their destination. Smith produced the pass Arnold had given him for transiting King's Ferry which terminated at Stony Point. They were quickly waved through.

"You look way more pretty than gritty," Joel quipped as he appraised Leah from behind. She rode at a sedate pace, hips rocking with the motion of her horse.

"You just keep your eyes on the trail."

The sun had nearly set before they reached Smith's house. It was anyone's guess what would happen to them if he and Leah were successful in spoiling Arnold's plot. He hoped they had plans to

436

get out of town quickly if the need arose, as it almost certainly would.

"By the time I find a boat, it really will be too late to make the crossing," Smith said. "The current can be tricky, especially for the likes of you."

"What do you mean by that?" Leah asked, none too casually.

"Have you ever rowed a boat across a river like the Hudson?"

"Well, actually, no."

"Then you have no idea how hard it can be."

"Give it up, Leah," Joel said.

Smith remarked, "We should get word to Arnold that we're not going to the *Vulture* tonight."

"We're almost there," Joel said. "You can tell him yourself."

"And risk getting shot? No." He looked up quickly. "You go!"

Leah chimed in, "We're *supposed* to be tenant farmers, remember? Besides, no matter how good our disguises are, he'll recognize us."

Smith muttered and groused but ultimately agreed. They had to find someone else. "When Arnold first told me about this, I thought right away of two fellows who live nearby," he said. "The Cahoon brothers, Joseph and Samuel."

"Where've I heard that name?" Joel asked.

"Mrs. Cahoon," Smith said. "You paid her to help my wife."

"Small world," Leah said.

~*~

Raines could almost feel the intensity of Chastity's startling green eyes as she stared into his boring brown ones.

"You're from the *future*?"

He nodded.

"How is that possible? The future hasn't happened yet."

"Well," he said, "much depends on how one looks at it."

"No, it doesn't! All we have is right *now*. We can't choose to occupy the past or the future. God might be able to, but as much as I love you, and believe in you, you *aren't* God!"

He dumped the contents of his valise on the bed they shared in a second floor room of City Tavern.

"Look," he said as he poked through the collection of miscellany from the 21st century, "do you see anything that could've been made here? How 'bout this?" He held up a clear plastic lighter and thumbed the tiny wheel that ignited the gas inside. It did little to improve visibility in the dark room. He wished they had a dozen more candle lamps like the one they huddled over on the bed.

"It's pretty," she said, "and quite clever. What do you call it?"

"A cigarette lighter."

Her eyebrows narrowed. "What's a cigarette?"

"It's-- Never mind." He reached for a ballpoint pen, clicked it to expose the point, and wrote her name on the back of his only copy of *Applied Physics Quarterly.* "There! How 'bout that?"

"'Tis passing strange," she said.

He showed her a small flashlight, his toothbrush, a roll of dental floss, a pencil and finally, his radio. "None of this could be made here. Not now, anyway, but perhaps someday soon."

Chastity looked bewildered. "How did you come by these wondrous things?" Suddenly, she grew intense. "Are you in league with the devil, husband?"

"No, sweetheart. I promise I'm not. If anything, I'm on the side of the angels. And despite anything Gabriel might tell you, I'm no sort of supernatural being."

She closed her mouth, put her hands in her lap, and looked at him--innocent and slightly fearful.

"I'm a scientist. I teach physics, which word comes from--"

"It's Greek, meaning 'nature,' I think."

He felt his smile stretch his cheeks. "Yes! And slap me the next time I forget how smart you are."

She crossed her arms but said nothing.

"We came here--Leah, Joel, and I--to stop a man from doing something terrible. If he succeeds, this war will never end. We're still fighting it in my own time, two hundred years from now!"

Chastity remained silent and spellbound.

"But, if we can stop him, there's a very good chance the war will end. Perhaps soon. King George will lose, and the colonies will have their freedom."

She waved her hands at the items spread out on the bed. "And these things will help make that happen?"

"One of them might." He picked up the

transmitter and turned it on. With luck, he'd be able to reach Leah. "This is called a radio. It's a device for talking over long distances."

"How does it work?"

He chuckled. "It would be hard to explain in just a few words, but it's not terribly complicated. I drew some diagrams and made a few notes for you and Gabriel. You'll see them when you get back to Boston."

He heard a crackle from the radio, then: "Daddy? Are you there?"

Leah!

"Yes, baby! I'm here," he said, completely forgetting to press the SEND button.

"Come in, Dad. Can you hear me? Dad?"

He pressed the button. "You're coming in loud and clear, baby girl! Are you all right?"

Chastity stared in shock at the voice coming from the little box in his hand. "It's... *her*. It's your daughter!"

Raines nodded enthusiastically.

"We're fine, Dad. This thing is supposed to go down at midnight tomorrow. Should've happened already, but Joel managed to delay things for a day."

"I can't wait to hear all about it," he said.

"Have you told Gabriel about us yet?"

He glanced at Chastity. "Uh, no. Not exactly."

"Oh, so he's not there with you now?"

"No," Raines said. "But Chastity is."

"*Chastity?*"

Raines could hear some talking in the background and assumed it was Leah and Joel. "I would have preferred to tell you this in person, but, uhm... Things didn't go exactly as we planned."

"I guess not," Leah said, "if Chastity's there with you instead of Gabriel." Her words were punctuated by a sharp intake of breath. "You two aren't... I mean... Does the Colonel know you're *together?*"

"Actually," Raines said, "he gave away the bride. Gabriel was my Best Man."

Though he'd played the scenario in his mind many times, and with many possible outcomes, Raines had no idea how Leah would really react when she got the news. Complete silence, however, was an option he'd never considered.

He pressed SEND again. "Are you still there, Leah?"

More silence.

Lord, please give me strength.

"Congratulations, sir." Joel's voice finally came through, shaky but easily recognizable. "You're a... a very lucky man."

"Yes, I know," Raines said. "Will you please put Leah back on. I need to explain--"

"Stand by."

"They sound as if they're in the next room," Chastity said, still amazed. "How is--"

"Okay," Joel said. "She's coming."

Raines tried to keep his voice calm, but failed. "I don't understand! What's the matter?"

Joel's voice came back at him. "She was laughing so hard she couldn't talk."

~*~

Benedict was alone in Smith's house when someone knocked on the front door. He limped over to answer it, knowing it was far too early for Andre' to have arrived. He picked up a pistol and cocked it before opening the door. Without his aides or his usual cadre of guards, he couldn't be too careful. The small escort he'd brought with him was camped at the rear of the estate where they were unlikely to interfere with Andre' when he arrived.

Setting his candle lamp on a table beside the entrance, he gripped the pistol and opened the door. A grubby-looking man in soiled and heavily patched clothing stood before him, a cloth cap twisted in his calloused hands.

"Gen'ral Arnold, sir?"

"Yes. What is it?"

"Name's Cahoon, sir, Samuel Cahoon. Master Smith sent me."

What now?

"'E sends 'is regrets, sir. An' most distressed 'e was, too. I'm to say 'e won't be makin' no river crossin' this night."

Benedict tried forcing himself into a state approaching calm but came up woefully short. Despite the whiskey he'd consumed to ease the pain in his leg, the growing tension and his sudden fury at Smith's ineptitude left him nearly rigid.

"Would ye 'ave me say anythin' to 'im for ye', sir?"

"No," Benedict said. "Not just now."

Cahoon bowed then stood at the door, waiting.

"What do you want?" Benedict asked.

"Well, sir, I thought ye' might gimme a bit o' sumpin' for me trouble. It's late y'see, and--"

Benedict slammed the door and went to refill his whiskey glass. Dawn could not come too early.

Unfortunately, he was wrong. He barely slept at all, and when he gave up the last pretense of trying, his jaws hurt from all the clenching he'd done during the night. Leaving the house at first light, he yelled for his horse and waited while his men scrambled to accompany him.

With barely half his escort ready, he swung into the saddle and whipped the horse into a run. He covered the two-mile stretch between Smith's house and King's Ferry with astonishing speed and roused the ferry operator well before the man's planned departure.

Having no use for anyone else's schedule, Benedict browbeat the ferryman to shove off at once and spent the short passage scowling and pacing the broad, flat, empty deck.

When he reached the eastern side, he found a letter waiting for him, supposedly written by the Captain of the *Vulture,* complaining about the behavior of some soldiers under Benedict's command. All of that was nonsense, of course. Benedict recognized Andre's handwriting the moment he saw it. The document had even been countersigned by "John Anderson."

The bloody fool may as well have taken out an advertisement!

But, the real message was only obvious to Benedict. Andre' would stay one more night. He would be ready, as before, expecting to meet

Benedict's contact.

Rather than risk yet another failure by leaving everything up to Smith, Benedict decided to remain nearby to personally oversee as much of the operation as possible.

While waiting to board the ferry for the return crossing to Stony Point, he was approached by Lieutenant Colonel James Livingston, a subordinate of the fiercely disfigured Colonel Lamb.

"A moment of your time, General," he said.

Benedict took a deep breath to keep from shouting at the interruption. "Whatever do you want?" he snapped.

Livingston was taken aback by Benedict's hostility. "I thought perhaps the General might be interested in reviewing some adjustments we've made for--"

"That's quite enough, Colonel. Do I look like I might be interested in something as mundane as field artillery *adjustments?* I am extraordinarily busy. I expect every officer in my command to be aware of that--and not waste my time!"

"Yes, sir. Of course. My apologies."

"You're dismissed, Colonel. Go finish your damned adjustments."

A red-faced Livingston saluted him, then turned quickly and departed. Benedict just as quickly forgot the episode and concentrated on preparing for that evening's rendezvous with Andre'.

This time, by God, nothing would be left to chance.

~*~

Leah and Joel stood upwind of Smith as he set another bowlful of tobacco alight. He generated a cloud of aromatic fumes which tempered the odor of the nearby barn. They heard the unmistakable sounds of mounted men approaching.

"It's Arnold," Smith said. "I suspect he's not going to be very happy with me."

"We should make ourselves scarce," Joel said. "There's no point in giving him anything to be suspicious about. He won't do anything stupid with so many of his men all around."

"But--"

"Just don't go anywhere with him. Stay here. We'll be in the loft, listening. If something dreadful happens, we'll be here to help you. Don't worry."

Smith looked anything but unworried, yet he somehow managed a reasonable attitude as Arnold rode close to the building and dismounted. He gestured for his men to deliver two other civilians, Samuel Cahoon and his brother, Joseph. Arnold had all three herded into the barn, then dismissed the troops who had accompanied them.

For the next several minutes, Arnold berated all three men for their failure to accomplish their mission the previous evening. The Cahoons tried to protest that they had nothing to do with it, but Arnold gave them no chance to explain themselves. He was well past explanations, and he certainly didn't want excuses.

The men kept their heads down while they shuffled their feet and grumbled. Eventually, Arnold made them swear they'd follow his orders and complete their mission. The boat he'd provided for them had been pulled up a nearby creek, and all was in readiness.

He left as abruptly as he arrived, and Leah and Joel waited until they were certain he'd reached the house before they climbed down from the loft. The Cahoons were startled to see them.

"Well," Leah said, "that's one man I wouldn't want to cross."

The Cahoons expressed their thoughts, though she struggled to understand the exact words. General Arnold, evidently, was either a horse's behind or something a horse *left* behind. She wasn't quite sure, but she agreed either way.

"The problem is," Joel said to Smith, "he's not going to let either of us get on that boat with you."

"Then, I'm not going."

The Cahoons rattled off a chorus of agreement.

"There's money in it for you," Joel said, flipping one of Leah's bogus Spanish dollars into the air with his thumb.

The Cahoon brothers immediately began to caucus while Smith aimed a skeptical gaze at Joel.

"If you three don't show up," Leah said, "the General will send soldiers to find you. It wouldn't do to make him any angrier than he already is."

Joel addressed the tenant farmers. "We'll pay you double whatever Master Smith offered you."

"What about me?" Smith asked.

"We'll match whatever Arnold gave you."

"But *we* does all the work!" said an indignant

Cahoon.

"That's true," Leah said. "But someone must be in charge, after all. And General Arnold has chosen Master Smith."

"We'll be hiding on shore, waiting for you, when you return."

Smith scowled. "Don't you mean *if* I return?"

"You'll be fine," Leah said. "The general has no one else to turn to." She gestured at the Cahoons. "And these gentlemen won't report to anyone else. So, you see, Arnold can't afford to harm you."

~*~

With dusk near at hand, Joel and Leah huddled in the woods near the river keeping an eye on the boat Smith and the Cahoons would use to retrieve Arnold's co-conspirator. "It's got to be Andre'," Leah said. "That's who he worked with before. There's really no one else."

"Sounds logical. But aside from that, we've got a decision to make," Joel said.

"About what?"

"How to prove Arnold's a traitor. You've already said that just stopping him isn't good enough. Otherwise, you could have just killed him."

"I told you we weren't planning to do that. I promised."

"You promised that *I* wouldn't have to kill him," Joel said. "You never said you wouldn't do it yourself. Another sin of omission."

"It was never more than an extreme option," Leah said. "Killing Andre' is more likely, if it means we can keep the British from getting Arnold's information about surrendering the fort."

Joel nodded. "Okay, so there's that. I'm also thinking about a couple things your Dad said once you stopped giggling."

She smiled but managed not to do it again.

"He said we had to conserve the batteries in the radios, so from now on, the only time we'll turn them on is at dawn and dusk, and then only long enough to determine if someone needs to talk."

"Right," she said. "Makes sense, doesn't it?"

"Absolutely. But I'm still working on the other part, about arranging for General Washington to talk to Sam Adams by radio. What's that all about?"

"It'll prove to Washington that we're not just charlatans--that we have something to offer that isn't available anywhere else on Earth."

"Yeah, but available for how long? For all we know, the radios could start to fade as soon as Andre' is arrested or killed. Right? *Everything* from our version of the future might just cease to exist." He snapped his fingers. "Like that. *Including us!*"

Leah held her palms up in a universal gesture of ignorance. "It's possible. I can't say for sure. Nobody knows."

He frowned. "Seems like you and your Dad could have worked some of this stuff out a little better before either of you went time traveling."

"Maybe," she conceded. "But it's immaterial now. We've gotta play the hands we've been dealt."

"Right," said Joel, "and the only way we can do that is to split up."

She stared hard at him, then dropped her eyes. "Yeah. I know. I just didn't want to talk about it, 'cause...."

"Because neither of us wants to do it."

She nodded. "But there's no other way. One of us has to keep an eye on Andre', and one of us has to convince General Washington to talk to Sam Adams on the radio. There's no way we can do that and stay together."

"I think you'd have a much better shot at sweet talking Washington than I'd have," Joel said. "Besides, if one of us has to live in the woods and monitor Andre', I'm the better candidate."

She couldn't help but look down at Joel's bad leg. "Even with that?"

"Yeah," he said, rubbing the ever-aching limb, "even with this."

Leah kissed him. "I don't have any idea where Washington is right now."

"Aw, c'mon. I'll bet you do. Think! Would anything that's happened so far change the timetable you memorized?"

"I don't think so." She closed her eyes and concentrated on a mental calendar. "Today is the twenty-second. In the *old* 1780, the redcoats already controlled West Point. They were just waiting for Washington to return from his talks with Rochambeau, the French Admiral."

"And where were those talks?"

"In... uhm... Hartford!"

Joel groaned. "That's what? Seventy-five, eighty miles away?"

"Yes, but the talks are over now 'cause

Rochambeau thinks the Americans are too weak to fight, and Washington knows it's true. So he's already headed back." She closed her eyes again picturing the embryonic network of colonial roads. "He'll probably spend the night near Litchfield and head due west in the morning. That's what he did when the British captured him."

"But this time around, the good guys still hold West Point."

Leah already felt better about the task ahead. "If I move toward him, and he moves toward me, we'll meet in the middle."

Joel scanned the growing darkness. "Yeah, but there's a helluva lot of 'middle' out there."

"True, but there are only so many roads." Still feeling a little deflated, she leaned against him. "Put your arm around me, okay?"

"Sure."

"Keep me warm while I try to get Dad on the radio. I want to make sure he knows what we're trying to do."

Joel hugged her. "You don't have to tell him *everything* we might try to do."

~*~

The radio came quickly to life bearing Leah's clear, distinct voice. Chastity continued to keep her distance despite Raines' repeated assurances that the device was harmless.

"Anything new to report?" he asked.

Leah explained her reasons for separating from Joel in order to find General Washington. None of it came as a surprise. If anything, he had expected her to tell him sooner than she did.

"I don't like it," Raines told her. "There's too much that can go wrong, too many ways you could get hurt."

"Please tell me you're not trying to convince me that *my* safety is more important than that of the whole country."

"It is to me!" he said, knowing he had no hope of talking her out of her plan unless he had something better to offer.

"Surely you can find someone to go with you," he said.

"I could grab a militiaman or a tenant farmer and drag 'em along, but I doubt I'd be any safer than if I traveled alone."

"You're not going to make this easy for me, are you?"

"Nope," she said. "I love you, Dad, but I'm not asking for permission to do this. It has to be done, so I'm doing it. I just wanted you to know, that's all."

"For what it's worth," Joel said, "I'm not wild about the idea either. But Leah knows how to handle herself. She's proven that often enough."

"Joel?"

"Yes, sir?"

"Shut up."

"Yes, sir."

"And Leah?"

"Yes, Daddy?"

"God speed. Call me at every opportunity."

~*~

Excerpt from the *Wilmington Dispatch*:

Texas Republic Assured Attack Not Imminent

Houston, Texas, Wed., June 27, 2012--Justin Stark, New England's Ambassador to the Republic of Texas, told reporters on Tuesday that his meetings with President Whit Pridemore of the Texas Republic had been "timely and productive." Stark said he had delivered "rock-solid" assurances from New England's Parliament that Texans had no reason to be concerned about the upheaval among the ranks of New England's armed forces or the deployment of military tankers bearing toxic agents.

"Anyone who claims New England would deploy weapons designed for the sole purpose of harming civilians, is clearly irrational. We have never used such devices on civilian populations, and we never will."

When asked about the alleged deployment of gas-dispersal vehicles in the rebellious midlands, Stark refused comment.

Chapter Twenty-four

"An election is coming. Universal peace is declared, and the foxes have a sincere interest in prolonging the lives of the poultry."
--George Eliot, *Felix Holt*

Benedict looked out over the water as he had for the past few hours. Smith and his oafish oarsmen should have made the round trip in a fraction of that time. The distance between the *Vulture,* moored near Tellers Point, and the creek on the west side of the Hudson where they were to land, couldn't have been more than a mile.

What were they doing out there?

Finally, he heard low voices and the shipping of oars. With his dimmed candle lamp in hand, he crept back into the cover of some fir trees and waited for Smith to lead Andre' to him.

But rather than greet Andre' when they arrived, Benedict demanded that Smith explain why he had taken so long to make such a short trip.

"It isn't the distance; it's the conditions. We

fought the damned tide to get back here. The men are bone cold and worn out."

Benedict snorted in response. He had expected excuses, and that's precisely what Smith had given him. When Andre' cleared his throat, Benedict dismissed the country lawyer and gave his full attention to the British spy chief. "We should go up to the house. We'll be more comfortable by the fire."

"I'd rather not. It's already quite late, and we have much to discuss. Let's get it done so I can return to the *Vulture*. I have no desire to be out on the water after sunup."

"But I have horses. We can make the trip easily."

"Let's not waste another minute. We can talk here while the oarsmen rest. They need it."

Benedict relented, and the two huddled over the lamp discussing every conceivable detail of the operation. Andre' took careful notes of the fort's defenses, armaments, manpower and supplies. General Clinton, he explained, needed explicit information about where and how his forces could strike the strongest blows and incur the least resistance. The surrender had to look good, too. At least in the short term. Once Benedict reached the safety of the British lines he would no longer be concerned about appearances.

In return, Benedict insisted on written confirmation that the rewards promised him would be made good, down to the last farthing.

The negotiations dragged on much longer than either of them had anticipated. Eventually,

Smith returned with a warning. "Gentlemen, it's nearly four in the morning. If you keep this up, the sun will rise before we're halfway back across the river."

Even by the weak light of Benedict's lamp, Andre' appeared anxious. He accepted one last document, folded it with the others he'd been given, and slipped them inside his boot for safekeeping. "I'm off, then," he said, giving Benedict a firm handshake.

They wandered back to the creek where the boat and the Cahoon brothers were waiting. Both men had fallen asleep, and neither appreciated Smith's efforts to rouse them. Any store of patience Benedict might have had for the men had been exhausted during the previous night's debacle. He stepped between them and used his boot to get them moving.

"It's time to earn your pay," Benedict said. "Get this boat in the water and man your oars."

Samuel Cahoon responded bluntly, "Can ye not see it? The tide's turned. Again! Ye'll not see me tryin' t' row no dinghy 'gainst 'at. Noways."

His brother echoed those sentiments.

Benedict's anger mounted, and his resolve allowed no quarter. He fought back by threatening the tenant farmers, and when that didn't work, he offered them more money. Neither man gave in.

"Enough," Samuel said. "We won't do 't. We *can't* do 't. Me arms still ache from the last time. No, sir! I'll row no more this day."

Nor did Smith offer anything helpful. "To reach the *Vulture* before dawn, we'd have had to leave hours ago. It's too late now."

Reluctantly, Benedict agreed.

"Then, I'm *stuck* here?" Andre' asked.

"I'm afraid so. There's nothing else to be done. Perhaps now we can ride to the house and rest. You'll be on your way soon enough; the hard part's behind us."

Andre' appeared too battered to protest. After enduring two nights without sleep and a marathon negotiating session with Benedict, the man could barely stand without support. He had nothing left with which to protest.

Benedict guided him to the horses he had standing by. They mounted and rode directly to Smith's house.

~*~

For Joel, the night had been long and grim. Watching Leah ride north, alone, on the road to West Point all but devastated him. How could he simply let her go like that? The dark forests of the Hudson Highlands provided shelter to brigands from both sides. And while he waited, hidden in a blind close to the very spot where Arnold would sell out his country, Leah risked her life to find Washington, a man who might not give her the time of day.

Yet, he had made the decision to give up Leah and observe the traitor.

Though his vantage point allowed him to watch what went on, Joel wasn't close enough to make out conversations clearly. Other than an occasional rise in volume, Arnold and Andre' remained civil and cold-bloodedly conscientious.

Smith's interruption came as blessed relief. The hours Joel had spent on the 18th century stakeout were about to be rewarded. He suspected Andre' was weary from lack of sleep and wrangling with the bull-headed general.

Joel knew they'd spend the night on shore because he had already drilled holes in the boat the Cahoons rowed up into the creek. While they slept, he'd augured three perfect circles through the flat hull. Between the opposing tide and those three holes, Andre' would have to walk on water to reach the *Vulture*.

He caught up with Smith after the conspirators rode toward the house, and the country lawyer confirmed where they would spend the night.

"He told me I wasn't welcome in my own home."

Joel responded with an all-purpose "what can ya do" shrug. "I'm sorry, but it was to be expected. Arnold's an ass. He and Andre' deserve each other. Oh, and I'm sorry about your boat, too. I put a couple holes in it."

"It's not mine," Smith said.

"Well, someone's not going to be happy the next time they take it out fishing."

Smith clapped him on the shoulder. "I'm sleeping in the barn. Care to join me?"

Joel chuckled despite the fatigue and his bruised heart. "I need the air. I've got a blanket. I'll sleep outside."

"Suit yerself," Smith said. "I don't know what

Andre's travel plans are."

"I think I do," Joel said. "I'll see you in a few hours."

~*~

Leah felt reasonably safe as long as she could see the trail which ran alongside the Hudson. She followed it as far as Fort Clinton which lay about halfway between Smith's house and West Point. There she unsaddled her horse and walked a safe distance into the woods before locating a likely looking spot in which to spend the night.

She found it amusing that the unyielding ground no longer represented a hardship the way it had when she first arrived in the past. Now, her primary concerns were removing large rocks and avoiding anthills. With those obstacles out of the way, and a clear sky overhead, she was content to roll up in a blanket and go to sleep.

That had been her plan when she finally settled down and pillowed her head on her arm. But sleep didn't come. Thoughts of Joel, however, did. They filled her mind with silly notions like where they might have a wedding ceremony and what were the chances that she and Chastity would both be pregnant at the same time.

She was up and moving with the first light, eager to find General George Washington if nothing more than to discover which of her father's theories about the "New Reality" might come true.

~*~

Benedict had ushered Major John Andre' to an expansive, second-story room of Smith's house. It had broad windows overlooking Haverstraw Bay, and the two men stood near them as the sun came up. In the distance they could just make out the silhouette of the *Vulture* floating at low tide near Teller's Point.

"I'm surprised you aren't asleep on the settee'," Benedict said.

Andre' yawned. "It won't be long, I promise."

Benedict doubted either of them could sleep. The combination of stress and nervous energy had fueled them all night, and just enough remained to keep them on their feet staring out at the river and the ship which promised their future.

And then something threatened that future. The distinctive sound of distant cannon fire rumbled across the water, and clouds of white smoke boiled up from Teller's Point.

Both men stood transfixed, staring at the *Vulture* in the distance.

What in hell is going on?

There were no heavy guns near Teller's Point. Benedict had certainly not given anyone permission to deploy them. Of course, managing the artillery was not his primary responsibility, but....

Suddenly, Benedict recalled the man he'd taken to task the previous day for bothering him with talk of artillery adjustments--Lieutenant Colonel Livingston. Benedict clenched his fists and jaws, wishing he had his hands wrapped around Livingston's throat so he could choke the life from the architect of those "adjustments."

Meddling fools--damn them all to hell!

If pacing provided either comfort or solutions, Benedict would have worn an even deeper path in the wooden floor of Smith's upper story. Instead, he forced himself to focus on the immediate crisis. For now, he had to do two things: get Andre' back across the lines to the British, and get himself back to West Point to prepare for the arrival of General Washington.

After writing a pass "Mr. Anderson" could use to get through American lines either by land or water, he summoned a yawning, belly-scratching Smith.

"I don't care how you do it," he told Smith, "but you will see that Major Andre' returns to New York City safely."

Smith pointed at the broad panorama of the Hudson. In the distance, the *Vulture* slowly rounded Teller's Point and slipped from view. Benedict shook his head as he acknowledged Livingston's cunning. The man had held his fire until the prevailing winds died and the current prevented easy navigation. Though distance prevented Benedict from making visual confirmation, he had no doubt *Vulture's* captain had been forced to use longboats to tow the gunship to safety.

"I'm leaving now," Benedict informed Andre' and Smith. "I suggest you rest during the day and start your return at dusk. Give those hot-tempered idiots across the river time to settle down. Now that they've got their blood up, they'll likely shoot anything that moves."

Smith promised to see to Andre's safety. "I'll let you know once he's in good hands."

Though bone weary, Benedict knew he needed only rest and luck. Surely, he'd earned both.

~*~

Leah rode all day, but her progress was tempered by caution. An unarmed female, traveling alone in an area frequented by militia and regular troops from both sides, faced an array of obstacles an armed male would find daunting. She took her time, approached crossings carefully and avoided all contacts with others she saw or heard as she traveled.

She likewise avoided farmhouses and woodland cabins. Without knowing the loyalties and temperament of a given homesteader, she couldn't chance an encounter that might prevent her from reaching General Washington.

Her intense focus, however, did not spare her from personal thoughts. Though she tried valiantly to suppress her own feelings and desires, the long hours of solitude gave her ample time to consider them. And how could she not? If she and Joel were successful in preventing Arnold's treachery, they would forever alter the future.

Their success would have repercussions beyond anything she could imagine, including--and in all likelihood--the end of her life.

The world, according to her father, would adjust to an altered reality, and while some people might briefly hang on to residual memories of loved ones and treasured moments, they would eventually fade, right along with every trace of their former existence.

So, why am I doing it?

It would be so much easier to just reverse course and ride back to Joel. He would offer no resistance. More likely, he'd welcome the change in plans. She could drag him away, far to the west, maybe somewhere in the future Texas Republic where they could watch their grandchildren's children grow and prosper.

And eventually fight their own never-ending war--with Mexico and Spanish California.

No.

Her mother had spelled it out from the start. Make a decision based on what is right, not for any one person in particular, but for everyone. And then stand by that decision no matter what.

And that, by God, was what she would do.

If George Washington was the honorable man she suspected him to be, he'd listen to her while there was still a chance the colonies could be saved.

And he'd give her a sleeve on which to wipe her tears before she faded away.

Forever.

~*~

Joel had begun to wonder if Joshua Smith would ever run out of tobacco. Any time the man stopped moving he seemed to be lighting his damned pipe. The aroma had once seemed pleasant, but its ever-presence now made it annoying.

And yet, here the man was, again, puffing away while he saddled his horse. "We'll be riding soon. Up to King's Ferry and across, then south as far as we can go."

"I'll be right behind you, then."

"Even on the ferry?"

"Why not?" Joel said. "Andre' doesn't know me, and when we reach the other side, we'll be riding on a common trail. I could pretend to join you on the boat. Is he going to look for the *Vulture*?"

Smith didn't know. "Where's your wife?"

"She's keeping an eye on Arnold and plans to disrupt him when he sets about moving his secret weapon into position."

"How will she do that?"

Joel had little difficulty imagining how Leah could charm some unsuspecting soldier into doing her bidding. With a provocative comment, a subtle touch, perhaps even a whispered hint of something pleasurable as a reward, she could recruit a dozen innocents to do her bidding.

"She has no trouble turning heads," Joel said. "I'm sure she'll find volunteers eager to make her happy."

"It must be hard to keep a woman like that under your control," Smith said.

Joel snorted. "You have no idea."

Smith paused after saddling a horse for Andre'. "Shouldn't we just tell Andre' what Arnold is up to? Why allow the fleet to sail into danger?"

Joel had been waiting for the question ever since he and Leah first presented themselves as spies sent by King George to operate outside the normal channels. He smiled in preparation for the whopper he was about to spin.

"You've done an amazing job thus far, Joshua. I've been impressed with your ability to deal with such a strong personality as Arnold, and it's obvious Major Andre' has great trust in you."

Smith responded like a praised puppy.

"But," Joel said, "you're still new to the craft. We were sent here not only to prevent a possible betrayal by Arnold, but to do two other things as well."

"*Two* more?"

"Indeed. Our mission has three parts: stop Arnold; steal or destroy his secret weapon, and see if he has other accomplices we haven't identified."

Smith seemed confused. "But, surely you can't mean Andre'."

"Probably not," Joel conceded. "But he's not working alone, as you well know. Who else in his organization has been corrupted by the colonials? It's our job to find out."

"I don't envy you that task."

"No, it won't be easy. But living in the shadows never is."

Joel swung up into his saddle, trying not to groan too loudly over the stress to his bad leg. "So, I remind you--keep this all to yourself. Play your part, and I'll see you at the Ferry."

The ride north to the crossing was short and pleasant. But by the time he arrived, he had conjured a new concern. What if Andre' had changed his mind and ridden south instead of north? What if they tried to reach Dobb's Ferry instead of King's Ferry?

As the minutes slid by, and the sun set lower on the horizon, Joel's fears grew. How could he have been so stupid as to trust Smith to follow a plan, no matter how simple?

He had just decided to mount up and retrace his route when the two men appeared.

Andre' had changed into civilian clothing, obviously borrowed from Smith, and they kept to themselves before, during, and after the crossing. More than once, Smith had cast a furtive glance in Joel's direction. Joel ignored him, and Andre' seemed not to notice him at all.

When they disembarked at the eastern terminus, Joel struck up a conversation with the ferryman while Smith and Andre' mounted their horses and rode off. Joel then followed at a discreet distance until they were stopped by a man in a Continental uniform.

He didn't seem overly interested in either of them and eventually pointed to a small farmhouse in the distance. Smith thanked him, and the two rode toward the building to which the soldier directed them. After speaking with the homeowners, the two came back outside and unsaddled their horses. It seemed painfully obvious where they'd be spending the night.

Grumbling to himself about the privations he endured, Joel rolled up in a blanket and tried to sleep. Unfortunately, his mind rapidly filled with thoughts about Leah. And when he pushed those aside, they were replaced by worries of what would happen should they successfully thwart Arnold.

He had one other line of thought that kept

him from sleeping: what to do with Andre'. The man was almost certainly armed, unlike Joel. And, he admitted to himself, even if Leah had hung on to Murchesson's gun, Joel would have insisted that she take it when she went looking for Washington.

That meant Joel's armory consisted of his wits and a T-handled auger sporting a two-inch bit, with which to counter a trained spy who was armed and quite capable of doing the drilling.

Joel's options boiled down to either killing Andre' outright, which didn't appeal to him at all, or arranging for his arrest. Joel settled on the latter choice, but knew he couldn't do anything about it while Smith remained at Andre's side.

Up and moving early, Joel spotted the two men when they emerged from the farmhouse to continue their journey. It was still dark. His stomach rumbled, and even though the sound wasn't nearly loud enough for them to hear, he gave them even more space.

By the time he had himself convinced things couldn't get any worse, it dawned on him that Smith might *accompany* Andre' all the way to the British lines. The closer they got, the greater the chance that they'd run into a militia patrol, since both sides kept men circulating in the area. The memories he had from his first encounter with the three loyalists who wanted his and Leah's clothing still haunted him.

Not knowing what else to do, he continued to follow them south along the Hudson, formulating and discarding one scheme after another. When the meditation proved fruitless, he settled on a direct approach--wait until they stopped to rest, then attack. He felt confident he could talk Smith into going home. Andre', on the other hand, would have to be disabled in order for Joel to keep him under control. Explaining that to Smith would be tricky.

"Don' move."

The disembodied voice came straight from the dark woods: flat, harsh and barely intelligible.

Joel did what anyone might when faced with so many uncomfortable unknowns. He moved.

"Said don move, n' ah meant it."

The synchronous clicks of four hammers, pulled back on four muskets, by four hard men pointing them in his direction, immobilized him.

"Good morning, gentlemen," he said. "You startled me."

One of the four responded, and while Joel recognized his voice from two previous commands, he struggled to get the meaning. Nor could he tell for which side the four armed men fought.

The speaker wore a crude epaulette of green cloth sewn to the right shoulder of his jacket. Aside from that, the four wore remarkably similar clothing: non-military, very old, and thoroughly soiled. In fact, it could have come from the same 18th century refuse bin used by the loyalist militiamen he and Leah had encountered earlier.

"How can I help you," Joel asked, in as pleasant a tone as he could muster.

"Shuddup!"

That command was followed by a few more unintelligible words which prompted two of the other three militiamen to pat him down. Though disappointed when they uncovered nothing of value, the soldiers backed away with their muskets pointed at the ground. "Nuthin', corp'ral," said the taller of the two.

The green stripe--of course! The man in command.

"State yer bizness," said the Corporal.

"I'm looking for the Officer In Charge."

The four men exchanged doubtful looks.

"Why?"

Joel cleared his throat and swallowed. If he was lucky, the squad at hand were patriots. If not, he was about to condemn North America to another 232 years of war.

"Before I answer, would you mind telling me how you feel about redcoats?"

The Corporal cleared his own throat and sent the resulting sputum spinning to the ground at Joel's feet. "Don' feel nuthin'."

"Would you rather salute 'em or shoot 'em?"

The two non-corporals smiled at each other, and Joel had his answer. "I'm trying to catch a spy."

The remark definitely got their interest, and all four spoke at once, thus eliminating any chance he had of understanding them.

"Look," he said. "I need your help. I've been following two men--"

"We know."

"Oh?"

So much for my stalking skills.

"Fine. But I'm only interested in one of the them. The other is harmless."

The Corporal said something Joel interpreted as meaning, "Which is which?"

Quite suddenly, all four men squatted down, and one of them pulled Joel down with them. His bad leg gave way, and he landed heavily on his backside. Before he could say anything, the Corporal gave him the universal sign for silence.

Joel bit his lip. Silently.

All five eased their heads up far enough to see over the undergrowth, Joel smiled at the view--a single horseman, Joshua Smith, was riding north.

"You want the other fellow," Joel said, pointing in the direction he'd last seen Andre'. "He's the spy. Look in his boots."

There followed a brief flurry of conversation in a colloquial patois Joel struggled to comprehend. As he waited for them to arrive at a decision, he tried to make himself appear non-threatening.

Eventually they finished. The Corporal ordered one of the men to take Joel to headquarters while the other three apprehended the spy.

"And you'll leave the first man alone?" Joel asked.

"Smith?"

Joel stared at him in wonder. "You *know* him?"

"'Course." He muttered something else ending in "lawyer," which detail proved sufficiently convincing.

Joel hoped whoever was on duty at "headquarters" spoke a version of English he could understand.

~*~

Excerpt from the *Albany Clarion*:

Chancellor Swears German Gas Not Used To Murder Royal

Philadelphia, Pennsylvania, Thurs., June 28, 2012--Gerhardt Stumpfel, Chancellor of Imperial Germany, issued a statement through his country's Embassy today vigorously denying rumors that the nerve agent used to assassinate Queen Elizabeth II had been manufactured in his country.

Analysts say the gas is similar to nerve agents used by Germany in the Great War. The difference, according to sources in the chemical industry, is that the new material is more concentrated and much deadlier than that used during the infamous trench battles of the previous century.

Consular relations between New England and Imperial Germany have only recently been restored. For most of the 20th century, diplomatic contacts between the former adversaries was channeled through Luxembourg, Switzerland or French Colonial Africa.

Chapter Twenty-five

"It's not denial. I'm just selective about the reality I accept."

--Bill Watterson

The most heavily traveled routes between Litchfield, Connecticut, and West Point, New York, were little more than deer trails. Leah had no chance of picking the exact one Washington and his entourage might use. Instead, she concentrated on choosing from the tiny clusters of homes and businesses which passed for civilization in the Hudson Highlands of the 18th century.

Few people would have been more surprised than Leah herself when she picked right. She had stopped for food at a tavern in Salem, about 15 miles east of King's Ferry. While she ate, a man dressed in the buff and blue of a Continental soldier entered the taproom and sought the innkeeper. For some reason he seemed familiar, but she couldn't place him and dismissed it as coincidence.

She concentrated on their conversation but

failed to understand what they discussed. The question answered itself a short time later when the proprietor produced a small keg which he exchanged for cash. Leah left money for her meal, then followed the soldier outside and watched as he struggled to mount his horse with the keg under his arm.

Pulling the brim of her hat low, she approached the man and offered to help. Though she'd meant to make her voice sound mannish, she worried that it just sounded suspicious.

The soldier gave her a long look, as if he, too, were searching his memory for a connection. Leah kept her head down. She couldn't imagine any good could come from whatever connection might exist.

"Thank you, lad," the soldier said, handing her the cask.

Having never carried such a thing before, she was surprised at its weight and staggered a bit as the soldier swung up into his saddle. She lifted it as far as her chest, and he leaned over and used both hands to haul it up into his lap.

"Party tonight?" she asked.

He laughed, then said, "That's a good one, that is!" as he rode away.

Leah scrambled to get on her own horse and give chase, albeit cautiously. She caught sight of him on the north side of the village where he rode to a halt among dozens of other horses.

She reined in and dismounted a reasonable distance from the light of their campfires. After securing her mount, she crept closer to observe. In response to the rider's call, two men exited a large canvas tent and retrieved the keg. All three of them looked happy about it, and Leah wondered if they might not be having a party after all.

Before she could get any closer to find out, she felt the sharp end of a bayonet pressing against the small of her back an inch or so from her spine. Slowly, she raised her hands above her head.

"I'm not armed," she said, making no effort to disguise her voice this time.

"Don't move," said someone behind her.

"I-- I've come to see General Washington."

Why had her voice suddenly grown so feeble?

"Stand up slow," he said. "And turn around."

~*~

"Headquarters" for the Continentals who found Joel turned out to be a commercial mill of uncertain vintage. It anchored the settlement of North Castle which had grown up around it. The mill consisted of several buildings, only one of which had the luxury of multiple windows. Joel's guard deposited him in a chair in that building where he faced a lieutenant colonel named Jameson, though he gleaned this intelligence only by listening to the garbled report of his captor. Jameson didn't bother to introduce himself formally, nor did he say anything to Joel for what must have been an hour or more. Without a watch, Joel had no way to tell time.

Eventually, however, Jameson tore himself away from whatever he was doing to conduct an interrogation.

"Now, what's this nonsense about a spy?" he

asked, his voice marked by a drawl Joel hadn't heard since a visit to Virginia Beach as a teen.

"There's a British agent passing through the area," Joel said. "He has information that will prove disastrous for West Point if he's able to reach New York City with it."

"And how do you know this?"

"I observed a meeting he had with the American traitor who gave it to him."

Jameson had been sitting behind a table which served as his desk. He stood and walked to the front of the table then leaned back against it, his arms crossed. He glared at Joel. "How do you know what they were talking about? Could you hear them?"

Joel shook his head. "I didn't have to hear them."

Jameson squinted. "You mentioned some sort of information. What kind is it?"

"I don't know the specifics, but I'm guessing the documents detail--"

"Documents?"

"Yes! Like I told the men who found me. The spy--his name is Major Andre'--has papers in his boots."

"Can you prove anything you're saying?" Jameson asked.

"No," said Joel, "but you can. Just grab Andre' and frisk him!"

"*Frisk?*"

"Search."

"Where is he?"

"How the hell should I know?" Joel yelled.

"You've had me sitting here under guard while the man you really need to catch is riding south to the British lines."

A commotion at the entrance to the room distracted both of them. The men Joel encountered earlier entered the room with John Andre' in tow.

"We caught 'im near the bridge over by Tarrytown," said their leader. "An he's got papers you need to see, Colonel."

"What do they say?" the officer asked as he accepted the documents. "Did you read them?"

"Paulding 'ere did," said their spokesman.

"They's 'bout the fort at West Point, sir," Paulding said.

Joel sat up. "You see? It's just as I predicted."

"Do you know this man?" Jameson asked the troops. "He says he told you about the spy."

The Corporal chose his words carefully. "We got 'im on 'r own. 'E warn't involved, so if'n there's a reward, he'll git none."

"All I want to 'git,' is gone," Joel said. "Outta here."

Jameson waved him to silence as he concentrated on the papers. Much head shaking and muttering followed. "This is unbelievable."

"I know!" Joel said.

"Will you not shut up? Speak again, and I'll have you gagged."

Lovely.

Jameson returned to his side of the table and sat down. He told the guards to leave the other prisoner, still bound, in a chair beside Joel. "Then go out and find Lieutenant Allen. Send him here."

The three men were clearly reluctant to leave. `Jameson looked up from his studies and asked, "What is it?"

"The reward?"

Jameson exhaled wearily. "What about it?"

"We want to be sure you have our names."

"I do. It's Paulding, Van Dart and Williams, correct?"

"Van *W*art it is, sir. Isaac Van Wart."

"Yes, yes, of course. Now, go fetch Lieutenant Allen."

After a considerable wait, the lieutenant entered Jameson's lair. "You sent for me, sir?"

"Indeed. I want you to assemble a detail and accompany a suspect to West Point."

Joel thought an escort might not be a bad way to travel. It would certainly be direct, and best of all, Leah would be waiting for him.

"Which suspect, sir?"

"That one," said Jameson, pointing at Andre'.

"Are you out of your bloody mind?" Joel said, his own brain reeling at Jameson's stupidity.

"I told you to be quiet!"

"Arnold is the man he conspired with!"

"You are speaking about Benedict Arnold, sir. Not only is he a General in the Continental Army and my superior, he is a true hero in every sense of the word."

Joel shook his head in desperation. "He's a damned traitor!"

"Silence!" Jameson roared. "I'll not allow you to slander a good man's name. Who do you think you are?"

"What about the papers in Andre's boots? Was he not carrying them to the British lines? Were they not written by General Arnold himself?"

"Lieutenant Allen, gag that man. I won't hear another word from him."

Jameson paused as he prepared a package containing the documents seized from Andre'. "Find me a courier who can take these papers to General Washington. We'll let him sort out the significance."

Joel shot a glance at Andre' who had maintained his silence throughout the exchange. He was smiling.

~*~

Raines had concluded most of his business in Philadelphia which didn't involve Samuel Adams. He made a number of investments on Chastity's behalf using just under half of the remaining Spanish dollars he and Leah brought with them. With any luck, those concerns would survive the rebellion and provide for Chastity's future. He had left an equal amount with Colonel Cotswold who agreed to make similar investments for both Chastity and Gabriel.

Satisfied with his provisions for the two young people who had done so much for him, he moved on to the rest of his agenda. The remaining items would be the most difficult to accomplish.

Pulling two chairs up to the table in their City Tavern room, Raines brought out a sheaf of papers containing notes and drawings he'd prepared in advance. He put the pile in front of Chastity along with a stack of blank paper, quill pens, a blotter, and a substantial supply of ink.

"What's all this?"

"Your future," he said.

"I don't understand."

"But you will." He waved at the documents. "I owe you an explanation and an apology."

Her look was one of consternation, and he wanted to take her in his arms and kiss her, hold her, and reassure her that everything would be all right. But he knew that would most likely be a lie.

"I've already told you how I came by the things in my valise which you found so interesting."

"You started to but never finished."

He nodded. "Right. So now I'm going to finish. I need you to bear with me. Some of it will be hard for me to say."

He cleared his throat, then dug in, "We're here because we want to change the future. In order to do that, we must interfere with the present. We want the rebellion to be successful. We want this country to grow and thrive under the guidance of the men leading the colonies right now."

"Adams? Washington? Franklin?"

"Yes," he said, "those three especially, but all the others, too. You would agree that's a good thing, wouldn't you?"

"Of course."

"The problem is, I don't know what will happen to us if we're successful."

"Us?" Chastity said. "Why would anything happen to us?"

Raines shook his head. "I'm sorry. I didn't mean you and me. I meant the three of us who came from the future. Technically speaking, we haven't been born yet, and won't be for many, many years to come."

"But you're here now, so what difference does it make?"

"It makes a difference to the universe," he said. "In my version of it, all my ancestors survived this era and the revolution. After Arnold's treason, however, the Continental Army dissolved. People moved to the wilderness. England posted troops everywhere and put their stamp on everything."

He raised his good arm and touched her face gently. "If we stop Arnold and save West Point-- along with General Washington and the Continental Congress--the fighting will likely *increase*. For a time, anyway, until the British are defeated."

"You won't be involved in the fighting, will you?"

"Not directly, no. But my ancestors might be. And if one of them is killed, or badly hurt, they may not have children. If there are no children to carry the line forward, there may be no Raines Kerr."

The reality of his words dawned slowly on her at first, but soon blossomed. "But you're *already* here. You wouldn't just disappear, would you?"

"I'm afraid that's exactly what might happen. I would simply cease to exist. And your memories of me would probably fade just as fast."

"But I don't want you to disappear," she cried. "I love you!"

"And I love you, too!" he said. "But this isn't about feelings. It's about the laws of nature."

"Then, you must stop doing what you're

doing! Tell Adams it was all a misunderstanding, a mistake. You ate some bad pork or something and suffered a moment of madness."

"Sweetheart--"

"I don't *care* what you tell him! I don't want to lose you." She hugged him fiercely.

He waited until her breathing settled, then went on with a thin smile. "I could be wrong. It may not happen that way at all. I have no concrete proof of it. But I can't take a chance on that."

She looked with dismay at the papers piled in front of her. "And that's what this is about?"

"Yes." He fanned the material out for her. "I've tried to write down the basics about everything I could think of that you might be able to use: simple versions of electrical generators, motors, radio. There's a great deal of information here, incredibly valuable information. You and Gabriel will be able to use it to create wonders. And not just for yourselves. The world will benefit from these gifts."

She stared at the documents in growing dismay. "But, I--"

"There's a problem, however," he said. "Just as I could fade away into nothing, so could every word I've written and every diagram I've drawn. It could all just... disappear."

"And you expect me to stop it somehow?"

"That's exactly what I want."

She threw up her hands in frustration. "If *you* can't figure it out, how do you expect me to?"

He smiled. "I want you to copy everything. Put it in your own handwriting on your own paper. Use pen and ink from the here and now, not from some future that may never exist."

"Copy... *all of it?*"

"Yes."

"That'll take forever!"

"I hope not," he said. "We've only got a few days at best."

"No!" she cried.

"Darling, there's no time to waste crying over what we can't control. We have to do the best we can. If I thought it would work, I'd copy these things for you, but I won't take the risk. I'll explain anything and everything you find confusing. I'll check your drawings and your notes to make sure they're correct."

"I'm not smart enough to--"

"Don't be silly! You're the brightest star in the sky. You can do this. I know you can."

"I wish Gabriel was here to help me."

Raines chuckled. "What makes you think he got off lucky? I left an even larger pile of papers for him to copy. The only difference is, I won't be there to check for errors. Fortunately, your father agreed to do that for me."

She sat quietly for a while, just looking at him. Her lip trembled from time to time. At last she asked, "How will you know if... if you're going to fade away?"

He shrugged. "I'm guessing that some of the things I brought with me will begin to fade first-- most likely the magazine, but it could be something else: my pen, a lighter. I don't know. It's not up to me."

She blinked her dazzling green eyes at him.

"Will you answer one more question, husband?"

"I'll try," he said.

"How do I explain this to our child?"

~*~

Leah's charms had precisely no effect on the man directing her toward one of the smaller tents which circled the largest one like planets in a solar system. Every attempt she made at either question or explanation was met with the point of the bayonet in her back, and while such thrusts lacked the energy to cut, she had no doubt that whoever delivered those jabs could easily make them deadly.

"In 'ere, dearie," said the man behind her.

"You tied my hands too tight," she whined.

"You'll live," he said. "Now 'ave a seat."

She looked in vain for a chair. "Where?"

A shove from behind propelled her to the ground where she landed with a yelp and all the refinement of spilled groceries.

"Ye'll do fine where y'are. Now stay there, and be quiet."

The sun was setting before anyone showed up other than the gruff old codger standing guard outside the tent. She tried lying down, sitting cross-legged, and pacing, but with her arms tied behind her, nothing felt comfortable.

"All right then," said a fastidiously uniformed man of approximately her own age. "Who are you, and what do you want?"

Quite ready to respond, and talk her way into an audience with General Washington, Leah looked up at the man and discovered her voice had gone missing.

I know you!

"Speak up. I haven't got all day."

"You're Alexander Hamilton, aren't you?"

He put his hands on his hips and frowned at her. "Have we met, Madame?"

"No," she said. "I-- I recognized your face from pho-- I mean paintings."

"I'm sure you're mistaken," he said. "I've never in my life sat for a portrait."

"Oh. Uh--"

"Now, please tell me what you want. the guard said something about seeing General Washington. But you must understand, almost no one gets to see him. He's terribly busy. In fact, *I'm* terribly busy. So get on with it; state your business."

Before she could say a word, he leaned out through the tent flap and called the guard. "Come remove the rope from her wrists. She's done nothing wrong."

"But," said the guard, "we be under orders about camp followers, an' I thought--"

"I'm not a camp follower!" Leah yelped.

Hamilton silenced her with a glare, then waited while the guard untied her hands.

"Thank you," she said, rubbing her wrists.

"All right, then. Be on your way. And watch out for loyalists. The woods are full of them."

"But I want to see General Washington. It's terribly important!"

"For whom?"

"For America. Someone he trusts is a traitor. I

can identify him."

Hamilton's brows drew down into a sharp V. "Who?"

"An officer close to him," she said.

"Here? On the General's staff? Impossible!"

"No. This man doesn't travel with him, but he is an officer."

Hamilton exhaled in frustration. "I have no time for riddles. Neither does General Washington. Say what you've come to say, or leave. It doesn't matter to me." He waited two beats, then held the tent flap open.

"It's Benedict Arnold," Leah said. "He's already met with John Andre', who--"

"I know who he is," Hamilton said.

"The British promised Arnold 20,000 pounds to give up West Point. He agreed."

Hamilton locked his hands behind his back and stared down at the dirt floor for a long moment. "General Arnold has proven his loyalty to this country many times over. I find it inconceivable that he would betray us."

"He already has."

"Can you prove it?"

"I can tell you where and when he made contact with Major Andre', and I can identify the man who is leading Andre', at this very moment, to safety in New York City. My only reason for coming here is to warn General Washington while there's still time for him to avoid being captured."

"Captured?" Hamilton's eyes went wide in surprise, but the moment quickly passed, and his expression became one of bored amusement. "And just what do you want in return for this outrageously valuable information?"

Leah stared at him in consternation. "I don't want anything."

Hamilton adjusted the ruffled cuffs of his shirt which extended beyond the sleeves of his military jacket. "Do you think you're the only one who's ever attempted to trade suspicious information for something of value? I should have you arrested."

"For trying to prevent a tragedy?"

Hamilton snorted. "The only tragedy here is the amount of my time you've wasted."

Leah felt a familiar wave of resentment rushing through her and knew that maintaining her composure would require all her will. She took a deep breath before responding. "I understand you don't have any reason to believe me. And, I have no doubt your intent is to free General Washington from interruptions."

"True. Now, if you'll excuse me, I--"

"Would you trust me if my introduction came from someone you know? Someone like Samuel Adams?"

"I know the man," he said. "If you have such a document, you should have given it to me the moment I came in."

"It's not a document."

"Madame, you have strained my patience to the limit. It's time for you to leave."

Leah shook her head. "No! Listen to me. I want you to *talk* to him. Actually, I want General Washington to talk to him, but that won't happen until you get out of the damned way."

"*Madame!*"

"I have a device which will make it possible for you to talk over great distances. If you'll allow--"

Hamilton took her by the elbow and walked her through the tent flap. "Go. Now. Back to your asylum. Be on your way before I become angry."

Leah grabbed his upper arm. "Don't be stupid."

He pushed her hand away.

"What do you have to lose?"

"Time," he said. "And I've lost enough of that already."

He signaled for a nearby officer. "Captain? Escort this woman from the camp."

Leah and the captain looked at each other in surprise. She'd seen him in the tavern earlier that afternoon and suddenly recalled why he looked familiar.

"I know you," the newly arrived officer said. "I saw you at Dobb's Ferry. You couldn't speak English."

"What?" said Hamilton. "Of course she speaks English. I've been talking to her for what seems like hours."

"I'm certain she's th' one couldn't say a word that made sense. We thought she might be addled, poor thing. And so pretty, too."

"I can explain," Leah began, "it's all--"

"Quite suspicious," Hamilton said.

"Colonel Hamilton?" asked still another voice.

"Yes, General?" Hamilton whirled around to face his commanding officer.

"Come see me as soon as you're free."

"Yes, sir," he said returning to Leah and the Captain. "Get her out of here."

"What about her suspicious behavior? And the odd language she spoke?"

Hamilton made no effort to disguise his growing irritation. "Go!"

Leah took a breath and screamed. Frustration lent strength and volume to her voice, and it echoed in the otherwise sudden silence of the camp. No one moved for the space of a heartbeat, and then everyone seemed to move at once. Hamilton shouted, a host of uniformed men dropped what they were doing to stare, and the Captain at Leah's side attempted to silence her by putting his hand over her mouth.

Leah reacted instinctively, grabbing the soldier's arm and twisting it as she had been taught by her martial arts instructor. The Captain's shriek mirrored his shock at the sudden debilitating pain. Completely incapacitated, he dropped to Leah's feet.

Hamilton reached for her, then stopped when she grabbed his wrist and pressed his hand down and past the point of pain-free movement. She stopped before doing any damage, but maintained enough pressure to keep Hamilton gasping.

Washington stuck his head from his tent and growled, "What's going on out here?"

Several soldiers had found their weapons and began a cautious advance.

Washington's face reflected an unaccustomed mixture of surprise and dismay.

"I need a moment of your time, General,"

Leah said. "But you make it awfully difficult to get an appointment."

"I could have you shot."

"Do it, sir!" Hamilton said.

Leah applied pressure between "Do it" and "sir," sending Hamilton's voice three octaves higher on the final word.

"I'm not here to cause harm or waste time," Leah said. "I promise you won't regret my visit."

Washington drew himself to his full height. After surveying the disposition of his cadre, he told his men to lower their weapons, then addressed Leah. "Do you intend to cripple my Aide-de-Camp?"

"No, sir."

"Then let him go and join me." He gestured to the interior of his tent, then disappeared inside it.

Leah released Hamilton who stepped away rubbing his wrist. "I won't forget this," he snapped.

"I hope you remember it," she said. "Things aren't always as simple as they appear, a truth multiplied ten-fold when applied to women."

"I don't ignore threats or insults," he said.

Leah nodded. "Down the line, you just might want to re-think that policy."

~*~

Treason, Treason!

Excerpt from the *Chicago Citizen*:

Colonial Leader Continues to Deny Assassination Claims

Chicago, Illinois, Fri., June 29, 2012--Lewis Cranston, President of the so-called 104th Continental Congress, issued yet another denial in the on-going investigation of last month's assassination of the Queen. Cranston said, "No Congressional approval has ever been granted for any plots against the Queen or other members of the Royal Family."

Evidence to the contrary, while circumstantial, has been made public and is widely seen as the reason behind growing demonstrations throughout New England over the past few weeks. Protestors have been demanding more military action against the rogue government.

"We had great respect for Queen Elizabeth and had hoped that together we might find a path to peace," Cranston said in a radio address to the North American midlands. "That opportunity, however, has been severely damaged by a person or persons hoping to profit from continued hostilities."

Chapter Twenty-six

"The only way to deal with an unfree world is to become so absolutely free that your very existence is an act of rebellion."

--Albert Camus

Benedict split his day between his headquarters office and his home. Though he and Peggy had been reunited for a week, his on-again/off-again attempts to meet with John Andre' had left them with little time to spend together. He would have been content to relax and spend the afternoon with her, but the imminent arrival of Washington required planning and preparation.

Adding to the situation was the appearance of Joshua Smith, beaming over the successful conclusion of his mission to return Andre' to safety behind the British lines. When Benedict's aides stepped out of the office, Smith gave his report.

"We parted ways just north of Tarrytown," he said. "Not once did we encounter any problems. The pass you gave us worked wonders at King's Ferry."

"You're sure he reached safety?"

"Oh, yes. If he'd been stopped by rebels, he would have produced your pass. The British will welcome him like the prodigal son."

A faint tickle of concern worried its way into Benedict's mind. "But you didn't actually *see* him reach British lines?"

Smith waved the query off. "There was no need. To my mind, traveling any further, together, would have raised more suspicions."

Benedict accepted the report and quelled his growing anxiety. "I suppose you'll be heading back home."

Smith shook his head. "I've done enough riding the past few days. Unless you have some objection, I'd prefer to spend the night with you and make my way home in the morning. I've never much cared for travel in the dark."

Against his better judgment, Benedict relented. "Just know beforehand that my staff will be dining with us this evening, and frankly, they're not overly fond of you."

"I shall be a perfect gentleman," Smith said. "You'll see."

"I can't wait," Benedict said.

Not wishing to invite any more criticism than he already knew he'd receive from Lamb, Franks, and Varick, Benedict sent Smith on ahead with instructions for Peggy to tell the cook how many would be at dinner. Benedict and his staff followed in his barge a short while later.

The evening meal was even less pleasant than Benedict had imagined. Though Varick and

Franks knew better than to openly challenge him, Colonel Lamb had no such compunctions. He glared at Smith constantly, which only distressed Peggy.

The meal became an exercise in hostility as Lamb found endless opportunities to call Smith's loyalty into question. Smith was either too smart to take the bait or too thick to recognize he was being baited. Either way, by the time the last course had been served, Peggy was too upset to remain at the table. Her exit captured the angst of an operatic death augmented by a torrent of real tears.

When the drama subsided, and Peggy's absence settled on the room like a curse, Benedict glared directly at Lamb. "See what you've done?"

"Kindly offer Mrs. Arnold my regrets," the Colonel said. "I didn't mean to cause her distress. My target was esquire Smith, not your wife."

The aggrieved lawyer wiped his mouth with a cloth napkin and rose to his feet. "Colonel, I've had quite enough. I'd challenge you, but I'm too fatigued, either to call you out or endure any more of your slights. I'm a civilized man, so I'll just take my leave."

"Best news we've had all night," Lamb grumbled. "And if you're serious about a duel, I'll gladly meet you on any field. It's your choice. I'm partial to four-pounders at, oh, a hundred paces. If you've got the balls, I've got the artillery."

Smith ignored him, thanked his host with a knowing smile, and departed.

Benedict relaxed, and the atmosphere in the room improved dramatically.

"You're a fool to maintain any sort of contact with Smith," Lamb said when they assembled a short while later on the porch for pipes and brandy.

Benedict skipped the tobacco and instead doubled up on the liqueur. "Rest assured, I have no plans to spend another moment with Mister Smith."

I certainly don't need the tiresome fool any more.

"A wise decision," Varick said.

Lamb and Franks agreed.

~*~

Rain began to fall as Leah approached General Washington's tent. She had risked the slight detour needed to retrieve her transmitter from the saddlebag on her horse. The same tight-lipped guard who had taken her into custody followed her and made sure she carried nothing but the harmless, rectangular box toward the General's tent. On the way, she thumbed the unit on, turned the volume low, and called for her father.

"I'm here," he said. "Are you all right?"

"Splendid," she said. "Who knew the rebels employed Neanderthals just like the redcoats?"

Her father chuckled.

"I'm about to meet with General Washington," she said. "I'm going to propose that he talk to Adams in the morning. Can you arrange things on your end?"

"Yes," he said. "And I think we can afford to leave both radios on for a bit longer than usual to ensure that we make contact."

"Good. I'll look for you and Adams at dawn," Leah said.

"Done."

They exchanged "love yous" and hung up.

Leah hurried to Washington's tent and announced her presence with a theatrical cough.

"Come in and have a seat," Washington said. He gestured to a chair opposite the table he used for a desk. "I don't have much time to spare."

"I'll be brief," Leah said.

"Good," said Washington. "I'm allowing this because I'm a fair judge of character, and I didn't see anything in you that I found threatening."

"Thank you," she said.

"With the exception," he continued, "of how easily you disabled two of my men."

"I'd be happy to teach you the technique," she said. "It's not difficult."

"Tell that to those you embarrassed outside."

Lacking a rational response, she relied on her smile. "I'll leave that to you, sir. You undoubtedly have a better rapport with them than I ever will."

"You might be surprised," he said. "Now, what did you wish to discuss?"

"Tomorrow morning," she said, "I aim to put you in touch with Sam Adams."

Washington frowned. "*Samuel Adams?* From Boston? He's here in the highlands?"

"No," she said. "He's in Philadelphia."

"But--"

"I'm going to make it possible for you to talk to him there. From here."

"Impossible!"

"Would you recognize his voice?"

"Of course. I've known Adams for years. Can't

say we always see eye to eye, but I believe him to be an honest man. And a fine orator."

"Then with your permission," she said, "I'll return at dawn, and you can talk to your old friend."

Washington sighed. "I never said we were friends."

"One can't always have everything," she said.

"What?"

"You need to talk to Adams before I say anything more, General."

"You presume a great deal, young lady."

"It wouldn't be the first time, sir."

~*~

In Philadelphia, Raines managed to keep Chastity occupied for most of the day. Periodically, she suffered bouts of intense grief, which pushed him near his own emotional boundaries. Sometimes he managed to console her. More often than not, they ended up weeping together.

Raines distracted her by wiping away smeared ink, or adding eyes, nose and mouth to smudges on her gently rendered copies. He didn't know if his doodles would survive him, but he doubted it.

If fortune smiled on them, whatever she copied might endure the universe's attempts to restore a single version of reality. If not, then they were wasting what little time they had together, a point Chastity made repeatedly.

He brought up the issue of her pregnancy several times, mostly to determine if she was positive about it. Though such a condition was entirely possible, not quite enough time had passed for her to be certain about it. Or so he thought.

"The point is," she said, "I *want* to have your children. I pray that I'm carrying one right now."

He tried to be as honest with her as possible. If she was indeed pregnant, the baby would almost certainly disappear along with him. And so too would any memories she had of him that weren't recorded in her notes.

Neither of them found much solace in that.

When he connected with Leah, and she asked him to have Adams ready in the morning, he suffered an attack of anxiety unlike any he'd ever known. Putting Adams on the radio with Washington would forever seal the changes they'd already made to history. Whether or not they stopped Arnold had almost ceased to be the essential element for the young nation's survival. That was on the verge of being eclipsed by the TALK buttons on a pair of souped-up transmitters.

~*~

Inside a drafty, plank-sided building connected to a grist mill in North Castle, New York, Joel sat bound and gagged in a straight-backed chair. His bad leg ached, but he couldn't reach it to rub out any of the pain. Worse still, he'd used up his supply of Leah's amazing little pills before he got there and had no hope of laying his hands on anything stronger than apple cider.

And he didn't even want to think about what

the gag in his mouth may have been used for.

He had been sitting in Colonel Jameson's makeshift office forever, or so it felt. To get his mind off his misery, he dreamt up different ways to tell the rebel officer how stupid he was to send Andre' to *Arnold*, of all people.

By late afternoon the rain came down in torrents, and the noise it made striking the roof added a new level of annoyance to an already dismal situation. Fortunately, a distraction appeared in the guise of a Colonial Army major.

"Good afternoon, Colonel," the new arrival said upon entering Jameson's office. He removed his soggy hat and jacket and hung them by the door.

"You're early Major Tallmadge," Jameson said, waving him to a chair near a wood burning stove.

"When I heard about the arrest this morning, I rushed here to question the suspect. Where is he?"

"Mister Anderson is under guard and on his way to West Point. He had suspicious documents in his possession, some signed by General Arnold. I felt the General would want to know."

Tallmadge appeared surprised. "Where are the documents?"

"I sent them to General Washington."

Tallmadge rubbed his face in obvious frustration.

Joel wished he were a ventriloquist so he might add his angry voice to the conversation, but all he could do was kick the floor and grunt.

"Who's he?" Tallmadge asked of Joel.

"Possibly another spy. But to be honest, I'm

not sure what to make of him."

Joel tried screaming through his gag, but his efforts failed to move either officer.

"Can you at least tell me about those documents? What sort of information do they hold?"

Jameson described what he'd read, coloring his commentary with expressions of surprise at seeing his commanding general's signature. How, he asked Tallmadge, could a merchant like Anderson have come into possession of such things?

Again, Tallmadge peered at Joel. "Perhaps *he* had something to do with it." The Major crossed the room and removed the gag from Joel's mouth.

Though tempted to lick the shoulder of his jacket to get rid of the taste of the gag, Joel contented himself with spitting out the worst of the fibers and residue. "May I have some water, please?"

"Of course," Tallmadge said, "but I need you to tell me a few things first."

Joel repeated what he'd told Jameson, adding details Jameson had not wanted to hear. Tallmadge poured him a cup of water from a pitcher on the Colonel's desk and untied him so he could drink it.

"We need to get Mister Anderson back here," Tallmadge said.

"His name is Andre', not Anderson," Joel said. "He's a major in the British army."

"I know who Andre' is," Tallmadge said. "I served General Washington in a similar capacity."

That explained the deference shown to the Major from Jameson, though he held a higher rank.

Jameson stood up and paced. "Why bring him back here? Surely General Arnold can explain--"

"I'm not concerned about the General's thoughts on this," Tallmadge said. "If Anderson is really Andre', then he's likely working with Arnold."

"That's outlandish!" Jameson said. "It's just not possible. The man's a--"

"Hero?" Joel interjected. "Have you ever *met* him? He's a complete ass--"

"Enough," Tallmadge said, giving Joel a stern look. "The issue is Anderson, not Arnold, and protocol says we bring him back for questioning."

Jameson went to the door of his office and called for one of his lieutenants. While waiting for him to arrive, the Colonel wrote a new note.

"Who's that for?" Tallmadge asked.

"It's for General Arnold. He needs to know we've arrested Mister Anderson. If the man really is a spy, I don't want him here. It's too close to the British lines. We need to move him farther away, so I'm ordering the detail to take him up to Salem."

"And what about me?" Joel asked.

Before responding, Tallmadge and Jameson held a brief discussion. The Major argued that they had no reason to hold Joel, but the Colonel wasn't comfortable letting him go free, even if his foray into the world of espionage was "nothing more than amateur adventurism."

Joel bristled at the remark but kept silent.

"I would rather keep him here for the time being," Jameson said. "At least until we can figure out what to do with him."

Tallmadge reluctantly agreed.

Joel concluded that some things would never change. The military version of middle management was forever doomed to the mediocrity of men like Colonel Jameson.

~*~

Leah spent a fitful sleepless night. Despite her bravado, and the noble words she shared with Joel, she could not ignore her growing anxiety. The future had never seemed so uncertain, and it was entirely her fault. Worst of all, she had no way of knowing if she'd even live to experience any of it.

Focusing on immediate tasks helped, but the jagged edge of worry continued to torment her no matter what she did.

Heavy rain masked the approach of dawn, and had she not already been awake, she would have missed it entirely. She rolled out of the miniscule tent Colonel Hamilton had grudgingly provided for her and was greeted immediately by the gruff continental soldier who had been assigned to guard her the previous day. Hamilton made sure he kept an eye on her, despite the almost cordial interaction she had with General Washington.

With the soldier at her side, Leah walked through the drizzle to an area set aside for use as a latrine. When they reached the shallow trench, rapidly turning into a waterway, Leah gestured for her guard to turn his back.

The man simply shook his head, no, without a change in his demeanor.

"Seriously?"

When he made no effort to respond, or look away, Leah shrugged and quickly took care of business. "I hope that made your day," she said, then headed toward her horse which someone had added to the cadre's picket line. Her saddle and other gear lay in a pile where the soldier who'd taken charge of the animal had left it.

Leah rummaged through the saddle bag, pleased to find that nothing had been taken. What little cash she still had remained in an inside pocket of her jacket, but everything else she'd brought from Boston had been squeezed into the saddlebag, including the radio.

Hurrying, as a band of gray appeared on the horizon, Leah and her guard proceeded to General Washington's tent, the largest of the temporary structures. Some of the others were already being struck as the General preferred to be on the move with first light.

Leah turned the transmitter on and called to her father as she waited outside Washington's tent for his signal to enter. Her father responded first.

"Adams and I are standing by," he said.

"Good. I'm about to enter General Washington's tent."

"Leah, there's something you need to know, before we get started."

"What's that?" she asked, noting that his voice lacked its usual vitality.

"My physics magazine--you know, the *Quarterly*--has started to fade."

"I-- Oh..." The knife blade of worry dug deeper into her resolve and cut her response short. "Does Chastity understand?"

"Yes. It's been... difficult here. Are you all

right?"

"For now," she said.

"Come in," said Hamilton as he pulled the tent flap aside and stepped clear.

Washington sat at a wooden table at the back of the square tent. "I don't have much time to spare."

A voice crackled from the transmitter in Leah's hand. "*George?* Is that you?"

Washington stared down at the device as Leah set it gently on the table. "Press this button when you talk, and hold it close to your mouth."

The General had no trouble following her instructions. "Adams?"

"Yes!"

Washington looked around the tent, then at Hamilton, and finally at Leah. He pressed the TALK button and said, "Where are you?"

"In Philadelphia. Where else would I be?"

The General looked straight at Leah, his face reflecting sudden optimism. "How many of these things do you have?"

"General?" Adams' voice came through before she could answer.

"Yes, I'm listening." In his excitement, Washington forgot to press the TALK button and had to repeat himself.

Adams said, "We ought to get a few of these things, don't you think?"

"As many as possible."

"That's going to be a problem," Leah said. "I'll explain why later."

"You'll find their story quite fanciful. In fact, too fanciful to believe," Adams said, "but now that

I've seen this thing, this--"

"Radio," Raines said from the background.

"--this radio, I believe them. I think they're telling the truth. We'd be wise to pay attention."

Washington stared from the transmitter in his hand to Leah and back, repeatedly. He kept his finger on the button. "You're saying we *can't* get any more of these?"

"Not right away," Raines said, his voice growing louder as he moved closer to the microphone in Philadelphia. "But we're putting a process in place to fix that."

"Please hurry," Washington said.

"In the meantime, George," said Adams, "listen to what they have to say."

Washington nodded, then spoke. "Of course."

There was no response, and when Leah tried to use the transmitter, she couldn't even get static.

"What's wrong with it?" Washington asked. "And can you fix it?"

She shook her head wondering how she could tell him the only way she knew to fix the radio was to let Benedict Arnold get away with treason.

~*~

Though no longer restrained, Joel remained in custody. His ongoing frustration at Colonel Jameson's blunders left him despondent. But more than that, he hated being stuck in North Castle when he could be on his way back to Leah for what little time they had left.

As he mused about finding and punishing the

moron who came up with the name "North Castle," a rain-soaked and mud-spattered Lieutenant Allen returned to Jameson's office with Andre' in tow.

"What are you doing here?" Jameson demanded of the lieutenant. "You were supposed to take this man to Colonel Sheldon in Lower Salem."

Flustered, wet, and weary, Allen managed a barely coherent explanation. Joel remembered a couple similar moments in his own military career, and instantly felt a bond with the young officer.

"You'll take him to Sheldon at first light," Jameson said before dismissing him.

Tallmadge, meanwhile, had been talking to the spy. Their conversation, carried on in low tones, seemed cordial enough and led eventually to a confession--Andre' admitted his true identity.

Joel wanted to scream, "See? That's what I've been saying all along!" but he feared Jameson would retaliate. He had wasted enough time already and was more than eager to find Leah.

Andre' asked permission to write a letter to General Washington, and when he finished it, Major Tallmadge read the brief missive out loud. He even kept a straight face.

"So," Tallmadge summarized, "it's not your fault that--" he ran his finger through the words Andre' had written "--yes, here it is. You were 'betrayed,' and that's why you're in the 'vile condition of an enemy in disguise within our posts.' This is what you want us to convey to General Washington?"

Joel knew the grim fate Andre' faced if he couldn't explain why he was traveling behind enemy lines dressed as a civilian. Still, his claim sounded amateurish. He seemed like a decent sort, but that didn't change the facts--he'd been caught actively engaged in espionage. He could spin it any way he liked, but short of intervention by Washington or God Almighty, Andre' was screwed.

Benedict Arnold, however, was still free.

Once again, Joel pleaded his case. Having been instrumental in identifying and capturing Major Andre', surely he had earned the right to leave. Knowing Leah, she had probably located Washington by now, and assuming she hadn't been captured, or worse, his best option of connecting with her would be to find the Commander-in-Chief.

Jameson, however, continued to waffle. He claimed there were issues "concerning the strange speech and mannerisms" Joel displayed, and an unexplained familiarity with the activities of the British spy. It seemed likely to him, if no one else, *including* Major Tallmadge, that Joel's part in the affair was to make Arnold look like a conspirator.

The three men were arguing about it when a second courier entered Jameson's office. The Colonel had dispatched him to Danbury, Connecticut, assuming that General Washington would simply reverse the route he'd taken previously.

Tallmadge shook his head. "He'd never do such a thing. He's too smart for that. Even if Arnold hadn't informed the British of his travel plans--"

"We don't know that!" Jameson protested.

"Based on what we've seen, however, it seems logical. Nevertheless, the General would not put himself at such risk. I could have told you that."

"Only if you'd been here," Jameson said, bristling.

"I suspect he took a more northerly route," the Major continued. "It's my understanding he planned to reach West Point today."

"He even travels on a Sunday?" Jameson asked.

"Yes, of course. But with all this rain, I wouldn't be surprised if he's delayed."

"Then I'll have the courier take the documents we got from our spy and deliver them to General Washington in West Point."

"I might as well go with him," Joel said. "That's where I'm headed anyway, the minute you let me out the door."

"He's harmless," Tallmadge said. "You said yourself he wasn't even carrying a weapon."

"He had an auger. In the right hands...."

Jameson's words died under Tallmadge's withering look--one which suggested the Colonel had just taken a misstep in a barnyard.

"The man's a cripple, Colonel. How dangerous can he be?"

Though incensed, Joel tapped a dwindling store of prudence and kept his mouth shut.

"Go, then," Jameson said. "If the courier doesn't mind your company, you have my permission to go with him. Just don't slow him down. Otherwise, you're on your own."

"Thanks, Colonel," Joel said. "You're a prince."

~*~

Excerpt from the *Portsmouth Press*:

Bizarre Document Discovered

Portsmouth, New Hampshire, Sat., June 30, 2012--Rachael Fineman, PhD, a history professor at Greeley College, today revealed a previously unknown diary which may shed new light on events surrounding the capture of West Point in 1780.

Fineman found the diary while researching a book on the early days of the colonial rebellion. It was written by Jedediah Slaughter, a junior officer on the staff of the rebel general, George Washington. In it, Slaughter describes a woman he met while guarding a Hudson River ferry crossing. She spoke a strange language that neither he nor any of the men in his command could understand. The same woman later had a private interview with General Washington at which she spoke "perfect English."

Slaughter, who later achieved fame as a portrait painter, sketched the woman. Professor Fineman commented on it, because the woman in the sketch bears an uncanny resemblance to Leah Kerr, whom authorities still seek in relation to the recent assassination of Queen Elizabeth II.

Chapter Twenty-seven

"Well, remember what you said, because in a day or two,
I'll have a witty and blistering retort! You'll be devastated
then!"

--Calvin, *Calvin & Hobbes*

Benedict finally got the quiet time with Peggy and their baby that he'd been wanting for so long. Neither the heavy rains nor the impending arrival of General Washington could dampen his spirits. Both knew that great turmoil loomed in the days ahead, and it would require careful planning to avoid tragedy, at least for them.

To that end, they made sure they were as ready as possible for an escape to the *Vulture* or whatever other craft General Clinton provided. What made such planning difficult, however, was the need to make it appear that no such planning was taking place.

As the hours rolled by, and no new word from Washington arrived, Benedict assumed he had been delayed by the weather. Of course there was always the chance that Washington had been intercepted on his return from his meeting with the French Admiral, Rochambeau. Benedict had been quite explicit in his note to Clinton about where and when Washington would be, assuming he didn't change his route.

That was the problem with the rebel Commander-in-Chief, he was not nearly as predictable as everyone thought. The British had made the discovery multiple times, yet they still couldn't accept it as reality. Benedict hoped to change that mindset when he assumed his new command. He would show them what real leadership looked like!

Peggy interrupted his musing about the campaign he'd wage to end the rebellion. Someone, it seemed, needed to have his nappy changed, and Peggy had a novel idea about who should do it at least once before their baby boy became a man.

~*~

Leah had gotten used to traveling on horseback, and if not for the weather might have found it almost enjoyable in the company of Washington's staff. Continuing rains, however, made conversation difficult and riding uncomfortable. The roads, such as they were, became little more than narrow streams of thick mud.

The riders pulled their hats low and those who had them wrapped themselves in cloaks. Leah used a blanket, which eventually became drenched and served only to make her colder. At that point, even if she'd had something to discuss with one of her fellow riders, her own chattering teeth would have prevented clear communication.

Though she desperately wanted to find shelter somewhere, Washington and his men kept on. She was reminded of what she'd read about him and his men at Valley Forge. Compared to that, a heavy rain would do nothing but slow them down.

Fortune smiled on her, however, as they approached the settlement of Fishkill. A coach bearing the French minister had stopped at a tavern. The driver was changing out the team of horses, and Washington took the time to meet with him.

Leah sat with some of the junior officers in the taproom while the General and his senior aides conversed with the Frenchman. Her companions felt sure their conversation was focused on the recent meeting in Hartford between Washington and Rochambeau.

Eventually Hamilton strode into the taproom and announced that even though the Robinson's house lay only a few miles away, Washington had decided to spend the night right where they were. The men were ordered to make camp as usual.

With painful memories of the rain and the pygmy-sized tent she had been given, Leah paid extra for a room in the tavern. She spent the night in a room by herself, in a dry bed, near a fireplace. Sheer luxury.

Retiring early, she reached the solitude of her room at dusk, or so she thought. The heavy cloud cover made it so dark, she could hardly tell if the sun had already set. She broke out her radio and tried once more to reach her father.

This time the on/off switch didn't even click, and the device actually felt lighter than she thought it should be.

Despite her fatigue, sleep did not come easily.

~*~

Joel and the dispatch rider from Colonel Jameson spent the day riding from one shelter to the next. Though they rode side by side, neither man spoke very much. Joel remained deep within his own thoughts most of the time, and the courier seemed to prefer the quiet.

They stopped at every settlement, farmhouse, and road crossing that offered any cover at all, but it didn't help. By the time they quit for the night, both men were soaked and miserable.

Fearing the packet of messages for General Washington might fall into the wrong hands, the courier rejected Joel's suggestion that they spend the night at an inn. The man implied that the security of his messages for Washington might be compromised. Joel argued that a room in an inn would most likely have a working lock. The clinching argument, however, had more to do with who would pay for the room. Joel was only too happy to oblige.

Though still well short of their West Point goal, the courier assured him they would arrive the next day, probably in the late morning.

Joel couldn't wait to reconnect with Leah.

~*~

Raines Kerr's breakfast meeting with Samuel Adams had been brief but fruitful.

"I must admit being impressed by your communications device," the patriot legislator said. "I assume it's not just a clever hoax."

"I assure you sir, the technology behind it is quite solid. Unfortunately, it's going to take time to produce a working version using materials currently available."

"What do you need?" Adams asked. "And how long will it take?"

"I can't answer the second question," he replied, "but I have faith that it can and will be done. As for what I need, the answer is simple. See to it that this young lady--" he gestured toward Chastity, "--the daughter of your old friend, Colonel Cotswold, returns to Boston safely. She and her associate, a young man named Gabriel, will do the rest."

"That seems reasonable."

"Oh, and one more thing," Raines added. "They will need an introduction to Benjamin Franklin when he returns from his ambassadorial duties in France."

"Doctor Franklin? What on Earth for?"

"He's a scientist, is he not?"

"Yes," Adams said. "Everyone knows that."

Raines gave him a smile. "I believe he will be able to give these two young industrialists a hand."

Adams shrugged. "Very well. I'll make the arrangements."

"Fine," said Raines. "And as promised, I'll pay for your lodging for the next year."

Though Chastity complained about the delay, Raines paid a year's rent on Adams' room before returning to City Tavern.

Once back in their quarters, Chastity quizzed the physicist again about his theories. "How can there be more than one reality?"

"There can't," he said, "and that's the most troubling aspect of time travel. A change made in the past can have huge ramifications on the future."

"I understand that part. It's what follows that mystifies me. You said you were going to disappear. To where?"

"Back to my own time, I hope." Raines smiled. "The problem is, there's no guarantee. If I don't return there, I'll just cease to exist."

The tears began anew, as they had every time the topic came up. "You'll be... dead?"

"Well, yes. Though technically, I will never have existed--like a child never conceived." He put his arm around her. "But if I'm right, the universe will adjust to the 'new' reality."

"I'm going to miss you so much!"

He smiled. "No, dear. In a very short while you won't remember me at all."

"But I don't want to forget you!"

"Believe me, I feel the same way about you, but that's the way it works. I can't change it. And in the long run, it'll be easier on everyone that way. Life will go on. And right now, we need to do just a little more preparation for that."

Chastity claimed that all the writing and copying she'd done the previous day had left her exhausted. Raines got her to do just a little more, choosing carefully from the few documents she had yet to work on. Eventually, her fingers cramped and her disposition grew contentious.

Raines plied her with compliments, food, and rum. Still she remained unhappy. Nor did the situation change until he agreed the documents she was copying had simply become too faded to read.

After that, and at her insistence, they spent the rest of the day in bed.

During a rare break, as he refilled their glasses with rum, he peeked at the materials she had copied. To his immense relief, none of them had faded.

"Come, husband!" she called. "'Tis time for you to return to work! I feel neglected."

"Yes, my dear," he said. Then smiled, albeit weakly, and promised to do his best.

~*~

Sometime during the night, the rain stopped. Someone pounded on Leah's door and advised that Washington would be leaving soon, and they hoped to have breakfast when they reached the Robinson house.

Leah hurried to avoid being left behind. Though she had been certain Washington would ask her about her radio transmitter and the cryptic advice Adams had given him about believing her "fanciful story," he had not spoken to her all day. Surely, she thought, things would be different that morning. After all, she hadn't mentioned Arnold's treason to him directly, although she felt sure

Hamilton would say something. The issue was too important for him to ignore.

As they rode away from Fishkill, however, Hamilton appeared beside her. He rode a beautiful horse with consummate skill, intimidating her by it. That feeling only grew as he maintained his position and prevented her from moving any closer to Washington.

"I need to speak with the General," she said.

"You already spoke to him."

"I'm not finished."

"Yes," he said. "You are."

"But I haven't told him about General Arnold."

He didn't respond.

"Did you?" she asked.

"He has enough on his mind," Hamilton said. "If there's any truth in what you say, it'll become evident soon enough."

"What's wrong with you?" she demanded. "He could be in danger."

"*All* our lives are in danger! The last thing we need is another charlatan to promise us the means to victory if only we pay for some new scheme or trifling invention."

"Long-distance communication is hardly trifling. Just think what such a thing would mean for men in battle!"

"It would be grand, I'll warrant. And the Congress would likely find the funds to pay for it. But your device doesn't work."

"It most certainly did! General Washington himself used it. You were there. You heard the conversation."

Hamilton smirked. "Oh, I heard something all right. I heard what even sounded *somewhat* like the voice of Samuel Adams."

"It was Adams. I guarantee it!"

"I'm sure you do. And for awhile, General Washington thought so, too. But once we had the time to reflect, we realized such a thing simply isn't possible."

"But it is!"

"Then show me! Turn your marvelous invention on. Let me talk to Adams. Or, better still, let me hear from Doctor Franklin."

"You know I can't do that," she said.

"No," he said. "We *both* know you can't do that. And so does the General. He's agreed to let you accompany us as far as Arnold's home. Afterwards, you will leave and not come back. Is that clear?"

Leah stared at him for a long moment, unwilling to back down, but unsure how to turn anything he'd said to her advantage. Finally, she gave up.

"Remember what I said about rethinking your attitude concerning insults?"

"Yes," he said, though the response was as much sighed as spoken.

"Just forget it."

"I already have," he said, reining his horse away from hers.

A short time later, they reached a trail leading to the first of West Point's outlying fortifications. Washington halted the party and announced that he wanted to conduct an inspection before they rode on to breakfast. The news generated a wave of grumbling.

"I know that all you young men are in love with Mrs. Arnold," Washington told them, and suggested that if they were that eager see her, they could ride on ahead. He intended to inspect the eastern fortifications first.

Two of his men, who considered themselves exceedingly lucky, rode on to alert the Arnolds that Washington would be delayed. Leah went with them. The two spoke of little else but the hostess for their breakfast. Evidently, they were already quite familiar with Peggy Arnold and couldn't wait to see her again.

Leah couldn't imagine what they saw in the woman and hoped she'd have time to get cleaned up before they all sat down to eat.

~*~

Benedict heard the riders approach and met them at the door. When he saw the exotic wife of Joshua Smith's relative trailing behind, he wondered how she had come to be traveling with them.

She smiled at him and reached for his hand.

"Thank God, I made it here safely. If not for these kind officers, I might've been in grave trouble." She squeezed his hand. "I'll explain later."

Though her claim sounded odd, he dismissed it with a dark look and allowed her in without comment. "There's food on the table," he told the new arrivals. "Mrs. Arnold is upstairs and will join us later. Have a seat and help yourselves."

Under normal circumstances, Benedict's aides, Colonel Varick and Major Franks, would have been dining with him that morning, but Franks was away on an errand, and Varick, who had not been feeling well, occupied a bed just down the hall from Peggy.

So, when a courier arrived from Colonel Jameson with a dispatch addressed to Arnold, he received it directly and sat down at the table to read it. Messages from field staff were quite routine and would normally be handled by his subordinates. This time, however, the message could not have been any *less* routine.

As he read the message, his heart raced.

A man named Anderson had been captured trying to reach British lines. Not only did the man have important documents in his possession, he also had a pass signed by Arnold. Jameson hoped Arnold could explain the mystery.

Benedict's entire world began to unravel. Feeling lightheaded, he backed his chair away from the table and continued reading.

Jameson had no orders covering such an unusual situation and had therefore sent the recovered documents to General Washington via a separate courier.

And Washington was set to arrive at any moment!

Rising as casually from the table as he could,

Benedict stepped away and hurried outside where he quickly caught up with the courier. He told the man to remain quiet about Mister Anderson--no matter who inquired--then ordered his horse to be saddled.

With that done, he raced upstairs to alert Peggy.

"My God!" she said, "We must flee!"

"Not with the baby," he said. "It's too dangerous. You'll have to stay here. I'm sure you'll be safe. They couldn't possibly connect you with what I've done."

Peggy was distraught. "You can't just leave me here! What will I do?"

He gripped her by her upper arms and stared directly into her face. "You *know* what to do. We've discussed it often enough. Just play your part, and no one will suspect a thing. We'll be reunited soon enough, I swear it!"

He would have said more, but someone knocked on the door to tell him that Washington and his men were approaching.

Barely avoiding complete panic, Benedict gave Peggy a hurried kiss then hobbled down the stairs and through the dining room. He hardly even slowed down as he announced that he had to cross the river to West Point in order to prepare for Washington's arrival. The General would be there soon, and would they kindly register his regrets for not joining him at breakfast?

He didn't wait for the obligatory answer. Instead he swung up into his saddle and kicked the horse into a run down the steep path which led to his barge.

He dismounted and without bothering to tether the horse, jumped aboard the flat-bottomed vessel and ordered his stunned crew to depart immediately.

~*~

Hamilton preceded Washington into the Robinson house where he and the rest of the General's entourage were greeted by the two officers who'd arrived with Leah. Hamilton spotted her immediately and escorted her out of the house.

"Enough," he said. "It's time for you to go."

"There's something going on," she said. "Someone arrived with a message for Arnold, and after he read it, he raced out of the house as if it were on fire. I think--"

"Silence!" Hamilton said, his voice bearing a harsh edge. "No one cares what you think. It's time you were gone. I've given orders that if you try to approach the General again, you're to be arrested."

"But--"

"Believe me when I say you don't want to be arrested. You wouldn't last a month."

"You're making a mistake."

"I doubt it," Hamilton said, but he'd already turned away. A few steps later he entered the house and disappeared from view completely.

Stunned, Leah walked away and found a spot beneath a tree where she could observe the building. Though she had every reason to believe her mission had been accomplished, she had absolutely no feelings of victory, and no reason to celebrate. If anything, she felt drained.

And abandoned.

Some time later, Washington and his men left the house, mounted their horses and took the well-worn trail toward West Point. Without priorities, Leah wandered aimlessly around the traitor's home hoping to find some solace in what she'd done or, lacking that, some function to which she could devote herself. More than anything, she kept moving to avoid breaking down and surrendering to a massive case of self-pity.

At some point, she figured, Joel would return, and that became her focus. It wasn't much, but it was all she had. She managed to doze off for a while but woke up when she heard a woman screaming. It had to be Peggy; she was the only other woman around.

The caterwauling continued for a long time, but eventually lessened. Though sorely tempted to enter the house and offer assistance, she recalled Hamilton's warning and maintained her distance.

Where the hell is Joel?

~*~

"We canna leave jus' now," the crew chief said. Like the others, he wore nothing to denote his rank. Benedict assumed he was simply the oldest of six privates.

"Why not?"

"We been towin' logs y'see, w' the barge, as ordered." He pointed at three stout tree trunks chained to the back of the craft and floating in the shallow water.

"Get rid of them!"

"We need 'em t' raise the chain, Gen'ral, sir. Ye said y'self--"

"It doesn't matter what I said. Unchain the logs and get this barge moving!"

"Aye, sir. Th' problem, y'see--"

"Silence!" Benedict barked. "Get the men aboard. The current's in our favor. They can put a bit more muscle into it and drag the damned logs behind. You can get rid of them later."

The crew chief scratched his head. "Beggin' yer' pardon, sir, but it seems a waste o' work t' me. If'n we--"

"Now!"

The six oarsmen clambered aboard and applied themselves to their oars.

"Look lively now," Benedict said. "I'm on a mission ordered by General Washington himself, and it must be concluded with all possible haste."

The oarsmen bent to their task and, aided by the current, propelled the craft with remarkable speed considering the three huge logs trailing behind. Yet, it wasn't fast enough to suit Benedict. He had no intention of coming within range of Colonel Livingston's four-pounders lest he receive a shellacking like the *Vulture* sustained a few nights earlier.

With a broad, white handkerchief fluttering in the wind, Benedict exhorted the men to ever greater effort. "Two gallons of rum for each of you," he cried, "if you can make way any faster."

The crewmen redoubled their efforts and flew by King's Ferry--and Livingston's guns--without incident. Within minutes, the *Vulture* came into view, and Benedict ordered the rowers to make directly for it. Not a single man objected. Nor, Benedict suspected, did they have any reason to since he kept the white handkerchief in plain sight.

In the distance, the *Vulture* executed a partial turn, orienting half of its fourteen gun complement on the approaching barge.

"Sir?" the crew chief said, "They don't 'pear 'appy to see us."

"Keep rowing," Benedict said. He raised a spyglass and focused on the deck of the *Vulture*. Standing at the rail, looking straight at him and gesticulating wildly, stood Joshua Smith. Another man Benedict didn't know stood beside him, and he was also pointing at the barge. The distance was too great for Benedict to understand what he was saying.

"But, sir--"

"Keep rowing, damn it!"

~*~

Joel reached the Robinson house late in the afternoon, still in the company of Colonel Jameson's second courier. He spotted Leah almost instantly and raced toward her.

They embraced as if the world were about to end, though neither was willing to admit the bald truth of it, at least for them. Shortly before Joel's arrival, Leah had looked in her saddlebag for the radio. What remained of it wasn't worth examining.

"The courier has proof of Arnold's treachery," Joel said.

Leah entertained a brief but satisfied smile. "I hope he gives it to Hamilton. He's such an ass. He needs to be the one to tell Washington their boy Arnold sold 'em out."

"It doesn't matter."

"Joel," Leah said, "let's go inside and find out what's happening. Let's see how they react. Let's see what Washington--"

Joel covered her mouth with his own, and their kiss lasted a wonderfully long time. "We've done all we can do," he said. "Whatever else happens is up to them."

"But--"

"No buts," he said. "We're done. If we have any time left, we need to spend it together."

"But General Clinton could still attack! And we don't know what will happen to Arnold, or... or Andre'!"

"No, we don't know," Joel said, watching as Leah began to fade even as he held her in his arms, "and we aren't going to find out."

"Joel," she said, her eyes going wide in fright. "I love you!"

"I love you, too," he said, softly.

And then they were gone.

~*~

Anthony Lancaster had never cared much for boats, especially small ones. The *Vulture*, however, while not as big as he would have liked, did offer some creature comforts. Fortunately, he wouldn't have to remain on board for long.

He had been quite fortunate while in a New York City tavern when approached by a press gang to serve on a British war ship. His status as a "gentleman" would have offered scant protection from the men searching for sailors to fill out the crews on the recently arrived ships.

Never more glib in his life, Lancaster convinced the leader of the "recruiting party" that he was already in the King's employ as a spy. That and a healthy bribe bought him one last chance at a meeting with Major Andre'.

Alas, Andre' remained unavailable, but the sergeant who listened to Lancaster's plea gave him a way out: sail aboard the *Vulture* for the next month, and alert the ship's master if he encountered anything suspicious.

Lancaster had readily agreed. Anything would have been better than serving for the length of a ship's commission, assuming he could have survived.

His status as a spy, while acknowledged to the Captain, was not shared with the crew who assumed Lancaster to be either a friend of the ship's master or someone with considerable political pull.

The arrival of Joshua Smith further enhanced Lancaster's status with the Captain since it provided corroboration of his story that General Arnold might be playing a deadly game of betrayal--not with the Continentals, but with the King.

Nor did it take long for Smith and Lancaster

to compare notes. Both men knew Joel Dawkins, though Lancaster held him in less esteem. Smith, however, was convinced Dawkins had been sent by George III himself to investigate the possibility of a new and deadly weapon. After seeing Dawkins in the custody of Continental militiamen, Smith had been tempted to return home and let things play out, but his dinner with General Arnold and his brazenly insulting officers changed all that. He knew it was time to warn the Royal Navy. He boarded the *Vulture* the next day.

When word went out that a barge headed downstream was making straight for them, the Captain called both Smith and Lancaster topside to inspect the rapidly approaching vessel.

Naturally, neither man had any inkling what Franklin's secret weapon looked like, but both were convinced the barge heading their way was towing it. The ship's Captain, having already endured one shelling by the Americans, had no desire to sit through another attack. He ordered the ship to come about and gave his gunners the order to fire.

The man standing in the bow of the barge waving a white flag provided a splendid target, and the barge went down in the first salvo.

Of the seven men on board the sunken boat, six survived. The American General was nowhere to be found.

~*~

Excerpt from the *London Daily Mail*:

Fitzwilliam Estate Sold For Use As Private School

Mole Valley, Surrey, UK, Wed., July 4, 2012-- Attorneys for Cotswold-Gabriel Industries, the world's largest privately owned manufacturing conglomerate, today announced the purchase of an estate once owned by Sir Bentley Fitzwilliam, a member of the House of Lords in the late 18th and early 19th centuries.

The estate, on over 500 acres of land, has an 88-room manor house and extensive out-buildings. It will be converted for use as a preparatory school. Cotswold-Gabriel maintains similar schools in 42 countries around the globe.

The company will only allow students earning scholarships provided by Cotswold-Gabriel to attend, but "they will be given everything they need to prepare for the rigors of higher education and the leadership roles we hope they will seek later in life."

Another feature of the Kerr-Gabriel scholarships is the inclusion of transportation and temporary housing for parents wishing to visit their children while enrolled.

Chapter Twenty-eight

"The quickest way of ending a war is to lose it."
                                          --George Orwell

Joel knew something wasn't right the moment he woke up, and it wasn't just the sound of someone in his shower. His bedroom looked... different. Try as he might, he couldn't identify anything specific which seemed odd or out of place. It all just seemed slightly *wrong*. He sat up and looked around.

He glanced at the bedside table and saw empty wine glasses and the remnants of candles. Clothing--both male and female--littered the floor. But that's *not* what he recalled. Instead, he remembered a wonderful moment with... *Who?* The name danced just beyond the edge of his memory, fragile and ephemeral. Fading like a dream.

But it wasn't a dream.

It had to be something... else.

When Mollie Evans walked out of the bathroom, wrapped in a towel that left deliciously little to the imagination, Joel almost let the dream memory go.

"Hungry, luv?" she asked.

Ravished.

Suddenly, and distressingly, his libido declared war on his conscience.

Mollie looked stunning.

But the damned dream....

"I know I'm going to hate myself for doing this," Joel said.

Mollie gave him a sly smile. "That depends a lot on me, doesn't it?"

"No, actually, I--" How could he make a graceful exit when he really didn't want to leave?

She advanced slowly, and softly, and stood directly in front of him as he sat on the edge of the bed. Then she let the towel fall to the floor.

The heat of her naked body warmed his face.

A drop of water glistened in her navel.

Oh. My. God.

"I-- I have to-- to go," he said.

She stepped away and gestured toward the bathroom. "It's all yours."

"No," he said. "I mean, I have to leave."

"Why? I thought Saturday was your day off."

"It is. But... There's something I have to do."

"Can I help?"

He shook his head.

"Are you all right?" she asked, suddenly concerned.

"Yeah. At least, I think so."

He stood up and quickly got dressed. Mollie watched casually while he brushed his teeth and ran a comb through his hair. She reached around from behind him and fiddled with his belt buckle and trouser clasp.

"Are you *sure* you want to leave?"

No. Not-- at all.

He gently pushed her hands away.

"You really are leaving," she said, mystified. "After last night. I thought we--"

"We were spectacular," he said. "No, you were--*are*--spectacular."

"Why are you in such a hurry to go? I thought we'd have breakfast and maybe, you know...."

Aw geez!

"Much as I want to, I just can't. I've gotta-- I've gotta run. I can't explain."

No, really, I can't explain--it's... It's impossible! I'm insane.

"When are you coming back? Should I stick around?"

"I don't know!" he said. "Feel free to stay as long as you like, but please lock up when you leave."

"Joel?"

"Yes?"

"I don't understand."

He shrugged. "Y'know, babe, I don't either. I'm all--" He shrugged. "If I figure it out, I'll call and explain. I promise."

"Is it something I said?"

"God, no!"

And then he left.

What the hell was wrong with him? How could he walk out on a woman like Mollie Evans? What was in his head, driving him--compelling him--

to pursue the remnants of a dream? Pieces of which continued to float through his mind as he strolled to the multi-story parking garage where he kept his 30-year-old Harley Roadster.

Traffic seemed even worse than usual, and he couldn't understand why everyone was driving on the wrong side of the road. Why weren't they on the left? Cars were lined up in both directions as far as he could see. And then he remembered. It was the 4th of July. There would be parades, concerts, and parties *everywhere*. But, he thought with a grim smile, *nobody* celebrated the Fourth like Boston. It made him laugh. It made him forget about Mollie Evans.

But it made him remember other things.

Like someone else's laugh. A woman's.

Wispy remnants of things he'd seen, or thought, or maybe even experienced flitted through his brain like a flood of butterflies.

Something haunted the outermost edge of his awareness--a place perhaps. Or a name.

He remembered someone holding on as he drove his Harley through the woods. Only it wasn't a Harley. And the someone holding on to him was a girl.

And she had a name.

Leah.

Without another thought he pulled out of the garage and headed west. Somewhere out there was a small-town college. He struggled with the name, but eventually it came to him, and he pulled off the road to punch it into the GPS on his phone.

Instantly, a map appeared. A glance was all

he needed to be on his way again, this time moving fast, before the butterflies in his head escaped.

Where had all the damned cars come from? And why were they clogging traffic in both directions?

Joel increased his speed, taking to the shoulders or center stripe to get to his destination. People honked, or blinked their lights, shook their fists, or gave him a one-finger salute, but he didn't care--he couldn't take the time to care.

He reached Millburn College in a state of anxiety. Something awful was going to happen here, he felt sure.

But as he drove around the heavily wooded campus with its ivy-covered buildings and immaculate lawns, he realized the tragedy had already occurred, but whether months ago or years ago he couldn't recall. If only the details weren't so damned fuzzy!

Leah.

That name, at least, wasn't fuzzy.

And she had something to do with the physics department.

I've gone completely nuts! What the hell is happening to me?

He stopped at an intersection, and a striking co-ed walked by in a short skirt and a tight top. Joel watched her pass thinking how pretty she was, but too young for him.

Way too young.

But Leah wasn't too young. That was a different butterfly.

He drove around a little more and came to

another stop outside a building that looked familiar despite the fact that he'd never seen it before. Not in this lifetime anyway. The sign outside it read: Jefferson Hall--Physics and Astronomy.

He parked the Harley and went inside. His footsteps echoed in the empty corridor as he made his way like some 50's movie automaton to the back corner of the second floor.

There he found the office of Raines Kerr, PhD, Chairman of the Millburn College Physics Department.

Kerr?

Still operating with the instinct of a cinematic robot, Joel tried the door. Unlocked, it swung open easily at his touch, and he came face to face with a vaguely familiar woman in her 60's. Her hair looked a bit like a skunk's pelt, but her demeanor was pleasant rather than stinky. She smiled up at him as he stepped closer, which surprised him. He had expected a frown.

"May I help you?" she asked.

"I'm looking for... Uh... Actually I'm--"

"Doctor Kerr?"

"Yes!"

"He and his wife, Beth, are attending a faculty luncheon. Millburn always makes such a big thing out of the whole July 4th celebration. Beth loves it."

"By any chance, does Doctor Kerr have a daughter?"

The woman smiled again, and once again it surprised him.

"That would be Leah. Such a dear."

"Do you have any idea where I might find

her?" he asked.

"May I ask what this is about?"

Joel smiled. "I-- I think we met once. And I thought... I wondered if--"

"She's probably in the Student Center organizing some sort of protest."

"Protests in the history department?"

The woman shook her head. "History? No. Political Science."

"Thanks," Joel said, retracing his steps through the hall and back to his bike.

Where's the Student Center?

Not surprisingly, it turned up near the middle of the campus. Joel parked his machine near two others and jogged up the steps of a modern and well-appointed structure. Once inside he didn't need to look very far.

A dozen college students labored over posters decrying the practice of human trafficking. He stepped carefully between sprawled bodies and pots of paint to reach a girl with light brown hair and a dark complexion.

She was too focused on her work to sense someone standing nearby, even close. He knelt beside her and gently touched her shoulder. "Excuse me," he said.

"Yes?" She rolled easily to a sitting position and regarded him with interest.

Joel found himself too tongue-tied to speak, so he just looked at her, studied her face, and tried to retrieve details from memories grown dim and getting dimmer.

"I know you," she said at last.

He nodded. It was all he could do. Words might break the spell, and he couldn't let that happen.

She held out her hand. He reached for it, gripped it, and smiled. The look on her face seemed to reflect the struggle he'd been having with his own memory. And then she relaxed, a grin tickling the corners of her mouth.

"It's Joel, isn't it?"

"Yeah."

"Help me up?"

She took his other hand and rose off the floor as if weightless.

"Come," she said, leading him to a bank of windows where bright sunlight flooded the open interior.

Joel still wasn't sure if he should risk saying something. He'd never experienced magic before and had no wish to spoil it.

"This is going to sound completely off the wall," she said, "but I think I've been waiting for you." Her smile grew even wider. "No. I'm sure of it."

She put her arms around him and hugged.

Joel's breath came out in a rush. He had no idea he'd been holding it.

She eased back but maintained a hold on his arms and stared deep into his eyes. "It's funny," she said, "but the guy I remember walked with a limp."

~ End~

Treason, Treason!

~ *Afterword* ~

There are a great many wonderful books available which detail the history of Benedict Arnold's fateful decisions, and I have tried to avoid straying too far from those historical accounts. The one book I found absolutely indispensable was Dave R. Palmer's definitive work, *George Washington and Benedict Arnold* (Regnery Publishing, 2006). A former Superintendent of West Point, Palmer's work is astounding. Don't miss it!

I freely admit that I made a major departure from the historical record when it came to Arnold's demise. The version in this novel is utterly fictitious. In the world where you and I find ourselves, Benedict Arnold escaped just before Washington arrived, but he made it safely to the *Vulture*. Later his treachery was rewarded by a commission as a brigadier general in the British Army.

I would have preferred to include details of the actual historical outcome--Major Andre's trial and execution, Arnold's command of British troops in an attack on Virginia and his subsequent, largely unsuccessful, business career. But it would have been difficult to do without introducing still more characters and conflict. Nor, do I believe, would readers have gained much from it.

Besides, I'm a romantic at heart, and I wanted to resolve the issue left hanging--Joel and Leah. I couldn't resist adding a touch of poetic justice for Smith (a real historical character) and Lancaster, a product of my imagination.

All the events surrounding Benedict Arnold, except his death in the final scene, have been rendered as accurately as I could manage. While I freely worked my fictional characters into the scenario, the movements, activities--and to the extent possible--*dialog* of the historical characters, is accurate and documented. This includes the Cahoon brothers as well as the three militiamen who captured Major Andre' and who received lifelong pensions from the Continental Congress for preventing the treachery that I believe would have cost the colonies the war.

Some readers have wondered about the low-tech nature of the 21st century described at the beginning of the story. That is based entirely on my conjecture about what might have happened if the Industrial Revolution had been interrupted by World War I, the so-called "Great War." It assumes England had been engaged in two wars on two different continents, with no United States of America available to join the fight. Under those circumstances, I believe Germany would have prevailed in 1918. That, it seems to me, would have caused the Industrial Revolution to suffer a huge setback resulting in the sad, largely rural, society of the *new* New England.

--Josh Langston
October, 2012
Marietta, Georgia USA

Made in the USA
Charleston, SC
11 January 2016